The Trial

考驗

Part I. Discovery

尋蹤

Cover by Axie Breen

Acknowledgments

I would like to offer my special thanks to editors: Elias Kopsiaftis, who was the preliminary editor. David Silver who had spent a lot of time in correcting my English in the first half of this novel. Finally, I would like to thank Mr. James Norman for the final editing, typesetting and publication of this novel.

I would like to thank my proofreaders: Nancy Hauser, Colin Borsos, and Susan Lau.

Plot Synopsis

Prior to retiring, a geology professor, in order to better understand how oil reservoirs are formed, takes his top students on an exploration of a depleted oil reservoir with the goal of retrieving rock samples. What they find instead leads the researchers to a shocking revelation about their own minds and bodies, and of life on Earth and elsewhere.

The team develops a submarine to enter the oil mine and finds, buried in stone that is millions of years old, evidence of an advanced civilization with technology far beyond today's modern science.

Their discovery of strange manmade crystals leads them onto a path of discovery into humanity's lost history, and of slowly realizing the true nature of mankind, now, and in the immediate future.

Preface

Actively searching for and learning about our history can help us understand the present time and foresee the future. I have long contemplated writing a novel that provides some insight into possible scenarios of our past. With this novel, I wish to accomplish three goals. First, I want to increase awareness of the actions we take that may impact the entire human race. In this novel, I write about both factual and fictional events in the hopes that we may learn from them, ultimately to prevent disasters from occurring in present-day real life. Secondly, by providing a perspective into our possible past, I hope that we will become more aware of where the human race stands today and how it may change in the near future. We should develop a sense for knowing whether **destiny** is about to dictate that history repeats itself. Finally, and most importantly, I would like to help bring the human race to a higher level of spiritual understanding and cultivation.

I am Chinese and have been influenced by nearly 7,000 years of Chinese culture. Within this extremely developed precious culture, spiritual cultivation has far surpassed the spiritual cultivation of the western world and is, in my opinion, one of the highest achievements of mankind. For more than 2,500 years, Chinese Buddhist and Daoist practitioners have quietly meditated and pondered the true meaning of life, hiding in the deep mountains without seeking the material desires of power, wealth, and glory. From this understanding and practice, they aim to reach the final goal of Buddhahood or enlightenment. In order to reach this goal, they must first study and comprehend the mysteries of human psychology and behavior. Through understanding themselves deeply and seeing their own true nature, they become deeply involved in searching for the meaning of life itself. Their final goal is to jump out of the human matrix through a gradual process of gaining insight and increasing their ability to sit in meditation, thereby achieving deeper levels of focused attention, or samadhi, to ultimately reunite with the Great Nature (Dao, 道), joining their consciousness with the universal consciousness. To achieve this goal, they must also undergo a physiological process to reopen the third eye, through which they may spiritually reunite with Nature. This is called "unification of heaven and human" (Tian Ren He Yi, 天人合一). The third eye is called "heaven eye" (Tian Yan, 天眼) in Chinese Qigong society.

With this novel, I hope I am able to deliver some crucial oriental spiritual development concepts to western society. This is a sincere attempt to help westerners to open their minds, especially about the process of spiritual cultivation, and to better understand the oriental perspective.

Since 1982, I have written more than 40 books about

Chinese martial arts and Qigong. After so many years of effort, I have realized that due to a prominent conservative mindset, very few westerners are willing to open their mind to deeply study, understand, and practice this method of spiritual understanding from the other side of the world. I have awakened to the fact that in order to reach the general public, instead of translating ancient spiritual documents and writing non-fiction on these subjects only in the martial arts Qigong worlds, I should write a novel which may possibly attract more mainstream readers.

I wish to inspire some readers to study more about the oriental spiritual concepts and training methods, especially today's Chinese. I also hope through this spiritual understanding, the cultural exchange between East and West can be expedited, and the final harmonization and peace of the world can be achieved more rapidly.

This novel is the first in a three-part series. This first part is entitled: *The Trial – Discovery*, the second part is entitled: *The Trial - The Past World*, and the third part is entitled: *The Trial - Beginning of the End.*

Dr. Yang, Jwing-Ming
Miranda, CA
May 17, 2006

Facts and Public Beliefs
Foundation of This Novel

This novel is written based on the following facts and public beliefs. Some of the facts can be quoted more precisely than others. However, many of them are from author's memory.

→ Coal is formed from plant remains that have been compacted, hardened, chemically altered, and metamorphosed by heat and pressure over long periods of time.

→ Oil is formed from the decayed remains of prehistoric marine animals and terrestrial plants. Over centuries this organic matter, mixed with mud, is buried under thick sedimentary layers of material. The resulting high levels of heat and pressure cause the remains to metamorphose, first into a waxy material known as kerogen, and then into liquid and gaseous hydrocarbons in a process known as catagenesis.

→ It is a fact that human's scientific spiritual development is far behind material development, consequently, we are on the path of self-destruction.

→ It is a fact that pollution has become more and more serious. Global warming has become common and the ice in the North and South Poles has begun to melt.

→ 604-531 B.C.

Lao Zi (老子) also called Li Er (李耳) or Lao Jun (老君) (604-531 B.C.) wrote a book: *Dao De Jing* (道德經). In Chapter 16, he mentioned the human's spiritual center and energy center (Qi center). When a person is able to keep his spirit and energy (Qi) in his center, he is able to trace back to the origin of his life. This has established the beginning concept of Chinese Qigong Meditation, Embryonic Breathing.

Lao Zi, in his book, also mentioned the "spiritual valley" (Shen Gu, 神谷) which is located between the two lobes of the brain. The spirit residing in this valley is called the "valley spirit" (Gu Shen, 谷神).

→ 0-200 A.D.

The concept of the body's Qi channels and vessels was recognized by Chinese medical science 2,000 years ago. It was also recognized by Qigong practitioners that a human has two polarities. One is located in the head called "Upper Dan Tian" (Shang Dan Tian, 上丹田) and the other is located at the center of gravity (c.g., i.e. center of guts) (Real Lower Dan Tian) (Zhen Xia Dan Tian, 真下丹田). The Upper Dan Tian is where the spirit resides (spiritual residence) (Shen Fu, 神府; Shen Shi, 神室) while the Real Lower Dan Tian is where the body's energy (Qi) is produced and stored (Qi She, 氣舍). These two polarities are connected by the Thrusting Vessel (Chong Mai, 衝脈) and synchronize with each other. The Real Lower Dan Tian produces the "quantity" of energy (Qi) while the Upper Dan Tian manages the "quality" of the Qi's manifestation. This human two-polarities concept has been interpreted by Dr. Yang, Jwing-Ming in his book: *Qigong Meditation - Embryonic Breathing*.

→ 0-2006 A.D.

In Chinese Qigong society, it is always believed that when a person meditates to a high level, he will be able to lead the Qi upward following the Thrusting Vessel (i.e. spinal cord) to the brain and activate more cells for function. When more brain cells are activated, the energy in the brain can be led to the spiritual valley (i.e. space between the two lobes of the brain) and vibrate. If the energy can be manipulated efficiently, he is able to cause synchronization or resonance of another brain. That means he is able to read other people's minds and also influence other people's thinking.

→According to traditional Chinese concepts, there are two worlds coexisting in this universe, one is called "Yang Jian" (陽間) (Yang Space or Yang World) and the other is called "Yin Jian" (陰間) (Yin Space or Yin World). Yang World is the material world where we are living in which there are three dimensions plus time (if time is considered one dimension, then we are in four dimensions). However, we know very little about the Yin World. The only thing the Chinese believe is that the Yin

World is an energy world, spiritual world (ghost world), or mysterious world where our spirits enter when we die. Therefore, scientifically, we are still in the path of searching for those dimensions we have not yet found and understood.

→ July 20, 1969 A.D.
Neil Armstrong became the first man to step onto the surface of the Moon. He was followed by Edwin Aldrin, both of the Apollo 11 mission.

→ 1970s A.D.
American navy forces aggressively research how to use meditation to control a missile's flight. In addition to America, Russia and China have also been involved in similar research. The movie "Star Wars," produced in the late 1970s about "mind control," was based on this discovery.

→It is reported in a Chinese newspaper that the Chinese, American, and Russian governments were searching for underground cities in desert areas. It is believed that these areas became desert due to nuclear bomb explosions in a previous civilization. Since the impact was so significant, even though most of the earth has returned to its original green state, these desert areas remain desert.

→According to Russian calculations, it would take ten

of today's regular nuclear bombs to raise the temperature on the surface of the earth at least 10 degrees. This would also melt the ice at the north and south poles. About 70% of existing land would then be covered with water. Any remaining survivors would die within a few days or weeks due to radiation. It would take 100 regular nuclear bombs to evaporate the ocean water and 500 bombs to destroy all lives and set the earth on fire. It would take Earth at least 100,000 years to cool down. Naturally, there will be no life during this period.

→The potential global atmospheric and climatic consequences of nuclear war are investigated using models previously developed to study the effects of volcanic eruptions. Although the results are necessarily imprecise, the most probable first-order effects are serious. Significant hemispherical attenuation of the solar radiation flux and subfreezing land temperatures may be caused by fine dust raised in high-yield nuclear surface bursts and by smoke from fires. For many simulated exchanges of several thousand megatons, in which dust and smoke are generated and encircle the earth within 1 to 2 weeks, average light levels can be reduced to a few percent of ambient and land temperatures can reach -15°C to -25°C. The yield threshold for major optical and climatic consequences may be very low: only about 100 megatons detonated over major urban centers can create average hemispheric smoke optical depths greater than 2 for weeks, and subfreezing land temperatures for months. In a 5000-megaton war, at northern mid-latitude sites remote from targets, radioactive fallout on time scales of days to weeks can lead to chronic mean doses of up to 50 rads from external whole-body gamma-ray exposure, with a likely equal or greater internal dose from biologically active radionuclides. Large horizontal and vertical temperature gradients caused by absorption of sunlight in smoke and dust clouds may greatly accelerate transport of particles and radioactivity from the Northern Hemisphere to the Southern Hemisphere. When combined with the prompt destruction from a nuclear blast, fires and fallout, and the later enhancement of solar ultraviolet radiation due to ozone depletion, long-term exposure to cold, dark, and radioactivity could pose a serious threat to human survivors and to other species.

→ February 21-28, 1972 A.D.
President Nixon visited China. Acupuncture, Qi, and Qigong concepts have been imported into America since then.

→1980s A.D.
Continue to search for signs of life on Mars

NASA was searching for the possible existence of an Atlantean culture.

→ 1985 A.D.
The book *Body Electric* by Dr. Robert O. Becker, M.D.

and Gary Selden was published. This book opened the westerner's mind to the Chinese concept of Qi and recognized that Qi is actually bioelectricity circulating in all living objects. Dr. Becker mentioned in his book that a blood cell has two polarities and therefore is able to charge and discharge the electricity. That means each blood cell acts as a small battery.

→ 1990s A.D.

Scientists announced that: The brain acts like a floppy disk and can be influenced by nearby magnetic fields. If there is some magnetic field influence near different parts of the brain, human emotion and thought can be affected. If there is some magnetic field influence in some specific area, recent memories can be erased.

Within the next 20 years, the memory, knowledge, and personality of a person can be recorded on a computer hard drive and this recording can be imported into another brain. Later this announcement triggered two movie productions, "The Matrix" and "Sixth Day."

Through the injection of human growth hormones, a person is able to live to be 120–150 years old.

A way to make brain cells divide was discovered, so the age of the brain cell can also be maintained. It is believed if we are able to pursue this longevity technique correctly, all humans will be able to live to around 700–800 years old.

Each cell has its own life, memory, and includes the entire genetic blueprint of a human body. From a single cell, we may be able to clone any life, including a human.

Scientists announced that it is possible to produce any part of the body from a single cell. It is also possible to produce a steak from a single cell of an animal. Future protein supplies could possibly be produced by an artificial meat industry through cellular multiplication.

Scientists announced that we are able to make plastic as strong as steel. Expended, Oriented, Wood-filled polypropylene (EOW-PP). SHW (Synthetic Hardwood) Technologies Inc. in Guelph, Ont. Canada.

Scientists announced that today's computer science is capable of making a computer as small as a human cell. Therefore, an artificial gland and a computer could be implanted into a human body. When the computer detects a decrease in hormone levels, the artificial gland could release extra hormones to balance it.

Some reports about alien abductions conclude that all aliens may have the life span of 700-800 years.

From some private studies, it is believed that aliens have the same genes as humans. Many times, human's eggs or sperm have been taken from an abductee and a new species of human-alien hybrid has been bred.

→ 1994 A.D.

The SDI-NASA Clementine spacecraft orbited the Moon and mapped its surface. In one experiment, Clementine beamed radio signals into shadowed craters near the Moon's south pole. The reflections, received by antennas on Earth, seemed to come from icy material. That makes sense. If there is water on the Moon, it's probably hiding in the permanent shadows of deep, cold craters, safe from vaporizing sunlight, frozen solid. So far so good, but... the Clementine data was not conclusive, and when astronomers tried to find ice in the same craters using the giant Arecibo radar in Puerto Rico, they couldn't. Maybe Clementine was somehow wrong. In 1998, NASA sent another spacecraft, Lunar Prospector, to check. Using a device called a neutron spectrometer, Lunar Prospector scanned the Moon's surface for hydrogen-rich minerals. Once again, polar craters yielded an intriguing signal: neutron ratios indicated hydrogen. Could it be the "H" in H_2O? Many researchers think so.

→ 1995 A.D.

The first phase of the International Space Station, the Shuttle-Mir Program, began in 1995 and involved more than two years of continuous stays by astronauts aboard the Russian Mir Space Station and nine Shuttle-Mir docking missions. Knowledge was gained in technology, international space operations and scientific research.

The International Space Station will establish an unprecedented state-of-the-art laboratory complex in orbit, more than four times the size and with almost 60 times the electrical power for experiments — critical for research capability — of Russia's Mir. Research in the station's six laboratories will lead to discoveries in medicine, materials and fundamental science that will benefit people all over the world. Through its research and technology, the station also will serve as an indispensable step in preparation for future human space exploration. Examples of the types of U.S. research that will be performed aboard the station include: Protein crystal studies, tissue culture, life in low gravity, flames, fluids and metals in space, the nature of space, earth observation, and commercialization.

→ 1995 - 1998 A.D.

NASA: Three moons of Jupiter - Europa, Ganymede, and Callisto - may have life forms.

→ January 23, 1996 A.D.

On January 23 of 1996, Dr. Michael Gershon announced the discovery of "the second brain" which is located in the guts. The second brain is able to store memory while the first brain located in the head manages thinking. These two brains are connected by the spinal cord (highly electric conductive material). Therefore, though physically there are two brains, in function, it is one since there is no resistance between the two brains. Therefore, they are able to synchronize with each other without delay. This matches the traditional Chinese Qigong concept that the top brain is the Upper Dan Tian, the second brain is the Real Lower Dan Tian, and the Thrusting Vessel (i.e. thrusting through rapidly) is the connection of these two Dan Tians.

→ August 1996 A.D.

"Of the 24,000 or so meteorites that have been discovered on Earth, only 34 have been identified as originating from the planet Mars. These rare meteorites created a stir throughout the world when NASA announced in August 1996 that evidence of microfossils may be present in one of these Mars meteorites." Information taken from the NASA website at

http://www2.jpl.nasa.gov/snc/index.html

→ 1997 A.D.
Human cloning is a possibility.

→ 1998 A.D.
NASA: The spacecraft Lunar Prospector was sent to the moon to check the water storage of the moon.

NASA: Plan to send a new spacecraft, Lunar Reconnaissance Obiter (LRO) to the moon to again check the water in 2008.

→ 2000 A.D.
Scientists had successfully decoded 85% of the human genome.

Scientists announced that the spinal cord has memory. This can be used to explain the reason for reflexes. Later, it was understood that the entire body has memory including individual cells.

Some private investors have invented "flying cars." They believe that flying cars will be the traveling vehicles of the near future.

→ June 25, 2000 A.D.
NASA announces discovery of evidence of water on Mars; At 8:03 p.m. ET on June 20, SPACE.com reported that NASA had found evidence of water on Mars. The tremendous discovery fuels hope for microbial life on the Red Planet. It also makes a human mission to Mars more practical.

→ 2001 A.D.
A cell has two polarities. When cells multiply and eventually become a human, that human should also have two polarities. These two polarities are the two brains of the human body which is connected by the spinal cord.

→ May 24, 2002 A.D.
Presidents Vladimir Putin and George Bush sign a treaty that will substantially reduce our strategic nuclear warhead arsenals from the range of 2,200 to 1,700, the lowest level in decades. This treaty liquidates the Cold War legacy of nuclear hostility between the two countries.

Olivine, a silicate mineral rich in magnesium and

iron, is found on earth in volcanic rock (basalts). It has also been spotted on Mars – most recently and in significant amounts by NASA's Mars Odyssey spacecraft (Geology, June 2005). Because life requires liquid water and because olivine dissolves in water, Amanda Albright Olsen set out to establish how long it takes olivine to dissolve. The answer could help scientists determine if there was liquid water on Mars long enough for life to develop.

→ 2003 A.D.

Dr. Yang, Jwing-Ming published a book: *Qigong Meditation - Embryonic Breathing*. In this book, Dr. Yang has compared the traditional Chinese Qigong understanding about the two polarities of the human body with that of the western scientific discoveries in recent years. This book has revealed the possibility of human brain wave communication. This has also triggered research on the possibility of fabricating a brain-wave machine which is able to control a person's thinking. If this can be done, it will become the most powerful method of warfare in human history. This will also lead humans to an age of mental and spiritual bondage even more serious than ever before.

Science: 99% of the human genome has been decoded. Producing a genetic baby free from disease and with a high IQ can be done.

→ 2005 A.D.

It will take about 100 years to change Mars into a human inhabitable environment like Earth. Each day on Mars is 24.6 hours of Earth time.

→ July 21, 2005 A.D.

Scientists announce that genes have memory called "genetic memory" or "ghost of genes."

→ 2006 A.D.

Dr. Yang, Jwing-Ming published the book: *Qigong Meditation - Small Circulation.*

→ March 23, 2006 A.D.

Announced by Seth Shostak, Senior Astronomer, SETI Institute:

Mars. Then and now, everyone's favorite inhabited extraterrestrial planet. While Mars's highly reactive and powder-dry landscape is practically guaranteed to be sterile, there is indirect evidence for watery aquifers a few hundred feet beneath the surface. If these liquid reservoirs exist, life may have found refuge within. Today's Martians − if any − would be alive thanks to internal, geologic heat sources that keeps these putative aquifers warm. Nonetheless, we classify the Red Planet as a Sun-powered world simply because any life would presumably have arisen during those long-gone days when liquid water pooled on the surface.

Europa. There's good evidence, mostly from its

changing magnetic field, that this ice-covered world orbiting Jupiter has an ocean lying 10 miles or so beneath its crusty exterior. At the bottom of this vast, cryptic sea, volcanic vents might be spewing nutrients and hot water into a cold, dark abyss, providing both the food and energy for simple life.

Ganymede and *Callisto*. Both of these Jovian moons show magnetic field variations similar to those of Europa, suggesting that they, too, might be hiding large, watery oceans. Given their thicker ice skins, finding that life – if it exists – would be even more daunting than for Europa.

→ November 4, 2013 A.D.

Astronomers suggested, based on Kepler space mission data, that there could be as many as 40 billion Earth-sized planets orbiting in the habitable zones of Sun-like stars and red dwarf stars within the Milky Way galaxy. They also reported that there may be more than two billion planets in our galaxy capable of supporting life.

Chapter 1
Meetings

Classroom

Dr. James C. Owen, beaming with an intensely focused smile, stood confidently in front of the classroom, clutching a small piece of chalk, and feverishly scribbling what seemed like utter gibberish on a cloudy blackboard. Geology. The endless sea of names and terminology seemed so foreign to most, but to Dr. Owen, it was his native tongue. No other professor at UCLA, or any other university for that matter, seemed to possess quite the same zeal and love for the profession more than Dr. Owen did. The students were as silent as the deepest reaches of space as Dr. Owen lectured on coal and oil forming beneath the earth's surface. Dr. Owen paused for a moment, leaning on the podium and sweeping his eyes from left to right to examine his class. They all seemed to be void of even the slightest trace of interest. Inside, he sighed.

The deafening silence was suddenly broken by a lone student in the front row. Stefani, the class pet, asked, "Is it true that we are recycling past lives when we burn oil today?" A few students snickered.

Welcoming the question, Dr. Owen jumped up. "Theoretically, it is true." Dr. Owen noticed the puzzled looks on some of the students' faces. "As we discussed earlier, before 2003 oil was believed to be formed entirely from the decayed remains of prehistoric marine and terrestrial lives. Over a period of thousands and thousands of years, buried under high levels of heat and pressure, these remains metamorphosed, first into the waxy material known as kerogen, and then into liquid and gaseous hydrocarbons. This process is known as catagenesis."

Dr. Owen paused for a little bit. "However, there are a few geologists, including Dr. Thomas Gold, who believe that there is another possibility of oil production. They believe that large amounts of carbon exist naturally in the planet, some in the form of hydrocarbons. Since hydrocarbons are less dense than aqueous pore fluids, they migrate upward through deep fracture networks. However, this theory is very much a minority opinion amongst geologists.

"When we burn oil today, in a sense, we are 'recycling.' Oil is converted to energy, energy is converted into life, life is converted into matter, matter is converted into oil, and oil is finally converted back into energy."

A burly looking student in the back row exclaimed, "So why is the EPA making such a big fuss about my Hummer?" The class broke into laughter as he gloated over his joke.

"From a purely theoretical standpoint this could be

considered recycling. However, the most important aspect of it all is not merely the fact that we can tap into this energy resource, but how we do it. And this, my dear Jason, is where the EPA shows up knocking on your door." The class livened up with smirks and grins as Jason shrunk back into his chair. "If we extract this energy the wrong way, the consequences can be dire. We are destroying the natural environment as we speak, and this will eventually have results of catastrophic proportions. Anybody look at the sky lately? Notice that big hole in the ozone?" Dr. Owen raised an eyebrow, never looking away from the class. "And what about global warming? We're setting more and more weather records each year. One day, the earth itself may become completely uninhabitable because of our actions. Only after the human race is extinct will the earth then begin a long process of recovery taking thousands of years. That is, of course, assuming that the earth is still here. And all of our dead bodies will be recycled as new energy throughout the entire process."

The class sat wide-eyed, unsure if they heard the latter, grim part of Dr. Owen's speech correctly.

"Is it possible that the oil we are burning today includes human bodies?" asked Stefani.

"Naturally. We are animals, aren't we?"

A chill ran up Stefani's spine as she fidgeted in her chair. "I'll never drive another car again," she thought. An eerie wind seemed to have swept through the lecture hall. Everyone was still thinking about a time when the remains of their bodies would be used for energy, some thousands of years in the future.

* * *

Dr. Owen, 65 years of age, was serious and solemn, though sometimes he could be a bit humorous during class. He was five foot ten with a gray mustache, and a little bit overweight due to his serious office work and study. He had always loved exploring and studying caverns since his childhood, especially the structure and the formation of their limestone columns, draperies, popcorn, and stalagmites. His wife, Jennifer, was 62 years old, and was a retired nurse currently working in a nursing home voluntarily. They had two sons, Ted and Robert. Ted was 35 years old, an astronomy professor at MIT, and had gotten married eight years ago. They had a boy, Ian, 7 years old and his wife Anna was expecting another baby girl in October. Robert was 32 years old and was an architectural engineer working at a firm in San Francisco. He was especially interested in ancient architecture and had a good imagination about future building structures and 'green' building design. During the last few years, he had begun to be interested in Chinese Feng-Shui.

Studying a depleted oil reservoir was to be Dr. Owen's final project, which he decided to undertake before he retired from his teaching career. It had been 35 years since he accepted his first position as professor, and he had always dreamed of accomplishing something that no one else had thought about or done. It was not until last semester that he finally convinced the government scientific research review board, which awarded him a $5,000,000 grant to study the depleted oil mine. Five million dollars, such a small portion of the funds needed for this scope of research, Dr. Owen thought. But he believed that once the project had taken off, he might get more funding from private oil companies, who might have a more financially based interest in a better understanding of oil mines. He approached Standy Firm, Inc. first because he had read that George Standy was a man of unusual integrity, known for his generous philanthropy and involvement in surprisingly forward-looking research.

* * *

Standy Firm, Inc.

Standy Firm, Inc. had an outstanding reputation of being a pioneering oil company. Its stocks had recently shot through the roof and it had been enjoying a plethora of boastful press. On a sunny afternoon in March, Dr. Owen sat with three of his top students, Tommy, Brian, and Joe, in Standy Firm Headquarters' main conference room. Everybody was neatly dressed. Tommy had slicked his long hair back, and Brian and Joe were clean-shaven. Dr. Owen seemed a little agitated, restlessly moving his thumbs back and forth and tapping his foot. The door burst open startling the four, and Stefani rushed in, taking a seat next to Dr. Owen.

"I'm, I'm sorry I'm late," Stefani exhaled, trying to

catch her breath. "I decided not to drive today."

Joe rolled his eyes in mocking disbelief. Just then, the door swung open again, this time by two men dressed in suits and a woman wearing a long skirt, a white button-up blouse, and glasses. They quickly took seats directly across from Dr. Owen and his students in an almost mechanical manner.

"Hello, Dr. Owen. Gentlemen." The more prominent looking man nodded at Tommy, Brian, and Joe. As he settled into his chair, he noticed Stefani and added, "And lady." Motioning to his left and right, "This is Mary and Michael. Shall we begin?"

This is it, Dr. Owen thought to himself. This is the time to shine. It seemed as if Dr. Owen had recited speeches like the one he was about to give all his life. He had an illustrious career as the "great geology professor." Sitting in front of him were two of Standy Firm's most veteran employees, true experts about the oil industry, as well as the CEO himself, George Standy. Dr. Owen felt himself almost about to stammer but recovered. Coolly, he said, "Yes, we're all ready to go."

Dr. Owen was actually in no way apprehensive about the presentation. It was his four students that he worried about, especially after seeing Stefani in such a frazzled state of hurry. Standy Firm had a long history of being cooperative with independent projects and research and had long been venerated as one of the most professional and environment-friendly oil companies to ever exist. Dr. Owen was almost entirely convinced that Standy Firm would accept his proposal and perhaps even fund part of his extensive, yearlong project. He had been waiting weeks to give this presentation.

"Gentlemen, the goal of our study is to understand Earth's past history through oil mines. We will be working to uncover the intricate mysteries of the earth's underground structure and how oil was initially formed. Through our discoveries, we will formulate hypotheses about Earth as it was either thousands or millions of years ago and, of course, present supporting evidence to sustain our claims. We hope that Standy Firm will take part in our endeavors by providing us with basic equipment and guidance for exploring some of your depleted oil mines."

George Standy answered in a challenging tone and sounded as if he was testing the knowledge of the individuals seated before him. "Dr. Owen, surely you must know that after an oil mine is depleted, it is filled completely with water. The water is so full of residue and dirt that any light would be useless. You'd be completely blind down there."

"Of course, we've planned for this. These are four of my top students, who will be working directly with professionals from various companies." Dr. Owen motioned to them. "This is Stefani, majoring in Oceanography and Engineering, Tommy, majoring in Electronic Engineering, Brian, majoring in Geology, and Joe, majoring in Computer Science with a focus on Scientific Visualization."

George looked at the four students, first rather sternly and then more astutely. Dr. Owen knew he had hit George's soft spot. The CEO of Standy Firm loved employing academics and research in industrial environments.

"Some of the major companies that I am in contact with include MarinaTech, Apt Technologies, and VisualSoft. They are all willing to contribute and are eager to work with us. We already have a submarine prototype that will be capable of carrying two or three people. It will be fully maneuverable in the mine. We will be starting with testing in small mines of course, for safety concerns, and mines that have been depleted for some time already so that the residue in the water is minimal."

The woman, Mary, now spoke. "Another problem is leftover gas. It poses a serious risk if the submarine hull is breached or some light should accidentally spark. And how specifically are you going to address the darkness?"

"The submarine is being specially designed for this task." Dr. Owen felt like he was on the defensive. "Tommy will be working with Apt Technologies to secure a robust sonic system onboard the submarine." Sensing that Mary was about to speak again, Dr. Owen went on quickly, "Tommy will be presenting the work in sonic technology thus far. Stefani will be working with MarinaTech to help design various components of the submarine, such as the oxygen supply, pressure control, and any additional tools or utilities. Joe and VisualSoft will be collecting the sonic data and generating computer imagery to visualize the findings. This means that Joe will be working above ground and possibly off-site." Dr. Owen paused for a moment and continued, "Brian will be the one analyzing and running the tests on the soil samples picked up from the walls and the ground of the mine."

The Standy representatives whispered amongst themselves briefly, as if to clarify who was doing what one more time.

"In addition to the above goals, being a geologist, I'm interested in discovering exactly why oil mines are almost always located in remote desert areas. Exactly what happened in the past?" Dr. Owen stopped to grab a glass of water and take one long refreshing sip. He took a look at everyone's face, but before he could continue, Michael uttered what he was thinking.

"Dr. Owen, in our experience the mine you describe will be very difficult to find. It will not be easy to find a depleted mine which has a shallow window that allows your submarine to enter."

Stefani looked at Michael, "I'll need to understand more about the window, of course." Naturally, this was the most important concern for Stefani since she would be responsible for designing the submarine.

Michael looked at Stefani and then the others, "The oil window is the drilled hole which reaches the shallow place of the reservoir. As we know, the typical depth of an oil window might be four to five kilometers, which is about two-and-a-half to three miles. Though sometimes we found windows could be only 150 meters, or 500 feet deep. Even at that, it is very deep for us to dig a hole which is big enough for even a small submarine to enter."

Suddenly the room was quiet, and everyone fell into deep thought, somewhat disappointed.

After a few seconds, Michael continued. "We will focus our efforts on locating a depleted oil reservoir in which the window is shallow. Hopefully, if we are lucky, it will be less than 500 feet. Then we must find a way to dig a bigger hole through this window that allows the submarine to enter safely. Naturally, it will cost a lot of money, a few million dollars, just for this project."

"More than half of the grant money," thought Dr. Owen. He stood up solemnly, looking at George Standy and Michael. "I know everything will be difficult, but I am confident it will come together with our teamwork." He paused for a second. "If Mr. Standy agrees, let us proceed from two sides. Standy Firm can spend some time during the next six months searching for a shallow window into a depleted oil mine, while my team continues our work of designing a suitable submarine, detection system, and computer simulation system. If we are not able to come up with a solution in the next six months, then we must meet and discuss our future alternatives."

In order to convince George Standy and his two top engineers, Dr. Owen decided to let them know what progress his team had already accomplished. Hopefully, through this effort, George would realize how enthusiastic and excited his team was about this challenging project. Therefore, without giving George a chance to respond, he continued talking.

"Ladies and gentlemen, in order to convince you of

the possibility of accomplishing this project, I would like Stefani, Tommy, and Joe to report on their progress thus far. As for Brian, his job is to analyze the collected samples from the oil mine, so he will not report at this time."

This caught the interest of George and his two engineers, so that they kept quiet and listened.

"Since the submarine is the first concern, will you speak first, Stefani?" Dr. Owen looked at Stefani.

* * *

Stefani Kim was 24 years old. Her parents immigrated to the United States from South Korea in 1982. She was in her senior year at UCLA, majoring in oceanography and engineering and was especially interested in deep-sea marine organisms. Stefani was an only child. Since she was small, she had always liked the ocean and marine organisms. Her dream was to study, research, and then compile all the knowledge currently existing about deep-sea organisms. She was from San Francisco and her father was a professor at the University of California, Berkeley. Her mother was a typical Korean housewife, staying at home, watching and educating the children, keeping the house clean, and also serving her husband. Stefani was extremely interested in deep-sea submarines as well, and desperately wanted to be involved with working with one. When she heard about Dr. Owen's project, she was very excited and asked Dr. Owen's permission to be one of the researchers on this project.

* * *

"I've visited MarinaTech in the Los Angeles area a few times. They have two submarines for deep-sea study. After talking to a couple of top engineers there, I am pretty sure that I have a very good idea of how to design a submarine that is suitable for our mission. MarinaTech has also instructed me on where I can have this submarine fabricated with the best quality.

"Basically, there are three areas in which the submarine we need differs from the submarines designed for the deep sea." She looked at Dr. Owen with a proud smile. She felt satisfied with the progress she had made in such a short time.

"The biggest difference is that we'll be blind, due to the darkness of the oil mine. Visible contact with the surrounding environment will be lost completely. We must rely on a sonic detection system, like military submarines in the deep sea. Second, I assume there will be many pockets of gas residue trapped in the oil cavern. To avoid any sparking from a regular motor, the entire submarine must be operated by battery. Of course, this will also significantly reduce the noise disturbance which can interfere with the sounds read by the sonic detector." She again looked at everyone for an agreeable reaction on their faces.

"Finally, in order to reduce the weight of the submarine, we cannot put too much equipment inside. The most important equipment will be a six-directional detecting system and two robotic arms. As the detector's information is collected, it will be transmitted to the surface for computer simulation, immediately producing a three-dimensional image. This image will then be transmitted back to the screen in the submarine so the submarine can be maneuvered without danger. This process will take only a second or two. Tommy and Joe will explain later how this can work.

"As for the two robot arms, there will be one in the front and one in the rear to dig samples and then place them into secure pockets.

"Naturally, some other systems, such as battery, oxygen supply, floating and diving, and propelling systems, must be included. However, since these systems are very similar with those of a deep-sea submarine, we should not have a problem designing them." Stefani looked at everyone, expecting some response.

"How long will the batteries last?" Michael asked.

"Conservatively, with the detection system and robot arm operation, it will provide about two hours for the submarine to move around. However, if we use too much robot arm operation, it could only run for one and a half hours," Stefani answered.

"Well, if we find a cavern which is about one to two miles long, and if the submarine can run five miles an hour, it should provide you enough time to move around. However, if you spend too much time searching, you may not be able to explore the entire cavern. To be more secure, can you increase the time frame to three hours instead of two?" Michael asked.

Stefani looked at Michael with a smile and said, "Yes, we can. But that means the weight will be increased, the floating system will be larger, and the submarine itself must be bigger. That means, as I know now, the entrance from the window to the reservoir must also be bigger."

"What size is the submarine? How many people will be inside?" Mary suddenly interrupted.

"So far, the size I have in mind is about five feet high, eight feet in length, and four feet wide. The lower half of the submarine will hold the two battery systems, one in front to operate the front propeller and one in the rear to operate the other. The floating and diving system will be at the center of the lower section. Naturally, two sample pockets and the robot arms will be situated on the lower half of the submarine as well." Stefani picked up a marker and drew a rough sketch on the dry-erase board behind her. "Two people will be in the submarine, one sitting on each end. I believe it will be Tommy and me, since I know submarines and Tommy knows the detection system, right?" She looked to Tommy for agreement, who then looked at Dr. Owen. Dr. Owen made a face as if to say, "well?"

Tommy sat up, smiled, and nodded, but thought to himself, "this sounds dangerous."

Stefani continued, "Both sides have a piloting system and monitors and the submarine can be piloted by either side. Having two people is not just to keep each other company, they will be able to help each other if one has an emergency."

"Will there be any windows?" Mary asked.

"Yes, there are two, in the front and rear. This will allow us to see outside visually when we are not in the cavern. In addition, I am curious to see inside the cavern...even though we can't see it." Everyone laughed.

"What is the submarine made of?" Mary asked.

"Of course, that's very important. The chemical residue in the mine will deteriorate any synthetic material that is sometimes used for small subs, like vinyl. I designed it using stainless steel to cover the exterior, with a plastic shell inside," Stefani answered. "The major concerns are weight and strength. The material must be light, but strong. So, the shell of submarine will be vinyl and stainless steel while the interior will be comprised of aluminum and lightweight plastic."

Dr. Owen waited for a few seconds to see if there were more questions for Stefani. Seeing there were none, he said, "If you do not have any questions, I will hand it over to Tommy. Thank you."

* * *

Tommy Wheeler was a 28-year-old post-doctorate research associate at UCLA. His expertise and interests were Electronic Communication, Real-Time Radar Simulation Systems, and Sonar Object Detection Simulation Systems. He obtained his Ph.D. in Electrical Engineering at MIT. He was hired six months ago by Dr. Owen specifically for this project due to his expertise. Tommy was a very social and handsome boy and wished to be very rich one day. He was involved with a UCLA graduate student, Cathy, whom he met just a few months ago. He had been very excited and happy to be involved in this new project. This had been especially true since he had become acquainted with Cathy in California.

* * *

Tommy stood up and beamed his attractive smile.

"Basically, we'll use sonic detection method." He looked at his notebook and then continued. "Unfortunately, this method can't detect objects far away, usually only those within a few hundred meters. Thus, the simulation will be slower. Usually it would take a few seconds to simulate the objects. But since the sub will be moving pretty slowly, probably about five miles per hour, the delay shouldn't really matter. You know, sound can travel about 331 meters per second in the air and faster in water, about 1,500 meters per second. The only concern is, if there is a high content of the oil residue and particles in the abandoned oil mine water, the information collected will not be as clear as we wish."

"Why don't you use radar detection method instead of sonic? It would be much faster, reach farther, and be clearer, wouldn't it?" Mary asked curiously.

"My understanding is that radar does not work well underwater. It uses wavelengths in the microwave range that can be absorbed by water just within several feet from the emitter," Tommy explained.

"Where on the sub are these detectors?" Michael asked.

Tommy picked up the marker and explained, using Stefani's submarine sketch. "There are six detectors which send out different signal wavelengths. These six signal emitters and collectors will be on the four sides and also the top and bottom of the sub." Tommy pointed them out on the sketch.

"Why do you have to use six different signal frequencies or wavelengths?" George Standy, who had kept himself quiet and listened, now showed his interest.

Tommy was a bit intimidated and nervous. "Well, Mr. Standy...different frequencies will offer us a clear distinction of the signals emitted and received from different emitters which are aiming in the different directions. This way, it will provide multiple sources of good and clear information to the computer for simulation. From this ton of information collected, the computer will be able to determine which data are correct and which are erroneous and create an accurate three-dimensional image of the surroundings." Tommy sighed. He was glad to have been asked this by George Standy himself. This implied George was very interested in the project.

"How can you be sure this system works?" Michael asked again.

"The Sonar Object Detection Simulation System has commonly been used in the fishing industry for years to detect deep sea fish. Oh, and of course, in the military... And in many other small sub missions before this one, though definitely not in a situation quite like this.

"So, once the system is installed and the sub is ready, I think we plan to test it a few times to make sure it's safe in the cavern, top to bottom, all systems, including the engines, batteries, detection systems, simulations..." Tommy continued.

"Actually," Stefani interrupted, "we've already talked to MarinaTech about this experiment at length. They've assured me that there are a few deep-sea caverns that are suitable for testing the sub. Working with the experts at MarinaTech, all the sub's systems will work as we hope." Stefani re-confirmed the possibility of the project. The group kept quiet.

Dr. Owen stepped in. "If you lady and gentlemen do not have more questions for Tommy and Stefani, I would like Joe to explain his part of the project," he said.

* * *

Joseph Oswards, 26 years old, was a smart and aggressive Ph.D. candidate of Computer Science at UCLA. He had obtained approval from his department to use this project for his Ph.D. thesis. His responsibility was to write a software program for the computer simulation configuration. He had to create a program that allowed the computer to simulate the visual three-dimensional image from information collected by Tommy's sonic detection emitters and receivers. He had already completed the required courses for his Ph.D. All he needed to do was to complete this project and write a thesis. He planned to complete his thesis within one or two years. Actually, due to his outstanding performance at UCLA, he already had a high paying job offer in New York City lined up. He planned to move there once the project was completed and his Ph.D. was awarded.

* * *

Joe stood up. Though a little bit nervous, he was pretty confident in his abilities. His manner of speaking had already earned him the nickname of Professor Joe from Tommy. He looked at the group from left to right and paused for a couple of seconds.

"Ladies and gentlemen, as you know, my job is complete technical oversight, and specifically designing and building a system which allows those within the submarine to see a three-dimensional image so they know exactly where they are and also what the environment in the darkness looks like. Naturally, the first step is to simulate a three-dimensional image from information collected by the six detectors. This will be done through a computer software program of my own design. Once this image is simulated, it will be sent back to the submarine. Practically speaking, it will take only a couple of seconds to complete this process for the computer. In order to allow the persons inside the submarine to know their surroundings there are eight monitors, four in front and four in the rear. Three of the four will show the image of the three sides and the fourth one will show the position of the submarine in the surrounding environment. For example, if I am the driver, there is one monitor on the left to show me what is on my left and how far the nearest object is. The same function for monitor number two on my right, and also number three in front. The fourth one, the most important one, is to show where we are in the cavern and where the surrounding objects are nearby. This will let the sub pilot, and those of us up on the surface, know the exact position of the submarine at all times," Joe explained while using his hands to point at the positions of the four monitors on Stefani's diagram.

"Two sets of four?" Mary asked curiously, confused.

"As mentioned earlier by Stefani, this submarine will seat two people, one facing front and one facing rear. The submarine can be piloted forward or backward, for maximum maneuverability. The safest way is to allow the person in front to handle forward movement and the person in the rear to handle backward movement," Joe answered. "Also, this of course provides a complete back-up for the navigation of the sub, should any issues arise.

"Naturally, this entire system will be tested in deep sea caverns. As we know, there will be only a very weak light in the cavern, and this means almost no visual at all, so this will be a very desirable place for testing," Joe added.

"Just out of curiosity, how many of these tests do you plan to conduct before you enter the depleted oil mine?" George asked.

"I believe that the plan is a minimum of three separate tests, in increasingly challenging locations. The two pilots," he looked at them with an unusually piercing gaze, "Stefani and Tommy, must first be entirely familiar with all the operations of the submarine and its instruments, the detection systems, and robot arms, but especially piloting in complete darkness," Joe answered.

* * *

After waiting for a moment, Dr. Owen saw there were no more questions. He stood up and addressed the Standy Firm team.

"You can see from my colleagues that there is a real possibility of success in accomplishing this project. However, I do now realize that it may be more difficult to find the right oil mine for this project than it will be to collect samples once we're there. We would very much appreciate your partnership in that aspect of this project. Once successful, the knowledge gained from this project will offer a far deeper understanding of the geology and formation of Earth, and of the structure and development of oil mines in particular, which we expect to be of great benefit to you. These samples collected from one of the most remote parts of the Earth will be analyzed by Brian and myself." Brian nodded and smiled. "Brian is one of my finest students, who is pursuing his Ph.D. His thesis will be the analysis of this depleted oil mine," Dr. Owen concluded and sat back, looking to George for approval.

"Lady and gentlemen, I am pretty impressed with your plan and progress so far. I believe our partnership will prove to be of great benefit to us all. This is some exciting new territory." Everyone in the room smiled, and relaxed. This was really going to happen. "Please allow us three to six months to search our historical data and mining records from the last 50 years. You know, even if we are able to find some candidates, we'll have to go down there and do extensive testing," George said.

"Even if we find a desirable old oil reservoir, getting the submarine in and out isn't guaranteed. Even once we've opened the window, we still don't know how wide the passage into the reservoir will be. It could be only a few meters or a few hundred meters. Before we dig, we'll need to study carefully and try to get as much detailed information as possible. Our Ultrasonic Detection System can only provide us with information to a certain level and depth. If we're lucky, I mean if conditions allow, such as the structure and the density of soil, we can sometimes collect information to a depth of 260 feet. That's still only 80 meters deep." Geoge paused a little bit and had a sip of water from the glass on the table.

"In addition, we'll also need to develop a way to pump out as much of the remaining gas as possible from trapped pockets in the cavern. This remaining gas can be very dangerous," he emphasized. George looked at Dr. Owen's face and saw that he was committed. However, he saw worry creep across Stefani's face. This project, though exciting and challenging, could be very deadly.

"If we do find a desirable cavern, we must first dig and make the window larger to the size of at least 15 feet in diameter. I suggest, lady and gentlemen, for the time being, that you design a smaller robot sub that can be a forerunner for the entrance. This robot submarine should be able to collect information from the surrounding environment including the size and shape of the window, and the passage into the cavern. You'll want this robot sub to be capable of testing whether there is any remaining volatile residue." Stefani's brow furrowed more deeply. "Anyway, what I mean is that before we send your people down, we should be certain the trip is safe," George suggested. Everyone around the table knew George spoke from his expertise and knowledge of oil mines.

"Your $5,000,000 grant won't get you too far in a project of this magnitude. Just finding a suitable mine and digging the window would run your funding dry. However, Standy Firm will be happy to help. Spend your funds and resources on that robot sub, and the manned submarine and detection systems. I'll handle the rest," George added.

Dr. Owen and his four students smiled at each other and looked at George Standy with deep appreciation. As Dr. Owen suspected, George Standy would not hesitate to support this sort of groundbreaking study and research.

Mary raised her right hand and, when everyone looked at her, she spoke.

"Why don't we just use a robot submarine to enter

the cavern and pick up the samples, so we don't have to risk anyone's life for this project?"

"Thank you, Mary. We're all concerned, of course," Dr. Owen answered. "We thought of that at first, but a small robot cannot pick up many samples. In addition, since the most desirable cavern will be very big, when a small robot enters the cavern it will be hard to make any decision about the next step from the surface. If there are people in the submarine, they can have a more accurate sense of the situation and can make a correct decision on the spot, especially if contact to the surface is lost."

"In our experience, there can be a serious risk of collapse or falling debris in these mines. The slightest disturbance sometimes causes rockslides or even collapse of the mine," Michael interjected.

Tommy stood up to answer. "Believe me, we take these risks seriously. Actually, Stefani, correct me if I'm wrong, but, using an electric motor should significantly reduce the interference of the ultrasonic detecting system, and also cut down all unnecessary disturbance to the surrounding environment. We're just going to sneak in and out quietly without making too much noise." Everyone laughed.

Brian had kept quiet all afternoon, knowing that all the subjects discussed were not his field. He was just part of the audience today. He would be excited only when he saw the samples actually brought back by the submarine. This is what he lived for.

Dr. Owen stood, and the rest of team followed. All Dr.

Owen and his crew could do now was wait for good news from Standy Firm and continue designing and conducting further tests. Now they also had to design a robot submarine as well.

"Thank you all so much. We'll be in touch," he said.

At MarinaTech Three Months Later

This was a very exciting day. It was a sunny and warm June afternoon in Los Angeles. Springtime in L.A. can be very pleasant, but it is also unhealthy when the smog levels start to rise to their legendary proportions. Dr. Owen pondered this on his Big Blue Bus ride to MarinaTech to see the submarine for the first time. L.A. became notorious for its smog in the 1940s when a Caltech chemist named Arie Haagen-Smit determined that the air pollution the city had been suffering from was the result of increasing auto exhaust. The problem in L.A. had brought this issue to international awareness, and eventually led to the creation of the Clean Air Act.

Dr. Owen entered the MarinaTech facility and saw his team working with the MarinaTech engineers, buzzing around the nearly completed sub in the large manufacturing bay. After three months of heavy work, it had finally reached the final stage of construction. They had decided to name the submarine 'Pioneer.'

On Mr. Standy's recommendation, Stefani had also fabricated the small robot submarine, making it about two feet long, one foot high, and one foot wide. Fortunately, the engineers at MarinaTech had some experience developing unmanned subs. Tommy had installed six small ultrasonic detectors on its perimeter. They had named this mini-sub 'Forerunner.' They were counting on 'Forerunner' to lead them to a safe passage into the oil mine.

MarinaTech was primarily a deep-sea exploration company. In order to have a submarine to serve their purposes, the company normally modified a sub that had been manufactured by other companies. They sometimes designed their own, and even had the facilities to fabricate small subs when necessary. When Stefani contacted them three months ago, they were very excited about the design and fabrication of this new and unique submarine, and they expanded their manufacturing capabilities to prepare for the project. They believed that through helping Stefani design and fabricate this submarine from the ground up, they would be able to learn something new. This experience would be very valuable for their future study and research.

Mr. Kyle Thomson was the manager of the submarine design and fabrication department assigned to help Stefani to design and fabricate 'Forerunner' and 'Pioneer.' They were small and not as complicated as the average deep-sea submarine, and MarinaTech had almost everything they needed for fabrication. Mr. Thomson and another engineer, Tony Graff, worked with Stefani on every aspect of the sub project. Tony helped with the design but was mainly the coordinator for the entire project. With Tony and two other technicians, both 'Forerunner' and 'Pioneer' were on schedule.

That morning, Stefani and Tommy had invited Dr.

Owen to see their progress, and to see if he had some suggestions or comments about the project.

"Good morning, Professor Owen!" Stefani and Tommy greeted him as he entered the MarinaTech factory. Stefani had been watching the door for his arrival for the last half hour.

She led Dr. Owen to the corner of the factory where 'Forerunner' and 'Pioneer' were. He walked between the two subs, looking them both up and down, and crouching to see underneath. It struck him how beautiful their shining stainless-steel exterior was, and it reminded him of the spaceships from the 1950s' science fiction he loved so much as a young boy.

"Wow. There they are. From imagination to reality in three months," he thought. 'Pioneer' was only slightly bigger than a mid-sized car.

Stefani introduced Dr. Owen, "Dr. Kyle Thomson, I'd like to introduce you to our fearless leader, Dr. Owen." They shook hands. Dr. Owen knew Dr. Thomson had helped greatly in the fabrication of these two submarines. Without his expertise, it would not have been possible for Stefani and Tommy to complete it in just three months. Dr. Owen also shook Tommy's hand, and they smiled at each other. Stefani then explained the structure of both subs.

"Professor Owen, 'Pioneer' is six feet high, four feet wide, and eight feet long, and weighs 1.2 tons. There are four small wheels underneath so we can move it around easily. These four wheels can be pulled in when the submarine is in the water. In that way they will not be in the way and become obstacles when the submarine is moving under the water. There are two lights, one in front and one in the rear. I don't expect we will use them too much in the actual cavern. However, I believe we will need them when we do our test drives," Stefani explained as she led Dr. Owen around 'Pioneer.'

"There are the six ultrasonic detectors, four on the four sides, one on the top and one down here on the bottom. As you can see, they're set within the main body, so they don't project outward at all. This way the drag is reduced, and they should be safe from damage if the submarine hits anything." She pointed out the location of each detector to Dr. Owen.

"As you can see there are two propellers, one in front and one in the rear," Stefani said.

"Stefani, how do you define which side is the front and which is the rear?" Dr. Owen asked.

"Yes, its symmetrical. Both sides are exactly the same. But I call my side the front and Tommy's side the rear," Stefani laughed and looked at Tommy who was standing beside them listening. "I'm the captain of this ship, right?" She giggled harder. "Actually, my weight is 140 pounds while Tommy weighs 185. To compensate for the weight difference, the captain's seat is higher and heavier so the submarine can be balanced." Tommy squinted at her, with a half-smile.

Dr. Owen hadn't considered the weight difference. He realized that they were very fortunate to have the detailed nautical engineering knowledge of Stefani and the MarinaTech team. Dr. Owen nodded and smiled.

"Here is the robot arm. There is another in the rear." Stefani showed him the robot arm, which was in its withdrawn position next to the submarine, situated beside the front propeller. "The arm will place the samples we pick up here in the secure sample pocket. It's just like a drawer that can be moved in and out. To help unload the samples, this pocket can automatically be turned upside down." Stefani used her hands to show Dr. Owen how the pocket could move in every direction.

"Behind the propeller, next to the seat inside, is the battery. There is another one exactly the same size in the rear. These two batteries supply all the energy for every function of the sub, including the motors."

"Which equipment consumes the most energy in the submarine?" Dr. Owen asked.

"Well, as you know, the propeller pulls a lot of energy, but we've done our best to make the sub as hydrodynamic as possible. The robot arm and the system that operates it draw a lot of power. Other systems are as energy efficient as possible and their consumption is pretty negligible," Stefani said. She then took Dr. Owen to the center of the submarine and said, "Here inside are the floatation system and the oxygen tanks."

"How long exactly do the battery and oxygen supplies last?" Dr. Owen asked. This was a major concern to him since these were the two most critical factors that could cause their death if they failed while they were in the oil mine.

"If we use the robot arms conservatively and gather our samples in minimal time, the battery should last from two hours to two hours and ten minutes. And so, the oxygen supply is designed to last at least that long, a little over two hours. If we need more, then the submarine will have to be larger and heavier, which then would pose a problem for passing through a small window into the cavern," Stefani replied.

Stefani smiled and brought him around to the other side, to the entrance of the sub. It was more like a window instead of a door. To get in, you had to raise one of your legs and step into the entrance and then squeeze in. The door could be opened from inside or outside. There was a stool in front of the entrance. "After you," she said.

Dr. Owen stood on the stool and stepped one leg in and then the other. He already knew the 'rear' was Tommy's side. Since he was almost the same size as Tommy, he went to Tommy's seat and sat down. Stefani also stepped in and sat on her seat.

"As you see, there are four monitors beside and in front of you, Professor," Stefani said.

"Your right-hand side shows the information collected from your right-hand side detector and your left-hand side shows the view of the left-hand side detector. The one on the top in front of you shows the front view and the one underneath it is the three-dimensional simulation image generated from all detectors.

"The switch next to the steering control is for me and Tommy to switch piloting."

Stefani explained each of the controls, how the floatation system worked, how to maneuver the robot arm and sample pocket. Dr. Owen looked at the oxygen supply meter and warning lights. "I hope this goes smoothly," he thought.

"Oh, yes! The gas warning light is above your head. It should flash if there is any gas outside the sub," Stefani continued. "There is a gasmask underneath each seat, just in case."

"Is the three-dimensional simulation imaging system operational yet? Can I see a demonstration?" Dr. Owen asked.

"Yes, of course." Stefani powered up the sub and put on the communication headset. There was a gentle humming sound and a series of beeps and clicks as the systems came online. From the window, she could see that Tommy was sitting right in front of Joe's computer station with a headset on.

"Tommy, Professor would like to see a demonstration of the simulation system. Can we give him a demo?" she asked. At the same time, Dr. Owen put on his headset.

"Yeah, but since Joe isn't here, all we can show is the images collected from three directions around your seat," Tommy answered.

"It is better than nothing," Dr. Owen said.

Stefani heard his voice in her earpiece for the first time, and thought, "I'll be hearing that a lot over the next year."

Tommy fired up Joe's computer control station. "Pioneer, you are cleared for liftoff," he said to himself before saying out loud, "Hello? OK, just turn on each of the monitors. The detectors are already functioning on their own, and the images should be visible."

Dr. Owen replied, "Yes. There they are, thank you." He was a little bit disappointed, however, since he had wanted to see three-dimensional simulation images. But he would have to wait until Joe was there.

"Stefani, you, Tommy, and Joe have done a great job. I am very impressed with your progress in such a short time. However, you have to keep pondering if there is anything missing in the design."

"Yes, Professor. We have had a lot of meetings with MarinaTech engineers. They have a lot of experience in designing submarines and have offered us many key ideas for our designs. Naturally, we'll continue meeting with them till we are satisfied."

They got out of the submarine and Stefani brought Dr. Owen to see the mini-sub, 'Forerunner.' Tommy followed them.

"MarinaTech has used this technology before and has made similar subs many times, so it was surprisingly easy," Stefani said.

It was essentially a miniature 'Pioneer,' complete with the six sensors, and propellers on each end. "This is 'Forerunner.'" It was one foot tall, one foot wide, and two feet long. It weighed only 38 pounds.

"How long can this little sub run?" Dr. Owen asked.

"The battery should support at least 30 minutes of exploration," Stefani replied. "This should give us enough time to explore the window passage."

Dr. Owen was very satisfied with all that Stefani and

Tommy had accomplished. It seemed all the necessary aspects they had discussed were implemented and functioning. All they needed were a few more days for the final touches, and they would be ready.

* * *

The next day, Dr. Owen called George Standy. "Hi George! I just faxed you the final design layout and dimensions of both subs. I wonder if you received them?" Dr. Owen asked.

"I believe I did. I am not at my desk, but I believe my secretary has already put them in my office. I will check later. These dimensions will help my engineers to visualize the subs moving through the right-sized window. Actually, I just received a report yesterday. I am told that we have found five possible candidates of old oil reservoirs from the nearly 200 we have in our database. All of these oil mines are small and should be the right size," Mr. Standy said. "Compared with a round lake, from the oil pumped out in the past, all of these reservoirs might have about a one-mile long diameter and about a 250-foot depth. However, my engineers have to conduct further tests to see how deep the windows are and how long the passage to the reservoirs are. It shouldn't take more than two months to get the final results," he continued.

"This is great news. Thank you, George!" Dr. Owen said. "On our side, we will conduct a few tests on the ground and make some necessary adjustments. After that, we plan to conduct a test in a lake in a few weeks.

I will keep you informed. Also, if possible, please ask your secretary to contact me with any good news. You know, I will be very anxious to know anything you can tell me about these five possible candidate mines."

"Naturally, James. It's a deal," Mr. Standy said.

Ultrasonic Detecting and Three-Dimensional Simulation System

Two weeks later, all fabrication of 'Forerunner' and 'Pioneer' was completed. Before the submarines were moved to Dr. Owen's garage, Tommy, Stefani, and Joe requested the opportunity to run a simple test to demonstrate the capability of 'Forerunner.' This would give them some confidence and experience of the possibility of exploration with the detection and simulation systems.

That Saturday morning at 10:30 it was sunny as usual in Los Angeles, and Dr. Owen and his three crewmembers were standing next to a swimming pool. The pool was part of MarinaTech's employee recreation park. They had obtained approval from MarinaTech to use the pool a couple of days ago.

Brian and his girlfriend arrived just before the testing was scheduled to begin. Brian had previously planned to spend this weekend with his new love, Xiaoling, a very nice Chinese girl he had met in San Francisco, but he wanted to be there to show support for the team as the sub went into the water for the first time. He also thought it was a good opportunity for Xiaoling to see the amazing sub he had been talking about.

"Tommy, explain to me again the details of how the ultrasonic detecting system works," Dr. Owen asked, though he already knew the basic theory.

"Yes, Professor. After consulting with an Apt Technologies engineer a few times, we believe that we can depend entirely on the ultrasonic system. Apt Technologies was able to provide me with the names of a few companies who are producing deep sea ultrasonic detecting systems. This kind of system is commonly used by fishing industries today."

"Why don't you ask Apt Technologies to build the ones we need?" Dr. Owen asked.

"Well, actually, they were not serious about getting involved in production. They just wanted to offer some engineering advice. To them, fabricating these devices is not economical. Furthermore, if it is too expensive, we cannot afford it and we will lose the chance and experience in building it," Tommy said.

"That is great! How about you, Joe? Can you explain this to me before your demonstration?" Dr. Owen asked.

"Naturally, Professor," Joe replied. "Actually, the most important part is the software. This software must have a few functions. Number one, it must be able to collect information from all six ultrasonic detectors and then get rid of information repeatedly collected from the different detectors. To distinguish the difference between one detector and another, Tommy was able to input six different ultrasonic frequencies, one for each detector. By calculating the scanning angle and speed of the sound rebounded, the software will be able to collect only the information needed. Number two, this software must be able to simulate a three-dimensional moving image while the submarine is moving. The time from information upload to simulation should not be longer than one-half to one second. Number three, once the simulation images are generated, they can be transmitted to the submarine immediately. With VisualSoft's engineering advice, I was able to generate the desired system. How clear the images will be is unknown since the system will be functioning in an oil mine and we don't know how much the particles or remaining oil residue will affect the detecting. It will not be the same as in clear water," Joe explained.

"Now, let us take a look at how this is functioning," Joe said. With Tommy's help, they carefully placed 'Forerunner' into the swimming pool. They had placed some pieces of rock, some pipes, and even a couple of chairs and metal desks in the swimming pool earlier.

Stefani had the remote control in her hands. She started the motor of 'Forerunner' and began to pilot it forward. When the motor was started, all of the detecting systems activated automatically and immediately. Dr. Owen was standing next to Joe and Stefani. The three of them were surrounded by seven monitors. There were three monitors on three sides of them except for in front where there were four monitors. Stefani sat right in front of the four monitors. To avoid the hot sun, the entire set up was under a big tree.

"These three monitors give us the images of the three directions of the 'Forerunner' while the middle one on the bottom in front of me is the image on the front side. The monitor on its left is for the bottom detector and the right is for the top detector. The one on the top, the most important one, is the three-dimensional simulation image." Joe used his fingers to point out the monitors one-by-one. Actually, Dr. Owen could see this already since on the bottom in front of each monitor there was a label stating its function.

As Stefani moved 'Forerunner' through the swimming pool, she became excited and felt a bit playful. It was like she was a nine-year old girl again playing with her robot submarine. She carefully maneuvered 'Forerunner.' From the three-dimensional images, she could easily see where 'Forerunner' was and the obstacles around it. She skillfully dodged the obstacles just like a fish swimming in a coral reef. This also reminded her of the trip her family took to Cozumel San Francisco Reef when she was ten years old. Her family, along with a few other tourists, had gone in a small submarine that took them around the beautiful underwater scenery of the coral reef and the sea creatures that lived there. It was the most amazing trip she had ever been on. That trip also triggered her deep interest in submarine deep sea exploration.

After 25 minutes, Stefani piloted 'Forerunner' back to the edge of the pool where Tommy and Joe picked it up.

When they were done, Joe got everyone to his area where he showed them a video of the entire process. It was a very clear moving image. The project was a good success so far. The entire crew felt comfortable about it; however, they all knew this was only a test. It would be the same as the real thing especially when 'Pioneer' began to run.

Chapter 2
Testing

Lake Testing

Dr. Owen and his crew were planning a series of actual tests for 'Pioneer' in a lake and deep ocean cavern. They decided to try a test in a lake first since it would be easier and safer. If there was any emergency, the submarine crew would be able to receive help without too much difficulty.

Before the lake test, Stefani and Tommy practiced five times on the ground. They learned how to communicate with each other without seeing each other's facial expressions since they would be sitting with their backs to each other in the submarine. They also had to learn how to read the images generated from the computer simulation quickly. However, these tests were not the same as if the submarine was in the water.

Wednesday, July 20 was the day chosen to avoid the weekend tourist crowd. This was a big day. This would be the first test to see if the submarine and the detecting system were as good as desired. They chose a small lake about one mile long, Lake Harrison, around 30 miles east of Los Angeles. Usually, this lake had fewer tourists since most of them were attracted by the bigger Lake

Matthews, which was nearby. In addition, Lake Harrison was shallow and only about 70 feet in the deepest place – that would be suitable for the primary test.

Dr. Owen had a truck and trailer that he normally used to carry his small boat to the lake or ocean for fishing or water skiing with his family. Now, both his children were grown up and independent, and he and his wife had lost interest in these kinds of activities. They rather enjoyed what little downtime they had, usually going for long walks in the woods.

The day before, Dr. Owen and Tommy had gone to the MarinaTech factory to pick up 'Pioneer' and 'Forerunner,' covering them with black plastic sheets. Then, they towed the trailer and submarines back to Dr. Owen's home to keep them overnight in the backyard to avoid his curious neighbors.

Stefani, Tommy, and Joe arrived at Dr. Owen's house as scheduled, at 6 a.m., with a rented mobile home. Joe had used his name to rent a mobile home to carry all the equipment and also then set the equipment up on site without being noticed.

"Good morning, Dr. Owen. This will be a good day," Joe greeted Dr. Owen when he stepped out of his driver's seat.

"All of you have your breakfast yet?" Dr. Owen asked. "If you haven't, go in the kitchen and get something. We must leave soon to avoid morning traffic. You know, Los Angeles traffic jams are quite famous."

Stefani had already had breakfast, so she stayed outside and talked to Dr. Owen while the other two quickly entered the house to grab some. Dr. Owen's wife, Jennifer, was still sleeping.

"Dr. Owen, do you think our funds will be enough?" Stefani asked.

"Well I've had a look at the accounting, and it has already cost us nearly $1,500,000 for the construction of 'Forerunner' and 'Pioneer,' as you probably know. If we have to pay more than $3,000,000 to Standy Firm, then we will be short. However, I believe Mr. Standy intends to help us," Dr. Owen replied.

"What are the odds that Standy Firm will find the kind of oil mine we need?" Stefani asked again. She had been worrying about the entire project. Money had always been an issue; opportunity was another one.

"We should know soon. Mr. Standy told me about a month ago that they had five candidates. I am just hoping that we are able to find one," Dr. Owen replied.

"How about the risk? This is a new exploration which no one has ever done before," she worried. "I feel like we really can't foresee the problems we'll face, since the cavern will be so different from the swimming pool we've been testing in."

"Stefani, that is why we must be thoughtful and careful. So far, I have confidence in you and Tommy. From your submarine design and construction, I know you and Tommy are very thoughtful in every aspect. I also know both of you are very careful in doing anything. I have the best team in my hands. I don't worry that much. Actually, I am more excited than worried," Dr. Owen replied.

Stefani was very happy to know that Dr. Owen appreciated her capabilities and accomplishments. To her, this was the biggest challenge of her life. While they were talking, the other two came out of the house with a satisfied look on their faces.

Dr. Owen and Tommy took the truck and trailer while Joe and Stefani brought the mobile home. They took off to Lake Harrison. Due to insurance, Dr. Owen had to drive the truck himself. Furthermore, he had had more experience than anyone else in towing the trailer since he used to do so when he went fishing with his family.

When they arrived, it was only 6:45 a.m. Joe immediately set up the equipment inside and out of the mobile home and conducted some tests. They had decided to keep the site of the test at the far end of the lake where there were not too many tourists around.

First, they tested 'Forerunner,' since this would be easy. Stefani and Tommy took turns piloting the little sub so that both of them would have some feeling and experience of how to handle it. However, the most important part for them was to gain some idea of how to read the monitors. Since the detecting system for 'Forerunner' was almost the same as 'Pioneer,' this easier test would provide them with a very good idea of how the entire detecting system would work, and how Joe's navigation could be simulated. Furthermore, since they were sitting right next to Joe in the mobile home, if they had questions, Joe would be able to explain it to them immediately.

Relying on the monitors, each of them tried to keep

'Forerunner' low and near the bottom of the lake so they had more chances to pilot it through rocks, sunken logs, and other miscellaneous objects. It was important to gain some experience for this since, for all they knew, they could be in a jungle when they piloted 'Pioneer' through the window or tunnel and into the bottom of the oil cavern. Since 'Forerunner' only had 30 minutes of energy supply, the test was soon over. It was satisfactory just like the test in the MarinaTech employee pool.

* * *

Next was 'Pioneer.' First, they placed a few wood boards on the sand at the edge of the water and pushed 'Pioneer' on top of them. Then Tommy and Stefani entered the submarine. After that, Joe and Dr. Owen together pushed it the rest of the way into the water. They rushed to the mobile home to watch the monitors.

Before Stefani piloted 'Pioneer' in the water, Joe called her on the telecom.

"Can you hear me clearly, Stefani?" Joe asked. "Please double check to see if the monitors function normally," he added.

"Yes, Joe," Stefani replied. After a minute or so, she said, "Everything is fine. Let's do it.

"Tommy, let me pilot it for about 50 minutes first and then you take over." Stefani felt that she should do it first simply because she was the one who designed it. She also believed she had more knowledge about deep-sea exploration than Tommy.

"No problem, Stefani. You are the captain."

Actually, during the nearly two months of design, discussion, and research that went into building 'Forerunner' and 'Pioneer,' Tommy had developed a great impression of Stefani's talent and firm decision making.

"She is a very talented woman with such a beautiful Asian looking face," Tommy thought.

The thought reminded him of his relationship with Cathy. It seemed that after a few months of acquaintance the honeymoon period was over, and they did not get together as much as they used to. He remembered the night a week ago when Cathy called him, "Hi, Tommy! It has been a while without talking to you."

"I am sorry, Cathy. I have been so busy designing submarines for my new projects. I will see if I can find a time when we can get together again."

"Tommy, actually the reason that I called is because I need to tell you something."

"What do you want to tell me? You can tell me when we meet."

Cathy hesitated for a moment, "Actually, I want to tell you that I have another boyfriend. I met him a couple of weeks ago when I was in the library. I was looking for a book and he helped me find it. After that, we met a few times. We really like each other and can talk for a long time."

Tommy was surprised and felt sad that he was being dumped. He did not answer for a few seconds.

"After six months with you, you feel more like a brother to me instead of a lover. I am very sorry, Tommy.

Can we just be friends?" Cathy continued.

"Well, if that is what you feel. We will see how the situation turns around," Tommy said, feeling lost.

They didn't talk much after that and Cathy hung up the phone.

Tommy was sad and depressed for a couple of days afterwards. He also realized that he might be in love with Stefani. However, he hesitated to pursue it for two reasons: first, he still had a relationship with Cathy, and he did not want to hurt her feelings. Second, he knew that Stefani was from an Asian Korean family. He did not know if he would be accepted by them since he believed all Asian families were very conservative. While he was thinking about all of this, he felt the submarine begin to move downward.

Stefani carefully piloted the submarine into deeper water. Since she could see an outside scene through her side window, she could not help taking a peek sometimes to make sure what the monitors showed matched with what was outside. After five minutes, when they had reached a depth of 32 feet, she realized that she was still piloting 'Pioneer' with her eyes on the window. She reached in her pocket and found her handkerchief and covered the window. Now, she had to rely on the monitors. She knew she had to get used to knowing her surroundings by using the monitors.

There was nothing around them but water and the occasional fish or turtle swimming by. Stefani realized that they wouldn't have much chance to practice if they stayed in the shallow area. Therefore, she decided to go to the deepest place in the lake, down to 70 feet. There they found some huge logs and rocks. Now, from the monitors, Stefani could see there were more obstacles for her to practice around. With four detecting monitors and also the three-dimensional simulation images transmitted from Joe, she moved 'Pioneer' around the bottom of the lake. She felt new and very challenged at the beginning, but after only 30 minutes or so she became bored.

"Tommy, there isn't much of a challenge here. It wouldn't take too much time for you to get used to it. If you like, you can take over now," Stefani said.

"OK!" Tommy replied and switched the controls on in front of him. Now, Tommy had control of the submarine.

As Tommy piloted the submarine, Stefani began to think about the difference between here and the oil cavern. "What are the possible dangers if this was an oil cavern?" she kept asking herself. She was afraid she had missed planning for something that could make a big difference in their destiny. Suddenly, cold sweat and a chill feeling emerged from her body. She thought, "If there was a leak in the submarine due to a collision, how could we escape?"

Since it was not too hard to pilot the submarine in this kind of environment, she began to talk to Tommy.

"What do you think if there is a leak in the submarine? It could potentially happen if there is an accident." She paused. "Especially in the oil cavern. We may lose vision if there is some damage or malfunction of the monitors. Or we may hit something and cause a leak. Or, some falling rocks could also damage the submarine."

The more she thought about it, the more she got scared. She realized she was trembling. Though she was confident in her design, this ominous feeling crept over her, and she began to visualize everything that could possibly go wrong.

"If there was some leak while we were here in the lake, it would be easier. If we have diving equipment and oxygen tanks, we can get out of here easily. But I don't know how much this will help if we have the same problem in the oil cavern," Tommy said. "We won't be able to see in there, and that water is most likely toxic. Even if we're able to get out of the sub, how would we know where to go?"

Stefani felt like there needed to be a viable escape plan before she could rest assured. The oil cavern was going to be an incredibly dangerous environment, and now that she was inside the sub, the full gravity of the situation was hitting her.

Their conversation was heard by the others through the telecom. Dr. Owen decided to shift their minds away from this worry and fear. It wouldn't do them any good to ponder these things right now while they were still in the water.

"Tommy, try to pick up some samples. We need to test the robot arm and storage system," Dr. Owen said over the telecom.

This brought Tommy and Stefani's thoughts back to the task at hand. Tommy paused a few seconds and said,

"Yes, Professor. I'll find a nice rock to pick up and put in the secure pocket."

Tommy piloted the submarine to about a foot from the bottom and extended his side of the robot arm outward. However, he couldn't see what he was picking up since the front monitor did not show the angle clearly, which was about 60 degrees downward. The monitor could see only about a 55-degree angle downward. If he wanted to see what he was picking up, he had to tilt the submarine at least ten degrees downward on his end. This was not quite as desirable as he wished originally.

"Okay. This is less than ideal." He managed to pick up some small rocks and sand on the bottom and moved the sample pocket out, but when he tried to put the samples into the drawer, he lost half of them. For the same reason, he could not see the operation clearly from the front monitor. He pulled the sample pocket back in first and then the robot arm. He knew what had to be done to correct this.

"Stefani, can you also pick up some samples and place them into your side pocket? This will make the front and rear more balanced. Also, you should practice using the arm and see how it feels," Tommy said.

Stefani did and encountered the same vision problem. In fact, due to her lack of vision, Stefani didn't realize that she had picked up a rock that was much larger than she intended. When she placed it in the pocket, the rock got stuck and the pocket could not be pulled into its secured position.

They had only 15 minutes left. They had to return.

They piloted the sub back to the shore without a problem, though one sample pocket stuck out.

Dr. Owen and his crew thought this lake test would be simple and easy. They began to realize, however, that this trip had offered them a valuable lesson. The the test results suggested several modifications were needed.

"It seems the submarine was still not as balanced as I thought. The weight on Stefani's side is still heavier than my side. I think it's because I lost almost eight pounds in the last few weeks," Tommy said.

"Yes, I felt the same. Tommy, why did you lose weight in such a short time?" Stefani asked.

"I guess I did not eat as healthy and sleep as well as before. I guess I spent too much effort on this project," Tommy answered with some embarrassment. He did not want to tell the group that the main reason he lost weight was because he lost his girlfriend, Cathy.

"Since your weights might be changing without our knowing it, we need to balance the submarine right before entering the water or oil mine next time. By the way, Tommy needs to redesign the front and rear ultrasonic detectors so the up-down angle can be adjusted," Dr. Owen said.

"Yes, Dr. Owen. It is on the top of my list. I will get started as soon as possible. However, I had a serious concern about safety. I believe we need an emergency plan in case the submarine is leaking. It could mean the difference between life and death," Tommy replied.

"I will talk to MarinaTech and see what suggestions

they may have. After all, they have more experience with this issue than we do," Stefani said. She was very worried about safety as well.

"At least both of you gained some actual experience piloting the submarine by watching monitors, picking up samples, and coordinating with each other. I will also see if I am able to fine-tune the simulator to the degree that you can see the size and shape of samples before you pick them up," Joe said.

"Tommy, how long will it take for you to modify the front and rear ultrasonic system?" Dr. Owen asked.

"If we return 'Pioneer' to MarinaTech, it would take about two days," Tommy replied.

"I still have a serious concern though. What should we do if the submarine has a leak? MarinaTech may be able to suggest some safety equipment, but we should train ourselves on using it in action," Stefani asked. Safety remained the most important issue in her mind. "Even with our diving equipment, how can we find our way out in the pitch black?" Stefani continued with a deeply concerned face.

"There is survival training for this kind of blind diving situation. Both of you have some diving experience, right?" Dr. Owen asked. He fondly remembered taking his own kids diving and watching them get their certification in their teens.

"No!" Stefani replied.

"A couple of times when I was in high school," Tommy replied.

"Obviously, we'll need to get you both some training

with a survival diving consultant. And, I want you practicing in the swimming pool a few times per week. You must learn to put the underwater gear on in under three minutes and how to use it in a blind situation," Dr. Owen said.

"If there was a situation, you must put them on before water fills up the submarine. Once the pressure of the inside and outside is balanced, you can open the door and get out. In our case, based on the size of our submarine, it would most probably give you only three to five minutes," Dr. Owen continued.

"Why can't we just wear the underwater gear the whole time, to be safer?" Stefani asked. She was not happy to now be picturing herself and Tommy clamoring in the toxic darkness of the mine.

"I'm sorry. I thought it was understood that these wetsuits are constructed of insulating material that will ensure that you have no contact with the water in the mine. They will be simply too warm for you to wear out of the water for any length of time," replied Dr. Owen.

Joe stepped in, "Each of these suits should have a signal emitter. Wherever you move, I will know where you are. The suits also have a telecom system for emergency situations such as this. I will direct you back toward the window, where you can be retrieved. Once we're there a short while, I should have a complete map of the surrounding cavern," he said.

"How long does the oxygen tank last?" Stefani again asked.

"About 30 minutes, if you breathe correctly. That

means if you panic, the oxygen supply will be shorter. You'll see when you begin training," Dr. Owen replied.

"I think we're panicking already," joked Tommy.

"Today is Wednesday. By the time Tommy completes his modification of the ultrasonic system, it will be the weekend already. Let us do the next round of testing on Monday. That will give Tommy more time to make his modifications. Furthermore, he and Stefani must also practice underwater diving a few times in the swimming pool," Dr. Owen said.

* * *

The next day, Dr. Owen received an unexpected call.

"Hi James. This is George Standy. I have good news for you," George said. "We found an old oil mine located in Austin, Texas that fits the bill for your project."

This really was good news. Dr. Owen knew that without a suitable old oil mine, even though they had a good submarine, everything would still be in vain. He was very excited.

"Really! Please tell me more. This really is good news," Dr. Owen said.

"The best part is that the depth of the window in this mine is only 285 feet. This, considerably, is very lucky since the depths of almost all windows is more than 500 feet," George said. "From our ground ultrasonic detecting system, we could see there was a tunnel connecting the window to the oil mine. The tunnel is about 157 feet long and has a gradient of about 57 degrees downward."

"Well! This is fantastic indeed," Dr. Owen said. "How big is the mine, I mean, the size?"

"The actual shape of the mine is still unknown since our ground ultrasonic detecting could not reach that far down. However, from the record of the oil pumped out in the past, if we compare it to a round lake, it will be about one mile in diameter and 260 feet deep," George replied.

"Now the question is, how long will it take to dig to make the window big enough for the submarine to enter," Dr. Owen wondered.

"Remember what I said earlier that the depth of the window is about 285 feet, but it does not directly connect to the reservoir. Once the submarine has reached this depth, it still has to get through a tunnel to reach the reservoir," George said. "It will take about two months of digging to make the window large enough for the submarine to reach the tunnel," he concluded.

"Are you implying that the hardest task will be getting through the tunnel?" Dr. Owen asked.

"Yes. We don't know very much about this tunnel," George replied.

Dr. Owen now realized that that was why George had stubbornly suggested building a robot submarine during the first meeting. He could see how necessary it was to send the robot submarine down first to explore the passage of the tunnel.

"If it's OK with you, we'll begin to dig in a couple of days," George suggested.

"Naturally, if you feel that this mine is our best option," Dr. Owen replied.

Actually, Dr. Owen knew that it was not easy to find a suitable oil mine for their exploration. The news from George was actually very good news. He had been worried about this since the beginning of the project.

"When will your team be ready to enter the oil cavern?" George asked, so his company would be able to co-ordinate with Dr. Owen's schedule.

"Well, today is July 21ˢᵗ. How about September 20ᵗʰ? Do you think your people could match this date?" Dr. Owen asked.

"That's a good day for me. I will be in Austin for a couple of days during that time. While I'm there I can also watch the progress achieved by your team."

"That will be great to have you there also," Dr. Owen said.

This was surely great news. Dr. Owen immediately called Tommy and asked him to pass the word on to the team. This news was sure to inspire and excite everyone.

* * *

Tommy had spent the last three days modifying the ultrasonic detectors in both the front and rear of the submarine. In addition, Joe had come and installed some additional sensors and software in 'Pioneer' to improve the simulation. This new modification would provide better information about the objects being picked up. Now 'Pioneer' was ready.

Tommy and Stefani had a schedule to meet at the swimming pool in MarinaTech for their practice and training. Tommy stood by the pool in his swimsuit waiting for her. He realized he was a bit nervous and was looking forward to seeing Stefani again. This was the second time that he was nearly naked in front of Stefani. The last time was the test for 'Forerunner' at this same swimming pool. He looked down at his muscular body and felt good that he was looking fit, though maybe a bit skinny.

"Somehow, I haven't been able to stop thinking about Stefani since the last swimming pool test. She is so different from Cathy. Though she does not talk very much or express her emotions openly, she is definitely a thinker and planner. Why do I feel that she has built a great wall between us that is hard to penetrate?" Tommy wondered.

He heard the dressing room door open and turned to see Stefani walking in wearing a one-piece swimsuit. Though he had seen other Asian girls in bathing suits at the beach with Cathy, he was struck by the sight of Stefani walking in now. She was surprisingly athletic, which he found extremely attractive.

When Stefani noticed that Tommy was staring at her, her face blushed and her heart beat faster. Tommy was a very handsome man with a well-tuned body. She felt embarrassed that the sight of him warmed her. After all, she was from a very conservative Asian family.

"Hi! You look very beautiful in that bathing suit," Tommy confessed to her once she stood next to him.

"Don't you have a dirty mind? You have a girlfriend, remember?" Stefani looked at him and laughed. Stefani did not know that the relationship between Tommy and Cathy had already ended.

"But I can't help it. It's not my fault that you are so beautiful. Furthermore, for your information, Cathy has found another boyfriend," Tommy said casually.

"Stop joking. Teach me how to use this gear," Stefani said, surprised that Tommy and his girlfriend were not together anymore.

"Yes, yes, OK." Tommy showed Stefani how to put the diving suit on and connect it to the oxygen tank. Then, they entered the water. First, Tommy taught her how to breathe through the mouthpiece connected to the oxygen. After a few times, Stefani felt very comfortable with the method, which alleviated her fears a bit. She began to dive and swim.

When she came out of the water, Tommy said "Wow, you're a serious swimmer. Were you a lifeguard or something?" Tommy had been hoping Stefani didn't know much about swimming so that he could have more time at the pool with her to teach her that as well. He felt unusually good spending time with Stefani. "Why have I not had this feeling before?" he wondered. "Maybe I do have a dirty mind."

"Actually, I grew up with a pool at my parent's house. I used to swim almost every day in the summertime when I was younger and more charming," Stefani joked, while watching Tommy's face.

They swam for at least two hours. This was a long

time for both Tommy and Stefani to spend in the water. Usually when they swam, it would be only an hour or so before they got bored. They enjoyed each other's company so much. This was also the first time they had had any real downtime together, and it was clear to both of them that they felt very close, especially when Tommy helped Stefani with getting the diving gear on and off. This training was fun, and the time flew by.

"Same time tomorrow?" Stefani asked.

"Yes, we need as much practice as possible," Tommy answered. He was so happy she asked and was already thinking about when he could see her again. It seemed that after nearly three months of hiding them, the emotions between them were beginning to emerge.

* * *

On the following Monday, July 25, Stefani, Brian, and Joe went again to Lake Harrison with the mobile home to set up their equipment, while Dr. Owen and Tommy went to the MarinaTech factory with the truck to pick up 'Pioneer.' When they arrived, they saw 'Pioneer' had already been moved to the trailer by MarinaTech technicians and covered by a black plastic sheet.

"Professor, I was hoping I could explain the new design of the ultrasonic detectors, but it seems the technicians worked faster than us, and they're already installed. Basically, the angle of both front and rear ultrasonic detectors can be changed manually from inside. It's just like when you are sitting inside of a car, and the angle of the side mirrors can be electronically changed. It's simple and safe," Tommy explained while they stepped into the truck.

"Isn't this going to affect Joe's three-dimensional simulation? You know, when the angles of these two detectors changes, all of the information collected for simulation will also be changed," Dr. Owen said as he started the engine.

"Yes, we've thought of this. Joe was here for the last two days and he connected a sensor to the front and rear detectors. Whenever the angles change, his computer will receive that information and correct for it accordingly," Tommy replied as the truck headed toward the MarinaTech gate.

"Joe's a computer genius, Professor! You know, he also wrote and installed some new software in 'Pioneer', so the sub is able to simulate a three-dimensional image independently whenever necessary. Just in case it loses contact with the computer up on the surface," Tommy said. "Just in case."

"Well then, do we still need any surface control from Joe?" Dr. Owen asked.

"Yes, I asked the same question and he told me that the computer on the surface is much more powerful and accurate. The images simulated will also be clearer and more detailed. And, if the control is on the surface, the surface team will know exactly what is going on in the cavern," Tommy replied. "I'm sure he can explain it to you much better than I can."

"That's good thinking. We're ready now," Dr. Owen

thought. "How about the diving equipment?" he asked aloud.

"Yes, we're comfortable with it and it's on board. Stefani and I have been practicing a lot the last week," Tommy said. "Joe has also put a signal emitter in the suits. When...if there's a situation, this will allow Joe to know our exact location. We are also equipped with two new telecom headsets operated by battery."

Dr. Owen was glad to hear that all of their concerns had been addressed and felt now his team was prepared for anything.

* * *

When they arrived at the lake, Joe, Brian, and Stefani already had the equipment set up and were waiting. Brian was also there to support the test this time. He had been sick last time and missed the first lake exploration. After the cover on the top of 'Pioneer' was removed, Dr. Owen went to the front and rear to see the modification of the detectors. Tommy walked next to him and indicated with his hand how the angles of these detectors could be controlled.

"Joe, Tommy told me that you have installed two sensors to these two detectors, so you are able to input the information change into your computer. He also mentioned you have generated a software program so 'Pioneer' is able to simulate its own three-dimensional image when necessary." Dr. Owen looked at Joe and felt proud of him. "Good thinking," he thought.

"Actually, the image generated in 'Pioneer' would not be as detailed and clear as my computer. My computer has a huge amount of memory and is much faster. The installation of the software in 'Pioneer' is to provide the basic critical information if there is a need." The group went quiet. "If Stefani and Tommy lose the navigation and simulation from the surface, they'll switch to 'SOS' mode and the sub's own simulation system will turn on automatically. Simple and easy." He looked at Dr. Owen with an expression of confidence.

Tommy nodded at Stefani. "No worries."

Dr. Owen felt so proud that he had such a perfect team with him. He knew they might not use these extra set ups, but it could mean life or death if a bad situation arose.

They carefully unloaded 'Pioneer' from the trailer. Since this was Monday early morning, there were only a couple of people fishing in the distance.

The same as before, Stefani and Tommy entered 'Pioneer' first, then Dr. Owen, Joe, and Brian pushed it into the water easily.

When 'Pioneer' reached the lake bottom, they first tested how to change the angle of the ultrasonic detector, pick up some samples, and place them into the pocket. Since they could see much better from the monitor now, they were able to avoid picking up samples that were too large without difficulty.

Once they had finished successfully filling the sample pocket, Joe's voice came over the telecom.

"Stefani, I am going to turn off the connection of the

simulation system here to yours for the next ten minutes. I want both of you to practice using your own simulation system to move around," Joe said, and he shut down the connection between his system and 'Pioneer.' Stefani then pushed the 'SOS' button and the simulation system in 'Pioneer' was on instantly. As expected, the image was not as clear as those images transmitted from Joe's system. However, it provided enough vision for them to move around. Both Stefani and Tommy tried it for about five minutes.

"Joe, please tell the Professor that we are going to spend about ten minutes here to practice putting the diving equipment on. You know, the space is limited and it's not the same as on the surface. We need to be sure we can manage," Tommy said.

"Good idea. Please do," Dr. Owen said loudly so they could hear.

It took more than three minutes for Stefani to put hers on. She could not believe it since she could put it on in less than three minutes on shore.

"I need to try again. It's much harder in here. This space is too small," Stefani said.

"Stefani, you think it's hard for you! It's even harder for me since my body is much bigger than yours," Tommy teased her.

So, Stefani tried again and again until she found a better position to put the diving suit on. Even with practice, it still took a little bit more than three minutes.

"We will practice more when we go home," Stefani said.

* * *

Tommy piloted 'Pioneer' back to shore. Everything had gone well in the test. The team took a rest and at the same time had a short meeting. They believed that they would need more challenging tests, but not in the lake. It had to be in the deep-sea cavern.

"What did the owner of the fishing boat say, Brian?" Dr. Owen asked.

Since Brian had not had too much to do in the last few days, Dr. Owen had instructed him to contact some fishing companies and check about the size, facilities, and cost of renting their boats. They had to find a good medium-sized boat which was equipped with a crane so 'Pioneer' could be lifted from the boat to the water's surface and vice versa.

"I checked three companies and only found one that I like. The owner, and also captain, is Greg. I don't know his last name. Both he and his brother have fishing boats. But I think his is larger and more modernized. Both of them are equipped with a crane. I talked to Greg and he wants $10,000 per day for 12 hours, from 6 a.m. to 6 p.m.," Joe said.

"Wow! Expensive," Stefani said, shocked about the price.

"Actually, Greg can make about $6,000 average per day for deep sea fishing. So, $10,000 is reasonable since he has to work with our schedule, and deal with the sub," Brian said.

"How many tests can we conduct in one day?" Tommy asked.

"I hope we can get in at least two full tests since we're paying big money," Dr. Owen replied.

"How long does it take to re-charge the batteries?" Joe asked.

"Fully charged, about 24 hours," Stefani said.

"In that case, we will need another set of batteries. Can we replace them easily on site?" Dr. Owen asked.

"Naturally, Professor, it was designed that way. The batteries are located under the floor on the side of the seats," Stefani said.

"How about the oxygen supply? We'll need a full backup for such a long day in the water," Tommy asked. He was concerned about spending so many hours in such a small space.

"That's also easy to replace. Simply open the cover located at the central floor of the submarine, you will see the oxygen tank," Stefani explained.

"OK then, we should have two tests in this deep-sea cavern for our next trip. Stefani, please contact MarinaTech and get the details on the locations of the caverns they mentioned," Dr. Owen said.

"I already have. They told me there were at least three caverns that some scuba divers always use. All three are close together and take about one hour to get to from the port. I'll visit the MarinaTech manager, Mr. Thomson tomorrow," Stefani replied.

Deep Sea Testing - First Trip

To avoid dealing with a crowd of scuba divers, they chose a Thursday, July 28, for the test. From MarinaTech's design manager, Mr. Kyle Thomson, Stefani had received the location, map, and details of three deep-sea caverns. All three were located between San Nicolas Island and Santa Barbara Island, about 50 miles northwest of Los Angeles. Actually, this area was near Channel Island National Park. All of the fishermen were very familiar with this place.

Early in the morning, around six o'clock, Dr. Owen and Tommy came to Malibu Port in Santa Monica about 20 miles from Los Angeles. As usual, Dr. Owen used his truck and trailer to bring 'Pioneer' and 'Forerunner' there. Ten minutes later, Brian, Joe, and Tommy also arrived with a minivan that Brian had rented to bring all the computers and monitors there.

"I am sorry we're late, Professor. It took me longer to pick up Joe and Stefani," Brian said as he stepped out of the van and greeted Dr. Owen. Then, he led the entire crew to the fishing boat, where Greg and his assistant, Tim, were standing on the dock and waiting for them.

First, Brian introduced Captain Greg and Dr. Owen to each other, and then the others. Greg then introduced his assistant to everyone. Greg was 42 years old. He had taken over his father's fishing business about ten years ago. Tim was a strong looking 21-year-old young man who had been working for Greg since he was 18.

"What a nice boat!" Dr. Owen said.

"It is still quite new, I bought it just two years ago.

All the equipment onboard is the most updated available, including the ultrasonic detection system," Greg said. This caught Tommy's interest of course.

"With this system, we can spot fish easily even 70 feet under the surface," Greg said.

"The poor fish don't have a chance nowadays!" Stefani said and everyone laughed.

"Usually, I have four or five people working for me when I go out fishing. However, I don't need so many today. Actually, Tim is the best guy I have," Greg said.

Brian, Joe, and Tommy unloaded 'Pioneer' and pushed it to the dock next to the boat. Tommy placed the hooks onto the hooking bars above 'Pioneer.' Greg used his crane to lift it up and then moved it to the deck of the boat smoothly. From the way he handled the operation, everyone could see how much experience he had.

Next, Brian, Joe, Tommy, and Stefani moved all the computer equipment, including the extra batteries and oxygen tanks, from the minivan to the boat. The boat took off on schedule around 7 a.m. Stefani had given the map and details to Greg, who was familiar with the area.

"So, as you know, we're interested in finding these caverns and testing the sub today," Stefani said to Greg in the boat's wheelhouse.

"I know this place. It is quite well known, one of the best fishing spots. I know exactly where it is." Greg looked at Stefani with a big smile. "Off we go."

It took about an hour and 20 minutes to reach the site of the smallest and most popular cavern first. It wasn't as deep as the other two and was a hot spot for scuba diving. When they arrived, there were only a couple of boats nearby. First, with Brian's help, Joe set up his equipment on the deck under the shade. Then, Joe asked Stefani to step into the submarine and turn on all the monitors. He and Stefani ran a routine test and checked the function of all the equipment. When all of this was done, it was already about 8:50 in the morning.

Now, everything was ready to go. Stefani and Tommy entered the submarine. The crane gradually lifted 'Pioneer' up and moved it into the water. It was considerably fortunate weather today. The wind was not too strong, and the waves were low. 'Pioneer' was just like a small boat floating on the water's surface. Tommy extended his body out of the door, removed the hooks from the top of the submarine and closed the door. "Here we go, Cap'n."

Stefani first allowed 'Pioneer' to sink to a level of about 20 feet and moved away from the boat. Relying on the monitors around her, she carefully steered 'Pioneer' to a deeper area where there were many coral reefs. Once they were closer to the area, they realized they were taking an unnecessary risk.

"Stefani, watch out. It seems the underwater current here is stronger than expected. Please put more distance between us and the reef," Tommy asked her.

"Yes Tommy, I also just realized that," Stefani replied, noticing the submarine was swaying from side to side. Stefani had a hard time maintaining a steady speed. Due to the disordered current in this area, it was very difficult to control the speed. A couple of times, Stefani almost let 'Pioneer' hit the coral.

"Let's circle around this area and find the entrance to the cavern," Tommy suggested. Stefani agreed. She realized that any unexpected strong current could cause a collision between the submarine and the coral. To the great force of the current, this submarine was like a leaf in the water. Stefani cautiously piloted 'Pioneer' for about 30 minutes; her shirt was already wet from sweat due to nervousness.

"Tommy, take over for a while. I feel dizzy. We're almost there," Stefani said.

"OK, just relax and take a few deep breaths. I've got the controls," Tommy tried to comfort Stefani. The force of the ocean currents had them both on edge. This was entirely different from their easy test in the lake. Tommy focused so intensely it reminded him of driving in a thunderstorm at night. Any careless action or momentary lapse of attention could be a disaster.

Tommy decided to keep an even greater distance, at least 30 feet, from the coral reef. He knew all of the information being collected by the six detectors would allow Joe to find an entrance to the cavern any minute. By the time he finished his circular exploration, at least 50 minutes had passed. As they were circling 'Pioneer' around, both he and Stefani had noticed two possible entrances. Now, they had only about 25 minutes left before they needed to return to the surface. Stefani felt better now. Tommy asked her to take over the controls so she could get more experience. She piloted 'Pioneer' to the side of the boat and then allowed it to float on the surface.

When Greg saw them, he immediately lowered the crane so that the hooks were above 'Pioneer.' The door was opened, and Tommy extended his upper body out and hooked up the submarine. He gave the OK signal to Greg and the crane lifted up 'Pioneer' and placed it on the deck.

When they got out, Stefani's face looked a little pale. Obviously, she was still uptight. On deck, the entire crew got together.

"I had a hard time simulating a three-dimensional image accurately. This was caused by the swaying of the submarine and the irregular speed. When I programmed the software, I did not expect the underwater current could be so strong," Joe said.

"Can you still offer some idea of the area? My concern is how we can find the entrance of the cavern if the simulation fails," Tommy said.

"I will try my best. Though I cannot guarantee 100% accuracy, we can at least get a 60-70% idea," Joe said.

* * *

Right after lunch, while the rest of the crew was taking a rest, Joe continued his work. He tried to adjust for the distortion factors caused by the current. First, he calculated the actual speed of 'Pioneer' and then deducted it from the controlled speed. This had given him a pretty good idea of the variability spectrum of the current's speed. In addition, from the detectors, he could figure out the angles of swaying. After about three hours, he came out with a three-dimensional image. Though it was not as accurate as he wanted, he believed that he had achieved at least 80% accuracy of the real lay of the land down there. This was a very good challenge for him since he had had only a few hours to complete the new software program. When he finished with such success, he was very happy that he had conquered another challenge. To him, it was just like a serious examination for his Ph.D.

By 3 p.m. the well-rested team had replaced the batteries and oxygen tanks and had prepared for the second test.

"Joe, this simulation looks amazing! Just like the view out the window," Tommy said. These three-dimensional images would be a reliable source of information for moving into the cavern, even with zero visibility.

"Yes, well, you still need to be very careful. The direction and speed of the current changes constantly down there. We can't predict it beforehand, but I think my new software patch will keep up pretty accurately in real-time," Joe said.

Stefani and Tommy got back into the sub, and Captain Greg lowered them into the water. Stefani let the submarine sink to a depth of 30 feet and then piloted toward the coral reef. They would try the entrance they both noticed about 30 feet below the reef. It took her only ten minutes to reach the area. She saw from her monitor that the current was much stronger, and she could feel the difference in the speed and sway of the sub as she tried to pilot it gracefully toward the cavern entrance.

Stefani carefully entered this new territory, paying close attention step by step, and watching her data update on her monitor as the software attempted to create a 3-D simulation in real-time. It was intense and unnerving as they traveled into the cavern entrance. Unfortunately, about 24 feet into the cavern, she discovered that the passage became very narrow, only about four feet wide and three feet high. It was good for scuba divers to enter, but not this submarine. In fact, she realized that it was too narrow to turn around, and that they were slowly drifting toward a collision with this bottleneck.

"Tommy, can you see this? We can't go forward anymore, and it's too narrow to turn. I need you to take over right now and bring us out backwards!" Stefani said.

"Yes! Aye aye, Captain," Tommy said nervously as he switched his controls on.

Tommy carefully piloted his end of the sub forward as the current swayed the sub from side to side, threatening to crash them into the entrance wall. He finally steered them clear and saw that this procedure had wasted 15 minutes.

"Nice work, well done," said Dr. Owen over the intercom. Immediately, Tommy piloted 'Pioneer' to the second possible entrance. All they hoped for now was that this entrance was big enough for 'Pioneer' to enter.

Unfortunately, they encountered the same problem.

Again, after Tommy brought the sub into the passage for about eight feet, the lights in front of him showed that it was too narrow. The current here was even stronger, making the sub unsteady, and bringing them dangerously close to the reef wall with each ebb and flow.

"Ah, Stefani, your turn! Get us out of here! The passage is too narrow again. It's even smaller," Tommy said.

Stefani took over the controls and led 'Pioneer' straight out of the entrance carefully.

"What should we do now?" Stefani asked.

"Let's try for an entrance lower down the reef wall. There may be another way in down there," Tommy said.

Stefani piloted the submarine down near the bottom. As she suspected, the effects of the current were not as strong at this depth. Stefani kept piloting 'Pioneer' along the bottom. Suddenly, Joe's voice came over the telecom.

"Stefani, try your left-hand side at about the nine o'clock position, 250 feet away. I saw a dark area there that may be an opening. Check that spot." Joe could see their surroundings from the information collected through the six detectors.

Stefani piloted 'Pioneer' to her left and she also saw the ominous black area. She approached cautiously, steering 'Pioneer' into what looked like an endless black hole. From her front monitor, she could see it was very deep and the entrance was pretty big. It could fit two or even three 'Pioneers' across easily. However, it was not very high, only about eight feet. She kept piloting 'Pioneer' forward slowly, waiting for the 3-D simulation to keep up. After they had traveled 56 feet into the darkness, suddenly there was a huge room right in front of them. They realized that they had just entered a huge cavern.

"Congratulations Stefani! It seems you have found the cavern," Joe said in telecom.

"Yes, we're in! Thanks Joe! It was your idea, remember, you helped me find it," Stefani said and laughed. They all breathed a sigh a relief.

Now, they had only about 48 minutes to explore the cavern and another 15 minutes to return. From Joe's 3-D simulation, they could see that the highest spot of this cavern was about 90 feet from the floor. Stefani began to move 'Pioneer' around. Tommy opened the cover of the window and took a peek outside. Though he saw some dark areas, he also saw some lights passing through gaps in the cavern walls and ceiling. It was beautiful. He saw some corals and many different kinds of beautiful fish swimming. But once they had gone about 250 feet, the cavern turned very dark. Tommy almost couldn't see anything through the window.

"It would be great if we could have a spotlight outside of the sub. Then I would be able to see how beautiful this place is," Tommy thought, even though he knew that this submarine was not designed for this purpose. Furthermore, a spotlight would make the submarine heavier and consume more of the batteries' charge.

This was a real test. The current in the cavern was

very weak and this allowed Stefani to easily pilot 'Pioneer' where she wanted. Stefani piloted for about 20 minutes and then passed control over to Tommy. Tommy practiced for about 25 minutes. Then he came to a spot near the corner of the cavern, adjusted the angle of the rear ultrasonic detector, picked up some samples and placed them into the sample pocket. He then asked Stefani to do the same.

With only 16 minutes left, they had to turn around and could not go any further. With the 3-D images, they knew exactly where they were and how to exit. They fully realized that if not for Joe's expertise in programming this 3-D simulation, they might have already been lost in the cavern. Fifteen minutes later, they were relieved to be on the surface near the boat.

Both Stefani and Tommy now had a very good idea of how to pilot the submarine and they had established a high level of confidence. Due to the limitation of a two-hour battery supply, they would not be able to get a deeper and bigger cavern for exploration. To avoid unnecessary danger in the deep-sea cavern exploration, they decided to stop further tests in the ocean. Now, they were ready for the oil mine.

Chapter 3
Entering the Mine

Forerunning

By September 20, as planned, Standy Firm had been able to dig a hole with a 15-foot diameter down to the entrance of the depleted oil mine. This hole was 185 feet long as originally expected. To prevent the wall from collapsing, many wood beams and panels had been used to support the internal wall.

A week earlier, September 13, Tommy and Joe rented a van and used Dr. Owen's trailer to move both 'Forerunner' and 'Pioneer' to Austin, Texas. It took them about three days of driving. The rest of the crew had flown in on September 17, three days before entering the oil mine.

After six months of effort the entire crew, including Mr. George Standy and his three engineers, were now standing next to a hole peering down into the darkness. Also next to the hole, a system had been installed to lower and raise the submarine. Most of the remaining gas in the hole and the oil residue on the water's surface had already been pumped out. About 30 yards from the hole a tent was set up as the headquarters of the project.

The crew moved into the headquarters. Inside, Joe

and Stefani sat in the center of the tent with seven monitors surrounding them. Dr. Owen, Tommy, Brian, George Standy, and his engineers took seats outside of this control circle.

Using the same set up as the testing in the lake, three monitors were on three sides of Joe and Stefani, two sides and rear. These monitors showed the three sides of the robot submarine, 'Forerunner.' Right in front of Joe and Stefani were four monitors. There were two in the center, one overlapping the other, while the other two were on the sides, next to the lower central monitor. The lower central one showed the forward direction of the detectors while the right one showed the topside and the left one showed the bottom side of the 'Forerunner.' However, the most important one was the one above the central one. This monitor would show the computer simulated 3-D images that had been created using the information collected from the six ultrasonic detectors.

Once everyone was in position, Joe radioed one of the Standy Firm engineers near the entrance of the hole. 'Forerunner' was then placed into a special carrier. The bottom of this carrier was flat and three times bigger than the length of 'Forerunner.' Both sides of the carrier were hung and hooked to the lifter. As 'Forerunner' was being lowered in, everyone had mixed feelings of nervousness and excitement. After about five minutes of descent, 'Forerunner' reached the surface of the water. The gas detector still detected some remaining gas; however, it was not enough to be considered dangerous or to cause an explosion. Once 'Forerunner' hit the water, Stefani took control.

She sat in front of a driving panel that had the same design as the big submarine, 'Pioneer.' First, Stefani carefully released the air in the floatation system of 'Forerunner,' and it began to sink. Using the monitor, Stefani moved 'Forerunner' very cautiously downward toward the entrance

'Forerunner' continued to sink for another five feet before the tunnel appeared. The entrance of the tunnel was about 12 feet wide and eight feet high. She sighed and looked at the professor. It was time to find out if this entrance would be large enough for 'Pioneer.' If the size of the entrance was smaller than 'Pioneer,' then they would have a big problem. Stefani believed with those dimensions, with caution, she would be able to pilot 'Pioneer' in. With 'Forerunner,' they could get a better look.

"Now, it will be a long trip," Stefani thought. As the Standy Firm engineer said, it was about a 160-foot-long tunnel. Stefani carefully manipulated 'Forerunner' forward. The computer showed that the tunnel sloped 57 degrees downward. After 16 feet, the tunnel had become wider. It was now about 25 feet wide and nearly 11 feet high. Stefani let out a long sigh and smiled. Dr. Owen noticed and could see Stefani was feeling a mixture of worry and confidence. Joe, at the same time, continued to check the data shown on the monitors to make sure everything was working as he wished.

About 62 feet from the tunnel entrance, it became

narrow again and the inclination changed from 57 degrees down to 30 degrees. However, this still did not bother Stefani. It seemed it would be no problem. 'Forerunner' reached the 108-foot mark as the team watched the monitors and documented their progress. The degrees of inclination kept changing, but it kept going down. However, when 'Forerunner' reached 138 feet, the size of the passage suddenly reduced significantly. Worry appeared on Stefani's face. There was a large rock situated right on the top of the tunnel that narrowed down the height of the tunnel. It allowed for only about five feet while 'Pioneer' was four feet in height. Worse, there were some rough surfaces on the bottom and the path curved slightly to the left. It seemed there had been some collapsing of the top of the tunnel. During the manned exploration, if 'Pioneer' was not manipulated correctly, any one of these obstacles could cause damage. Even worse, if a collision caused further collapse, they could be trapped in the tunnel.

"The biggest challenge will be to get through this area," Dr. Owen looked at George and said.

"I am sorry that we could not spot this problem beforehand. The signal of the ground ultrasonic detector cannot reach so deep," George replied.

At this critical moment, they did not want to say too much and influence Stefani's concentration. They turned their eyes to the monitor right in front of Stefani again. Finally, Stefani got 'Forerunner' through the bottleneck and the sub entered a bigger space. Immediately, about four feet further in, from the monitor Stefani could not see anything in front of 'Forerunner.' It had come to the edge of the oil reservoir, which appeared to be vast and dark.

Stefani stopped 'Forerunner.' "Should we enter the reservoir, or should we return?" she asked.

Dr. Owen looked at George's face and the others. "The purpose of 'Forerunner' is to explore the window and the entrance tunnel. Now that mission is accomplished and we have all the necessary data. Will we have further need for 'Forerunner?'" Dr. Owen asked.

"The only concern is that if this cavern is not as good as we wish, will we continue to another oil reservoir?" George asked. "How much trouble would it be if we need to create another mini-sub?" he continued.

Stefani looked to Tommy and Joe, and said, "Since we have the experience of building this one, it won't be too difficult to build another. In fact, we can build another one in just two months with about $50,000."

"In that case, it would be worthwhile to use this robot to explore further. Even if we lose it, it shouldn't affect our project significantly. The more info we can get ahead of time, the better, both for safety and to get more acquainted with the reservoir," Dr. Owen said.

Everyone agreed. Stefani continued her operation and directed 'Forerunner' into the oil reservoir. However, since the detection distance of 'Forerunner' was only about a hundred feet, Joe couldn't get much information beyond this range. Not only that, it seemed that the chemical residue dissolved within the water also shortened the detection distance more than anticipated.

This caught Brian's attention. He was very excited and said, "Can we collect some data about this water or even pick up some samples so I can analyze it?" Analyzing the material in the oil mine was his responsibility and interest.

"Sorry, Brian," Tommy replied. "It was not the original design for this robot. From the sound collected, we cannot tell what chemicals have been dissolved in the water."

Since the remaining mission of 'Forerunner' was to pick up as much information as possible, and there was not much concern for keeping 'Forerunner' alive, Stefani proceeded. From the monitors, it seemed that there were many columns, especially near the lower part of the cavern. They were just like the structures and the formation of limestone columns, draperies, popcorn, and stalagmites in caverns. However, due to the short detection range of 'Forerunner,' the images were not quite clear. To the others, these gigantic structures seemed normal and were probably common in caverns. But to Dr. Owen, a geology professor and expert in cavern study, it seemed the shapes and arrangements of these structures were weird and not normal. He also knew he should not compare what he was seeing of the structures in the oil cavern with those of a natural cavern. He kept his silence.

The movement of 'Forerunner' was very slow, with the fastest speed being only about 16 feet per minute. It did not get very far before the battery died, but they felt that the data they collected was invaluable. The battery was initially designed only for the purpose of surveying the tunnel once and returning within 30 minutes, 15 minutes in and out.

"'Forerunner' is lost," said Stefani. To Stefani, the data collected in these extra 16 minutes had increased her confidence significantly. She felt ready to enter the mine.

A few hours later, Joe had completed the 3-D simulation of the entire tunnel and entrance into the mine. "That little robot provided some critical data. Nice work, Stefani," he said, as he handed her a copy of the simulation on disc. She and Tommy sat and watched the simulation down the tunnel, through the bottleneck, and into the mine, over and over. They needed to gain a feel for the entire entrance process since they were the ones who would have to pilot 'Pioneer' into the reservoir.

* * *

Tommy and Stefani had known each other for more than six months since the project began, but they hadn't had much time to get to know each other better. They had met together more often only in the last few months during 'Forerunner's' and 'Pioneer's' fabrication. Tommy knew that Stefani, like many Asian girls, was always shy and conservative. He kept a polite distance between himself and her but wished they could be closer. Today's success gave both of them some excitement. Somehow, he felt they were closer than ever. This afternoon, after they watched Joe's three-dimensional simulation together, Tommy asked "Would you like to have dinner with me? I have a rental van and I know the Austin area quite well, so I can show you around."

"How do you know Austin? Have you been here before?" Stefani asked curiously.

"No, but I studied the Tourist Guide before I came. There are a lot of historical sites in the Austin area, like The Alamo in San Antonio which is only 80 miles away," Tommy said. This caught Stefani's interest, but she hesitated a moment in answering.

She was remembering her trip home three months ago, when she went back to San Francisco for the weekend. Her parents had arranged a meeting with another Korean family for dinner. "Why don't you have a boyfriend? You should marry a Korean boy and keep the same blood. Our dinner guests tonight have a son who is handsome and smart. We know them very well. They have just immigrated to the United States. Would you be interested to meet this boy?" All of these voices appeared in her mind during the last three months.

Her parents had already arranged this family meeting without telling her in advance. When she arrived home, she was shocked to find the guests already there. On the one hand, she did not want to upset her parents, on the other, she thought, "I want to choose my own boyfriend."

To be polite, after dinner, she talked to the boy on the deck. He was almost as tall as her with eyeglasses. He was nice, but not what she wanted. In addition, they shared no similar interests at all. He liked the new exciting western music while she liked the classics; he talked more about material things, like money and his car, while she was more interested in spiritual cultivation, and living a simple life. "No, definitely, this is not the boy I dream of," she thought.

"Wake up, Stefani. What is your answer? Yes or no?" Tommy asked her again.

Since there was nobody she knew in Austin, and furthermore, she already knew that Tommy had lost his girlfriend and was available now, she looked at him and nodded, "OK. But remember, we are just normal friends," she said.

That evening they had dinner in a Mexican restaurant and listened to nice music near the canal. They talked about the past six months and also about the future project. Both of them knew that the next few days or weeks would be the most crucial and critical time of their lives. They had to cooperate with each other in the submarine. As a matter of fact, it would be great if they were able to communicate with each other without too much talking. This project, though exciting, was also very dangerous. They walked and talked for hours, the conversation sometimes turning to serious topics like mortality, and their mutual respect for Dr. Owen and the rest of the team. When they returned to the guesthouses of Standy Firm, it was almost two in the morning. Many of the Standy Firm's guest rooms were empty since there were not as many oil projects being conducted in the Austin area as there used to be.

After they said goodnight, neither of them could sleep when they returned to their rooms. They felt anxiety and excitement, and both felt that the time passed so fast when they were together.

* * *

The next morning, the entire crew met at 10 a.m. A schedule of three meetings had been set for before they would enter the mine, and this was the first.

Stefani wore some light make-up on her face and Tommy had shaved neatly and was wearing a tie.

Joe noticed this sudden change. "Wow! What's so special about today, folks? Why are you both so clean cut and dressed up?" he asked.

Tommy and Stefani looked at each other. "The next few days will be exciting. I just want to make it special," Tommy replied. Stefani did not say anything and simply bowed her head down and looked at the teacup right in front of her.

Dr. Owen stepped into the room and everyone stood up to show respect. "I hope you had a nice sleep," he smiled at everyone. This was only just the beginning of his final project before his retirement.

Tommy and Stefani looked at each other. Tommy made a funny face at Stefani. Both of them knew they did not sleep well last night.

"The most important thing we need to talk about is how to deal with the narrow neck area at the end of tunnel," Dr. Owen said.

"I talked to George last night about the possibility of making the neck area wider and taller. George did not believe it would work. He thinks any effort to make this narrow area wider may cause more damage or narrow it down. Furthermore, we would have to design another robot to carry explosives to the bottleneck. And then, create another, larger robot to clear the debris created by the explosion. It's impractical, and quite possible that the path could be sealed by collapse," Dr. Owen continued.

"So, our best bet is to just carefully pilot in, as is. Can we do it?" Joe asked.

"It depends on how well Stefani or Tommy can manipulate 'Pioneer,'" Dr. Owen replied. "Though Stefani has designed 'Pioneer' and also gained more experience in manipulating 'Pioneer' from the last few tests, when the situation arises, it ultimately depends on how much confidence you have. If you don't have a high level of confidence, then even if you have good skill, mistakes can be made.

"It is a narrow and curved entrance, but I know a light scratch would not jeopardize the mission or cause any leaks. However, if the contact between the submarine and any obstacle causes any collapse, the submarine could be buried and get stuck, or possibly crushed," Dr. Owen continued.

This was the main concern for Stefani. She did not know if she could handle that area. She knew from her past experience that whenever she was too cautious, mistakes occurred. Correct and fast decisions were usually needed in an emergency situation. But, above all, she knew that if she chickened out now, she would regret it for the rest of her life.

"I will do it. I will practice it first. I wonder if it is possible to set up a prototype model so I can practice for a few days," Stefani said.

"Let us meet again tomorrow morning and see if Joe is able to provide a more detailed three-dimensional image in this area," Dr. Owen replied.

"I will work the whole night tonight. I'll provide a more detailed 3-D model tomorrow," Joe said.

After the meeting, Tommy sensed that Stefani was wound up tight.

"Do you want to go out with me again, Stefani? It will ease your tension," he asked.

But Stefani was too worried and not in the mood to go out again. She also needed to catch up on the sleep she had missed from the night before.

"Sorry, Tommy. I need sleep. I am exhausted," Stefani replied.

* * *

The next morning, the entire crew met again. George Standy and a couple of local engineers were also invited by Dr. Owen.

"Ladies and gentlemen, yesterday we concluded that we need a prototype model for our pilots to practice with. Mr. Standy and a couple of his engineers are here today, and we will see how we can build a prototype model in this facility," Dr. Owen began. "Joe, could you please show us your simulation of the tunnel and bottleneck?"

Before the meeting started, Joe had connected his computer to the projector provided by Standy Firm. He had spent the whole night making this presentation possible and had finished it only an hour ago. He turned the lights off and the projector on.

Before he pushed the 'play' button on his computer, he said, "This entire simulation movie will take about 35 minutes including entering the hole until the end of the battery in the robot. After we finish the entire movie, then we will again play the critical five minutes of passing through the problem area."

Joe demonstrated his expertise, showing a 3-D movie of the area as 'Forerunner' entered the hole and dove deeper into the water. Often there were split screens which provided two synchronized images, one looking forward in 'Forerunner.' It was just like you were sitting inside the robot and saw things appearing right in front of you. The other image was a three-dimensional image which showed the detailed structure of the passage and the location of 'Forerunner.'

When 'Forerunner' reached the bottle neck area, all that could be seen were split screens since this was the most important area. Most amazing to Dr. Owen and Mr. Standy was to see that Joe had drawn a virtual 'Pioneer' in the passage. This offered the crew a clear idea of how narrow the passage was in relation to the actual size of

'Pioneer.'

When the movie was over, you could see from Stefani's face that she was very nervous. The passage looked even tighter than she had envisioned.

"Joe, would you play that narrow passage section several times for me, please?" Stefani requested. In fact, the entire crew was curious to see it again and again. He showed the section twice. Though it took only about five minutes each time, it seemed to take an hour.

"I will show it again in slow motion so you can see it more clearly. However, if you see something and need me to freeze the image, please don't hesitate to tell me so," Joe said. Once again, Joe played the section, this time at only half the regular speed. Now, everyone could see more clearly and also think while watching.

"Stop!" Dr. Owen yelled. "Please go back about two seconds or so."

Joe did. Dr. Owen went up to the screen and pointed out a small area which protruded out from the piled dirt on the lower right-hand side of 'Forerunner.' Without looking carefully, it would have been easy to miss the protuberant area. It was very small indeed - small, but sharp.

"This could be a problem. This object protrudes from the ground here. It may be fragile and might not do anything more than scratch the sub, or it may be a serious hazard. Since this object is in the narrowest place, you must be very careful," Dr. Owen said to his two pilots.

"From the image shown, I believe we will be able to create a prototype model of the passage in two to three days. We have a swimming pool at this facility, 100 feet long and 60 feet wide. It will be ideal to create a model in the swimming pool, so Stefani and Tommy are able to practice with it," George stood up and said. While George was standing up, Joe also turned on the light.

"Wow," thought Stefani, "I only thought that I might practice with a virtual prototype! I can't believe we're going to have a life size model to practice in!"

George then looked at one of his engineers and said, "Eric, can you handle this assignment? This is very crucial for this model. It is one of the key elements to succeed in this project."

"Naturally, Mr. Standy." Eric felt very delighted and somewhat proud that his top boss, the owner of the company, recognized and appreciated his talent. He had never thought that he would receive an assignment directly from Mr. Standy. "I will do my best," Eric continued. He then turned his head toward Joe. "May I have a copy of this movie, and an export of the data? I need to study it carefully."

"Of course. I can have a copy for you in an hour," Joe replied.

"How long will it take to build this model, Eric?" Mr. Standy asked.

"I hope to complete it in three days. However, it depends on how much cooperation I will be able to receive from any related departments," Eric replied.

"Let everyone know that you have a direct order from me. You will need all of their cooperation," Mr. Standy said.

Wow! Eric had never felt so important and powerful since he began his job at Standy Firm seven years ago.

The faces of Dr. Owen and his crew reflected their appreciation for everything Mr. Standy and his firm were doing for them.

Dr. Owen looked Mr. Standy in the eyes and said, "George, this is so great! I don't know how to thank you for your extraordinary help."

Joe looked over at Stefani, "I'll also give Stefani and Tommy a copy of this more-detailed movie in an hour or so."

* * *

The meeting lasted until almost 2:00 in the afternoon. Tommy asked Stefani if she wanted to have a light lunch in Standy Firm's cafeteria and she agreed, though she didn't say much during lunch. Tommy could sense that her worry was getting deeper and deeper. He tried to get her mind away from the project.

"Would you like to go out tonight? We can find a nice restaurant for dinner and then go to a movie," Tommy said.

"I think I should spend more time watching the simulation movie and think more about the project," Stefani replied.

"I understand. I want to do the same. But maybe if you take some time off tonight and try to relax, your mind will be clearer tomorrow. Normally, the more nervous you, the worse off your mind is at concentrating." Tommy smiled at her. "And, Eric said it will take at least three days to build the model. We should have plenty of time."

"OK. But promise me we won't be out too late. We were so late last time and I was very tired the next morning."

At 6:30 Tommy went to Stefani's room to pick her up. She was watching the movie of the passage simulation she had received about three hours ago from Joe. Tommy had just shaved and wore a nice shirt with a red tie. He looked very handsome that night.

When Stefani opened her door and saw Tommy, she was shocked. "I did not realize so much time had passed. I thought it was only 6:00. Please give me a few minutes to get ready," Stefani asked.

"No problem. Just take your time. Anyway, it is too early for dinner," Tommy replied.

While Stefani went to the other room to get dressed, Tommy began to watch the movie and got absorbed into it very quickly, pondering their options and visualizing their success.

Stefani came back 20 minutes later, dressed very attractively for a night out. She looked at Tommy and smiled. "Hey, wake up! I thought I was the only nervous one. Promise me we won't talk about this project tonight. I want to relax and enjoy the evening," Stefani said.

"Naturally, my queen. It's a deal," Tommy teased her. She raised her eyebrows at him, and they both laughed.

Stefani suggested going to a Korean restaurant. She missed Korean food a lot, especially rice. She missed her mother's cooking most of all. Though she didn't think any Korean restaurant was able to cook any dish as well as her mother, at least it was better than Mexican or American food. Even though Tommy had never tried Korean food, he was open to her suggestion and wanted her to be as happy as possible. He really felt that Stefani was just like a princess or a queen to him at that moment. His feelings of attraction for her had grown, but he had also developed a great deal of respect for her character and intellect over the last few months.

They found a Korean restaurant in downtown Austin. They couldn't tell how good the food would be, but the outside looked elegant and promising.

Tommy let Stefani order the meal, listening to her speaking Korean for the first time. At that moment, he felt like he would eat anything she ordered. Tommy believed he was in love. "How can it be? It's been only two days since our first date," Tommy thought. "But I guess I've been interested for months." The more he thought about it, the more he felt the sweetness of the relationship between Stefani and him.

After dinner, Stefani said, "How was it? Did you like it?"

"Not bad! However, I must be honest, it is new to me," Tommy replied.

"You should wait and try my mom's cooking. It is much better than this," Stefani said with a smile.

"Yes, my queen," Tommy said.

"Stop calling me queen. That's ridiculous. My name is Stefani. Understand? Stefani!" she laughed and made a funny face at him.

They chose to go to a romantic comedy movie that neither of them knew anything about, but it was obvious that both of their minds were not on the movie. When Tommy reached over to take Stefani's left hand, she did not withdraw her hand. The connection gave them a special feeling neither had ever experienced before. They felt light and high. Their eyes continued to face forward, but both their minds were intensely focused on the connection of their hands. It seemed time had stopped, yet it went so fast. The movie was over.

They returned to Standy Firm's housing and, in front of Stefani's door, Tommy held both her hands and looked into her eyes. They looked at each other for a moment that lasted forever, and then kissed each other. This was Stefani's first kiss. It had been many times for Tommy, but it was different this time. He felt the entire world was spinning. They said goodnight and smiled at each other as Stefani closed her door. When Tommy returned to his room, he couldn't help thinking about what had happened that night, over and over. He believed he had found the girl he had been dreaming of.

* * *

"How should I tell Mom and Dad?" The thought was hanging in Stefani's mind. She knew her parents wanted her to marry a Korean boy, not an American. "Will they like Tommy? Will they be upset about my choice? After all, it is my life," Stefani thought. "What should I do? Well, I just have to wait and see what develops. For the time being, I need him. He is my partner and he has given me so much comfort and encouragement."

* * *

The next morning at 10, back in the Standy Firm's conference room, Eric met with Dr. Owen and the team. George Standy had to go somewhere and could not be there. Today, Eric was to report on his plan and when the prototype model would be operational.

"Ladies and gentlemen, I have contacted the necessary departments and obtained agreements for their complete cooperation. If everything runs smoothly, we should be able to conduct the first test in the swimming pool in three days, on Saturday morning," Eric said. "We'll pump the water out of the pool today. Tomorrow, a Standy Firm architectural engineer, Mike, will oversee construction of the model in the swimming pool. The material will be wood and plastic since we don't expect to use this model for a long time. By using wood and plastic, the model can be fabricated easily and quickly.

"In one and a half days, with three of the company's most experienced model technicians working on it, it will be done. For the time being, we should move 'Pioneer' over to the swimming pool. We'll also move a small crane there to move the sub into the water when it's time. We should have this done by tomorrow after-noon," Eric continued.

* * *

That afternoon, Tommy and Stefani were in her room watching the simulation movie on her laptop. They watched, talked, and discussed excitedly for hours. It seemed they were enthusiastic about the project, but truly, they just wanted to be together. They had watched the simulation at least ten times, until they were able to remember the entire path in detail. They felt like they were even able to get through it with their eyes closed. They eventually fell asleep holding each other. When they awoke, it was almost 8 p.m. Though Tommy had a strong desire to make love to her, he knew if he rushed it, he would ruin everything. This was especially true for a conservative Korean girl. He calmly controlled his de-sire.

Stefani warmed up some of the leftover Korean food they had brought home last night. They ate their simple meal and then Tommy returned to his own room.

* * *

Friday morning, at Eric's request, the team came to the swimming pool located at the corner of Standy Firm's ten-acre housing area. The pool had been iso-lated by a fence and, in some areas, yellow ribbon. Eric took them into the pool area. When they looked down into the dry swimming pool, they saw a model about 60 feet long had been built. Both ends of the model had enough space in the pool for 'Pioneer's' entry and exit.

"Can I go down and check it?" Stefani asked.

"Naturally. Both you and Tommy should go down and have a walk through," Eric said. As a matter of fact, almost all of the crew wanted to enter the swimming pool and try walking through the model.

"Please gentlemen, it's not a good idea that all of you go through the model tunnel. Too many people stepping on the bottom may damage it. The fewer people the better," Eric said loudly to everyone.

In the end, only Stefani and Tommy were permitted to enter, and they were very careful to not damage it. They knew any damage caused would only delay the project.

Stefani and Tommy stepped into the model tunnel. Though it was 60 feet long, the crucial area was only 26 feet. There were some lights on in the tunnel. Since it was only completed late yesterday afternoon, the electric connections had not yet been removed. They were scheduled to be removed that afternoon and the swimming pool would be refilled by Saturday morning.

Stefani and Tommy walked through the model tunnel, stepping carefully and lightly. Halfway into the entrance, they could see the sharply protruding area. They could see how narrow the area was and how dangerous it could be. It was only 26 feet long but posed the most serious risk in the entire project thus far. Finally, they exited from the other side.

They went through again, and again, sometimes moving backwards as if they were in the submarine, stepping backwards cautiously. They changed positions and took turns being in front. After they had made 12 passes through the tunnel, they came out.

"Now we know why it can be so dangerous in that narrow area. It really doesn't give us much space to make the turn," Tommy said to Dr. Owen.

"When did you say they'll refill the pool?" Stefani asked Eric.

"About 4:30 this afternoon," Eric replied.

"If possible, I think that Tommy and I should come here early this afternoon and repeat the entrance and exit a few more times until we're completely familiar with it," Stefani said. Though Tommy was confident he had it memorized, and thought this was not necessary, he would do it to be alone with Stefani. He kept quiet.

"I can arrange this for you," Eric replied. He turned away, walked over to a technician standing nearby and said a few words to him. The technician looked at Stefani and Tommy, smiled and made the OK sign with his thumb and index finger.

That afternoon, Stefani and Tommy returned to the swimming pool and repeated the path, spending more time looking around the tunnel, until they agreed they knew they could make it through without incident.

* * *

Saturday morning, the entire crew was once again by

the pool. This would be the real test. Joe had moved all his equipment there so he could conduct the simulation image.

Stefani entered 'Pioneer' first followed by Tommy. The crane lifted the sub and moved it to the surface of the water. The crane moved away, and 'Pioneer' was free floating on the pool's surface.

Stefani skillfully allowed the water into the ballast tanks and the submarine began to slowly sink. All of the monitors were turned on. Stefani covered the windows. They were supposed to pilot the submarine without seeing any surrounding things. They had to be capable of relying on the images shown on the monitors. When 'Pioneer' had sunk about two feet under the water, Stefani moved it forward.

Stefani piloted forward carefully, and 'Pioneer' entered the tunnel. Relying on the four monitors around her, she was able to move 'Pioneer' smoothly. From the experience of walking the tunnel, she anticipated and easily navigated past some bumpy areas and difficult corners slowly and steadily. Finally, they came to the most critical narrow area with the protuberant bump. Stefani carefully turned 'Pioneer' toward the left and tried to avoid the protuberance while at the same time, avoid hitting the surrounding wall of the sharp turn.

There was a sound of collision on the left topside of 'Pioneer,' and the sub rocked to the side. It seemed Stefani had turned too much to the left. Though both Tommy and Stefani knew that this collision would not hurt the structure in the model tunnel, it could be a real disaster when they were trying to enter the cavern. When 'Pioneer' turned toward the right, it hit something again. Stefani became very nervous and upset.

"Don't worry, Stefani. This was only the first try. After a couple more times, I'm sure we can handle it," Tommy said, trying to comfort and encourage her. Stefani was nearly in tears. Finally, they reached the other end of the tunnel.

"Let me try this time and see if I can do any better," Tommy said. Since 'Pioneer' was designed for two-sided operation, they didn't have to turn the sub around.

Tommy drove 'Pioneer' back into the tunnel. In just a couple of feet, they had entered the most critical area. Tommy carefully and confidently maneuvered 'Pioneer' through the narrow, sharper turning area and got through smoothly. This made Stefani even more upset.

"I don't think I am a good pilot in 'Pioneer.'"

"Actually, you did pretty good. I just learned what to avoid by watching you. Without your mistakes, I don't think I would have gotten through so easily," Tommy replied, trying to point out some truth so Stefani would not feel so bad. However, both of them knew that Tommy could get through easier simply because he was more confident.

"You should try again, Captain. It will be smoother sailing this time," Tommy urged Stefani, trying to help her build her confidence.

Stefani took a couple of deep breaths and once again piloted 'Pioneer' forward. She was calmer this time. Tommy's success had given her great hope. "If Tommy can do it, so can I," she thought.

When 'Pioneer' came to the crucial red zone, Stefani tried not to move 'Pioneer' so much to the left. She kept her hands steady. She did it smoothly and they came out of the tunnel without a scratch.

"See, I told you all you need is your confidence. Now, you have it." Tommy smiled and turned his head trying to see her facial expression. It was not easy since they were facing opposite directions, but he could feel Stefani was smiling inside.

"Let us try a few more times this way. You go forward entering and I will go backward returning. Once we feel comfortable, we can switch our path, and each practice going through the opposite way," Tommy said.

They practiced a few more times and it seemed there was no problem. When they returned to the entrance for the last time, they turned 'Pioneer' around so Tommy could pilot forward this time, while Stefani went backwards. Even though there were a couple of touches, basically, the drive was smooth.

Both of them were satisfied and confident. They told Joe that they had completed the drills and ten minutes later, they all were standing on the side of the swimming pool.

Dr. Owen could see from Stefani's face that she was calmer and more confident. It seemed as if she had grown up so much in just a couple of hours.

"What is the weather supposed to be like next Monday, Joe?" Dr. Owen asked. Joe had been assigned to check the weather every day.

"There will be some rain tonight until tomorrow noon. Then it should be sunny until next Wednesday," Joe replied.

"Splendid! Let's do it Monday. Take a nice break tomorrow. Monday will be the day." Dr. Owen looked at everyone as he announced the exciting news.

While they were talking, George Standy arrived.

"I am sorry that I couldn't be here to offer any support. I have been so busy taking care of some business in Mexico. How is everything?" George asked Dr. Owen.

"Well, we are ready. We were just talking about moving on to the real thing," Dr. Owen replied.

"What date have you set up?" George looked at everyone with a hopeful expression in his eyes.

"Monday. Monday is the day," Dr. Owen told him.

"That's great. I thought I would miss the big day. I'll be here next Monday, but I must leave and return to Los Angeles Tuesday morning. I'm very much looking forward to watching the operation."

"George, you know how much we appreciate your help. It is outstanding that you can be here to see it happening." Dr. Owen looked at George with deep appreciation.

"Why don't we have a cookout tomorrow afternoon. It looks like the weather should be good," George said.

"A fantastic idea!" Dr. Owen thought. Even though he and Mr. Standy had met a few times before, they had never been together for an informal occasion. This would provide them with a good opportunity to get to know each other much better.

"Where?" Dr. Owen asked.

"Right here next to the swimming pool. This place will be cleared by tomorrow morning, and the pool can be re-opened by 2:30. I'll arrange everything. Let's celebrate and prepare for our success on Monday. I'll also invite the other engineers and technicians who've worked on the project to the cookout."

Tommy had been hoping to get to be with Stefani alone. But since they played two of the most important roles in the project, it seemed they should and must be at the cookout. On second thought, it might be better like this. The event would allow them to relax and get more acquainted with all the people involved.

When everyone arrived at the cookout Sunday afternoon, they saw that Mr. Standy had managed to transform the pool area overnight into an elegant party, with sunshades, a band, and full catering. It was his way of showing the team his appreciation and giving them a well-earned day of rest and relaxation to prepare for the serious challenge ahead.

* * *

The relationship between Stefani and Tommy had grown deep very quickly. It seemed that the conservative wall of Korean tradition that Stefani had built up since she was a child had completely broken down. They wished they could be together all the time. Introducing Tommy to her parents and persuading them remained the biggest obstacle to their relationship. Stefani began to write e-mails to her parents more often than ever. Occasionally, she would attach some photos, beginning with the group, and gradually, with her and Tommy alone. This caught her mother's attention.

"Hi, Stefani! It's Mom." Stefani's mom called Stefani's cell phone Sunday afternoon as the guests began to arrive for the party.

"Hi, Mom. It is great to hear from you." Usually, her mom did not call her. Why did she call this time? This was somewhat strange, especially since Stefani reported what was happening with the project almost every two days. "Did anything happen?" she wondered.

"Anything urgent, Mom?" Stefani asked.

"No, everything is all right. I just miss you and want to hear your voice," Mom answered.

"Mom, we're in the middle of a party. Tomorrow we enter the oil mine. Everything is working as planned. I don't have too much time right now though. I need to be social with the people who have just arrived." More and more people were arriving, some with children and friends. Stefani believed since she was so involved in the project, she should be there to greet them, at least at the beginning.

"OK, well, I am just curious... the good-looking young guy next to you in the photo you sent, how is your relationship?" Well, at least Mom had gotten the hint.

"Good looking guy! Doesn't sound too bad. It seems she has a good impression of Tommy from the photos," Stefani thought.

"That's Tommy. We are just friends," she told her

mom.

Her mother could sense she was smiling as she spoke. "Mm-hmm?"

"Well, I won't deny that we can talk for days without getting tired since we have many similar interests, and we're very involved, I mean, with the project. Mom, can I call you back tonight?" Stefani thought it wasn't a good idea to get any deeper into this conversation with her mom right now. A hint was good, but she didn't want to confirm.

"OK, I will be waiting for your call. I just want to remind you don't be too emotional and jump into something too fast," Stefani's mom said. Stefani understood her mom was talking about sex. It is still Korean tradition that a girl must be a virgin before she gets married.

"Don't worry, Mom, I'll call you tonight. OK? Bye..." Stefani closed her phone and felt her heart racing.

* * *

Stefani knew that it was easier to convince her mom than her dad. She felt that her mom did not like the Korean boy very much either and thought he was too quiet. Stefani decided to try not to talk too much about Tommy when she called her mom back that night. She didn't want to get herself or her mom upset, especially on the eve of the big day. And she knew that her mom would need some time to think about it and subtly pass the hint on to her father so he could prepare psychologically. However, her mom's call also reminded her not to rush into getting emotionally attached. They should maybe take more time to really know each other, and maybe she had been rushing a bit. She hoped Mom wouldn't press too hard for details later tonight. She decided to keep her distance with Tommy as a very good friend.

During the cookout, Tommy sensed the sudden change in Stefani. He felt that her defense wall was back up and could tell that she tried to control her emotions and keep a bit more distance. He figured Stefani's strange change was because the big day was ahead of her and decided to leave her be. They didn't talk very much at the party, and he kept watching her from across the pool, feeling this new distance between them. They went back to their own rooms right after the party.

Emotionally, Stefani began to get confused. She missed Tommy already. She liked Tommy a lot, but she kept reminding herself that she should keep her distance. She sat on her bed and cried. She wished there was someone wise who could answer this confusing question for her. As she sat there, suddenly her cell phone rang. "It's Mom," she thought.

"Hi Mom, I was just going to call you," Stefani said a bit sadly as she answered the phone without even checking the number of the incoming call.

"This isn't Mom. It's your daddy's good friend, Tommy." Stefani recognized Tommy's voice. Her face turned red.

"Oh, hi, sorry! Why did you call? Is everything OK?" Stefani asked.

"I'm just checking if you are OK. You were nervous

and distant the whole afternoon."

"I'm OK. I'm just tired and need some rest. I'm expecting my mom to call. Can I talk to you tomorrow?" Stefani didn't want to talk to him, especially right now when she was confused and emotional.

"OK, well. I'm here if you need me. OK? Talk with you later, I guess. Bye."

After a few minutes, Stefani felt calmer and emotionally stable. She picked up her phone and dialed her mom's number.

"Stefani, I have been waiting for your call. How was the big party?" Mom asked.

"OK. It was just a social cookout so everyone in the project could get acquainted with each other." Stefani decided not to mention Tommy at all, to try and cool down her mom's excitement. However, her mom knew she would do this in advance, and she would not be deterred. It was the main reason for her call.

"About Tommy, do you like him? You know your dad and I wish you to marry a Korean boy," her mom said.

"Mom, I'm telling the truth! I like him a lot, but...we are not in love yet. I think we are just friends," Stefani answered, questioning her own words.

"I just want you to slow down your pace. This kind of thing can be too fast and make your head spin. Later, when you wake up, it is only a dream. I trust you and believe your wisdom mind is stronger than your emotional mind. You were always strong since you were a child," Mom said. Stefani believed her mom was talking about sex again.

"I am not absolutely against your friendship with him. I just want you to take time to get to know each other better. I think you and Tommy have only know each other about seven months. It is too short a time to know each other," her mom said again.

"Wow! I cannot fool Mom. She knows me too well," Stefani thought. However, from her mom's speech, it seemed her mom was not as stubborn as her dad. "Mom is right. Earlier, I was searching for a wise one to advise me. Who can be wiser than Mom? Truly, who can love me more than Mom?" Stefani thought.

"Mom, thanks for your advice. It has helped me a lot, more than you know." Stefani made up her mind to keep more distance until she and Tommy knew each other better. "Only time can tell," she thought.

"Mom, I need a good rest tonight. Tomorrow is a big day for me. Your advice has calmed down my mind. I want to focus entirely on this project now. That's my first priority, not my friendship with Tommy."

"I am so glad to hear that. Have a nice sleep tonight. Wish you success tomorrow. Please be very careful and safe in that submarine."

"Good night, Mom," Stefani answered.

"Only a few minutes ago, I was so confused about myself. Now, after talking to Mom, I feel so calm and wise," Stefani thought and smiled. She had a very nice sleep that evening.

* * *

Big Day - First Exploration

Next to the entrance of the cavern window, all the equipment was set up and an operations tent erected. 'Pioneer' had been moved back to the site the previous morning. Joe and Tommy had arrived the day before to help the Standy Firm technicians and workers handle the shipping and installation. They didn't want any accidents right before the big day. They also wanted to make sure everything was arranged appropriately.

Other than Tommy and Stefani, Dr. Owen, Joe, Brian, and all the technicians were present. Surprisingly, Eric was also there. After the successful model tunnel dive, he had become very interested in the project. He felt he had to be there to see what happened, and Mr. Standy had granted him this.

Tommy and Stefani both wore loose clothing and comfortable sneakers. They had discussed it and decided tight clothes would only make them more tense and nervous. Five minutes before launch time at 10 a.m., Dr. Owen wondered if Mr. George Standy would arrive in time for the launch. While he was wondering, a car came, and Mr. Standy stepped out and waved to everyone. This made all the Standy Firm technicians and workers a little bit uptight and excited, but they were used to his sudden arrival at go-time.

Dr. Owen shook hands with Mr. Standy and led him into the operations tent. Dr. Owen took a few minutes to explain how everything was set up and what the purpose of all the equipment was. Now it was time. They were about five minutes behind schedule. Everyone stepped out of the tent except Joe, who stayed inside in his control circle to monitor the simulation images.

Stefani and Tommy stepped into 'Pioneer' feeling very excited and nervous. They felt like astronauts about to launch, or maybe movie stars about to shoot an action movie scene. Tommy crouched down and closed the door from inside. Two technicians used ladders to place hooks on top of 'Pioneer.' After they removed the ladder, one of the technicians gave the OK sign to the crane operator.

'Pioneer' was lifted up from the ground and moved to the entrance of the window. To avoid unnecessary bumping against the wall, 'Pioneer' was lowered very slowly. Soft cushions had been placed around the sub to protect it.

One foot, two feet... 265 feet, and finally 'Pioneer' reached the water's surface. Joe's system reported that there was very little gas left at the surface. After 'Pioneer' was stable on the surface, Stefani told Joe that it was OK to release the hooks. To avoid sparking caused from the friction of the hooks and bars on the top of 'Pioneer,' a nanocoating insulation had been used on all the metal surfaces. Rubber wasn't an option since it would be dissolved quickly by the oil residue in the water. It was easier this time to lower 'Pioneer' down to the water's surface and release it since the hooks could be released by surface control. However, when they returned, Tommy would have to open the hatch and place the hooks on the bars by hand. Stefani had considered using a magnetic method for 'Pioneer's' lifting and lowering; however, she had a concern that magnetic contact might cause friction and initiate sparking. This would be very dangerous if there was too much gas residue on the water's surface.

Stefani released the air inside the floatation device. 'Pioneer' began to sink, one foot, two feet...five feet. From her monitors, Stefani could see the entrance to the tunnel located on the left-hand side of 'Pioneer.' She carefully turned 'Pioneer' 90 degrees to her left, being very cautious since there was little space for her to maneuver. Outside 'Pioneer' it was completely dark since the entrance of the window was nearly 300 feet up. The view out the sub's window was blackness, a vast and haunting blackness that caused claustrophobia to sink in. Brian, Mike, Dr. Owen, and Mr. Standy had returned to the tent and were staring intently at the monitors surrounding Joe. Not even the slightest sound was heard as everyone was holding their breath.

After Stefani had corrected the forward direction of 'Pioneer' toward the entrance of the tunnel, she began to pilot 'Pioneer' forward about 15 feet per minute. As she remembered, in about another 15 feet the tunnel would open up a bit. After a minute or so, the tunnel grew bigger just as they had experienced with 'Forerunner.' However, that lasted only about three minutes before it became a bit narrower again. It still was not too much trouble for Stefani to pilot through the area.

Seven minutes had passed. Everything looked and felt very familiar to Stefani. She deeply appreciated their hours and hours of study and practice a few days ago. In only a couple of minutes, 'Pioneer' came to the red zone bottleneck, the most crucial area that everyone was worried about. They had progressed 137 feet from the entrance of the tunnel. Everyone was very tense, especially Stefani and Joe. Tommy deliberately kept himself very quiet and as relaxed as possible so that Stefani was able to concentrate.

Twenty seconds later, 'Pioneer' arrived at the protuberance; the narrowest area. Stefani carefully and skillfully avoided making contact between 'Pioneer' and the sharp rock that she knew to be there, jutting out, threatening to end their mission right then and there. She knew she had to turn and tilt 'Pioneer' to the correct angle to the left to fit in the curved path and avoid colliding with the wall. Right after 'Pioneer' passed, she inhaled with a sigh of relief only to hear "Watch out!" through the telecom. It was too late; at the last moment Joe had seen on his monitor that the bottom of 'Pioneer' had already touched the piled dirt on the bottom of the tunnel. Stefani and Tommy felt a sudden bump and were jolted in their seats. However, 'Pioneer' had entered a wider space again. Stefani saw ahead of her that they had made it to the entrance of the oil mine. She stopped 'Pioneer' and took a break, dripping with sweat.

"OK, OK. Nice, Stefani. We're OK," Tommy reassured her.

"Stefani, I've lost signals from the bottom detector. It could be damaged, or the signals might be blocked by debris," Joe said over the telecom.

"I am very sorry, Joe," Stefani said. She paused for a few seconds. "Should we continue even though we have lost this detector?"

"Please stay at the same position, let me talk to Dr. Owen," Joe replied.

There was a short, urgent meeting in the tent on the surface.

"Joe, I need you to answer this question so I can make a decision." Dr. Owen looked at Joe. "How much information will be lost if we continue? Will it cause any significant danger?"

"Well, all we lost was one bottom side detector. We still have quite good vision of the surroundings. The front ultrasonic detector can still see the lower part of the path since it covers nearly a 120 angle in front. That means Stefani can use the data from the front detector, and easily adjust the height of 'Pioneer' to avoid any danger. Of course, we won't have as much detailed information on the bottom side," Joe said. "However, I must point out one thing. Realize that the 3-D simulation image will not be as detailed as I want since we've lost one-sixth of the information detected. If and when we decide to pick up some samples, it will be more difficult since the bottom detector is designed to detect the distance between the bottom of the submarine and the ground. They will have to rely on their other sensors and intuition."

Dr. Owen looked at Mr. Standy and tried to read the expression on his face. Dr. Owen and George had become good friends in just a few days. "What do you think, George?" he asked.

As leader of one of the largest companies in the

world, George had demonstrated his ability to function under extreme duress many times and answered instantly, saying, "I believe this is not a one-time mission. We may have to reenter the mine many times. Maybe we should not take a risk and try to pick up some samples this time. Without a bottom detector, it could be very dangerous since Stefani and Tommy will be blind on the bottom side. Any further mistakes could damage 'Pioneer' and risk the lives of our crew," George replied.

"That is exactly what I was thinking," Dr. Owen said. "Let's take it easy this time and just learn more about the oil cavern. We'll try to pick up some samples next time," he continued.

Disappointment appeared on Brian's face since he was very anxious to see the samples and analyze them.

"Stefani, the decision is made. Do not pick up samples this time. Simply move around and try to collect as much information about the cavern as possible. The first mission is to acquaint our systems and yourselves with the cavern," Joe over the telecom.

Actually, Stefani and Tommy were relieved and in agreement with Dr. Owen's decision. They also worried about the lack of information from the bottom detector. They now had about one and a half hours of oxygen supply, leaving them at least one hour of time to explore the cavern.

Stefani piloted 'Pioneer' forward, entering the blackness of the cavern. From the monitors, especially the main one in front of her, she could see the depth of the cavern and related data. Stefani now began to realize how important their practice in the deep-sea cavern just a few weeks ago had been. However, there was something here that was very different from the deep-sea cavern. There were a few longer columns in front of 'Pioneer' and many various shorter ones down near the lower section of the cavern. All of them were crossing each other.

A giant long column stood right beside the exit of the tunnel. Stefani moved 'Pioneer' around this column and then moved in deeper. From her front monitor she could see there was more wide-open space above, on the top half of the cavern. Looking down again, she realized it was very complicated and chaotic on the lower half of the cavern, as if there had been a major collapse in the past.

"This is very strange, indeed," Joe said, staring wide-eyed at his monitor. "Based on the more precise data I'm receiving from 'Pioneer,' I can see that the entire cavern looks like a dome, with a very round ceiling. It's unusually symmetrical."

Actually, Dr. Owen and George were also surprised by this.

In the wide-open area, Stefani moved 'Pioneer' faster, about 100 feet per minute, nearly the maximum speed designed. She calculated that if the cavern is about one mile in diameter, with this speed, she might cover nearly half of the cavern in this trip. She knew she had only one hour to play around with.

"Stefani, Dr. Owen believes that you will not be able to cover the entire cavern this time. You should cut the entire cavern into two or three zones, and just investigate one zone this time. We'll need to go down again," Joe said, telling Stefani exactly what she had been about to tell him.

Stefani spoke to Tommy and decided to cover the right-hand side of the cavern. The exit was located about 180 feet from the bottom of the cavern. It seemed the highest central area was about 260 feet high. Stefani decided to take the first scan at the depth of 160 feet and the next at 80 feet. It would take them at least 60 to 70 minutes to cover this area. Tommy agreed.

From the monitors, both Stefani and Tommy could see the three-dimensional image become clearer as they covered more area. The first run was easy since there were not too many very long columns standing high. However, when they ran the second run at the lower level, there were more columns to navigate around. These columns were shorter, and randomly located. Even so, Stefani was able to dodge them without any problem. Now Stefani and Tommy could really feel their appreciation of Joe's work. Without Joe's computer simulation images, it would be impossible for them to pilot the submarine. Naturally, without Tommy's ultrasonic detection system, nothing was possible either. Deep inside Stefani's heart, she admired and respected their talents more than ever.

Nearly 70 minutes passed. Then Joe's voice came over the telecom, "Stefani, just to remind you that you don't have much oxygen left. It is time to return."

"I understand. I will complete this run in three

minutes and then we will be heading back," Stefani said.

Tommy was amazed that Stefani, after their earlier, unsmooth entrance into the cavern, had been able to calm down and rebuild her confidence quickly to handle the situation skillfully. She was the most talented woman he had ever met.

When the second run was completed, Stefani piloted 'Pioneer' slightly upward, so they were able to reach the tunnel entrance. It looked to Stefani that it would take about five minutes to reach the entrance. The oxygen meter showed that they still had 22 minutes of air left. It should take only ten minutes to get through the tunnel, if everything went smoothly of course. That meant they still had 12 minutes extra for them to play around if there was any delay.

The crew on top could see their entrance from the monitors.

"Eric, Mike, can you tell the outside crew to be ready to pick them up? They have about ten minutes," George announced.

" Yes, sir." Eric smiled and nodded. He knew he had contributed a great effort to make this project possible.

In a minute or so, Eric returned. "Mr. Standy, they will be ready in five minutes," he said.

After speaking with Tommy, Stefani decided to pilot 'Pioneer' through the tunnel herself. Tommy agreed.

Everything went smoothly. It took them only nine minutes to get through. It seemed Stefani had become very familiar with the path of the tunnel and piloting 'Pioneer.'

When they finally reached the bottom of the window, Stefani allowed 'Pioneer' to emerge from the water's surface slowly and gradually. Once they reached the surface, Tommy prepared to open the door so he could set the hooks on top of the submarine. Tommy stood up and went to open the door.

"Wait, Tommy," Stefani said. "Underneath your seat, there's a gasmask. Please put it on, just in case." Stefani also picked up the gasmask underneath her seat and put it on. She was just trying to be more cautious since the gas detection light was not even on. That probably meant the gas content at the bottom of the well was too low to even register.

Tommy opened the door wearing the mask, extended his body out, and placed the hooks on the hooking bars. Then he closed the hatch and sat down

"We're ready," Stefani said into the telecom, still wearing her mask. Both she and Tommy knew that when the submarine door was opened, some gas might have entered the submarine.

In a minute or so 'Pioneer' was rising. It took about 18 minutes to reach the top, and then the crane placed 'Pioneer' down gently.

When Stefani and Tommy stepped out of 'Pioneer,' everyone was there smiling and applauding. Dr. Owen stepped forward and gave Stefani a big hug. Then he turned to Tommy and shook his hand.

It was a great success.

After the First Exploration

When Joe, Tommy, and Stefani examined the bottom of 'Pioneer,' they could see that when Stefani entered the red zone area of tunnel, some dirt had filled up the hole where the ultrasonic detector was. This surprised them since the dirt should have come off later when they entered the cavern. However, when Tommy took a closer look and tried to clean the dirt, he began to realize that there was a small piece of rock coated with oil just the right size to fit in the hole. He used a screwdriver to dig the rock out and saw the detector had been pushed in and damaged. Originally, Stefani and Tommy had thought of using fiberglass to cover the hole and protect the detector, however, since anything in front of the detector would affect the effectiveness of the signal's emitting and receiving, they had decided not to put any cover over it.

"We just have to be more careful next time. We'll need this detector so we can see the bottom more clearly, and to be safer picking up samples," Tommy said to Stefani with a smile. Both Tommy and Stefani still could not believe that they had entered the oil mine and come back alive.

The next exploration was set for Wednesday. According to Joe, Wednesday would be a nice day. This would give Joe an entire day to analyze the data collected from the five ultrasonic detectors. It would take some time for him to clean up the signals received and generate a clearer three-dimensional image simulation. Furthermore, Tommy would need some time to repair the damaged detector.

Joe just could not wait for another trip. He knew the more trips Tommy and Stefani went on; the more data would be collected. He intended to make this cavern known as clearly as possible since this was his Ph.D. project at UCLA. He now believed and had the confidence that he would do an exceptional job and would deliver a groundbreaking thesis.

* * *

To celebrate this first success, Dr. Owen hosted a small party in the Standy Firm's cafeteria for everyone involved.

"Ladies and gentlemen, I would like to express my deep appreciation to all of you. Without each one of you, it would be impossible to make this happen. Naturally, I want to especially thank Mr. George Standy. You know, without his generosity and great leadership, this project would have been unattainable." He looked at George who was sitting next to him smiling. The group applauded him loudly.

"Finally," Dr. Owen went on, "I feel so lucky that I have four aggressive and brave students. Without them, my dream of exploring the oil mine would not have happened either." He looked at Tommy, Stefani, Joe, and Brian with great sincerity. Though Brian had not gotten very involved yet, Dr. Owen knew his future job would be harder than, if not equal to, the others.

Halfway through the party, Tommy brought a glass of beer to Stefani.

"I don't really drink beer," Stefani said. "I've never liked beer. It doesn't taste good to me." She looked at Tommy and smiled.

"What do you prefer, then, my queen?" Tommy had not called Stefani 'queen' for a couple of days, but he felt that that night was the right moment for him to express his emotional intention again. He could sense the defense mechanism that Stefani had rapidly rebuilt between them in the last couple of days.

"Just call me Stefani. Please?" Stefani smiled at Tommy. "Sometimes during Korean festivals, my family will drink some sweet wine," she said.

"Then, let me bring some for you," Tommy said, trying to demonstrate his gentleman's courtesy. He could feel that she was closing down to him and moving farther and farther away. What happened? He began to feel very concerned. Stefani didn't reply, so he just walked away to see if he could find 'sweet wine' here.

Stefani's mind began to get confused again. "I really like him. He is very sincere and trying so hard," she thought. However, she had to keep her distance. She didn't want to sink into emotions so deep that she could not pull up if needed. Anyway, tonight was special. She had conquered herself. She had established a confidence that she never had before. It was a night to celebrate. A few minutes later, Tommy returned bringing her a glass of sherry.

"This is sherry, made from white grapes." Tommy

handed the wine to Stefani and smiled. "The sweetest thing they have."

"I've had this before. I like it. My mom also likes it a lot," Stefani said. Oh no! It seemed her mom was there to remind her of the conversation they had a few days ago. However, she didn't want to think about it. This was her night of celebration. She had earned it.

"Cheers." She raised her glass. Tommy also lifted his beer and said, "To you, Stefani."

They sat together talking, a little bit drunk, and the time passed very quickly. Around 9:30 p.m., people began to leave the party. Mr. Standy left early since he had an early flight to Los Angeles. They continued to sit together, holding hands, until it was time to leave. When Tommy took Stefani back to her room, he kissed her again.

* * *

Stefani slept until 10:00 in the morning. When she woke, she had a little bit of a headache. She did not drink wine often. "Maybe I drank too much last night," she thought.

Around 10:30 a.m., Joe called everyone together for a meeting.

In Standy Firm's conference room, at 2:30 p.m., Dr. Owen, Tommy, Stefani, Joe, and Brian were all there. Tommy had gotten up early that morning and replaced the damaged detector.

"Hi everyone! I have just completed the updated 3-D

image. This meeting was called because I believe that we should take a look at the image and then decide what the next step is for tomorrow," Joe said.

Joe turned the light off and began to project the 3-D image. It took only about 20 minutes. To everyone's surprise, a very clear picture of the cavern appeared. They could see that the dome-like cavern had a height of approximately 20 stories and was very wide. One side of the cavern was clearly shown. However, the other side was a blur. Not only that, nothing could be seen of the lower half of the cavern. Everyone knew this was due to two reasons. One was that only a portion of the cavern had been explored. The other was because the bottom detector was not functioning. In spite of that, this 20-minute movie gave them a much clearer understanding of the shape of the cavern.

Joe turned the light on.

"As you saw, we only have a clear understanding of part of the cavern. As to the other side, the edge, and the bottom, we still don't know," Joe explained. "I believe we need a very detailed plan for the next couple trips."

Everyone looked at each other and agreed with Joe's suggestion.

"What's on your mind Joe? Since you have thought about this, you must have already had some ideas," Dr. Owen said.

"Since we have only two hours of oxygen and battery supply, my suggestion is that we collect information for the other side of the cavern on the next trip. Actually, the hardest part will be the lower section since there are so many columns and so much debris and dirt piled up at the bottom. I estimate we will need about three trips to understand the lower section better," Joe looked at everyone and said.

"Four more times total?" Stefani asked. Stefani's face had shown an expression of impatience and worry. She knew that each time they went in was a risk. Nobody could be sure that all the trips would be safe. In addition, if there were any danger, Tommy and Stefani would be alone down there. There would be no one that would be able to go down and rescue them. She just hoped they could get some samples as soon as possible.

"Yes. Maybe more. The reason for this is being able to get samples from the very bottom of the cavern, not from the piled dirt that's fallen from the ceiling. The real samples we need to analyze are located on the bottom of cavern," Brian said and looked at Dr. Owen seeking his agreement.

"It's true. The samples we want are on the bottom of the cavern since they will offer us the true age and history of the cavern. These samples will be the hardest ones to obtain, especially in light of the amount of debris. As to the samples on the wall or the dirt, we can pick them up easily," Dr. Owen confirmed Brian's statement.

"That means we need to have a solid understanding of the bottom of the cavern. This area is the most important, and the most dangerous. I will need as much detailed information as possible before you try to work down there," Joe said again.

"Since there is such a huge pile of dirt covering the floor bottom, it may take forever to find samples from the bottom of the cavern," Tommy expressed his opinion. He was showing the same worry as Stefani.

"Once we have a better picture of the bottom, we may find an area where the debris is thinner or, with any luck, locate some area which has not been covered by dirt," Joe said. He paused a moment and looked at Tommy and Stefani. "If we are able to find an exposed spot, we can just focus on that area, and save a lot of time."

"Let's now decide on three more trips. One will explore the second half of the top area and two more near the bottom area. After these three trips, we will see what we've accomplished, and go from there," Dr. Owen said.

"I'll call Mr. Standy about our decision. We'll need his crew to help keep us going," Dr. Owen continued.

Now the immediate mission was clear. They set up three more explorations: tomorrow, and then the two days following for the next two trips. This would provide some time for Joe's analysis and simulation.

Second Exploration

On Wednesday morning, the entire crew gathered around the cavern window. Everything was going according to plan. There was almost no problem or difficulty this time due to the experience gained from the last trip. The best part of the trip this time was that they would have more information about the lower section of the cavern since the bottom ultrasonic detector had been replaced and was functioning.

When Stefani and Tommy entered the cavern, they began to see that the structure of the unexplored side of the cavern was almost identical to the side they had explored last time. This time it only took about 15 minutes for Stefani to get through the tunnel and through the bottleneck without hesitation. She skillfully circled around the huge column near the tunnel and piloted 'Pioneer' downward to a height of 160 feet. Since there were only a few long columns sticking up from the ground, the ride was much smoother. It took Stefani about 38 minutes to circle around and collect information. She then piloted 'Pioneer' down to a height of 80 feet and repeated the ultrasonic scanning. It took longer for Stefani to scan this time, 43 minutes, as there were more gigantic columns sticking out from the bottom. Not only that, the area they covered was wider.

When they were returning to the tunnel, Tommy told Stefani what he thought about the other side.

"Stefani, it looks like there are more areas where the roof caved in over here than on the other side. That probably means there is more dirt piled up on this side as well," Tommy said.

"Yes, also from my monitor I'm seeing an empty air pocket across the way over there. Do you see it?" Stefani asked.

Tommy was paying attention to the monitor that scanned the bottom side of the submarine and hadn't noticed it until Stefani pointed it out. There could very likely be gas accumulated in the pocket. The empty space could have been created due to dirt falling from the ceiling at some other time. Stefani calculated that this place was less than five minutes from the tunnel entrance. That meant it was about 2,000 feet from the tunnel entrance if they kept moving at full speed. They knew they should keep themselves away from the empty space since any sparking could cause an explosion.

After concentrating so intensely on her piloting, Stefani felt tired.

"Tommy, can you take over? I am exhausted. I may lose my concentration in the tunnel. And besides, I believe it is also good for you to experience it."

"Aye aye, Captain!" Actually, Tommy had been hoping to experience the piloting as well. He skillfully piloted the submarine through the tunnel without a problem. They returned safely.

After the Second Exploration

Again, the next morning at 10 a.m., the entire crew gathered in Standy Firm's conference room.

After everyone sat down, as before, Joe turned the light off and the projector on. Everyone was still very anxious to see more about the cavern, especially the new side. They also knew the bottom of the cavern would be clearer since the bottom detector was fixed.

Joe pushed the play button on his computer and the movie began. Everyone could see the structure on the other side clearly. In addition, the lower section of the cavern on this side was also much clearer. However, the other side was still blurred due to a lack of information from the first time.

When it was finished, Joe repeated the entire simulation one more time. He then turned on the light and the projector off.

"From what you have seen, we can come to a few conclusions. One, more of the ceiling fell in the past on this side. Two, more debris piled up on this side. And three, there is a pocket of air trapped on the top of this side, most likely full of volatile gas," Joe concluded his analysis. Everyone agreed.

"My suggestion is since there is more dirt piled up on this side, we should focus on the lower section near the bottom on the other side for the next trip. Clearly, we have a better chance of reaching the bottom on the other side," Joe continued.

Dr. Owen had come to the same conclusion as Joe. He had already concluded this while he was watching the movie. The new mission was set, and the next trip was planned for the next morning at 10 a.m.

Third Exploration

Since they were much more familiar with the tunnel and cavern, Tommy asked Stefani if he could pilot 'Pioneer' again this time. He knew scanning the lower section would be more dangerous, but he wanted the challenge. Stefani agreed. It was only fair to let Tommy pilot 'Pioneer' sometimes.

After 'Pioneer' had been lowered to the water's surface, Tommy released the air and the submarine began to sink. When it reached the entrance of the tunnel, he piloted 'Pioneer' to the right to enter the tunnel. He carefully steered through the entire tunnel without much difficulty, having gained experience on the previous trips.

When they entered the cavern, Tommy was mainly interested in searching for samples on the bottom of the cavern. He kept 'Pioneer' as low to the ground as possible. He knew Joe would be more interested in knowing the entire cavern's structure. But to him, samples were the first priority.

He only had about 90 minutes to scan the bottom area, so he drove 'Pioneer' a little bit faster than Stefani, even though it was more dangerous near the bottom. This made Stefani nervous at first, but after 20 minutes, she could see the skill of Tommy's piloting, and she began to feel more relaxed and comfortable.

After scanning nearly the entire bottom, Tommy found at least seven areas that had lower levels of dirt piled up. He turned the sub to the left, trying to decide which area to search first. Directly in front of him was a massive structure, some kind of phenomenon he had not yet seen down there.

"Stefani, can you see the far end of the cavern? There's a huge pile of columns in the shape of a pyramid," Tommy said.

"Yes, I see it! It just looks like a collapsed section of stalagmites to me," Stefani replied.

Tommy felt differently though. His mind was racing, and he had a strange feeling that this area was special. All of the columns were about 50 to 100 feet long. It was fantastic to see the structural difference between this area and the others. However, they were running out of time. They had only about ten minutes to return to the tunnel entrance. Tommy regretted not being able to get more information about this pile.

Though it was time to return, Tommy piloted to the nearest area below them and managed to pick up some dirt from the bottom with his side of the robot arm and placed it into the sample pocket safely. Before reentering the tunnel, he asked Stefani to scratch some of the material as a sample from the wall of the cavern also. Stefani did it carefully. They now had two samples from two areas, the bottom dirt and the wall.

When they returned to the surface, Brian was very happy to see some samples finally reaching his hands. The most valuable were the small rocks that had been picked up. They would help him determine the age of the cavern and also how the oil had affected the structure of the soil.

After the Third Exploration

As usual, the crew gathered in the conference room at 10:00 the next morning.

Again, Joe waited for everyone to get ready, then he turned the light off and the projector on. This time the movie was considerably clearer than the previous two times. Each time 'Pioneer' went in, they collected more data for Joe's simulation.

After the show was over, as usual, Joe stood up and

said, "From what you have seen and what I have analyzed, the biggest problem is with the dirt on the bottom. This sediment has piled up over the years, and even in the shallowest places, it's still at least 20 feet deep. If we wish to reach the bottom for samples, we must first dig away the dirt on top. I think it will take at least ten hours using the robot arms to complete the job. This means it will take at least ten more trips if we are lucky," Joe said.

This made Tommy and Stefani very depressed and unhappy.

"In that case, it seems this mission is impossible since it will take more trips and, naturally, more risks," Stefani said.

To support Stefani's argument, Tommy said, "In addition, we don't even know how thick the dirt piled up on the bottom is. It may take us forever to reach the bottom even if we dig."

The group suddenly fell silent and entered into deep thinking. From what they now knew, it seemed it was impossible to make this happen. However, without the bottom samples which were the main objective of this project, it would be as if they were eating a meal without the main course. Everyone looked at Dr. Owen and waited for his response and decision. None of them had ever thought this might be a problem.

After a few minutes, Tommy suddenly spoke up.

"Joe, can you enlarge the pyramid pile of columns near the far end. I am very curious about this area," he requested.

"Naturally, I will try my best," Joe replied. It took

only a few minutes for Joe to set up and locate the structure in the 3-D simulation. He enlarged the pile and played the section repeatedly, five times in a row. Though the image was quite clear, what it showed was very strange indeed. During the last showing, Tommy suddenly shouted,

"Stop here! Can you freeze this, Joe?"

Joe rewound back a couple of seconds and then froze it. Tommy stood up and went to the screen. He used his finger to point out a hollow area located about one-third of the way from the top of the pyramid pile and near the cavern wall.

"As you see, we cannot see what is inside this pile; however, this hollow area looks like an entrance or opening to the inside of it. If we are lucky, since most of the falling dirt would have been shielded by these columns, if we can enter, we may have a chance to see the bottom of the cavern," Tommy said excitedly.

"Tommy, you should know, even if it is worthwhile to take a look, it could be extremely dangerous. If there is any collision or scratch between the submarine and the columns, this pile could collapse and bury you alive in there," Dr. Owen expressed his worry sincerely.

However, Tommy insisted that it was worth a try. He believed that as long as they were cautious and did not take any unnecessary risks, they should be OK.

"Brian, what do you think? It is your call since you are the one who needs samples more urgently than the others," Dr. Owen said.

"Well, from my preliminary analysis, the samples on

the wall were the same material as the dirt piled on the floor bottom. Though they are able to offer some past history, the whole story is not quite clear. These samples can offer us only part of the cavern history. The history of the top part of the pile can possibly be very different from that of the dirt near the bottom. Naturally, this is inconclusive. I will need more time and better equipment for my analysis. I'll have to use the lab at UCLA," Brian replied. That meant Brian also agreed that they should find a way to pick up samples from the floor bottom.

The decision was made for the next day.

Fourth Exploration

Before going into the tunnel, Tommy told Stefani that he insisted on piloting 'Pioneer' this time when they entered the new unknown territory since it could be more dangerous than ever. From their last three experiences, Stefani realized that Tommy was not just a skillful but also a cautious driver. Not only that, she felt and knew that if there was any crisis, Tommy would probably react and handle it better than she would.

"Yes, Tommy. After we enter the cavern, you take over. But be careful," she replied.

Stefani piloted 'Pioneer' into the cavern and then Tommy took over. Since they knew the way pretty well, it took them only 35 minutes to reach the pyramid pile. Tommy circled the pile a couple of times before he carefully approached the hole or the opening gap in the pile. He slowed 'Pioneer' down to 16 feet per minute. From the monitors, he could only see the superficial structure of the passage. He could not see anything beyond the columns, and he did not know the way. The worst part was that he lost telecom communication with Joe once they entered the pile. All four monitors directly showed that the four detectors were functioning, but not the three-dimensional simulated one. They were now completely isolated from the outside world. It seemed the information being collected could no longer be transmitted to the surface for simulation. They were in a completely new place and half blind. Tommy turned on the on-board simulation system, 'SOS,' which had been installed on 'Pioneer' by Joe. He remembered that when Joe told him about this installation, he had thought it redundant and unnecessary since Joe's computer could process all the information and then send it back to the submarine. Now, he could see the wisdom of Joe's decision.

When Stefani saw that they were out of touch with the surface, she became very nervous. She began to sweat and held her breath. She noticed that her legs were trembling and tried to keep herself as calm as possible.

After they traveled for about 20 feet, Tommy could see what looked like a path going almost straight down. The size of this path was just big enough for 'Pioneer' to get through. He warned Stefani about his intention to go down and told her that if he got stuck and could not advance forward, she would have to pilot the submarine backward so they could get out. This made Stefani even more nervous. They double-checked to make sure they were tightly secured by their seat belts.

Tommy piloted 'Pioneer' downward very carefully. Once they had gone about 20 feet, he could see there were no more obstacles in front of him. They entered a big space about the size of a basketball court hidden inside of the pile of columns. Stefani and Tommy were amazed to see there was such a big space hidden inside the pile of columns. They were very excited and felt their tension ease. From the monitor, they could see the bottom floor of the cavern. It was covered with only a couple feet of dirt and some miscellaneous objects. Tommy first circled the area a couple of times and allowed the detectors to collect as much information as possible and store it in the submarine's computer. He then went to the spot that appeared to have the thinnest layer of dirt over the cavern floor. He was very excited and used the robot arm to dig a couple of scoops of samples and place them in the storage pocket. He asked Stefani to do the same at the other end. They both knew the samples from this area would be much more valuable than those collected from other places. Time was running out. They had only 40 minutes to get back.

Tommy piloted 'Pioneer' upward through the same hole they had come in. The computer in the submarine had already simulated a three-dimensional image of this small tunnel from the information collected. It helped Tommy a lot and allowed him to come out of the pyramid column pile smoothly. Again, they were so glad that Joe had installed the simulation software in the submarine's computer. They really appreciated Joe's talent and thoughtful planning.

Once they got out, Tommy telecommed Joe immediately.

"Joe, you will not believe it! We got the samples from the bottom of the cavern," Tommy told the good news with a very excited voice.

"Thank God you're safe! We have been worrying about you guys for the last 30 minutes. What happened?" Joe asked.

"I don't know. Once we entered the pyramid pile, we immediately lost your signal and three-dimensional simulation image. It seems those columns create a shield that blocks the signals. All we relied on were the four monitors that showed the information collected by the detectors, and also the images simulated by the submarine's computer. Anyway, we will report to the entire crew when we return to the surface," Tommy said.

When they returned to surface, the entire crew was waiting. This was another time to celebrate. As a matter of fact, they had scared everyone to death, especially Dr. Owen.

On the ground, the samples were released into two large strong plastic containers. Brian was very excited to see them. Even though everything was coated by black oil, they were priceless to him.

When Stefani and Tommy stepped out of 'Pioneer' everyone came forward and hugged them.

After the Fourth Exploration

That evening at about six o'clock, Brian called Dr.

Owen.

"Hi, Professor. I wonder if it is possible for us to meet and talk alone tonight?" Brian asked.

"Is there anything wrong, Brian?" Dr. Owen asked.

"No, Professor. It's just - I have found something strange in the samples brought back today. I need to show you and talk to you about it."

"Have you talked to anyone else about this?"

"No, I think we should talk alone first tonight," Brian answered.

Dr. Owen could sense that Brian must have found something in the samples he could not explain. It must be something very obvious since the equipment here was not good enough for him to conduct any analysis in depth.

* * *

Right after dinner, Brian came to Dr. Owen's room. It was 8:00 p.m.

When Dr. Owen opened the door and let him in, Brian greeted Dr. Owen and sat down. Then he carefully brought from his pocket an object that was wrapped in his handkerchief. He opened it and handed it to Dr. Owen.

"Professor, I need you to take a look at this. I found it in the sample pile," Brian said while Dr. Owen took the object from his hand. Most of the oil coating on the object had been removed and cleaned by Brian.

It was a transparent rhombic crystal, like two equal

sized pyramid crystals glued together at the bottom. Why was this thing in the cavern? Dr. Owen was shocked and speechless. He looked at Brian with a wondering and confused expression on his face.

"Professor, please take a careful look <u>inside</u> the crystal." Brian brought a magnifier out of his pocket and gave it to Dr. Owen.

Dr. Owen brought the crystal and magnifier near the light and took a close look. His eyes opened even wider in surprise by what he saw. The top half of the crystal had a gap that divided the top pyramid into two sides, while the bottom pyramid was a solid piece. The crystal was cut so neatly and cleanly that no defect could be found. The most amazing thing was that there was a tiny metal wire connecting the center of the pyramid on the top to the center of the bottom one. At the two ends of the metal wire were two tiny round metal balls. Anyone could tell that this was not a natural product.

"Why was this there?" Dr. Owen wondered.

"Brian, can you keep this a secret only between you and me? At least until we know more about this crystal?" Dr. Owen asked. "When we return to Los Angeles, I will have this crystal analyzed by an expert. Also, can I keep it for the time being?"

Naturally, Brian agreed.

"Remember, don't tell anyone," Dr. Owen again reminded Brian as he left.

Dr. Owen could not sleep the whole night. He kept taking the crystal out and inspecting it with the magnifier he had borrowed from Brian. He tossed around for three hours and could not fall asleep. Finally, he decided to get up and inspect the crystal again. He looked and looked at it again with the magnifier.

"Definitely, this is not a natural material. Nature does not form this type of shape and structure with a perfect metal alignment within," he thought.

"Where did this crystal come from? It had to have been manufactured by some highly intelligent being in the past."

He wondered.

"What is the purpose and function of this crystal? There might be a hidden advanced technology inside."

He was almost sure.

"Definitely, until we know more about it, we should not reveal this secret to the outside world, especially to the government. It might cause a huge disturbance, or it might be abused," he thought.

He asked himself the same questions repeatedly in his mind. Then he thought of the Roswell UFO crash incident. He wondered how many advanced technologies might have been received from that incident and were being used for weapons development by the government. Top authorities were not interested in promoting human benefits and peace. They were interested in developing more advanced weapons for their wars. Finally, Dr. Owen made the final decision that this secret must be kept till he and Brian knew more about the crystal.

* * *

The next morning, at 10 a.m. as usual, the entire crew gathered in the conference room. Joe stood up behind the projector and addressed the group. "Great news everybody! I was successful at taking the SOS data and adding it to the 3-D simulations we've already collected." Joe turned on the projector and started the movie. He had been able to create a much clearer three-dimensional image of the entrance and passage of the pyramid pile. Not only that, he had also created a three-dimensional image of the room hidden inside the pile.

They now had to decide if they wanted to continue on with another trip or if they should stop there. However, before they came to a decision Tommy sat forward in his chair and spoke up. "Joe, I saw a hole near the far end of the room. Can you enlarge it for me please?" Tommy asked.

"Naturally." Joe brought the pointer on his computer to the place and then enlarged it. Now they could see clearly that there was a hole that was as large as the submarine at the far end of the room. What was behind this hole was unknown.

"I am very curious about what's on the other side of that hole. I understand it could be a dead end since it is at the very edge of the cavern," Tommy said. Somehow, though, he had a feeling that this hole was something worth investigating. Furthermore, he was interested in getting more samples that were closer to the edge of the cavern.

"I would like to attempt to go back and take a look at it. I may find something there," Tommy said. However,

Stefani's face wore a nervous expression. She had been hoping this was the end of her part of the project so that she could go home.

"I think you and Stefani should go back at least one more time," Dr. Owen agreed. This surprised everyone.

"I talked to Brian last night and it seems that we will need more samples from the same area," Dr. Owen told them. He looked at Brian with an expression of apology for the lie he had just told. Actually, they had not talked about this last night. However, Dr. Owen hoped to find more crystals or other strange items in the same area. He had had a strange thought hanging around his mind since the night before. He could feel there was some huge secret hidden in this room.

Since Dr. Owen said so, the decision was made. This could be the final trip for Tommy and Stefani, therefore they had to collect as many samples as they could. If they still had time, they would investigate the hole at the far end of the room.

Fifth Exploration

The next morning, they again met at 10 a.m. They knew that each time they went in they were taking a risk. This was especially true on the last trip when they had explored the pyramid pile. They had more confidence this time due to two reasons. They had already had one experience entering the column pile, so they knew what to expect, and Joe had provided them with a better three-dimensional simulation image of the entrance and the room.

Since the mission was clear and straight forward, Stefani again took the responsibility of piloting 'Pioneer' into the cavern and over to the column pile. Tommy then took over. This shifting strategy provided each of them with some time for relaxation and rest. This was very important since the two-hour trips were very mentally intense. High concentration was needed.

To Tommy, this trip had an extra purpose. Somehow, he had a strong and strange feeling about the hole near the other end of the room in the column pile. Not only that, this might be the last risky trip in which both Stefani and he worked together.

When 'Pioneer' had reached the column pile, Stefani turned it around so that Tommy was facing the entrance.

"It's yours, Tommy. Be cool," Stefani said.

"Aye, aye, Captain," Tommy replied confidently with a smile.

With the help of the three-dimensional simulation, Tommy carefully entered the hole and reached the vertical downward tunnel. Even though he had some experience from the last time, and was also helped by the simulated images, he was still a little bit uptight. Finally, 'Pioneer' entered the room without any problem. Amazingly, since this trip had gone so smoothly, they had at least one whole hour to explore the room and the hole.

"Stefani, I would like to explore the hole at the other end first and dig samples later. This way we won't have to carry unnecessary weight until the last moment. You know, we must conserve our energy," Tommy said. He paused a little bit. Before Stefani could express her opinion, he continued, "In addition, I would like to know the area better first and see where the best spots are to get samples. We were in too much of a hurry last time."

"What a wise idea!" Stefani thought. She believed, in many ways, Tommy was showing his wisdom and foresight.

"Naturally! You are the pilot now and can make the decision," Stefani said.

Without hesitation, Tommy piloted 'Pioneer' to the hole. Again, due to the lost connection with the surface, Tommy had to rely on the submarine's detectors and its own simulation system. From the front detector, he was shocked to see the depth of the hole. He had thought the hole would be shallow since this column pile was located near the edge of the cavern. Soon, he began to realize that there was another huge space on the other side of the hole.

The entrance of the hole was about 45 degrees upward and small. It was barely wide enough for the submarine to get through.

Once they entered the other side, Joe's voice re-appeared over the telecom.

"Tommy, I can see you and read your detectors again. I guess you are out of the column pile, right?" Joe asked.

It was like hearing a sweet angel's voice. Both Stefani and Tommy were so happy that they had connection again with the surface.

"Yes, Joe. How great to hear your angelic voice! When we lost contact, we felt like abandoned children in the wild," Tommy said with a laugh.

"It seems you have entered another space. The computer is showing you in a new area," Joe said.

"Yes, behind the hole there was another huge space. Since I still have 50 minutes to play here, I intend to spend at least 40 minutes exploring this new space," Tommy said.

"Understood. Just be careful," Joe replied.

First, Tommy carefully circled around the new space. He kept 'Pioneer' about 60 feet high from the bottom to avoid any collision with columns laying down there. He spent about 30 minutes circling the new cavern. He could see that this cavern was much smaller than the other one. The height was only about half of the big one, nearly 130 feet. The diameter was about half a mile across. Strangely, the structure of the smaller dome was almost exactly the same as the big one. Again, there were countless numbers of columns, short or long, laying down on the bottom. After 30 minutes, Tommy could see the entire cavern very clearly from the three-dimensional image transmitted down by Joe from the surface.

He could also see that the dirt piled up on the ground was not as deep as in the big cavern. He noticed some areas where the dirt was in fact very shallow. Finally, he decided to go to an area that was the closest to the hole where they had entered. This area was near the bottom and near the boundary of the big cavern. Tommy chose this area for two reasons. First, it was closer to the hole so they could get out quickly whenever necessary. Second, this area was near the edge of the cavern. That meant he would be able to pick up samples from both the bottom and also the edge.

He carefully piloted 'Pioneer' lower and lower. Finally, it was only about two feet from the bottom. He manipulated the robot arm and dug up some samples from the bottom and placed them into the sample pocket carefully. After that, he secured the pocket so the sample would not come out even when the submarine was tilted.

"Stefani, it's your turn now to dig some samples for your sample pocket. We have a bigger harvest this time," Tommy said.

"Where should I dig?" Stefani asked.

"Your choice is as good as mine. You may have better luck than me," Tommy said with a laugh.

Tommy let Stefani pilot the submarine and find her chosen spot. She went to a corner that was not very obvious and began to dig with the robot arm.

Tommy was glad that Stefani chose a different spot. This would offer them more chances for different samples.

After Stefani finished her digging and secured the sample, Tommy contacted Joe. They had only ten minutes to get out of here, re-enter the empty room, and get out of the column pyramid pile. After that, they would have only about 20 minutes to reach the entrance of the tunnel.

"Joe, we are re-entering the column pile through the hole again. You may not see us for about ten minutes," Tommy said.

"Okay, be careful!" Joe replied.

Tommy piloted the submarine and 'Pioneer' re-entered the hole and entered the room again. It took him about five minutes to reach the other end. Then he piloted the submarine upward through the same path they had come in. Finally, they got out of the column pile in just eight minutes and 16 seconds.

"I see you again, Tommy!" Joe said over the telecom. "Take your time, you have plenty. Enjoy your last trip. It will be a great success this time!"

Brian, standing next to Dr. Owen, was very happy that they finally had some samples he wanted. However, he was still wondering about the crystal they found last time.

At last the submarine was lifted to the surface. When Stefani and Tommy stepped out of the submarine, Dr. Owen and all the others were there to welcome them. Dr. Owen stepped forward and hugged Stefani first and then Tommy. The most difficult part of the project, obtaining samples, was accomplished. However, deep in his mind, he could not help but keep thinking about the strange crystal they found last time.

"Maybe they found more crystals this time," Dr. Owen hoped.

A couple of Standy Firm technicians released the security lock on the sample pockets and poured black and dirty looking samples into four plastic containers. Then they helped Brian load the samples onto the bed of the company pick-up that Brian had borrowed from Standy Firm for the last few days.

After the Fifth Exploration

That evening, there was a good-bye party hosted by Dr. Owen. Everyone involved was again invited but this time, Dr. Owen did not see Brian. It seemed Brian was very busy with something. He guessed that Brian might be more interested in the samples than the party.

Halfway through the party, Brian came in. Without stopping, he went straight to Dr. Owen who was talking to Mr. George Standy's secretary, hoping she would be able to pass a message to George and tell him how much the entire crew appreciated the Standy Firm's assistance.

"I will call Mr. Standy and thank him myself when I return to Los Angeles," Dr. Owen said.

"Mr. Standy will be very happy to know the project was such a success," George's secretary replied. While they were talking, Dr. Owen saw Brian approach. He could see Brian was looking for him.

"Excuse me. I need to talk to Brian," Dr. Owen apologized to her and went to meet him.

"Hi, Brian! You're late," Dr. Owen said.

"Can we find a separate place so we can talk alone?" Brian asked.

"Naturally! Come with me," Dr. Owen replied and led Brian outside.

They went to a picnic table and sat down. With the help of a streetlight, Dr. Owen could see Brian was not only nervous but also excited.

"I searched the entire pile of samples picked up today. I found six more crystals. Amazingly, they are <u>exactly</u> the same size and same structure. I just finished cleaning them right before I came to the party." Brian looked at Dr. Owen. "Like the last time, I could not clean the gap area completely."

"It's a jackpot! Six more?" Dr. Owen asked. He just could not believe it.

"Yes, Professor. Should we tell the other people?" Brian replied with excitement.

"Brian, I still believe that before we know what they are, we better keep them secret. I just feel it is very strange. I need time to think and conduct more experiments," Dr. Owen replied. "If you don't mind, let me keep all of the samples. I will take them to an expert and have them analyzed."

"Yes, Professor. I will bring them to your room," Brian said.

Brian followed through later that evening and brought all the crystals to Dr. Owen's room, then left.

* * *

Since the mission had been accomplished, Dr. Owen and Brian decided to return to Los Angeles as soon as possible while the others decided to stay one more day for relaxation and sightseeing. Again, Tommy and Joe would be responsible for towing 'Pioneer' back to Los Angeles. Brian could not wait to get the analysis started at UCLA. However, Dr. Owen's mind was on the crystals. He just needed to know what these strange crystals were and why they were there in the cavern.

On their last day, Joe, Tommy, and Stefani went on a nice tour of Austin and had a good time. Tommy and Stefani knew they might not see each other as often as they want once they returned to Los Angeles. Stefani would be very busy preparing for her final examination for her degree. Then, after her graduation, she had already accepted a job offer from MarinaTech. During the construction of 'Pioneer,' MarinaTech had seen first-hand Stefani's talent and enthusiasm for deep-sea exploration. She would be a great help to the company. The job offer was what Stefani had always dreamt of. She accepted the job delightedly.

Tommy would also be busy preparing his final report for the project. He also needed to see about making a plan for his future. Dr. Owen had hired him just for this project and his grant would run out soon. Dr. Owen would not be able to hire him anymore once they returned to Los Angeles. Even though Stefani still treated him as a good friend, not as a lover, he hoped he could stay in the Los Angeles area so he could still see her.

As for Joe, the project was a great success for his Ph.D. thesis. He had done a great job. It was just the beginning of November and he had already completed the simulation project of his Ph.D. thesis. Since he had completed his required courses in the first two years of studying for his degree, all he needed to do now was write a nice thesis and present it to his advisor. This would take him about one and half years instead of two years as he originally thought. After that, he needed to prepare for his final presentation and oral test in front of his thesis committee. He had received a job offer in New York City and planned to move there in June right after graduation.

Chapter 4
The Crystals

Way Back

Since he was purchasing the tickets last minute, Dr. Owen was not able to get on the same flight as Brian. Otherwise, he would have been very happy to talk to Brian about the crystals and his project all the way back. But they could not make their reservations earlier since they had not been sure when the project in Austin would be finished.

On the way back, on the airplane, Dr. Owen kept thinking about a few things. Why did both the large and small caverns have similar shapes, and why like a dome? Why were they not shaped as other regular natural caverns? What were these crystals? Their shape and structure were very unique. He had never seen any natural material like them. He was almost one hundred percent sure that these crystals were not natural. Why were the crystals there? As far as he knew, after so many years in the oil, any material should have been somewhat eroded by the chemicals. However, all seven crystals had shown no damage at all. They had perfect shape, the same size, and the same structure. Were there more crystals in the cavern? Were there any other crystals in other oil mines?

All of these questions and many more kept playing over and over in Dr. Owen's mind during his flight home. He could not help but play the three-dimensional simulation image of the cavern on his laptop. He played it again and again. He pondered and tried to figure out many unknowns.

Dr. Owen had hundreds of questions. For the past few days, since Brian had shown him the first crystal, he had been continually working, curious about the mysteries hidden behind the crystals. Now he was very tired and felt like he could collapse. He finally relaxed and, before he knew it, he fell asleep. When he woke up, the airplane had just landed and was taxiing on the runway.

Dr. Owen felt it was just like a dream. Yes, it was a dream. But when he opened the briefcase, he saw the crystals.

* * *

Preliminary Analysis

By the time Dr. Owen arrived home, it was nearly 10 p.m. He decided to rest first and worry about the crystals the next day.

The next morning, he ran some tests in his lab on the material the crystals were made of. However, there were a few elements that could not be identified. All the information he could discover with the equipment he had was that these crystals were as strong as diamonds or stronger. He could not even learn how these unbreakable crystals could be constructed in such a shape with some metal inside. When he tested the metal inside, he could not find a match to any existing metals on earth. He repeated the tests several times and ended with the same results.

Finally, he called his good friend, Dr. Matthew Kaufman, a well-known material analyzer in the United States. Whenever Dr. Owen could not obtain an answer from material analysis in his lab, Matt was the first one he asked for advice.

It was still early in the morning when Dr. Owen called Matt's lab. "Good morning, Matt! How are you doing? I have not seen you for a few months. How is your family?"

"Hey, James. Long time, no see. My family is good. Thank you! I heard you were in Austin for your oil mine exploration project," Matt said when he answered the phone.

"In fact, I just returned last night. I have found some material in the oil mine which needs your expertise for analysis," Dr. Owen replied.

"What material is so troublesome for you? I thought your lab was able to handle almost any analysis," Matt asked.

"Not this time. Can we meet for lunch? My treat."

Dr. Kaufman and Dr. Owen had been high school classmates. Once they graduated from high school, they went to different universities and pursued different careers. After more than 45 years, Dr. Kaufman had become one of the leading authorities in material analysis in the States and, as a matter of fact, almost the whole world. Due to some connection through their jobs and research, they had gotten together again about nine years ago. Since then, they had often talked to each other just like old friends.

"OK, I will find time for you, James," Dr. Kaufman replied.

"I will come to your company and we can have lunch in the cafeteria or at a restaurant nearby. How about 12:30 p.m., Matt?"

"I will be waiting for you," Dr. Kaufman replied, and at the same time, he wondered what kind of material it could be. He knew Dr. Owen's lab was able to analyze nearly everything on earth.

* * *

At 12:23 p.m., Dr. Owen met Dr. Kaufman in the main hall of the building where Matt worked. They greeted each other.

"There is a Chinese restaurant just a couple blocks away. The food is good, and it should not have too many people there at lunch time," Dr. Kaufman said.

They walked down the street to a Hunan Chinese restaurant. There they chose a corner table so they could talk without bothering other people. In addition, Dr. Owen did not want others overhearing their conversation, especially this time. After they sat down, the waiter brought some ice water and tea, and handed them two menus.

"Let's order first. While we are waiting for food, we

can talk," Dr. Owen suggested. Dr. Kaufman agreed. Once the waiter had gone Dr. Owen brought out an object wrapped in a cloth from his briefcase. He put the object right in front of Dr. Kaufman.

"Take a look Matt, can you tell me what this is?" Dr. Owen looked at Dr. Kaufman's face and gave a challenging smile.

Dr. Kaufman carefully opened the cloth and saw a crystal inside. His face immediately reflected an expression of confusion.

"It's just a man-made crystal. I don't know the purpose, but it's very obvious that it is man-made. There is no natural material that has this kind of shape, in fact, a perfect shape," Dr. Kaufman said.

Dr. Owen handed a magnifier to him and said, "Look again, Matt."

"The structure is very strange. Two tiny metal balls connected by a metal stick inside and situated exactly at the center of the pyramids," Dr. Kaufman said after he took a detailed look. He began to wonder what the purpose of this special structure was.

"Matt, I need you to analyze the material of this crystal and the metal inside. If you are able to also tell me when it was fabricated, it would be great," Dr. Owen said. But Dr. Kaufman's face still wore an expression of confusion.

"James, why are you taking this so seriously? From the look of it, this was either made with glass or artificial crystal. I believe your lab is able to handle this kind of simple analysis," Dr. Kaufman said.

"Matt, I have already tested it repeatedly in my lab. It is not glass or artificial crystal. It is harder than diamond, if not more. Furthermore, there are a few elements inside which are unknown from all our data. The metal connecting the top and bottom pyramids is also unknown."

"Really, James. Where did you find it?"

"Matt, we found it in the oil reservoir. Any material inside this reservoir has probably been there for at least one million years," Dr. Owen said.

"What did you say? You found it in an oil reservoir?! That's impossible." Dr. Kaufman stared at Dr. Owen with his eyes wide open. He began to get excited and could not believe what he had just heard.

"Yes, Matt. We found seven of them. All of them are exactly the same size and structure," Dr. Owen said. "I need you to analyze them. By the way, I need you to keep this a secret between you and me. This is very strange, and we should not cause any unnecessary disturbance before we know more about it," he continued.

"I think so too. Let us study this crystal first and then decide on the next step," Dr. Kaufman agreed.

After lunch they separated, Dr. Kaufman taking the crystal with him.

* * *

The next morning at about 10:30 a.m., Dr. Kaufman called Dr. Owen's office.

"Hi, James. I spent the whole afternoon and the

154

whole evening yesterday analyzing the crystal you gave me. I finally got the data back this morning. Listen carefully, James." Dr. Kaufman paused a moment, then continued.

"This is not a man-made material. It is also not a natural material. As you said, the crystal material is as strong as diamond. And the metal inside," he stopped, and then continued, "I don't know. It does not exist on Earth."

"I need to know more about this. It is very strange, indeed." Dr. Owen was shocked to hear this.

"I need more time to figure out how this crystal could be fabricated. From what I know, there isn't an artificial diamond cutter big enough to make this anywhere on earth. I don't even know how it could be cut into the shape it is. It is impossible for any technology existing today," Dr. Kaufman added.

Dr. Owen listened carefully and was very confused. "How about the metal inside?" he asked.

"I just don't know what to tell you. From spectroscopic analysis, this material is mixed with natural material and some strange metal that is unknown. I only know, it is as strong as steel and as flexible as rubber."

"Is there any other organization which can analyze this in more detail?" Dr. Owen asked.

"Come on, James! I am the authority. If I don't know, I believe you cannot find anyone who knows," Dr. Kaufman said with confidence and pride.

"OK, Matt! I believe you. If you find more information, please let me know."

"Allow me one week and I'll see what I can find," Dr. Kaufman said.

* * *

A week later, Dr. Kaufman called Dr. Owen and set up a meeting in Dr. Owen's office at the UCLA campus.

"James, I still don't know what to tell you. As I know from theory, these materials were not produced on earth, not in the environment of air and gravity. These materials could only have been produced in an air and gravity free environment. That means they were fabricated in outer space," Dr. Kaufman said. "As we all know, there is no such factory in outer space today."

"It seems the more we know about these crystals, the more we don't know. In this case, we must continue to keep our mouths closed. Any news revealed will cause significant disturbance. I will continue to look for an alternative means to study this crystal," Dr. Owens said and took the crystal back from Dr. Kaufman.

* * *

Family Reunion

Progress was now stuck. Dr. Owen did not know what to do next. Nearly two months had passed, and no progress had been made. He was very frustrated and depressed. Christmas was coming. His eldest son Ted, and Ted's wife Anna, came from Boston with their son, Ian, and their newborn daughter, Tracy. His second son,

Robert, had also come back from San Francisco.

It was Christmas time, a time for family, but Dr. Owen's heart was very heavy. He had been troubled by the mystery of the crystals during the last two months. He had to find the answer.

Brian, his doctoral candidate student, was also stuck on the project. Both of them had already known by now that the oil cavern might not have been natural. "How will Brian be able to write his thesis?" Dr. Owen thought. It seemed many things in the cavern were not natural.

One night after dinner Dr. Owen's grandson, Ian, was watching a Superman movie on TV while Dr. Owen was sitting on the couch and pondering. When Dr. Owen saw Superman place a crystal into the reading tube to read the recording of his parents halfway through the movie, he suddenly jumped up. Everyone was shocked by his action. He smiled and began to laugh since he had discovered a possible use for the crystals. These crystals might be recordings of the past. All he needed was to find a way to read them!

When his whole family looked at him with surprise, he looked back at them, and said, "I just discovered a solution to a big question in my project."

To his wife, Jennifer, Dr. Owen's behavior was normal. He had been acting strangely ever since he returned from Austin. She knew something had been bothering him. As usual, she kept silent. She knew from being married to him for many years, he would always come to a solution.

Meetings

"What should I do next? Where can I find a way to read these crystals?" Dr. Owen's mind kept thinking. A couple more weeks passed. In the third week of January, he had a conference in Washington D.C. At the conference, he met an old good friend, actually an old master's degree classmate from Stanford University named Richard Moore. They had not talked to each other since graduation, 35 years ago. They barely recognized one another. They talked about the past. With two other girls, they used to climb mountains and go to the beach. They had had such a good time together.

"Where have you been, Richard?" Dr. Owen asked. "After graduation, I tried to contact you several times but failed. It seemed you just disappeared from the world."

"I am sorry. After graduation, I moved to Italy with my parents and worked there for 20 years. I moved back here 15 years ago. Now, I am working at a high-tech firm in D.C."

"If you are working in the high-tech industry, you must know many high-level scientists?"

"Of course. We also have a wide range of connections with other high-tech industries in the world," Richard replied with pride, since he worked in such a high intelligence industry. "How about you, James?"

"I have been teaching at UCLA since I received my Ph.D. I am thinking of retiring in a year or two."

As Dr. Owen said that, he realized there were only a couple of minutes before the next session would begin.

"Can we have dinner tonight? It's been a long time. Let's talk about the past, the time when we were young and aggressive," Dr. Owen suggested.

"Sure, I know a nice seafood restaurant in D.C. Let's eat there. I haven't been there for a whole month," Richard said.

Since Richard had been working in the D.C. area for the last 15 years or so, he knew the area very well. And, since Richard had never married, he also knew a lot of restaurants.

* * *

Richard went to the Hilton Hotel to pick up Dr. Owen with his car. They drove about 35 minutes and finally came to the restaurant where Richard had made a reservation in advance. Once they were seated, they talked and drank some wine.

"James, that is enough for me. Remember, I'm driving. However, I had such a good time tonight. It feels just like the old days," Richard said.

In just a day, Richard had already re-earned Dr. Owen's trust. "Just like the same old Richard," Dr. Owen thought in his mind.

After they'd been talking for a couple of hours, Richard asked, "What will you do after you retire? I still don't know what I will do when I retire. Time has passed so fast. James, we are old now."

For more than two months now, Dr. Owen had kept his crystal secret. He was frustrated and felt the need to talk to someone he could trust. He also thought that Richard might know someone in his high-tech industry who might be able to untie the mystery of the hidden secret in the crystal. He began to tell Richard about his exploration of the oil mine. Then he said, "Actually, there is one thing that has been bothering me for the last couple of months. Since you have known so many researchers and scientists in the D.C. area, you may be able to offer me some suggestions."

Dr. Owen then told him about the crystals they'd found in the old oil mine. He said he suspected these crystals were some sort of recording device. At the beginning, Richard just looked at Dr. Owen with a confused expression. To him, this was impossible. But after a few moments, he became excited and looked at Dr. Owen with shining eyes.

"Memory crystal," Richard said.

"What did you say? Memory crystal? Do you know anything about this?" Dr. Owen opened his eyes wide and stared at Richard.

Richard hesitated for a minute and finally said, "I am sorry, James. Truly, I was not in Italy after my graduation. Actually, I was involved in some government research projects in the 70s. Since some of the projects were classified as top secret, all the researchers were encouraged to isolate themselves from outside lay society. This was to prevent any government secrets from being revealed to the outside world," Richard explained with an expression of apology.

Dr. Owen felt somewhat uneasy since he had been

fooled by Richard into thinking that he had been work-ing in the high-tech industry. But, after he thought it over, he realized that Richard did not have a choice but must keep his government's research secret from the outside world. He began to understand.

"Are you still working on secret government re-search, Richard?" Dr. Owen asked.

"Of course not. I was transferred to another depart-ment ten years ago where the research is not as exciting and challenging. There are not very many secrets to be kept in this department. All they want now is the new generation to work on the exciting stuff," Richard re-plied.

"Then, how much do you know about memory crys-tal?" asked Dr. Owen.

"This was an old secret in the government's scien-tific research. You probably already know that the gov-ernment has a secret scientific research group that spe-cifically focuses on weapons development. About 12 years ago, a group of scientists was ordered to research crystal memory technology. After ten years of heavy re-search, the project was suspended," Richard said.

"How do you know this?" Dr. Owen asked.

"Though there were a few different groups working on different projects, due to information and technical support, we often communicated with each other. We all knew in general what the other group was doing, but the details were unknown and kept secret. They came to our department for some advice about four years ago. In or-der to receive assistance from our group, they needed to tell us briefly about the project they were doing. This was common cooperation among various groups."

"Why was it suspended?" Dr. Owen asked.

"Two years ago, they realized that in order to produce memory crystal, the crystal had to be fabricated in outer space where there is no air or gravity. They found out that it was not possible to do this at the time. Actually, the project was suspended indefinitely, until we are capable of building a lab or factory in outer space," Richard answered.

Dr. Owen was shocked at what he had just heard - outer space, without gravity and air. "Isn't this what Matt Kaufman said?" he thought. For a moment, he could not say a word.

"Do you know anyone who may be able to help me resolve the secret of these crystals?" Dr. Owen asked.

Richard pondered for a few seconds and said, "The director of the original project, Dr. John Torr, may know something that I don't know. He may offer you some recommendations."

"Do you know him, Richard?" Dr. Owen asked urgently.

"Yes, I do know him. We used to work on some other projects together. I have known him for about nine years," Richard said.

"Do you think you can arrange a meeting for me? It would be a great help, Richard."

"I can try but cannot promise. There are many strange people in that research group. Dr. Torr is one of them," Richard said. "I will contact him tomorrow and see if we can meet for dinner. We will have to come up with an interesting subject so that he actually meets with us."

"Just tell him that I know something about memory crystal or crystal memory. I believe this will catch his interest," Dr. Owen suggested.

* * *

After Dr. Owen returned to his hotel, he had an uneasy feeling. "I want to keep this secret from the government, but now, I realize that it may have been foolish to reveal the discovery of the crystals to Richard. After this meeting with Dr. Torr, this secret will definitely be revealed to the government, without question," he thought. He kept blaming himself with regret. However, on second thought, "If there is anyone who can reveal the mystery of these crystals, it has to be a member of the government's research team since they had a huge group of intelligent scientists."

"At least the secret, even if revealed, will stay with the American government," he tried to comfort himself.

The next day during the conference's morning break at about 10:00 a.m., Richard went to Dr. Owen's conference room. From the doorway he passed a signal to Dr. Owen to join him in the hallway. Dr. Owen was talking to another conference participant at the time. When he saw Richard's signal, he apologized to the other guy and came out of the room.

"Your suggestion was correct and excellent. Dr. Torr

could not reject our invitation since he is so attracted by the subject. We'll meet tonight," Richard said.

To Dr. Owen, the prospect of the meeting brought on a mixture of excitement and serious concern, though this meeting might give him a hope of finally finding some answers.

"I suggested to him that we should have dinner in a Japanese restaurant nearby. This is because this restaurant has isolated private rooms. In this case, we can talk about any subject without too much concern," Richard said and continued, "I hope you like Japanese food."

"It does not matter. As long as Dr. Torr is happy, I will be happy," Dr. Owen said. Food was not his main concern that night.

* * *

As he had the night before, Richard went to the Hilton Hotel to pick up Dr. Owen at 7:00 p.m. Dinner was reserved for 7:30 p.m. and it would take Richard only 20 minutes to get there.

"Don't forget to bring your crystal," Richard reminded Dr. Owen in the hotel lobby.

"It's here." Dr. Owen used his finger to point at his briefcase. Actually, he had carried one crystal with him at all times during the last two months. He kept the other six in a safe in his office.

When they arrived at the restaurant, Dr. Torr was already there. It seemed he was very anxious about tonight's subject.

Dr. Torr, a genius in material science, had become the director of the project. He was known as smart, wise, and had a unique character and strange personality; he had especially good leadership skills. Many people said he had a genius level IQ. However, there was one problem. He did not talk much and did not like to socialize with people unnecessarily. He only talked when necessary. He seldom smiled either. He was still single, and it seemed any woman would be scared just to look at his serious, solemn face.

"Hi, Dr. Torr. I am sorry that we are late. This is Dr. Owen whom I talked to you about on the telephone," Richard introduced them.

"You are not late. You are on time," Dr. Torr said, looking at Dr. Owen and extending his hand to shake Dr. Owen's. "You better really have something which interests me. Otherwise, you are wasting my precious time," he thought.

After they ordered their food and the waitress had closed the door behind her, Dr. Owen opened his briefcase and brought out the crystal. He handed it to Dr. Torr.

"Where did you get this?" Dr. Torr demanded. He was immediately shocked to see the crystal in his hand. Nobody was supposed to know of these crystals except the researchers in his group. The similar shape structure had been developed for memory crystal about three years ago in the research lab. There were two polarities in the crystal which were connected by a highly conductive material. The memory should have been recorded in the crystal molecules when the two polarities synchronized with each other and vibrated. Though the shapes of the crystal in his hand were slightly different from what his group had designed, the theoretical concepts were the same. Dr. Torr stared at Dr. Owen with surprise.

"From an old oil mine in Austin," Dr. Owen replied.

"What did you say? Can you repeat that?" Dr. Torr asked urgently.

"From an old oil mine in Austin, Texas," Dr. Owen said again slowly, word by word.

"I just cannot believe it!" Dr. Torr said. "Please tell me every detail." Dr. Torr had changed his attitude; he had become enthusiastic and excited. He looked at Dr. Owen with eyes eager and anxious.

Dr. Owen repeated the history of how they found the crystals in more detail than when he had talked to Richard last night. Both Dr. Torr and Richard kept very quiet and listened carefully.

Suddenly Dr. Torr interrupted. "Seven! You said seven?"

"Yes, seven. I personally believe if we searched more, we would find more," Dr. Owen said.

After finishing the story, Dr. Torr and Dr. Owen did not feel like strangers to each other anymore. Both were scholars and top scientists; both shared the same interest.

"Now, Dr. Torr, can you tell me something about these crystals since you seem to know so much about them?" Dr. Owen asked.

"Actually, as I mentioned earlier, the government

had been involved in the development of crystal memory technology for some time. In theory, we had reached a conclusive and feasible achievement. However, practically, we didn't know how to produce these crystals. As you know already, these crystals must be fabricated in a gravity and air free environment," Dr. Torr said.

"The government suspended this project two years ago until we have the capability of fabricating these crystals in outer space. Actually, all the equipment we used is still in the research room ten stories underground in Virginia in a secret research center," Dr. Torr continued.

By this time, Dr. Torr had established his trust in Dr. Owen. He believed if they wanted to communicate with each other honestly about this subject, he should not hesitate to share what he knew with Dr. Owen.

"Can you explain what the theory is behind it? Or is it classified as top secret by the government?" Dr. Owen asked.

"To others, it will still be secret. However, since both of you are already involved in this subject, and also to help you understand, I will explain it to you," Dr. Torr said.

"Theoretically, many scientists believe the universe is shaped like an ellipse which has two polarities. Therefore, any life form formalized within the universe will copy this energy pattern, or formation, and also have two polarities. Through the energy vibration between the two polarities, an energy shield in the shape of an ellipse covers the entire universe. These two polarities synchronize with each other and oppose each other. Inside of this ellipse shield, all living things are created and derived." Dr. Torr paused and had a sip of the green tea sitting in front of him. Then he continued.

"Everything happening in this universe can be recorded in the energy field existing in this ellipse energy domain. As you know, today scientists have confirmed that there are two polarities in a tiny cell, and in theory, we should be able to clone a human from a single cell. Once this cloned human has grown, he should also have two polarities. On January 23 of 1996, scientists discovered these two polarities in a human. Actually, these two polarities are the top brain in the head and also the center of the guts, the enteric nervous system. These two polarities are connected by highly conductive tissue, the spinal cord. These two brains or polarities synchronize with each other and communicate with each other without any signal delay. That means physically there are two, however, in function, it is one.

"As you know, this is what is called the central nervous system by medical science," he added.

Even though Dr. Owen had read and heard something about humans having two brains, he had never connected it with the dynamics of nature. He was so surprised and curious about this whole theory, especially since it was related to the crystal memory.

"According to updated scientific understanding, the entire human body has memory. This memory is possible due to the synchronized vibration of the two brains, or polarities. When the energy trapped between the two polarities vibrates, all of the material within the field is able to record any event that happens. That is why I said earlier that the entire universe has memory." Dr. Torr looked at Dr. Owen and Richard who were engrossed in his explanation of this topic. "As you know, our top brain is constructed of two hemispheres with a space between them. It was understood in the 1960s that this space acts like a resonance chamber. When energy is trapped and vibrates in this chamber, it can generate resonance with other things, whether they are alive or dead. This vibration is commonly called a 'brain wave.' That means when the frequency of vibrations match, the brain is able to resonate and synchronize with other objects and cause vibrations. That is why some sets of twins are able to communicate with each other even when they are a far distance apart – because twins came from the same genetic source and may have the same brain vibration frequency," Dr. Torr continued.

This had caught Dr. Owen's curiosity. Without thinking, he picked up the crystal and magnifier on the table and looked at the crystal while listening. It had exactly the same structure as a human. There was a gap in the center of the top pyramid. Not only that, the top center and the bottom center were connected with a highly conductive material as his friend Matt had said.

"As discovered by our research group, the bottom brain is able to supply energy while the top one is controlling the vibration of the energy. When these two work together, memory can be recorded throughout the entire body," Dr. Torr continued his explanation. "Now, you can see why I was so shocked when I saw this crystal." He looked at Dr. Owen.

"What did you mean about memory recording in the universe? Would you explain that further, Dr. Torr?" Richard asked.

"As we have already known, the entire universe is changing constantly. When this process occurs, all energy is changing, and all of the materialized matter is also changing. During this changing process, any energy disturbance can change the structure of the entire energy pattern and naturally the material structure as well. For example, if there is a rock in a field which has been degenerating since ancient times, during this degenerating period any energy change or event occurring around the rock would influence the degenerating process of the rock and the information recorded." Dr. Torr looked at Richard and tried to read his facial expression. Then he continued, "Until now, we haven't had the technology to retrieve these memories from the rock. If we did, we would be able to see what had happened around the rock in the past. In this case, all of history could be re-written. All truth could be retraced."

Dr. Owen nodded his head in agreement.

"What do you think, Dr. Torr? Is it possible to use the facilities equipped by the government to conduct some experiments on this crystal?" Dr. Owen asked.

"I believe I will be able to get in the lab, but not both of you. You would need a special pass to get through security. This whole area is under the highest security protection," Dr. Torr replied. "Do you have all seven crystals with you, Dr. Owen?"

"No, just this one. All the others are in Los Angeles," Dr. Owen replied.

"May I keep this crystal for a few weeks and see if I am able to learn something? I intend to read the recorded memory if I can," Dr. Torr requested.

"Naturally, Dr. Torr. I just hope you are able to untie the mystery of this crystal," Dr. Owen replied.

"Furthermore, can you also send a copy of the three-dimensional simulation image of the cavern to me? I am very, very curious about it. I suspect those columns inside the cavern were fabricated by some intelligent beings instead of being a natural formation. I also suspect that the entire cavern may have been an underground city before," Dr. Torr said.

"Naturally, first thing when I return to Los Angeles. That will be in two days," Dr. Owen replied.

Before they left the restaurant, Dr. Torr solemnly looked each of them directly in the face.

"Both of you must know that this secret cannot be revealed to lay society. The influence and disturbance of such a disclosure could be huge. Furthermore, if other countries learn about these crystals, such as the Russian or Chinese governments, they will no doubt try to find a way to acquire them. The secrets hidden in these crystals could be used for advanced weapon development. Richard, you must have known that. You work for the government and know the consequences of revealing this kind of secret."

"Dr. Torr, I know the consequence. I am not stupid. But since this is your department, will you report to the government?"

"Yes, when the time comes. First, I must find a way to read the secret inside. I may not acquire it since we don't have this kind of knowledge and technology." Dr. Torr turned to Dr. Owen.

"Where are you living and when will you return to Los Angeles?"

"I am staying at the Hilton Hotel on Connecticut Avenue N.W. I will return to Los Angeles tomorrow afternoon."

"Great, let me take you back to the hotel. I'm going that way. Richard, I hope you don't mind?"

Richard was so surprised that Dr. Torr could get along with Dr. Owen so easily and fast. "Certainly. It is getting late. After two days of conference, I am tired," he said.

* * *

When Dr. Owen got into Dr. Torr's car, Dr. Torr asked him, "Are you tired? If you don't mind, I'd like to talk to you more and get to know you better."

"That will be great! I would like to know you better as well. And actually, ten o'clock here is only seven o'clock in LA. It is still early for me."

Dr. Torr drove his car to Meridian Hill Park near the Hilton Hotel. After he parked the car on a side street, he led Dr. Owen into the park and found a bench to sit on.

The park was almost empty except for a few couples walking on the path.

After they sat down, Dr. Torr said, "Dr. Owen, you must have realized how much your discovery will shock the world? This is a revolutionary discovery in human history."

"Yes, I know, Dr. Torr. But I worry that once these crystals are handed over to the government, the truth in them may be hidden from the general public - like the Roswell UFO incident and the Philadelphia Experiment."

"That is the reason I want to talk to you and understand your position. Furthermore, I would like to point out a few concerns. If the discovery of these crystals becomes known by the Russian or Chinese governments, and you still keep these crystals, you may be in serious danger. They will definitely use any means possible to acquire them since the secrets hidden inside may help them develop more powerful and advanced weapons."

"But if you submit them to the government, will the government reveal their secrets to the public and use the advanced technologies to promote peace? I don't understand why there are already more than 6,000 nuclear bombs in this world. That is enough to eliminate the entire human race a few hundred times. Why are we still searching for more powerful ways to kill each other? I am afraid that once these crystals are submitted to the government, a new upgraded level of weapons competition will occur among nations."

Dr. Torr smiled when he heard Dr. Owen's concerns.

"That's the reason that I want to talk to you. The discovery of these crystals must remain hidden from all governments until we know what was recorded inside them."

"But I thought since you work for the government, you would report this discovery to your higher authority?"

"Dr. Owen, to tell the truth, after working for the government nearly 35 years I really comprehend that all highly talented scientists who are recruited by the government are only the tools or puppets of politicians. They use us to develop weapons to satisfy their pursuit of power and glory. Once we are used, we are dumped silently and disappeared from the world. I have regretfully and deeply realized that almost all politicians are not concerned with the peace and harmony of the world."

Dr. Owen was so surprised to hear what Dr. Torr said. He realized that Dr. Torr had the same thoughts and concerns that he did.

"Then, what should we do about these crystals?"

"Let's find a way to read them first and then, only then, we will decide if we should reveal the secret to the general public, or to the government, or not. So far, there are so many unknowns."

To Dr. Owen, this was a huge relief since he had been worrying about the consequences of releasing the discovery of these crystals to the government.

"Dr. Owen, remember what I said. Keep the secret

hidden. If Russian or Chinese spies know you have crystals, you will be in serious danger. Let me take you back to the Hilton. I will contact you once I find a way of reading the crystal."

* * *

Two Polarities

Two days later, Dr. Owen went back to Los Angeles. The first thing he did was to send a DVD copy of the three-dimensional simulation image to Dr. Torr. However, another thing bothered him greatly. He had to figure out how Brian's thesis could be done without revealing the truth about the cavern. One morning, Brian came to his office.

"Dr. Owen? How are you? You know I am stuck on my thesis. I have analyzed all the samples we picked up. However, there is nothing fantastic to report. There is some history, but I am not sure if this history is even accurate," Brian said.

"I know, Brian. Actually, everything was a big surprise to me," Dr. Owen replied. Dr. Owen knew it would be unfair not to tell Brian the truth about the crystals, so he told Brian what he knew about them and also about the meeting with Richard and Dr. Torr in Washington, D.C. He, again, reminded Brian to keep their discovery a secret.

"Tell me more about your soil analysis," Dr. Owen asked.

"Well, from the small pieces of rock collected, it

seems this cavern was built or formed around 12 million years ago," Brian replied. "From the three-dimensional simulation image, we already know that it is not a natural cavern and that those columns are not the same columns you would find in a natural cavern. I am almost sure those columns were fabricated in the past."

"Will you be upset if you cannot complete your thesis? We might have to change to a different project or topic for your thesis," Dr. Owen told him.

"Actually, I can write something about my analysis of the soil collected. But I will have to hide most of the truth."

"I understand. Just try your best and let me read it when the draft is completed."

"I am very curious, Dr. Owen, about the two human polarities that Dr. Torr told you about." Brian looked at Dr. Owen. "In fact, I have studied about it recently from reading a few books," he continued.

"Really? I will be very interested in knowing more about this," Dr. Owen responded.

"My girlfriend, Xiaoling, is Chinese. Even though she was born in the states, she has been very interested in Chinese culture. Recently she has gotten more and more into Chinese meditation. Actually, due to her influence, I have also started meditating with her often, especially on weekends. She has a great collection of books that talk about the theory of these two polarities," Brian said.

* * *

Xiaoling Chen, a 22-year-old senior UCLA student, was majoring in oriental philosophy. Her parents had come to the States from Taiwan in 1984 to study and later decided to stay. Xiaoling was an only child and her parents were living in the San Diego area. Due to her parents' influence, Xiaoling had always been interested in Chinese culture, especially ancient philosophy and practices. A couple of years ago she became interested in studying more about Chinese Daoism including the philosophy of the *Dao De Jing* and *Yi Jing*. Because of this interest, she was attracted by the Chinese Qigong meditation that was developed from Chinese Yin and Yang theory. Since then, she had been serious about collecting any information related to Chinese Qigong meditation. The books that had influenced her greatly were *Qigong Meditation - Embryonic Breathing* and *Qigong Meditation - Small Circulation*, by Master Dong, and also *The Second Brain*, by Dr. Gershon. These books had helped her understand the two polarities theory of the human body. She realized that all of these practices could be traced back over two and half millennia in China.

"If you like, I can borrow some of her books and let you read about it," Brian offered.

"Of course, only if it is convenient. I will also see if I can find them from Amazon.com," Dr. Owen said with excitement.

After Brian left, Dr. Owen could not help thinking about what Brian had said. "Twelve million years ago?" "Two polarities of a human body?" All he could do now was wait for further news from Dr. Torr.

A few days later, he was surprised to receive all three books from Amazon.com in his office. They were gifts ordered by Brian. He was very touched and began to read them immediately.

A Shock

By using his security pass, Dr. Torr did not have any trouble entering the secret research center in the government's underground facility. He had gone there often before to find necessary materials for his research. In fact, he occasionally slept in his old office and stayed there for a few days. Therefore, his appearance in the facility again did not draw too much attention.

When Dr. Torr entered the lab, since the project was terminated there was no one else there. He tried everything he knew; however, he could not find any way to read the crystal. He became frustrated and depressed. Two weeks passed and there was still no result. He knew Dr. Owen was waiting for his good news anxiously. Again, for two days straight he had stayed in the lab and tried to figure out a method of reading the crystal. He had tried all possible methods he knew, sleeping only six hours in the last two days.

Now, he had run out of ideas. From the clock, he could see it was about 2:00 a.m. He had just repeated a method that he had tried several times already using various frequencies over the last couple of days but failed again. He picked up the crystal and brought it to a table light next to his computer. He used the magnifier and also a microscope to investigate the crystal again and again, hoping to gain some inspiration or hint. He was very tired. He needed some of the coffee that was sitting on the table about ten feet behind him. Without thinking, he placed the crystal on top of the computer and turned around to pour a cup of coffee. He had relied on coffee to keep him awake during the last two days.

As he poured the coffee into his cup, suddenly a three-dimensional moving image filled the entire room. Even though it lasted only a couple of seconds, he could see clearly the scene that appeared was a recording of a strange new world. He saw a flying car that was flying toward a city in the sky. He was so shocked. He was frozen for a few minutes. It took him a few more minutes to realize what had happened.

"Why was the crystal's recording revealed? There wasn't any electric connection with the crystal at all! The computer isn't even turned on. How could it be read?" he asked himself.

Suddenly he noticed a red light in the corner of the room was blinking. The light was the signal that an earthquake had just occurred. Obviously, it had been too small for him to feel, but this highly sensitive earthquake detection system was designed and installed there to signal any slight movement of the earth. Actually, the lab had been built underground to avoid any vibration on the earth's surface.

He began to understand the recording could be accessed by vibration. This changed his tactics completely. Instead of using electronic methods, he began to use vibration methods. Again, he tried everything he could think of, but failed.

After another two days, he knew he had to stop and rest for a while. He left the lab with a long beard and mustache.

* * *

After a long sleep, Dr. Torr felt better. Around two o'clock in the afternoon he decided to make a call to Dr. Owen.

"Hi, Dr. Owen, how are you doing? I believe you have been waiting for my news," Dr. Torr said.

"Hi, Dr. Torr! It is so good to hear your voice. I have been wondering about the results of your crystal investigation," Dr. Owen replied.

"I am sorry to tell you that I could not recover the memory recorded in the crystal. However, by accident I saw a couple of seconds of the recorded scene. A flying car and a sky city," Dr. Torr said.

"What? A flying car and a sky city? That's unbelievable! How did you recover that scene?" Dr. Owen asked curiously.

"There was an earthquake at the time. Somehow, the quake released the information recorded inside."

"I wish I could have been there to see that." Dr. Owen was very excited.

"But when I tried to copy the vibration of the earthquake hoping to read the crystal, I failed. I don't know what I was doing wrong. All I know now is the reading can be done through vibration instead of electronic methods." Dr. Torr paused.

"I wonder if it is possible for your team to go back to the oil cavern and find something for me?" Dr. Torr asked.

"What are you looking for, Dr. Torr?" Dr. Owen asked.

"A reading device from the past. If there are so many crystals there, I believe there must also be a reading device around the same area. I just don't know how much luck we might have getting it," Dr. Torr said.

"The difficulty is all of the crew have separated. There is only one, Brian, still with me. In addition, I would have to contact Mr. George Standy about this and get his approval. Without his approval, it will be impossible. I will need his crew to help me. I'll contact Mr. Standy this afternoon. I will also ask Brian to contact the others and see if it is possible for them to return," Dr. Owen said.

"That is great! I will be waiting for your news. Oh, there is one more thing. Through watching the three-dimensional simulation image, I believe those columns in the cavern are fabricated and not natural. If you are able to go down again, is it possible to hit one of the columns and record the sound? We would then be able to analyze the sound and see what material they are made of. I suspect these columns were used to support the cavern or underground city in the past," Dr. Torr said.

* * *

After finishing the conversation with Dr. Torr, Dr. Owen pondered and reviewed the project again. It seemed the goal of the original project had changed. Now, they were searching for the truth of a past civilization instead of just the history of the oil mine. This would be the biggest archaeological discovery in human history. He knew that he would become very famous if he found the truth and revealed it to the general public. He could also understand how much of a disturbance he could cause. As he knew from his life experience, the truth was never really what it seemed. It had always been distorted by human minds. Normally those who lie receive glory and those who are truthful suffer shame. Truth has never been stronger than reality in the human matrix. It did not matter who the person was, humans were still under the heavy bondage of the human emotional matrix. He had to think about it carefully before he revealed the truth of the cavern. Furthermore, if the government found out about it, there could be another cover-up just like the UFO's crash in Roswell, since the information in these crystals could be used for possible weapon technology development. However, the most important step now was to find the truth hidden in the cavern. Only after that should he decide what to do next.

The next morning, he called Mr. Standy. He had not talked to him since he had come back from Austin two months ago. He called him and thanked him again for his support and assistance. A busy schedule for both of them had kept them away from talking or meeting again, however, this was important now. He had to talk to Mr. Standy again.

"Hi, George! It's been two months since I last spoke with you. How are you doing?" Dr. Owen began.

"Fine, busy as usual. How is progress on the project? Everything smooth?" Mr. Standy asked.

"Not bad. Well, actually, we have encountered a difficulty. That is the reason for my call."

"Is there anything I can do for you, James?"

"We need more samples from a specific area in the oil mine. The samples we obtained last time are not enough to verify some of the theories we've developed. We believe we may get answers if we go in again and find more samples," Dr. Owen said. He did not tell Mr. Standy the truth or give more detail of what they were looking for. However, since Mr. Standy was not a geologist, he did not ask too many questions.

"That means you need to go to Austin again with your entire crew. Is this right?" Mr. Standy asked.

"That is correct. I am just wondering if it is possible for us to use your facility and people again? I promise that this will be the last time. It will take only a few days at most," Dr. Owen said.

"OK, I will contact the Austin department this afternoon about this. I should be able to give you an answer late this afternoon," Mr. Standy replied.

"George, you are great. You are more than a friend," Dr. Owen said.

* * *

At about 4:40 that afternoon Mr. Standy called Dr. Owen and told him everything was arranged. All he needed to do was to set up the dates and call Eric in the Austin department of Standy Firm.

Dr. Owen now had to find a way to contact Tommy, Stefani, and Joe since they had all moved to new apartments when they returned. He knew Brian might have contacted them since the last exploration in Austin, so he called Brian's cell phone.

"Brian, I talked to Dr. Torr yesterday. He found some information about the crystal," Dr. Owen said.

"Really! Please tell me more, Professor." Brian was very excited to hear the news.

"By some accident, Dr. Torr saw a scene recorded in the crystal, a flying car and a sky city."

It took a few seconds for Brian to reply. He was shocked and speechless.

"You said a flying car and a sky city?" Brian could not believe what he had heard.

"Yes. Now this project has a new meaning and a new goal, you understand? We will be searching the oil mine for the truth of an ancient civilization," Dr. Owen said. "Dr. Torr requested we go back to the cavern one more time to look for some specific samples. He needs to find some answers."

"How do we go back? Is it possible?" Brian asked.

"I have talked to Mr. Standy. There is no problem on his side. The question I have now is: do you have contact with Tommy, Stefani, and Joe?" Dr. Owen asked.

"Yes, I do. Tommy is still in the Los Angeles area

looking for a new job. Stefani is working for MarinaTech now. And Joe is busy writing his thesis. I should be able to talk to them today," Brian said.

"You mean Stefani is already working for MarinaTech before her graduation?" Dr. Owen asked.

"Yes, Stefani has completed her required courses. All she needs is to take the finals. MarinaTech had a job opening two months ago. She took it as part time for now, and will be full time after graduation," Brian replied.

"That is a surprise," Dr. Owen thought. "Not too many people begin working before graduation. But after all, she is a very talented girl."

Brian continued, "But what do I tell them? What excuse should I give them? Should we tell them the truth, Professor?"

"No! No! It is not the time to tell them the truth yet. The fewer people who know about it the better. I did not even tell Mr. Standy," Dr. Owen said. "Can we come up with any reasonable explanation? You know, they have completed their mission. They don't have to go again."

"I know. This will be a favor for both you and I, Professor," Brian said.

"Tell them that after I checked your report and samples, I found that we would need more samples from the same area. The samples we have will not be enough to conduct our experiments," Dr. Owen said. "In this case, we are not lying to them even if we do not tell them the whole truth." To Dr. Owen, based on the team's previous experience, he was confident that there would be not much danger this time. Hiding the truth was more important right now.

"I can try Professor," Brian replied.

* * *

Arrangements

"Hi, Tommy, how are you doing? I haven't talked to you in a couple of weeks. Have you gotten a job yet in Los Angeles?" Brian called Tommy and asked.

"Hey! How about yourself? How is your project going? I am still hanging around here, even though I got a job offer to work for NASA in Houston. Actually, I had another offer in the Boston area from my MIT professor's recommendation, but I don't have the heart to leave here," Tommy replied.

"Is it because of Stefani?" Brian joked with Tommy.

"I will tell you more in the future. I am confused about what I should do. Tell me about your research. I am part of it, remember?" Tommy asked again.

"Well, to tell you the truth, that's why I'm calling," Brian said. "After I talked to Professor Owen yesterday, we realized that we would need more samples for our experiments, especially from the corner area where Stefani picked up her samples. We need more samples, Tommy! Professor Owen asked me to ask you if it is possible for you to go back to the cavern again? He said we just need one more time. Naturally, he will be responsible for all the expenses."

A few seconds passed, then Tommy said, "There is

no problem for me, you know. I have nothing to do right now anyway. However, it is a surprise to me. What did Stefani and Joe say?"

"I haven't asked them yet. You are the first one," Brian replied.

* * *

When the entire crew came back from Austin last time, on the last day of sightseeing and relaxation Tommy felt Stefani's defenses had become lowered again. He was very happy about it. However, after they returned to Los Angeles, Tommy had a hard time getting Stefani out often. In fact, they had gone out only twice in more than two months. Tommy was frustrated and emotionally depressed. He felt like he was living in hell for the last couple of months. He just could not put Stefani's smiling face behind him. He missed the old days when they were so close together in the Austin cavern.

For her part, Stefani was very confused about her relationship with Tommy. On the surface, she showed him a defensive wall, however, deep inside of her heart she felt like opening the gate wide for Tommy to enter. Whenever she felt like opening the gate, though, her mom's warning continually rang in her ears. Fortunately, her new job working for MarinaTech had attracted her interest and attention. This had somehow eased the pain inside. But when she was calm, Tommy's face and laughter appeared in her mind. Under this complicated emotional confusion, she had gone out with Tommy only twice. She was afraid that once she had put herself in too deep, she would not be able to pull out.

* * *

"Hey, are you still there, Tommy?" Brian's voice was heard again.

"Oh, yes. I am sorry. I was wondering if Stefani would go again?" Tommy woke up from his deep thinking.

"Why don't you try to talk to her? You are still old friends, aren't you?" Brian asked.

"Yes. But I think it will be better if you talk to her. Anything I say will make her very sensitive and doubt my motives," Tommy replied.

Brian could sense that both Tommy and Stefani were in a period of testing each other. Both of them were very cautious of any action they took. He said, "OK. I will call her later."

"Please let me know immediately, can you, Brian?" Tommy asked. He really wished Stefani could go and they could be together again.

"Naturally, young lover," Brian replied.

* * *

Before Brian talked to Stefani, he thought he should talk to Joe first. It would be easier to talk to Joe than Stefani. Joe was still on campus and busy writing his thesis. He headed to the study room that Joe shared with his advisor. When he came to the Computer Science Department, on entering the room he saw that Joe had also just stepped in with his lunch in his hands.

"Hey, Brian, nice to see you here. Have lunch yet?" Joe asked. They had become such good friends since the Austin trip.

"Truth? No! Is that lunch for me?" Brian joked.

"Yes, it's for both of us," Joe replied with a big smile.

"No, I'm joking. It's your lunch."

"Brian, don't be silly. Yours is mine and mine is yours, right? I can share it with you. Actually, it's too much for me anyway. Whenever you order takeout from a Chinese restaurant, they always give you a lot. Please help me eat it," Joe said with a laugh.

They went outside and found a stretch of lawn near the building and sat down. Joe opened the lunch and put it between himself and Brian.

"Help yourself. This is dim sum. You can use your hands. Otherwise, there is a pair of chopsticks and also a fork inside the bag. Which one do you prefer?"

"I'll use the fork. You use chopsticks better than me," Brian replied.

"You came to see me because you miss me, right, old friend?" Joe said.

"Yes, it's true. We had such a good time in Austin. Even though it has been more than two months, I still dream about it sometimes. But the real reason why I'm here is because Professor Owen and I have a favor to ask you." Brian looked at Joe with such a sincere expression on his face that Joe could tell he wasn't joking.

"Anything. What can I do to help?" Joe said.

Brian told Joe the story about why they had to go back to the cavern one more time.

"Actually, I am pretty bored with writing my thesis. I need something more exciting to stimulate my soul. There's no problem. It will be a good chance for all of us to get together again, just like the old days." Joe paused a moment to swallow his food.

"What are the dates? Have you and Dr. Owen set any yet?" Joe asked.

"We think the best time will be the beginning of March. That's three weeks from now. You know, the submarine was brought back to Los Angeles. We'll have to move it back to Austin. We also have to clean it and conduct some tests to make sure that all the systems are still functioning."

"That's a good time for me. My graduation will be mid-May. My Ph.D. final dissertation presentation is the third week of April and my thesis is almost done. This will be a good break for me," Joe said.

"Now you must convince Stefani. She will be the hardest one to persuade," Joe continued. He knew Stefani had already begun her new job and she did not have any vacation days accumulated yet. Furthermore, the up-down relationship between her and Tommy would be an obstacle.

* * *

The next morning, Brian called Stefani at her office just as she was taking her 10:30 a.m. break.

"Stefani, how are you doing? This is Brian," he said.

Stefani felt very happy that morning. She was in a good mood because her boss had told her how great her contribution was to the company in just two months.

"Hi, Brian! I miss you guys so much. How have you been? How is your project?" Stefani asked. She was very happy to hear Brian's voice. They had talked to each other just once since they returned from Austin. He had called her about a month ago when he needed some detailed information about her sample picking for his thesis.

"It's great, but..." Brian paused.

"Problem, Brian?" Stefani interrupted.

"Yes. I wonder if you can help me solve it," Brian asked.

"What problem? You know I will help you if I can," Stefani said.

That was a good sign, Brian thought.

"Actually, Professor Owen and I just realized last week that we don't have enough samples to conduct the experiments we want. We are just wondering, is it possible for you and the others, I mean, the same old crew, to go back to Austin again and pick up more samples? Of course, this will be the last time. I promise," Brian explained.

Stefani was shocked when she heard this. She did not know what to say. This was something she had to consider and reconsider. She thought everything was done on her side. Actually, she was a little bit afraid to go back into the dark cavern. She held her phone and paused for a while. Her memory of her dangerous adventure in Austin reappeared in her brain. She had almost forgotten the whole thing. The only thing she could not forget was Tommy's shadow that kept following her everywhere. Whenever she calmed down, she thought of him. "Oh! I miss him so much and at the same time, I am afraid to step in," she thought.

"Stefani! Stefani! Are you still there?" Brian asked.

"Very strange, indeed! Both Tommy and Stefani reacted the same way," Brian thought.

"Brian, let me think about it. First, I need to talk to my parents. Second, I don't have any vacation time yet at MarinaTech. Third, truly speaking, I am a little bit scared. And fourth," she paused and did not continue.

"Has everyone agreed to go?" Stefani finally asked. Actually, all she thought of was Tommy.

"Yes, everyone including Tommy," Brian said. He knew Tommy and Stefani had an up-down relationship.

Stefani's mind was split. Both sides were in conflict again. One way she wanted to go and the other, she wanted to avoid it. Actually, her parents and MarinaTech were only excuses. She knew from the last trip that her parents had learned to trust her decisions. Her mom told her several times that she had grown up so much since she came back from Austin. As for MarinaTech, the worst that would happen is she would have to take time off without pay. She had demonstrated her potential and talent in the last two months. She knew if she requested it, she would get a few days off. However, she had to think about it.

"Brian, give me a couple of days and I'll see if I can arrange something," Stefani said.

"Naturally, Stefani! But please give me an answer soon. You know we need you very much," Brian replied.

* * *

After Brian hung up the phone, he immediately called Dr. Owen and explained the situation to him. Now, Dr. Owen thought he should pay a visit to Stefani and also to her boss. To Dr. Owen and Dr. Torr, this new project was extremely important since it dealt with a great, hidden mysterious secret that needed to be discovered. Without Stefani, Dr. Owen would lose a right-hand person. The next morning, Dr. Owen went to MarinaTech. He first went to see his old friend, Kyle Thomson, who had helped them build 'Pioneer.' Mr. Thomson was the manager of the submarine design and fabrication department. He went to Mr. Thomson's office, where the secretary notified Mr. Thomson of Dr. Owen's arrival and then led him to Mr. Thomson's office.

* * *

"Hi, Dr. Owen! What a surprise," Mr. Thomson said when Dr. Owen stepped in his office.

"Hi, Mr. Thomson. I came to see you for two reasons. The first one is to thank you and MarinaTech for all of the help a couple of months ago. And, second, I wonder if you could help me one more time," Dr. Owen said.

"Tell me, Dr. Owen, how can I help you?" Mr. Thomson asked.

Dr. Owen then explained to Mr. Thomson the progress they had made and then mentioned the need for more samples from the cavern.

"We will need Stefani to go with us again. However, she does not have vacation time since she has been working at MarinaTech for only two months," Dr. Owen said. "I wonder if you could explain the situation to her boss and allow me to borrow her for a week or so."

"She is working in the research department, isn't she? Her boss is Dr. Edward Whiley," Mr. Thomson said. "I could talk to him and see. Dr. Whiley and I are old friends. We have both been working in this company for more than ten years. Let me try."

Mr. Thomson picked up his phone and dialed. "Hi, Ed, this is Kyle. How is your grandson?" Mr. Thomson asked. Dr. Whiley had just become a grandfather a couple weeks ago. He had been showing his grandson's photo to everyone he could.

"He is great! Sleeps the whole night. So cute, just like me," Dr. Whiley joked.

Before Dr. Whiley could continue, Mr. Thomson cut in. "Ed, actually, I have a friend here who needs your help." Mr. Thomson knew if he let Dr. Whiley keep talking about his grandson, it would be more than five minutes before they could get down to business.

"Let us have dinner together tonight and we can talk

about your grandson. We haven't gotten together for a while. I can tell you about the Chinese antiques I just collected, and you can talk about your grandson. Right now, I have a friend here who needs your help," Mr. Thomson said.

"OK, Kyle, let's meet after work. What can I do for your friend?" Dr. Whiley asked.

"His name is Dr. James Owen and he is a professor at UCLA. Here he is," Mr. Thomson said and gave his phone to Dr. Owen.

"Hi, Dr. Whiley, it's nice to talk to you," Dr. Owen said politely.

"Dr. Owen, I feel like I know you. Stefani talks about you all the time. You are her idol. She talked about the Austin cavern exploration a couple of times too. What can I do for you?" Dr. Whiley asked.

"Well, it seems the samples we picked up a couple of months ago are not enough to supply all of the experiments we want to conduct. We need more samples. I just wonder if I can borrow Stefani for a week or so. I need her to go back to Austin and pick up more samples for me." Dr. Owen paused a second, then continued, "You know she is the key person of this entire project; I cannot accomplish my project without her. As you know, she does not have any vacation time yet since she has started working for MarinaTech two months ago."

"I understand. You need special permission from me, is that right? But that will be against the company's policies and rules." Dr. Whiley paused for a couple of seconds. "Wait. I can send her to Austin on one of our research projects. The project can be the comparison of deep-sea cavern structures with the oil cavern. What do you think?"

"Wow! It is a splendid idea. That won't be against the company's policies and also gets the project done. Dr. Whiley, you are so generous and kind. This is a huge favor you are doing for me. I owe you one," Dr. Owen said. He knew that Dr. Whiley just wanted to help him since this project was so important. He appreciated him deeply in his heart.

"Can you ask Stefani to your office and explain it to her? I will come to your office in ten minutes so we can talk together. Is this OK?" Dr. Owen asked.

"OK, I will see you in ten minutes," Dr. Whiley said.

* * *

It took only about eight minutes to walk to the next building where the 'deep sea research department' was. Dr. Owen had been there a few times when 'Pioneer' was under construction. He had no problem finding it.

When he arrived Dr. Whiley's secretary led Dr. Owen to Dr. Whiley's office. Dr. Whiley had already notified Stefani about Dr. Owen's arrival. When Dr. Owen stepped in, he could see Dr. Whiley was talking to her.

"Hi, Dr. Owen, it is so great to see you here. We have not seen each other since Austin. How have you been?" Stefani smiled and was very happy to see Dr. Owen. She already knew the purpose of Dr. Owen's visit from Dr.

Whiley. Now, she could really sense how desperately Dr. Owen needed her. With her boss's approval, it seemed that she could not refuse. This would now be the company's project as well - her assignment.

* * *

A Visit

Later, Stefani called her mom. "Hi, Mom, how are you doing? I haven't talked to you for a week."

"Hi, Stefani, I miss you a lot. When are you coming back to San Francisco again to visit? I have not seen you since you came back from Austin," Stefani's mom said.

"Mom, you know I am working now. I am not in school anymore. Actually, I want to tell you that I am going back to Austin," Stefani said. "This time it's for a company project. This is a rare chance for MarinaTech to see the difference between an oil cavern and a deep-sea cavern. This is my assignment."

"How are you going to do it? You cannot go to the cavern alone," Mom asked.

"Of course not, Mom! Actually, the entire crew will go back one more time. Dr. Owen needs more samples. This trip will serve two purposes, Dr. Owen's and also my company's," Stefani explained.

"I will tell your dad. Before you go, can you come home at least once?" Stefani's mom requested. She paused a second then said, "This means you and Tommy will be together again for this new assignment. Right?"

"Yes, Mom!" Stefani said.

"Is it possible for you to bring him home so I can meet him myself?" Stefani's mom had sensed Stefani's emotional confusion and conflict over the last three months whenever they talked. Her mom decided to step in and see if she could do something about it. However, the first step was to know Tommy better, especially his personality, morals, and attitude.

"Mom! We saw each other only two times since we came back from Austin. It wouldn't be right for me to ask him to come to our home," Stefani said.

"But this will be the real test. If he really loves you, he will come," Mom said.

"I know he will come if I ask him. The problem is I will be embarrassed to ask him since I have been semi-rejecting him for the last three months," Stefani said.

"Do you like him, Stefani? I mean the feeling from deep in your heart?"

Stefani kept quiet and felt uneasy answering her mom's question.

"If you really like each other, then there is no such thing as embarrassment," Mom said.

"Mom, I don't know. But I will tell you if he comes. Anyway, I will come back next weekend. We have only two and a half weeks to prepare for the next exploration," Stefani said.

"At least Mom is on my side. I don't know what Dad's reaction will be." Stefani kept guessing in her mind.

* * *

From Dr. Owen, Brian learned that Stefani had agreed to go and he was very excited. He couldn't wait to tell Tommy the good news. He knew Tommy had been anxious to know the answer.

"Hi, Tommy, this is Brian. I have some good news. It seems everything is set. Stefani has agreed to go with us. The date for entering the cavern is set for March 20th. That means we still have 15 days," Brian said.

Tommy was very happy to hear about this. He had been very anxious to get together with Stefani again. However, he tried to calm his voice and hide his emotions.

"Who is going to drive 'Pioneer' to Austin this time?" Tommy asked.

"Tommy, think about it. Who else? Joe went with you last time. I will go with you this time. You know, it will be hard work, two days of driving. And once we arrive, we must clean it immediately. When the crew comes, we need to conduct a series of tests before we go into the cavern," Brian said.

Tommy was hoping Stefani could go with him this time. However, he knew deep in his heart that was impossible. Stefani would not have so many days of vacation and it was a four day drive round trip between Los Angeles and Austin. In addition, Stefani would not agree to have four days alone with Tommy in the same hotel. "I'm just dreaming," Tommy thought.

"In that case, when should we take off?" Tommy asked.

"I think the latest is March 14th. Two days of driving

and one day of rest. The crew arrives on March 18th. Testing on March 19 and 20. What do you think?" Brian said.

"What's Dr. Owen's opinion?"

"This was Dr. Owen's idea. Actually, he has already contacted Standy Firm in Austin about the dates," Brian replied.

* * *

The timing meant Tommy had only nine days before Brian and he took off. He hoped he could meet Stefani at least once before he left. After he finished talking with Brian, he was wondering if it would be okay to call her. He struggled for a while, then finally picked up his cell phone and dialed her cell phone number, but she did not answer. He left a message.

"Hi, Stefani, this is Tommy. I heard that you are able to go to Austin with the crew again. I am very excited. I wonder if we can meet and talk about it tonight? I have missed those few days very much."

Tommy was disappointed that he had not been able to talk to her again. "Should I call again later, or should I wait for her call?" he wondered.

After 30 minutes, when he had received no answer, he could not help but call her office.

"Good afternoon! This is MarinaTech Research Center, how can I help you?" the secretary answered.

Tommy asked for Stefani, but the secretary told

Tommy that everyone in the department was in a meeting. She said it probably would not finish until nearly 5 p.m., so Tommy left a message. He was very disappointed. He had never felt such high anxiety before. He never had this feeling when he was with Cathy. More and more, he was sure that Stefani was the one he loved.

"It's only 3:30 p.m. Should I call her again at about 5?" he wondered.

Tommy found a coffee house near MarinaTech and sat there alone quietly with a cup of coffee. He had to calm down and review the entire situation starting with when he first met Stefani. Why was there such a strong attraction between her and him? This relationship was able to affect his emotions significantly. Suddenly, his cell phone rang.

"Hi, Tommy, what is so urgent?" Stefani asked.

"Hi, I thought you were in a meeting," Tommy said.

"We have a ten-minute break. These long meetings really kill me. I am tired mentally. I don't have too much time. How can I help you?" Stefani said.

"There are many things you can help me with, my queen," Tommy joked. Tommy had not called her 'queen' since Austin.

"Don't be silly. Tell me what you want," Stefani said.

"I wonder if we can have dinner together tonight?" Tommy said.

"Will you offer me some mental relaxation, or will you give me more pressure?"

"I promise, we'll just talk. I miss the old days. Since we will be going exploring together again, I think it will be good for us to get acquainted from the beginning," Tommy replied.

"OK, the meeting will be over at about a quarter to five. Can you pick me up at my company?"

"Yes. I have been here in the coffee house on the corner by your company since 1:30. I will be waiting for you here."

"Is it the one next to McDonald's?" Stefani asked.

"That's it. I will be here," Tommy answered.

After Stefani hung up the phone, she could feel some sweetness and warmth in her heart. Actually, she was anxious to talk to Tommy, especially about her mom's idea of inviting him home.

* * *

At 5:05 p.m., Stefani stepped into the coffee shop. Tommy was very happy to see her.

"What would you like to eat tonight? Some Korean?" Tommy asked.

"I thought you don't like Korean." Stefani looked at him and smiled.

"Actually, I have eaten in Korean restaurants many times the last couple of months. The more I eat it, the more I like it."

"OK then. Let's have some Korean food tonight."

"There is one near Beverly Hills. The food is good. One of my favorites."

"But I heard the food is very expensive at that restaurant," Stefani said. Actually, Stefani knew this restaurant very well as she had been there a few times with friends. Now she knew what Tommy said was the truth, that he had been eating Korean food.

"It's worth it since we have not talked for some time. It's still early. Let's go to the beach for a while, OK?" Tommy asked. Stefani agreed.

On the beach, they took their shoes off and walked along the coastline. They talked about the past and the present, feeling like old friends meeting again after a long, long time. They felt close again. Tommy had missed that feeling for nearly three months.

Suddenly, Stefani said, "What are you doing this weekend?"

"Nothing. I hope we can be together again this weekend since you have more time," Tommy said with eagerness in his eyes.

"I promised my mom I'd go back to visit them, I mean my mom and dad, this weekend." Stefani paused for a few seconds. She could see the disappointment on Tommy's face. She continued, "Why don't you come with me? Maybe my parents would like to meet you."

This was a surprise. Tommy knew this was unusual. It was beyond what would be expected in a normal friendship, especially in conservative Asian cultures. It was a sweet gesture and Tommy felt a rekindling of the love that had started to develop during their time in Austin.

"What will your parents say? Will it be OK with them?" he asked.

"If you agree to come, I will arrange it," Stefani said.

"Aye, aye, Captain!" Tommy replied with a big smile. Stefani looked at him and felt he was just like a 15 year old boy.

They had a nice time with the best dinner they had ever eaten. Of course, this was mainly because they were in a very good mood that night. Stefani insisted it was her treat since she had begun to make money already.

* * *

When their taxi arrived at Stefani's home in Berkeley, Tommy was very nervous. Since Stefani's father was a professor who taught at the University of California, Berkeley, their home was near that campus. On the airplane, Stefani had already educated Tommy on the manners of how to face an old-fashioned Korean couple: "Don't sit when they stand. Sit only when they ask. Bow instead of shaking hands. When you eat, wait until the elders begin first, etc."

Tommy had never spent time with an Asian family. He did not want to embarrass himself in front of Stefani's parents. This was a big day. To him, it seemed like he was going to meet his parents-in-law for the first time. He had dressed for the occasion, wearing a nice suit, and was neatly shaved for the first time since their return from Austin. As a matter of fact, this was the first time in the last 15 years that he had had his hair cut short. He looked so sincere and solemn.

When Stefani's mother opened the door, Tommy

bowed politely. He knew if everything went smoothly, all of the obstacles between Stefani and him could be removed this weekend. Stefani hugged her mom and said something unimportant to try and ease Tommy's nervousness. As they were talking, Stefani's mom kept asking questions about Tommy's family, his interests, and his plans for the future. "Gosh, Mom! This is just like giving a test to a candidate son-in-law," Stefani thought in her mind. However, she could see that her mother had a very good impression at the first sight of this handsome young man. There was no question that Stefani's mom liked Tommy a lot.

"Anyone home?" Stefani's father opened the door and stepped into the house.

Stefani hugged her father first, then introduced Tommy to him. Tommy tensed up again. "This is more nerve wracking and harder than piloting 'Pioneer' in the cavern," he thought. He tried to keep himself calm with deep breathing. After only 30 minutes, Professor Kim and Tommy had already gotten acquainted. This was because they shared the same interest in science. They talked about Tommy's research at MIT and Professor Kim's job at the University of California, Berkeley. To Professor Kim, this young man, a Ph.D. from MIT, was special. It didn't hurt that he was also good looking.

While Tommy and her dad talked, Stefani helped her mom cook; however, she constantly peeked and watched the development between her father and Tommy. After a while, she released the worry that she had felt ever since she knew Tommy would be coming with her. She knew now even her father's stubborn old-fashioned mind had accepted Tommy. This made her very happy since she knew if her father was against their relationship, he would be the biggest obstacle. When the food was ready, they had a nice dinner.

"As Stefani has said many times, her mom's cooking is the best." Tommy believed it now.

It was a great visit. The gap between Stefani and Tommy shortened very much in just one weekend. Stefani's defense wall was getting lower and lower. After they went back to Los Angeles, they met almost every night.

On March 14, Tommy and Brian left driving a tow truck carrying 'Pioneer.'

* * *

Final Exploration

Before Tommy and Brian left for Austin, Tommy called Stefani.

"Hi, Stefani. I found a better battery that could supply us at least ten more minutes of charge in the submarine. I found it by accident a couple of days ago when I talked to one of my friends at MIT. They often use the same size battery for their experiments. What do you think? Should we change our batteries to this brand?"

"What do you think, Tommy? This is the last trip and I don't expect anything will happen. The batteries we had before were working fine," Stefani replied.

"However, when it is a critical situation, even ten

minutes can mean life or death," Tommy said.

"Why don't you get two of them and take them with you. We will see if we need them in Austin. If we don't use them, we can always return them," Stefani suggested.

Tommy went to a marine battery shop to purchase the two new batteries. At the shop, he realized that this was a new product from a German battery company that had been introduced to the market only two months ago. The next morning, Tommy and Brian left Los Angeles for the last exploration in Austin.

Tommy and Brian arrived at Standy Firm in Austin on March 16. As soon as they were settled in, Tommy began to charge the new batteries. They took a day to rest and then began to clean 'Pioneer.' Brian did not know very much about the structure, ultrasonic detecting system, or computer simulation system; all he could do was remove any oil residue or rust. In the end, Tommy decided to replace the old batteries with the new ones.

After Tommy and Brian had been working for five hours, the rest of the crew arrived in a car Standy Firm had sent to pick them up from the airport. The entire crew had a very happy reunion. They drank and talked about the last exploration. They all believed that everything would go very smoothly this time.

"By the way, I would like to tell you that I replaced the old batteries with some new ones. These new ones are more efficient than the old ones and should give us ten extra minutes," Tommy announced to everyone.

"Great idea, Tommy. I believe there will be no problem this time since we have already had so much experience. As a matter of fact, if Dr. Owen likes, we can even go down a few times and pick up all of the samples he needs." Joe was joking.

Actually, Dr. Owen would like it if they made many more trips down since he knew the more samples they got, the greater the chance he and Dr. Torr would be able to discover the past secrets hidden in this cavern. However, he said, "We'll wait and see. If we have time and if everything goes smoothly, then we can talk about it. You all should know that Brian and I are very appreciative of all of you about this surprise exploration."

"What are we looking for this time? We all know we need more samples from the same area, but what are we searching for?" Joe had been wondering about this trip.

"Brian and I found a few pieces of rock which could give us a more accurate history of the cavern. However, it seemed strange that different rocks had different historical backgrounds. We will need more of these rocks to verify our theory," Dr. Owen replied. Naturally, Brian knew that Dr. Owen was hiding the truth of the crystals. Dr. Owen continued, "Another thing that needs to be verified are those columns. We need to also know the structure and the material of those columns. They are different from columns existing in natural caverns."

Everyone was excited and felt there was nothing to worry about. All they needed to do was to pick up more samples and gently knock a column and record its sounds.

The crew met at 10:00 the next morning and had a meeting with Standy Firm's technicians and engineers led by Eric. They reviewed the mission and anticipated a smooth ride this time.

Joe and Tommy spent the whole afternoon setting up the detecting and simulation system just like last time. At dinner, they reported to Dr. Owen that everything was ready to go.

* * *

The next day, Tuesday morning, the entire crew met each other at the entrance of the mine's window. After Tommy and Stefani had entered the submarine, they each checked the oxygen supply and battery on their sides. Then Tommy extended his head out and said, "Let's go, everything is ready."

As it had nearly six months ago, 'Pioneer' entered the cavern without any difficulty. Both Tommy and Stefani still had good piloting skills and their memory about the tunnel and cavern was clear. To them, it seemed like they had never taken a break since their last exploration. Again, Stefani piloted 'Pioneer' through the tunnel and then approached the column pile. "It's yours, Tommy," she said.

Tommy took over the controls and piloted 'Pioneer' into the column pile carefully. After all, this place was the most dangerous place and he had not gone through it for the last six months. Everything was smooth as they entered the room. To save time, Tommy piloted 'Pioneer' straightforward to the hole, the entrance to the other cavern. Once they entered, he asked Stefani, "Do you remember where you dug your samples last time? Why don't you fill up your sample pocket first?"

Stefani took over the controls and piloted 'Pioneer' to the corner where she had picked up the samples last time. With just a couple scoops, the pocket was already filled.

"Now, it is your turn, Tommy!" Stefani told him.

"What do you think? Should I try different spot?" Tommy asked.

"No. Professor Owen asked for the same spot specifically. I believe he had a reason for it. Maybe the material here is more desirable for his purpose."

"Tommy, please keep to the same spot," Dr. Owen's voice came over the telecom. He had been able to listen to their conversation as soon as Stefani and Tommy had entered into the smaller cavern.

"OK, Professor!"

Tommy turned 'Pioneer' around and aimed at the same spot where Stefani had dug. He dug more samples and placed them securely in the pocket on his side.

Mission accomplished. The only thing they had left to do was to hit the column with a robot arm and generate a sound. That should be easy. They decided to do this when they approached the entrance of the tunnel.

After they deducted the time necessary to return to the surface, they still had 25 minutes extra. With the old batteries, they would have had only had 15 minutes remaining. Stefani and Joe both noticed it.

"Tommy, just to remind you, you still have 25 minutes," Joe said.

Tommy was curious and wanted to use the extra time to explore more about this smaller cavern. He had mentioned the possibility to Dr. Owen over the telecom when they entered the small cavern.

"Dr. Owen asked me to remind you not to do anything risky and remember to check the remaining time constantly," Joe said. That meant Dr. Owen agreed with Tommy's suggestion.

Tommy piloted 'Pioneer' carefully near the lower edge of the small cavern and scanned around. Actually, there was nothing fantastic which could attract their attention. All of it looked the same. When 20 had minutes passed, they decided to return to the big cavern. Tommy piloted 'Pioneer' to the room in the column pile and then to the other side where the entrance was. He carefully tilted 'Pioneer' upward so they could get out like before. However, it seemed it was more difficult to go up than the last two times. The charge in the battery was running out very quickly. The only reason he could think of was that they carried more samples; that meant more weight this time. He had to be very careful even though he had a new set of batteries; otherwise, it could be a disaster. It took three minutes longer than he expected.

"Stefani, please let me pilot 'Pioneer' to the entrance. We don't have too much time," Tommy asked. Stefani agreed.

They were quickly running out of the time. When they reached the tunnel entrance area, the red warning light for the battery came on. That meant they were using reserve power. Stefani began to worry and some panic showed on her face. When she checked the oxygen supply, it indicated they had about eight minutes.

"Tommy, we are running out of oxygen! We don't have enough time to get out!" Stefani's face was scrunched up tightly and tears began to fall from her eyes.

Tommy quickly took from behind his seat the spare oxygen tank that was originally planned to be used for escape purposes. He released the oxygen into the 'Pioneer.' Though this small tank could supply 30 minutes of oxygen in a personal diving situation, it would only supply about ten minutes when it was released into the vessel.

"Stefani, please release the oxygen of your spare tank as well. If I calculated correctly, this will provide us at least 20 more minutes of oxygen supply," Tommy said.

When Stefani realized that they actually would have 20 more minutes of oxygen supply, she felt much better. She took the tank out from behind her seat and released the oxygen.

Now they had only one more thing to do and that should not take too long. This would still give them enough charge and oxygen to return, Tommy thought. He came to the mid-section of the long column next to the tunnel and used his robot arm to hit it. The sound seemed very weak the first time. Again, he operated the robot arm and hit it a second time. The sound was louder this time, louder than they expected. While they were wondering at the sound, an echo, a resonant vibration, caused all the other columns that had the same length to vibrate. Suddenly they realized the vibrations were causing the cavern to collapse.

Stefani's face turned pale and her breaths came faster and faster.

"Tommy, watch out! The cavern is collapsing. According to your top detector, it looks like the rock at the top of the entrance has fallen and sealed the entrance. You must think quickly and act quickly. You must find a solution quickly!" Joe's voice shouted over the telecom.

Back on the surface, everyone's face had turned pale, especially Dr. Owen's. "What have I done? I've killed them," he thought.

Tommy and Stefani were very nervous now. The path to get back had been sealed by the falling rock. They had only 25 minutes of oxygen and probably 17 minutes of charge. Usually, it would take 15 minutes to get through at a speed of five miles per hour. One minute passed and then two. The situation became more and more urgent. It seemed they would die in the next 17 minutes or so. Stefani had completely flipped out. Her breathing got faster and faster. She could not stop crying.

"Stefani! Keep strong. I need you now. You must be calm." Tommy turned his head and tried to see Stefani's face. However, Stefani was quiet and did not know how to react.

Tommy piloted 'Pioneer' back near the entrance and

used the robot arm to hit the rock blocking it. It was hopeless. He could not move the rock at all. He tried a few more times but failed. Every minute passed too quickly. Now, they had only 17 minutes of oxygen and 12 minutes of charge. The oxygen was running out more quickly due to their rapid, panicky breathing, especially Stefani's.

"I need some force strong enough to re-open this entrance," Tommy thought. "The only way is..."

"Stefani, I am going to hit the column one more time and see if it can cause another vibration," Tommy said.

Stefani turned her head and with a trembling voice asked, "Are you sure? We could be buried."

"It doesn't matter anymore. If we don't do it, we'll die for sure," Tommy said and without waiting for Stefani's answer, he quickly piloted 'Pioneer' to the mid-section of a column. The position was about 20 feet under and beside the tunnel entrance. He raised the robot arm and hit the column hard. Again, resonance occurred. The entire cavern vibrated, causing more and more collapse.

"Tommy, watch out! The rock sealing the entrance is falling," Joe's voice said over the telecom.

It was great news, but Tommy had to watch to keep 'Pioneer' from being damaged by the falling pieces, especially the big rock that had been sealing the entrance. 'Pioneer' shook here and there from the falling pieces. Finally, the big rock fell, just barely passing Stefani's side of the sub.

"Stefani, watch out!" Tommy quickly released the

hook of the sample pocket on his side; all of the samples on his side fell away into the darkness. The submarine's load lightened, it tilted, with the head of Tommy's side heading upward.

Tommy quickly piloted towards the entrance and entered. They had only nine minutes to get through the tunnel. Tommy kept the speed at 12 miles per hour, nearly three times faster than what they had done before. 'Pioneer' was moving through falling stones. They hit the surrounding wall, ceiling, and ground a few times because of the uneven balance between Tommy's side and Stefani's. Every time they hit, more of the tunnel fell in. When they were two-thirds of the way through, their oxygen supply had nearly come to an end. Both Stefani and Tommy could feel that breathing was getting harder and harder.

"Hang in there, Stefani! Just three more minutes," Tommy kept encouraging and comforting her.

"Put your gasmask on now, Stefani," Tommy yelled. But Stefani's body was trembling so much that she had a hard time picking up the gasmask and putting it on.

"You must try, Stefani! Please! For me and for you," Tommy turned his head shouting again. Suddenly, Stefani became calm and her desire to survive took over. She took the gasmask out and put it on. Seeing that, Tommy quickly took his own gasmask out and put it on.

When the submarine entered the window, the engine stopped, and the oxygen ran out. From the rear detector, they could see that the entrance was almost completely filled by the falling dirt. The tunnel had been sealed.

Both Stefani and Tommy were having a hard time breathing. Tommy tried very hard to reach the door of the submarine. He knew this was the last challenge and their last hope of survival. The gas detector gave a warning that there was some accumulation of gas just outside of the submarine. Obviously, this new accumulation of gas was caused by the collapse in the cavern. Finally, Tommy got the door open and air mixed with gas flowed into the submarine. With their masks on, both of them could breathe again.

They stopped there for a few minutes until their breathing became more normal. Then Tommy stuck his head out to place the hooks on the hooking bars and told Joe that it was OK to pull.

When they came out of the submarine, Tommy went out first and removed his mask. He then helped Stefani out. When Tommy helped Stefani remove her gas mask, he could see her face was still pale and wet with tears. Her body was still shaking.

When Stefani looked into Tommy's eyes, she could not help holding him tightly and begin to cry. Tommy hugged her close. All of the people surrounding them were quiet. Dr. Owen's eyes were wet. In his heart, he thanked God for sparing their lives.

Now, they all knew that this really was the last trip. The collapse made it impossible for them to go back again. Furthermore, after this experience none of them would think of another adventure like this again. It took almost five minutes for Stefani and Tommy to get their emotions to settle down while the others stood by still and quiet. Even though they had lost half of the samples, at least they had their lives. Samples or no samples, to Dr. Owen it was not important anymore. Both Tommy and Stefani knew that if Tommy had not made the quick decision of hitting the column again, they would have died inside the cavern. Furthermore, if Tommy had not dropped the samples from his side the extra weight would have slowed them down and it would have taken more time to circle around in the falling rocks and dirt until they could reach the tunnel entrance.

Finally, Dr. Owen stepped forward and hugged Stefani first and then Tommy, saying thank you with tears in his eyes. Then everyone stepped forward to hug them. All of the Standy Firm technicians and engineers started to applaud. Both Tommy and Stefani's eyes were wet.

A couple of Standy Firm's technicians helped Brian put the samples that Stefani had picked up into a plastic box and placed it on the truck. Dr. Owen announced that he would host a party that evening and invited everyone. He did not know if they had been able to find the crystal reader. He knew the chance was very small, especially since they had lost half of their samples. But it did not matter now. And, at least they had recorded the sound of the columns. This would provide Dr. Torr with some of the information he hoped for about this cavern.

* * *

Just two hours after the final exploration, Brian

called Dr. Owen. His voice was excited.

"Dr. Owen, I believe we have gotten what we were looking for. There is a device in the sample dirt that was made by crystal but is a different shape. In addition, there is another crystal shaped the same as the others," Brian said.

"Do not move. I will come to your room," Dr. Owen said. He was afraid if Brian brought this new discovery to his room, Brian might encounter someone who would ask him questions. Now, keeping the secret was more important than ever. He believed his and Dr. Torr's theory was correct about the past history of this cavern. He could not let anyone see these new crystals.

It took him only five minutes to get to Brian's room. When Brian opened the door and let him enter, he could see the big mess in Brian's room. All of the samples were divided into different groups: some rocks, some dirt, and all covered by the black oil.

"Here they are, Professor Owen," Brian said, removing the crystals from the drawer where they had been hidden and handing them over. They were wrapped in a cloth and were still coated with oil since Brian had not had enough time to clean them. He had called Dr. Owen as soon as he saw the two pieces.

Dr. Owen was very excited and happy, knowing that this was the biggest success of their exploration. However, when he thought of the danger Tommy and Stefani had been in, his eyes became wet again. He appreciated all his students, but especially Tommy and Stefani.

As Brian said, one piece was just the same as all the

others. But the other had a strange shape. It was bigger than the others and in the top of this crystal, there was a pyramid shaped hole, just the right size for one of the smaller crystals to fit in. Surrounding this hole was a chamber that was empty. It seemed this space was to be filled up with something. It did not matter what, both Brian and Dr. Owen knew this piece was related to the crystals found before.

"Brian, you know that we must continue to keep quiet about this. If we release the news now, our fate will be out of our hands. What I am worried about is, if the government knows, they may want to keep it a secret from the public, especially if it could be used for weapons technology development," Dr. Owen said. "Politicians will take over the study of the crystal for their own glory. We will just be the victims of their glory."

"I understand clearly, Professor Owen. I am not stupid," Brian said.

"I will keep you informed about any discovery Dr. Torr and I make in the future," Dr. Owen went on. "Please keep these two pieces for now. I can't put the big one in my briefcase. It's too big."

"I can put them in my backpack and bring them to you tonight before the party," Brian suggested.

"OK but be careful. If you encounter anyone and are questioned, what would you tell them?" Dr. Owen asked.

"I'd just say I have some questions about the samples which I need to ask you. But I hope I don't encounter anyone," Brian said. "Since the dirt samples we have picked up are so black and oily, no one has even shown interest in touching them anyway."

"OK, it does not matter what, just don't reveal the secret," Dr. Owen warned.

* * *

About half an hour before the party, Brian brought the crystals to Dr. Owen's room without any problem. Then he left to get ready for the party that night. Dr. Owen carefully placed the samples in his luggage.

The evening party was great. It eased all of the nervousness and tightness of the daytime adventure. Tommy and Stefani stayed together the entire time except for some social greetings. Their relationship had never been so close. There was no wall between them anymore. Tommy brought some sherry to Stefani. They were silent and simply held hands or hugged each other quietly. In Stefani's heart, Tommy was her hero. Without Tommy in the cavern today, she would not have survived. She knew Tommy's bravery, wisdom, and quick reactions were the keys of their survival. He was a man rarely found in the world.

Both of them got a little bit drunk. Tommy brought Stefani to the door of her room about 10 p.m. Once there, she pulled him into her room. They lay down on the bed, hugging and kissing each other. The next morning when Tommy left her room at 9 a.m., Stefani had already considered him as her lover, or even husband.

Stefani, Joe, and Dr. Owen would leave in the afternoon together. Tommy and Brian stayed behind to clean the oil coating off of 'Pioneer.' Now, 'Pioneer' did not look as beautiful as it used to since there were so many damaged areas caused from falling rocks. Finally, when Tommy and Brian brought 'Pioneer' back to Los Angeles, it was placed in the university's warehouse. This would be a piece of history, an incredible history indeed.

Chapter 5
The Truth

Testing

A few months after the entire crew returned to Los Angeles, Tommy and Stefani announced their engagement on July 15th. They first had a celebration party in Los Angeles for all their friends. Naturally, the entire crew was there to celebrate. The following weekend, they had another party and formal ceremony in San Francisco for Stefani's family and friends. Tommy's mom also came from Chicago. Tommy's father had died in a car accident when Tommy was only 9 years old. Because of his father's death, Tommy learned to be independent and mentally strong even as a tiny boy. He was an only child and did not have any brothers or sisters.

The wedding was set for March 20th of the next year to remember the date they had entered the cavern for the last time. To Tommy and Stefani, this date, the date of life and death, was a day that would never be forgotten.

As for Joe, after returning to school, he added another whole chapter to his thesis. The chapter and DVD explained and demonstrated the collapse of the cavern. Amazingly he was able, from the random information collected, to produce very vivid images. This work had a high level of difficulty since many parts of the data collected were incomplete due to the collapsing of the cavern. This was a huge opportunity for him to demonstrate his talent in computer simulation. His adviser was surprised and impressed with the results and quality of the thesis. After his graduation, Joe moved to New York City.

* * *

When Dr. Owen arrived in Los Angeles, he called Dr. Torr in Washington, D.C. about the good news. He also told him, briefly, about the entire exploration process and that it was impossible to return to the cavern anymore. Then he arranged a flight to meet Dr. Torr three days later. This would give Joe some time to finish his three-dimensional simulation of the final exploration. The afternoon before Dr. Owen took off, Joe brought him the first edition of the three-dimensional simulation images. Dr. Owen brought the simulation, along with a recording of the sound made by hitting the column and all of the crystals, with him to Washington.

Dr. Torr came to the airport to pick him up. They were so happy and excited to see each other again. Dr. Owen stayed in Dr. Torr's home this time. Since Dr. Torr was not married and did not have any children, it was easy for them to talk without fear of being overheard. After a couple of days, Dr. Torr realized they had another similar hobby, drinking good Chinese tea. Since Dr. Owen could not go with Dr. Torr to the underground lab, he stayed in the house, and studied and wrote on his laptop.

One day, when Dr. Torr returned home, he handed a couple of pages of a report to Dr. Owen, and said with a proud and cheerful tone, "The testing of the sound has been done; this is the report. As I suspected, this oil mine was an underground city. All of the columns were made of very strong stainless steel. It seems these columns were used to support the structure of the cavern in the past."

"No wonder there were so many different sizes and such a great number of columns in the cavern. This explains why the sound generated by a single column could trigger so much resonant vibration in the cavern. You know, the group of columns with the same size and length would have the same vibration frequency," Dr. Owen said. Naturally, Dr. Torr had already thought of that.

Now, their curiosity regarding the secret of this underground city had never been so strong. They had so many questions and both of them knew the possible answers were all recorded in the crystals they had found. Dr. Owen stayed for about two weeks waiting for more good news. However, it was not easy for Dr. Torr to find the secret to reading the crystals and eventually Dr. Owen had to return to Los Angeles. Even though he did not teach many classes now, he still had to return to handle necessary business on campus. It was near the end of the semester.

* * *

After Dr. Owen left, Dr. Torr spent almost all of his time in the underground lab. He was so excited and anxious to find a way of reading the crystals; he just ignored his regular research job. About three weeks after Dr. Owen gave him the crystal reader, this caught his boss's attention.

Finally, in the fourth week, Dr. Torr decided to use some liquid that was heavy and had good electrical conductivity. According to his analysis of the vibration from the earthquake, the frequencies and amplitudes of the vibration had to be accurate. In addition, the material inside the chamber also had to be a good electrical conductor so the energy could flow without stagnation. Finally he came to an answer: mercury. He filled up the chamber of the crystal reader with mercury and designed a device that was able to adjust the height of the mercury in the chamber through an existing tiny hole located on the side and near the bottom of the reader. He did not know if it had been designed for this purpose. But surely, it would serve the purpose.

Dr. Torr also connected a vibration device to the center bottom of the reader. Through this device, different frequencies and amplitudes of vibration could be produced and controlled. Once he had this new idea, it took him almost a whole night without sleep to find the right frequencies and amplitudes. Finally, in the early morning, at 4:32, when he tuned the electronic vibrator to a very low frequency, the image recorded in the crystal appeared. This was the most exciting moment. He was so tired and had thought of quitting only a half-hour ago. Now, he continued to try different frequencies and realized that the band was very narrow. He therefore re-adjusted the electronic vibrator so the frequencies in this band could be tuned finely.

Next, he tried different amplitudes by increasing the power of the vibration and realized that through differ-ent amplitudes, he would see different parts of the re-cording. However, he could never come back to the same spot, even if he used the same amplitude. He knew the reading system was not as good as it would have been originally. But considering his lack of knowledge at the moment, whatever information he could gather was good news.

Dr. Torr also connected a sound magnifier to the three edges of the upper crystal pyramid and was then able to hear sound. He discovered that he could adjust the loudness of the sound through the magnifier. This made him very happy. However, it did not matter what he tried, he still could not figure out how to stop, rewind, fast forward or backward, go in slow-motion, or any of the other functions found in any of today's VCR or DVD players. By now he was very tired and needed to go home for some sleep.

He slept until 2:20 in the afternoon. Knowing it was 11:20 a.m. in Los Angeles, he decided to call Dr. Owen and tell him the good news.

"My friend, I have good news for you. I found out how to read the crystals," Dr. Torr told Dr. Owen on the phone.

"Really? That is great! Tell me about it," Dr. Owen asked anxiously and excitedly.

"Mercury was the answer. I have tried all kinds of liquids and solutions to fill up the chamber. Through the vibration device, I tried to read the recording but failed. Now, I know mercury is the answer. Once that was in place, the other connections were easy and not too complicated," Dr. Torr said.

"Have you seen the whole recording?" Dr. Owen asked.

"No, I was really tired and came home to sleep. In fact, I just woke up a few minutes ago. I still cannot find the way to stop, rewind, fast forward, fast backward, play slow-motion, or any of the features we have in our DVD system. But I believe I could figure it out with my knowledge and today's technology," he continued.

"The most amazing part was, I was able to control the size of the images by controlling the height of the mercury. The higher the mercury surface is, the larger the images are. When it reaches the highest point, the three-dimensional image is large enough that you are inside the image. However, when you lower the mercury level, the image shrinks and becomes smaller. It can be the size of a baseball hovering above the tip of the top pyramid. That means the size of the three-dimensional images are controlled by the quantity of mercury in the chamber," Dr. Torr explained.

"Wow! I wish I could be there to see it," Dr. Owen said. Then, he continued, "Could you find a way to get me into the underground lab? I must see this."

"James, I am sorry. It is impossible. In addition, even if I am able to get you in, it will catch the authority's attention. That would not be wise," Dr. Torr replied. Since they had become good friends, Dr. Torr began to call Dr. Owen by his first name.

"Let me see if I am able to set it up in the basement of my house so you can watch it. It should not be hard. If you come in a couple of days, I should be able to move all of the equipment from the underground lab to my house," Dr. Torr said.

"Very well. I will book the ticket today. I will see you in two days," Dr. Owen said.

* * *

Two days later, again Dr. Torr came to the airport to pick up Dr. Owen. Dr. Owen was very excited. He had heard twice now about watching a crystal's recording of the past, however, he had never had a chance to see it even once. It was a 45-minute ride back to Dr. Torr's home and they chatted all the way, Dr. Torr telling him in detail how to read the crystals.

"I finished setting up and testing last night, however, I must tell you the truth. The images are not as clear as when I watched them in the underground lab. In addition, the images keep jumping from one spot to another," Dr. Torr explained.

"Do you know the reason?" Dr. Owen asked.

"I believe it is interference caused by surrounding vibrations. As I believe, they must have had some special device that was able to eliminate surrounding vibrations in their time. However, I don't think we have this kind of technology today," Dr. Torr replied.

"Does that mean the only possibility of understanding the crystals is by conducting experiments a few stories underground?" Dr. Owen asked.

"It seems that way," Dr. Torr said and turned on the system in his basement.

Even though what Dr. Owen saw were just pieces here and there, he was so shocked by what he could see of the past world. He guessed the technologies he saw from the images had to be at least 500 years more advanced than today's; flying cars with sky cities! To him, these ancient beings looked just like humans today, though their clothes were different as well as their hairstyles. In addition, they had to have already unlocked the mystery of gravity; it seemed anti-gravity technology was already commonly applied at that time.

To learn more about the past, they had to find an underground lab. It would not be easy, since any attempt they tried would bring attention. After a few days, Dr. Owen flew back to Los Angeles. Dr. Torr continued his research to see if he was able to improve the reading system.

FBI

Unfortunately, in time Dr. Torr's visits to the underground lab caught the attention of security. In addition, his boss had reported the strange behavior Dr. Torr had displayed for the last couple of months. They suspected he was doing something secret without government approval. Due to national security reasons, the FBI had reactivated a bugging system that had been secretly installed in Dr. Torr's phone and in his house back when he began to work for the government on the "memory crystal" project. Fortunately, this was initiated a couple of days after Dr. Owen left Dr. Torr's home. Now, even Dr. Torr's cell phone was traced, and his conversations were listened to. He was followed and watched secretly.

Dr. Torr became aware he was being spied on the third day after Dr. Owen left. He had gotten up early in the morning and saw a strange car parked a couple of blocks away. He had never seen this car before, and usually, there were no cars parked on the street since all the neighbors had garages. When he thought about it, his sixth sense told him that he was being watched. Even though he had known that, sooner or later, his abnormal behavior would catch the government's attention, he did not expect it would be so soon.

Once he realized this, a cold sweat broke out on his forehead. He knew that he had to do something before the investigation got any deeper. He had to remove the crystals and all of the reading equipment from his house as soon as possible before they found out. Not only that, he had to pass a message to Dr. Owen about what had happened here without being noticed by the FBI.

He called Dr. Owen and another good friend, Dr. Peter Wong, as a three-party telephone call. He knew that with the third party, Dr. Owen would not mention anything about the crystals in conversation. He knew that the FBI was listening. His call shocked Dr. Owen, who did not know what had happened; however, since there was another person on the phone, he knew he should not talk about the crystals at all.

"James, I would like to introduce a good friend of mine, Professor Wong. I have known him for more than ten years. He is teaching at Maryland University. His major is archaeology," Dr. Torr said. "Since your field, geology, is very close to what he is doing, I thought both of you could become good friends as well. He is on the phone as well."

"Hi, Dr. Wong. It is nice to talk to you. Though we have never met, I have known about you from papers you have published," Dr. Owen said.

"You are very kind, Dr. Owen. You are pretty well-known yourself too. It would be great to meet you," Dr. Wong said.

"I would like to invite both of you to my 60th birthday party. It will be Wednesday of next week," Dr. Torr said.

"Where will it be and how many people will be there?" Dr. Wong asked.

"Actually, I would like to have a peaceful and quiet birthday. I am only inviting you two," Dr. Torr said. "Since I like deep ocean fishing, I wonder if you would like to go deep sea fishing with me. We will check into the hotel near the port next Tuesday and take off Wednesday early morning. You know, you must get up early to catch fish. I have already hired a boat for only the three of us," Dr. Torr said with a laugh.

Dr. Owen could sense something was going wrong and that Dr. Torr was trying to arrange something. This invitation and the three-party telephone call were a surprise. This meeting might be crucial for their investigation about the past world. Before Dr. Wong could say anything, he said, "That will be great. Especially since this will offer me a great opportunity to get to know Dr. Wong. I have been anxious to meet him."

Because of what Dr Owen said, it seemed impolite for Dr. Wong to refuse the invitation. Furthermore, as Dr. Owen said, it would be a good opportunity to get to know each other. It was summertime anyway and there was not too much to do on campus.

"It will be an honor to meet you too, Dr. Owen," Dr. Wong said.

They made an appointment to meet at the Marriott Hotel near Virginia Beach next Tuesday.

* * *

Four days later Dr. Owen flew to Washington, D.C. and Dr. Torr came to pick him up with his car. When they saw each other, before Dr. Owen could begin talking Dr. Torr shook his hand and signaled with his eyes that they were being watched. Dr. Owen therefore acted as an old friend and did not say anything but a general greeting. Both of them knew, through modern technology, any spy was able to secretly record any conversation, even from a few hundred yards away.

When they got into the car, Dr. Torr gave Dr. Owen a cup of tea and said, "James, I know you like Chinese tea. I cannot wait for you to try this one. It's the best I have found, and I think it's better than the one you treated me to last time."

Dr. Owen accepted the tea, however, he felt that the cup was empty inside. When he opened the lid, he saw a few lines had been written inside the cup, "We are being watched. Be casual. The car might have been bugged." With just a peek, Dr. Owen suddenly understood everything. He pretended he was drinking the tea.

"Still hot! John, it is pretty good. But I think mine was still better than yours." Both of them laughed, then they just chatted about something unimportant and did not mention anything about memory crystal.

When they arrived at Dr. Torr's home, they were even more cautious. Both of them knew any place where Dr. Torr used to go had been bugged, especially his home. In addition, he might be followed and watched 24 hours a day. Therefore, they avoided anything related to the crystals. They simply talked and drank tea until they went to bed.

They took off the second morning to go to the Marriott Hotel near the beach. After they had checked in, Dr. Torr demanded to be changed to another room where they could see the ocean better. Dr. Owen knew that Dr. Torr suspected that even the hotel room might have been bugged since the FBI would know where they would stay. However, this last minute's switch would surprise them. At least, it would provide them some time to communicate until the new room was bugged.

Once they entered the room, Dr. Torr found a notepad and wrote, "Keep talking. They were listening outside. We will communicate by writing."

Then, Dr. Torr spent the next hour explaining how the government might have known their secret. He said he had to move all the equipment and crystals over to Dr. Owen. The longer he kept them, the more at risk they would be. He quickly opened his traveling bag and gave Dr. Owen all of the crystals and also the reading device.

Dr. Torr wrote, "It is easy to set it up again. I will give you directions on how to set it up before we separate again." While at the same time, he said aloud, "How are your wife and kids? You are a grandpa of two grandkids now. James, we are old." Dr. Torr laughed.

Dr. Owen quickly placed the crystals and the reading device into his own traveling bag.

"Take these with you all the time. They will search the room later on," Dr. Torr wrote.

Later, Dr. Wong arrived and Dr. Torr introduced him to Dr. Owen. They immediately liked each other since both of them shared the same interests, especially good Chinese tea. Dr. Wong stayed by himself in a single room that evening.

Early the next morning, on Dr. Torr's birthday, they went out fishing. During the first three hours of the trip, Dr. Torr went to the toilet at least five times.

"I don't know what I ate last night. I had diarrhea last night and I still have it this morning. I am sorry,"

Dr. Torr said.

Originally, they had planned to fish for five hours. But now, due to Dr. Torr's sickness, they decided to cut it short. They asked the captain to steer the boat back to port. When they were near the port, while the captain was busy docking, Dr. Torr secretly passed five sheets of writing to Dr. Owen. He had spent the last three hours, off and on, writing them in the tiny toilet located in the lower section of the boat. Dr. Owen immediately placed them into his pocket.

Back at the hotel, Dr. Torr apologized to Dr. Owen and Dr. Wong for the disappointing trip. He said he felt weak and wished to go home. Naturally, the other two agreed.

When they arrived home, Dr. Wong left and they continued talking casually, saying absolutely nothing related to the crystals. A few minutes after their arrival, Dr. Torr fixed some good Chinese tea for Dr. Owen.

"Enjoy your tea, James. I want to show you something. Wait here. It is in the basement," Dr. Torr said with an excuse and went to the door to the basement. After he opened the door, he noticed that two slippers that he had put on the stairs in a special arrangement had been moved. He knew someone had entered the house while they were away. He also knew that the basement might have been searched and bugged. It was lucky that he had taken all the crystals and the reading device to the beach and passed them to Dr. Owen in advance. He went down, found a nice fountain pen, and came back upstairs.

"James, this is an antique. It is a very old design. I

know you are collecting these kinds of old pens and I want you to keep this one as a good friend." Dr. Torr gave Dr. Owen the pen. Though it was a surprise to Dr. Owen, he knew everything Dr. Torr said or did must have some special reason. He accepted it delightedly.

The next morning, Dr. Torr took Dr. Owen to the airport and said good-bye. By now, the FBI did not suspect Dr. Owen. They were convinced that Dr. Owen was only a good friend Dr. Torr met a few months ago. Since Dr. Torr was a strange guy and did not have too many friends, the way he treated Dr. Owen was understandable.

New Lab

On the airplane, just to be cautious, Dr. Owen did not dare to take out the sheets of paper Dr. Torr had given him on the boat. He suspected he now might be followed as well. Only after he arrived home did he begin to feel that he was not yet suspected. This gave him some level of freedom and release.

Dr. Owen went into his study and carefully took the crystals and reading device out of his traveling bag. Then, he took out the five sheets of paper from his pocket. He began to read.

Basically, Dr. Torr told him that the FBI had suspected him due to his constant visits to the government research lab. He could not continue his investigation anymore. He told him that once the government knew and owned the crystals, the truth might never be discovered. These sheets also gave Dr. Owen instructions on how to construct the reading system by himself. It was not hard; he just needed a quiet and secret place.

Dr. Owen kept searching for a place to read the crystals and eventually he asked Brian to come help him. A few days passed and he could not find any desirable place. However, the desire to read those crystals made him decide to construct a small lab in the basement of his house.

With Brian's help, Dr. Owen was able to assemble a system according to Dr. Torr's directions. It was an exciting moment when everything was set. Dr. Owen turned the main lights off and only left a small table light on so they could see. They turned the vibration machine on and kept changing frequencies slowly and gradually. When the vibration had almost reached zero, a three-dimensional image appeared.

As Dr. Torr had said, the image was off and on and jumped from place to place. Dr. Owen remembered that Dr. Torr said this was caused by surrounding vibrations. Since they didn't have any idea or knowledge of how to design a device that was able to eliminate the surrounding vibrations, they just had to watch the show this way. However, through the off and on watching, they were shocked to see the recording of the past world. Both of them began to learn the Utana language, the language spoken on the recording. Gradually, they grasped words here and there and began to learn what the world was like in the past and what the problems were at the time. At the same time, Dr. Owen kept searching for a vibration free environment. Dr. Owen and Brian kept watching the recordings of the past world whenever they had time. What was amazing to both of them was that the recording seemed to never come to the end in just one crystal. There was so much information recorded in just one crystal.

A couple weeks later, Dr. Owen found out there was an empty room in a lab that was six stories underground. The lab belonged to the Physics Department and was home to a particle accelerator. The empty room was situated and isolated at the corner of that floor and had been the office of Professor Zhang, who had just passed away due to a brain tumor.

Dr. Owen went to the Physics Department to talk to the chairman, Dr. Rones, a scientist well-known throughout the world. Both Dr. Owen and Dr. Rones had met each other on several occasions.

"Dr. Rones, I have a favor to ask you. I am conducting an experiment and I need an environment that is free from vibration. I have heard you have such a room or office in the underground lab. Is that right?" Dr. Owen asked after they greeted each other.

"Yes, Dr. Owen, it was Professor Zhang's office. He just passed away a few weeks ago. How long will you need this room?" Dr. Rones asked.

It was very common that almost all of the professors on campus would support each other for their research whenever they could. So, it was not a surprise to Dr. Rones about Dr. Owen's request.

"I am not sure. A couple of months. Maybe longer,"

Dr. Owen answered.

"We have a new professor who will come to replace Dr. Zhang's position at the beginning of the new semester. That means he will be here at the end of August to get ready for the new semester. What date is it today? Yes, it is June 25. This will give you only about two months of time. Will that be long enough?" Dr. Rones asked.

"I will take whatever I can get. I deeply appreciate your assistance," Dr. Owen said.

"I will notify my secretary to give you a special pass to the underground lab. Do you need extra ones for any of your students?" Dr. Rones asked.

"Yes, I will need passes for two more other than myself. I will pick them up on the way out." Dr. Owen shook Dr. Rones's hand and showed his appreciation.

"Remember, August 25 you must move out. I am sorry," Dr. Rones said.

"Understood." Dr. Owen closed the door when he stepped out.

On the way to the secretary's office, Dr. Owen thought this was the best, and probably the only, chance that he and Brian would have to be able to see the images clearly and continuously. He had asked for an extra pass just in case. When he came to the secretary's office, she already had three passes ready. She asked him to write his and the students' names on the passes. He wrote his name and Brian's and told the secretary he might need another one, but he did not know for whom yet. The secretary told him that he could always come to see her for a new pass. He took only two with him.

* * *

They now had only two months of time to study the huge quantity of information recorded in the eight crystals. Dr. Owen and Brian were so excited and immediately went to the room to clean it. It was a small office; however, it was very comfortable for two people. They just had to re-arrange some of the chairs, sofa, and a desk. This would provide them enough space to set up the system.

The next morning they moved all the equipment to the underground office. It took them all morning to set up. At the same time, Brian set up a video recording system with four cameras situated at the four corners of the room so they could record the recording. They also spent some time insulating the room for soundproofing. This was to prevent outside people from hearing the conversations in the recordings since these sounds would be so strange to other people. They just didn't want to attract any special attention from other curious students or professors. To prevent someone who still had the key from entering the office, they put up a sign saying, "private research room, do not enter." Usually, out of mutual respect, this kind of sign would stop people from entering. This was very common on campus.

That evening they finished setting up. They could now watch the recording continuously; however, whenever they stopped and restarted it, the recording began from a different place. Dr. Torr had said he could not figure out how to rewind, stop and replay, or fast-forward or backward. Now, neither could they. They had not gotten any idea of how these functions worked.

Dr. Owen and Brian ignored almost everything else except watching the recording nearly ten hours per day. After they went home, they watched the DVDs they had made of the recordings and tried to learn the Utana language. They both knew that the more they learned of the language the better they would understand what was going on in the past. Brian postponed his thesis for one more year and Dr. Owen temporarily suspended his research at UCLA. Since this was summer vacation time, everyone understood. The last thing Dr. Owen needed to do before his retirement was to help Brian complete his thesis.

Eventually, they began to realize that all the features such as rewinding, stopping, replaying, etc. were done by oral command through some sort of controlling device like a computer. In addition, they also understood that the way to eliminate outside vibration was to place the entire reading device in an anti-gravity chamber in the air. But they did not know how such a chamber worked and they could not figure out how to make one anyway. It might be some technology far beyond today's. They had to be satisfied with watching pieces here and there.

After only one month, to help each other learn the new language, whenever Dr. Owen and Brian were alone, they spoke to each other in Utana. In just six weeks, they were able to speak the Utana language somewhat fluently. They had only two more weeks left to watch the recordings. However, they knew they might have watched only about five percent of the entire recordings on the eight crystals. They recorded to DVD as much as possible. During the last two weeks, they even took turns to record it, so they were able to record 24 hours per day.

On August 25, they moved out of the small lab and returned to Dr. Owen's basement. They continued to watch the recordings off and on and, at the same time, Dr. Owen kept searching for possible new secret vibration-free environments. But it was not easy.

One important recording they viewed was about the two polarities of the universe or of any living form. This had encouraged Dr. Owen to read more about the polarities whenever he could. The new semester began, and Brian began to focus on his thesis again. Dr. Owen studied more about the two polarities. He kept reading Master Dong's book, *Qigong Meditation - Embryonic Breathing*. The more he read, the more he understood.

Dr. Owen could not reach Dr. Torr anymore. It seemed he had just disappeared since Dr. Owen's return from Washington, D.C. Dr. Torr must have been moved to some secret place for interrogation. Dr. Owen would not doubt that the FBI might have found some evidence of what he was doing in the lab or from his basement. He just hoped all this interrogation would not lead the FBI to his door. He believed that he did not have much time to keep the secret hidden. Now, he also tried to eliminate any linkage or connection of the crystals' study with Brian. He simply did not want Brian to get involved with the FBI. He told Brian what had happened to Dr. Torr and encouraged him to concentrate on his thesis.

* * *

The FBI had, in fact, searched the underground lab and Dr. Torr's home again and again. From what they found, they concluded that he had conducted some experiments about memory crystals. However, they could not find any crystals. For further interrogation, the FBI moved Dr. Torr to a secret place where Dr. Torr explained to them what he was doing in the underground lab.

"Actually, I had figured out a possible theory of how to record and read memory crystals once we know how to fabricate them in outer space. My theory was that the entire recording and reading process must be done by molecular vibration. I was so excited and tried to prove my theory was correct. However, before I submitted it to the authorities, I felt I should conduct some experiments and verify my theory was correct. That is the reason for my frequent visits to the underground lab," Dr. Torr explained to two interrogators and also one young new scientific researcher.

"After nearly three months of testing, I realized that I could not conduct my experiment successfully, simply because we don't have the capability to fabricate memory crystals yet," he added as he looked at them and then sipped a mouthful of water right in front of them.

Since his explanation was reasonable and also, they could not find any proof that he was doing something against the government, after six months of studying the documents and material collected from his home and lab they began to believe him, and his life returned to normal. However, Dr. Torr knew he would still be watched for a long time. He did not know how long but he knew they would. Therefore, he did not contact Dr. Owen for a year. After a year, he resumed his contact with Dr. Owen but still avoided any topic related to memory crystals.

* * *

For a year, Brian concentrated all his efforts on writing his thesis. In his thesis, he simply wrote down his analysis about the cavern. He did not mention anything about the discovery of crystals or the reading device. Only he and Dr. Owen knew that his thesis had left out the history of 12 million years of a diminished past world. To anyone reading it, Brian's thesis was about 12 million years of oil cavern history. His thesis earned public recognition since it was the first published report for this kind of research. He graduated as an honored Ph.D. student. After his graduation, to avoid the FBI's suspicion, he also seldom visited Dr. Owen but continued watching his DVD recordings of the crystals in secret.

A couple of months after Brian's graduation he found a job in the San Francisco area and moved there. His girlfriend, Xiaoling, also moved there after she was awarded her master's degree in Oriental Philosophy six months later. They had been more than friends for a couple of years already. She worked for a Chinese trading company since she was able to speak Chinese and English fluently. Both Brian and Xiaoling had also become more and more interested in Chinese Qigong Meditation practice.

* * *

After Brian's graduation, Dr. Owen retired from teaching at UCLA. He continued watching the crystals' recordings in the basement of his house. He rebuilt his basement so that he could have a private room. This way he could spend time studying the past world without being disturbed.

He also improved the reading system. He discovered that if he insulated the whole reading device with spongy cushions and soft cotton, he could eliminate at least 70% of the surrounding vibrations. Though it was not as good as it had been underground, his improvement provided him some sense of the continuation of history.

After his retirement, Dr. Owen also began to be more and more interested in the theory of the "Two Polarities" and its relationship with meditation. He meditated at least two hours a day. After a year of meditation, he could begin to feel what Master Dong's book described about the two polarities. However, he still encountered many questions and difficulties with his practice.

Three years later Dr. Owen's wife, Jennifer, died of liver cancer. He felt very sorry that he had not spent more time with her during the last few years; instead, he had spent almost all of his time on his crystal studies. The only comfort he had was having a much better understanding of the secrets of the past world. In addition, it seemed he knew more and more about Chinese Qigong meditation. To him, the most amazing part was that the two polarities theory mentioned in Master Dong's book was almost the same as what he learned from the crystals. The more he watched the crystals, the more he was interested in this two polarities theory.

Dr. Owen felt like spending the rest of his life learning the theory of the "two polarities." He knew he had to also meditate so he would be able to experience the feeling of the two polarities and hopefully, through this understanding, he would be able to re-open his third eye. He sold his house in Los Angeles and moved to Garberville, in Northern California. According to what Brian told him, this area had a very strong and healthy energy, or Qi, and was one of the most desirable places for meditation. Actually, Master Dong's retreat center was not too far from this town.

Dr. Owen's new house was a couple of miles outside of the town and near the mountainous area where the closest neighbor was at least half a mile away. He felt peaceful and calm there. He called Dr. Torr and told him that he had moved to Northern California and gave him his new address. They didn't talk at all about the crystals. Both of them were afraid that Dr. Torr was still being watched. They just chatted like old friends who missed each other. It was true that Dr. Owen missed Dr. Torr very much, especially now. He had many things he wanted to discuss with him; especially what he knew about the past world and the synchronized vibrations of the two polarities. He also missed him because he was lonely, and he believed Dr. Torr would be good company.

Though he had a lot of memories to recall in his life, Dr. Owen still had ambitions and was interested in his future. Instead of waiting like most retired older people do, he decided to create his future. Now, he had two new very challenging projects. One was to complete his study about the 'past world.' His interest was not just to understand this past world, but also to learn and practice the knowledge recorded, especially about spiritual cultivation. He knew that spiritual science had not even taken its first step in the scientific development of today. Humans were still attracted by material enjoyments. Though humans had reached a very high level of material science, their understanding of the human spirit was still nearly empty. Human spiritual understanding was far behind material development. Because of this reason, humans were encountering a possible catastrophic crisis. They had the capability of destroying the entire human race but still did not understand the meaning of their lives.

"The American and Russian presidents agreed that each country could own 3,000 nuclear bombs," Dr. Owen recalled from announcement in the news a few years ago, "but it would take only 100 nuclear bombs to wipe out the entire human race. Why do we need more than 6,000 nuclear bombs on the earth? Are we crazy? Are we on the path of self-destruction? Will humanity have any hope for the future?" Dr. Owen asked himself.

He also believed the only way to prevent the same destiny as the past was to develop spiritual science. Human emotions had to be studied and understood. Humanity must learn how to jump out of its human emotional bondage. Spiritual cultivation was the only way, as he knew, not continuing material development for the satisfaction of material desires. Dr. Owen believed he would be able to re-open his third eye and become enlightened through studying Master Dong's book and from what he had learned about spiritual cultivation from the recordings of the 'past world.'

After he had been living in his new home for half a year, Dr. Owen decided to participate in Master Dong's upcoming summer Qigong retreat in the remote mountainous area that was only about 25 miles from his home.

Chapter 6
Spiritual World

Reunion

One early morning in June, the Northern California weather was beautiful, especially in the mountains. The top of the mountain was covered with white clouds and the woods were filled with mist. "In just a couple of hours, when the sun rises, all of these beauties will be gone," Dr. Owen thought as he walked up the mountain.

A few months after he moved here, Dr. Owen finally made up his mind to go see this old Chinese man, Master Dong, who had retired to this remote mountain area for spiritual cultivation through meditation. On the one hand, Dr. Owen was nervous and on the other, he was excited. It seemed strange that in one way he knew there was some truth hidden on this mountain and in another, he was nervous to face it. It was like he was stepping into a mysterious new dimension.

As he climbed up the mountain step-by-step, he felt like he was walking through his life - every step was difficult, but rewarding when accomplished. Life was a challenge, but every step was a mixture of sweetness and bitterness. He remembered Brian telling him that only a four-wheel drive car could reach the top, so he had parked his two-wheel drive car at the base of the mountain.

After nearly an hour of climbing, he was very tired. For his age, nearly 70 years old, this was hard work. He realized that his wish of searching for the truth was so strong that he did not mind the challenge. When he reached the top of the mountain, he could see a round house and a greenhouse. "This must be the center. Everything is just like Brian's description," he thought.

Master Dong's retreat center included 243 acres of mountain land that was classified as a Timber Production Zoning area. There was little commercial value. All the neighbors were at least a mile away. This was a most suitable place for Master Dong to build his retreat center. The mountain's Qi was so strong that it could be verified from hundreds of acres of huge redwoods along the Avenue of the Giants. At the bottom of this valley, the water flowed in the Eel River from the south of the mountain area to the north, and entered the Pacific Ocean at the town of Eureka.

When Master Dong purchased this land 15 years ago, from his first look he could already see that the landscape of this land was just like a three-dimensional Taiji Yin-Yang symbol. Near the Salmon Creek area there were five acres of flat land that would be suitable to build a studio for physical training and also for meditation. This place was considered to be the Yin polarity of the Yin-Yang symbol since it faced the North (Water) and the creek. This area was at an elevation of 200 feet. The environment of this area was able to bring the fire Qi down and make a person feel calm and peaceful. In the future, when the time was proper and finances allowed, Master Dong wanted to build a lodging house and a studio there.

On the very top of the mountain, on the Yang side of the Yin-Yang symbol, there was a small flat area that faced the South. This area was at an altitude of 1,050 feet. The round main house was situated in this area. Right in front of it were a few acres of meadow declining downward. In the far distance was another mountain with pine covered flanks that made for a beautiful view. Often, the top of this mountain area was covered by the clouds, especially in the winter and spring time. On the left-hand side, there was an old volcano called Bear Butte that reached an altitude of 2,200 feet. Clouds also often covered the top of this volcano area. It was said by local people that the energy was strong in this area due to the existence of this old volcano.

Between the top Yang and low Yin part of this Yin-Yang land, there was a dividing road that became the boundary line of the Yin and Yang domains. Amazingly, on the Yin side under this boundary line, water was abundant and there were three springs emerging out from the ground. On this side, there were many redwoods since redwoods needed plenty of water for their growth. On the Yang side, above this boundary line, the land was drier. The Qi was stronger there and good for nourishment.

* * *

It was nearly 7 o'clock in the morning when Dr. Owen arrived at the entrance of the house. He could hear the chanting sound of "Mmm" coming from inside. He was very excited and believed that he had found the correct place. When he stepped in, he realized that he had arrived at the end of a morning meditation session. The whole group of about 20 people noticed a stranger had suddenly appeared at the entrance to their meditation room. Among them were Brian and Xiaoling, who were very surprised to see him. They had not seen Dr. Owen for a few years now and were very excited and happy to see him.

"Hi, Professor Owen, it's Brian," Brian stepped forward and called Dr. Owen, who was standing at the entrance and did not know what to do next. When he saw Brian and Xiaoling, Dr. Owen also was very happy and excited.

"Hi, Brian and Xiaoling! I am so glad to see you here," Dr. Owen said when he saw them. "Actually, I didn't expect that you would be here." He smiled at them warmly.

"Yes, we have been coming here for the summer meditation retreat for the last three years," Brian said.

While they were talking, many people came to surround them. Brian introduced the students to Dr. Owen, then looked over at Master Dong. He saw Master Dong was answering the question of a student. Brian brought Dr. Owen to Master Dong's meditation place just as Master Dong finished his conversation with the student.

"Master Dong, this is Dr. Owen, the professor I've mentioned to you several times. He is one of the few people I admire and respect deep inside my heart," Brian introduced Dr. Owen to Master Dong.

"It is so nice to finally meet you," Master Dong said.

"Same here. Brian has told me about you many times. I finally had a chance to come visit you. Actually, I have moved to a town called Garberville near here," Dr. Owen said.

"Yes, it is only about 15 miles from here. We get most of our supplies there," Master Dong said.

"Master Dong, the reason that I've come here is that I'm hoping you can accept me as one of your meditation students. I have been reading your books for a few years and have become more and more interested in knowing more," Dr. Owen asked.

"Naturally, you are quite welcome. We are having our summer meditation retreat now until the end of this month. Come join us, if you have time," Master Dong said.

"I will stay here today and will begin to come every day starting tomorrow," Dr. Owen replied.

Dr. Owen joined the group for breakfast. After that, there was a one-hour break followed by the morning lesson beginning at 9 o'clock.

* * *

After breakfast, Dr. Owen, Brian, and Xiaoling went to a meadow near the lecture building. It seemed there were so many things they wanted to talk about. However, because of Xiaoling's presence, Dr. Owen hesitated to talk about the crystals. Brian could sense Dr. Owen's concern since he knew the crystal study had been both his and Dr. Owen's common subjects whenever they were together in the past.

"Professor Owen, I have told Xiaoling about the crystals. She also knows how serious it would be if the secret were revealed to the government," Brian told Dr. Owen. Dr. Owen knew they had been lovers for a few years already. It made sense that Brian would not hide this secret from her.

So Dr. Owen told Brian about what had happened to Dr. Torr and what he himself was doing. He also told Brian about the new place where he now lived.

"What made you come here for Master Dong's seminar, Professor Owen?" Xiaoling asked.

"Actually, after I read Master Dong's books about Qigong and Embryonic Breathing, I have become more and more interested in meditation. Especially after studying the recordings of the crystals, I have realized how deep the theory of the two polarities is and how much it can be applied to our lives, especially science. To understand it better, I decided to come here. Furthermore, the place I live now is not too far from here," Dr. Owen replied. "How much have I missed in the last two days of the seminars? I didn't know it began two days ago."

"Well, we have talked about the basic concepts of Qi

and Qigong and its relationship with nature and a human's health and longevity," Brian replied.

"Though I have studied Master Dong's books, would you summarize these concepts for me briefly? Actually, this will be a good review for you, too. Don't you think so?" Dr. Owen said.

"Basically, to the Chinese, Qi is any type of energy existing in nature. This energy includes those types we have understood and those we have not discovered or understood. The examples of those energies we have understood are heat, light, or electromagnetic energy, etc. The examples of those we have not yet understood are gravitational energy, cosmic energy, spiritual energy, or many others. However, when the Qi is applied to the energy circulating in a human body, it is bioelectricity, or some people prefer to call it bio-energy," Brian explained. "According to Master Dong's interpretation, the word Qi (氣) in Chinese is constructed by two words: air (气) and rice (米), meaning oxygen and glucose. This was because after a couple thousand years of Qigong development, the Chinese realized that the main energy supplies to our bodies actually were air and rice."

Dr. Owen nodded his head. Even though he had read about Qi, he had never thought it could be so simple and clear. He knew that was because he had paid more attention to the theory of the two polarities in Qigong.

"What does Qigong mean then?" Dr. Owen asked.

"Essentially, most of the Chinese who studied and practiced Qigong were more interested in humanity's health and longevity, therefore, nearly 70% of Qigong study in the past talked about human Qigong or, in other words, how to improve bioelectric energy circulation in the human body. As you know, all of our cells are alive and to keep them alive and healthy, they require the proper amount of Qi supply. Therefore, the quantity and the quality of the Qi's circulation have become the main issues of human Qigong study," Brian replied.

"How do you increase the Qi quantity in the human body?" Dr. Owen asked.

"Actually, there are many ways. You may receive extra Qi from various foods or herbs. You may also receive extra Qi from the trees or other living things. However, the most powerful practice is learning how to absorb extra Qi from cosmic and spiritual energy existing in nature. As you know, we are a part of nature. We are nature and nature is us. It cannot be separated. That means all types of energy are communicative and transportable from one to another. Only if you know how can you then absorb this energy. You know, we have isolated ourselves from nature and have lost this natural instinct of energy transportation," Brian said.

Brian was talking about Grand Qi Circulation between humans and nature, a topic that had not yet been written about by Master Dong. It caught Dr. Owen's interest, however. He asked, "These ways of increasing the quantity of Qi in Qigong practice are different from what Master Dong mentioned in his books. Didn't Master Dong write about improving the quantity of Qi in the area called the 'Dan Tian' (丹田) or 'elixir field?'"

"Yes, that's true. For any beginning Qigong practitioner, the first step to gaining extra Qi is through abdominal Dan Tian breathing. Through this abdominal breathing, the fat or the food essences stored in the body can be converted into extra Qi," Brian explained.

"Yeah, I read about that. How about the quality of the Qi's circulation? The second crucial key to health and longevity?" Dr. Owen asked.

"Well, as you know, Qi is a bioelectricity. In order to have a circulation of electricity, we must have an electromotive force or EMF. The whole key of improving circulation is finding all the possibilities of creating this electromotive force. It is just like an electric current. If there is no potential difference in the circuit, then electricity will not circulate," Brian explained. Of course, as a scientist Dr. Owen understood this simple concept of electric circulation.

"According to past Chinese experience, there are at least six ways of generating this EMF. The first one is food and air. Remember this was how the word Qi was created. Actually, the Chinese have discovered hundreds of herbs that are able to improve or enhance the Qi's circulation in the body. For example, Ginseng (人參) is one of them. This is the field of Chinese herbal medicine.

"The second way of generating EMF is through exercise. As you know, when you exercise, your blood circulation is enhanced. According to Dr. Becker's book, *The Body Electric*, a blood cell is a small battery which is able to store and release charges. That means if you improve the blood's circulation, you also improve the Qi's circulation. Third is Qi nourishment from nature. We are influenced by natural energy. For example, when there is a full moon, we are more energized. When the clouds are low, we feel energy is more trapped in our bodies. Our daily activities follow the sun's rising and falling. There are so many ways of gaining Qi from nature. As I mentioned earlier, this is called 'Grand Qi Circulation.'

"The fourth is through improving proper hormone production in the body. Hormones are called 'original essence' in Chinese Qigong society. As you know, hormones act as a catalyst for the body's biochemical reactions. That means improving the body's metabolism. Therefore, how to maintain proper production of the hormones is also a crucial key of improving Qi's circulation. The fifth is through artificial manipulation. Through methods such as acupuncture and massage, EMF can be created in the body to improve the Qi's circulation.

"Finally, the most important one is the mind. Through our thinking, the Qi can be led to a specific area so that physical action can be initiated. For example, if you wish to lift your arm, you must think first and then the Qi is led to the arm to activate the nerve system and muscles for action. We are still in the process of discussing the mind. Since this is a huge subject in Qigong practice, which is related to the two human polarities, Master Dong plans to take time to explain it over the next few days," Brian concluded.

"Wow, what a lecture! It seems that you understand

the subject pretty well, Brian." Dr. Owen was very impressed that Brian was able to use such a short time to explain a subject of a few thousand years' of study.

"I have been practicing with Master Dong for a few years now, remember? Actually, it took me some time to understand it to such a level," Brian said.

It seemed their one hour of break had passed very quickly. It was time for the next lecture.

* * *

Lectures and Discussion

Master Dong's lecture, actually, was a mixture of lecture and open discussion. A participant was encouraged to ask questions and initiate an open discussion whenever he or she wanted. Master Dong believed through this kind of teaching, it would be more interesting and more open minded. The lecture included all aspects of Qigong meditation practices.

First Lecture

Today's subject was about the Chinese concepts of Yin (陰) and Yang (陽). Chinese Yin and Yang theory was passed down from *The Book of Change* (*Yi Jing*, 易經) which was written more than 4,000 years ago.

"Chinese have always believed that there are two worlds or dimensions which are coexisting and mutually influence each other in this universe. One is called 'Yin Jian' (陰間) which means 'Yin world' while the other is called 'Yang Jian' (陽間) which means 'Yang world.' The Yin world belongs to the spiritual world where all spirits reside while the Yang world belongs to the material world where we are living. After any life dies, the spirit will separate with the physical body and enter into the spiritual world while the physical body re-enters the natural recycling process. When the time and opportunity allow, the spirit will re-enter the Yang world and be re-born. This is the concept of reincarnation. Today's science already understands a great deal about the Yang world, however, it knows very little about the spiritual world," Master Dong said.

"How did these Yin and Yang worlds begin?" one of the participants asked.

"Well, according to *The Book of Change*, there is a Taiji (太極) existing in nature. Taiji can be translated as 'Grand Ultimate,' however, it does not mean anything if you don't have a clear idea. The term 'Grand Ultimate' is pretty vague," Master Dong explained.

"Would you please explain it more specifically? This Taiji concept or theory is very difficult for us to understand, especially to non-Chinese," another participant asked.

"Naturally! Let's use an ancient document to explain the concept of Taiji. An ancient Qigong master, Wang, Zong-Yue (王宗岳) said: 'What is Taiji? It is generated from Wuji (無極) and is a pivotal function of movement and stillness. It is the mother of Yin and Yang. When it moves it divides and at rest it reunites.' From this, it is known that Taiji is not Wuji, and neither Yin nor Yang.

Instead Taiji is an invisible power of the natural world that controls pivotal functions of the universe. That means through Taiji, the Wuji can be derived into Yin and Yang and also through Taiji, the Yin and Yang can be reunited into the state of Wuji. This invisible natural power is called 'Dao' (道) and natural pivotal function of movement and stillness is called the 'De' (德). If I say it more clearly, 'De' is the manifestation of the 'Dao.' All of these 'Dao' and 'De' have therefore become the 'rule' of great nature," Master Dong explained.

"Then, what is Wuji? Can you tell us more?" another participant asked.

"Wuji means 'no extremity' which implies there are no polarities or discrimination of Yin and Yang. That means the 'emptiness' or 'a tiny spot of space.' You may say Wuji is nothingness or emptiness," Master Dong said. "Due to the existence of Taiji, all things are created from emptiness and discriminated. It is from this Taiji the Yin and Yang worlds were created from nothingness. As I said earlier, this power or Taiji is also called 'Dao.' This Taiji or Dao may be called 'God' in your society," he continued while using his right hand to draw a Taiji and Yin-Yang flowing chart on a large flip-chart pad at the front of the room.

"These Yin and Yang worlds mutually relate to and influence each other. It seems there are two worlds, but actually in function, there is only one since they cannot be separated from each other. Again, as I said earlier, according to *The Book of Change*, everything can be classified as Yin or Yang. Due to Taiji, Wuji can be discriminated into Yin and Yang, and also due to Taiji, Yin and Yang can be reunited into Wuji again. During this creation and reunification process, spiral patterns are commonly seen. That means when 'Dao' has been manifested into 'De,' it has commonly shown the spiral action. For examples, black holes, tornados, hurricanes, seashells, or even things as tiny as DNA are all spiral manifestation of the 'Dao,'" Master Dong continued, realizing that this concept was very difficult for Westerners to understand.

"Originally, I thought that Taiji meant Yin and Yang discrimination. Now, it seems that Taiji is something invisible between Wuji and Yin-Yang," a female participant said.

"Yes, this is a common mistake in today's Western Taijiquan society. Most of the people practicing Taijiquan today misunderstand and think that Taiji is Taijiquan. This is a mistake. Taiji is actually a philosophy dating back more than 4,000 years and is recorded in *The Book of Change*. Taijiquan is a martial art style that was created based on the theory of Taiji. Remember, whenever Chinese specify fist (Quan, 拳) or palm (Zhang, 掌) behind a phrase, it usually implies a style of martial arts, such as Taijiquan (太極拳), Changquan (長拳), Shaolinquan (少林拳), or Baguazhang (八卦掌)," Master Dong explained. "Therefore, Taijiquan is a martial arts style which uses the concept of Taiji. If I use a circle to represent a universe, and there is nothing inside, it is a Wuji state or emptiness. However, if there is a discrimination of Yin and Yang in this circle, then it is in a Yin-Yang state," Master Dong continued, flipping the paper over and using the marker to draw a circle and Yin-Yang symbol.

"Then, what is the symbol for Taiji? Can you use a symbol to represent it?" Xiaoling asked.

"Actually, Taiji is an invisible power and cannot be illustrated by a drawing. However, due to Taiji, Wuji has gradually been derived into Yin-Yang. If we choose the middle point of this derivation, what we should see is a spiral." Master Dong again drew an illustration that showed the manifestation of Taiji.

"Remember, what I have drawn is a two-dimensional manifestation of Taiji. If it is expressed in the three-dimensional world, it should be a three-dimensional spiral. That is why I said earlier that when Taiji or Dao have been manifested into De, it is a spiral motion such as a black hole, tornados, or even DNA," he looked at the students and said.

"Can this Taiji be called the spirit of nature?" one participant asked.

"Naturally. In the Western world, you call this spirit 'God' and in China, it is called 'Dao,'" Master Dong said.

These basic Chinese concepts of Wuji, Taiji, and Yin-Yang had interested Dr. Owen greatly. He asked, "According to what you said, because of the existence of Taiji, the Yin and Yang worlds are created. Can Taiji again discriminate Yin into Yin-Yin and Yin-Yang, and also Yang into Yang-Yin, and Yang-Yang?"

Actually, Dr. Owen had read about the derivation

concepts of Yin and Yang, Two Polarities, into Four Phases. Eventually, the Four Phases could again be derived into Eight Trigrams, and so on. However, he wished to hear Master Dong's personal explanation.

"Yes, if you are inside the Yin world or Yang world, you will be in the Wuji state. From this Wuji state, it can be again divided into Yin and Yang through the influence of Taiji. Everything is relative and hardly absolute. For example, if you are outside of a moving vehicle, what you see is a moving vehicle. However, if you are inside of the vehicle, you will see no moving vehicle and feel still. That means when you are in the moving vehicle, you are in a Wuji state. From this Wuji state, Yin and Yang can be discriminated again," Master Dong replied and again drew the derivation of Yin-Yang into Yin-Yin, Yin-Yang, Yang-Yin, and Yang-Yang.

"Does this mean that if we are in the Yang world or material world, then this material world can be again discriminated into Yang and Yin? Isn't this the theory of matter and anti-matter claimed by Einstein and some other scientists in the 1940s?" Dr. Owen's thinking got deeper and deeper.

"I believe so. Actually, as I heard, the theory of matter and anti-matter was proven correct only in the last 20 years in Germany," Master Dong replied.

"In that case, is it reasonable to assume that this universe has two polarities? One being the center of matter and the other the center of anti-matter?" Dr. Owen asked again.

"Yes. Dr. Owen, your questions are very profound.

Actually, according to Chinese belief, any living matter formalized in an energy field of two polarities will also have two polarities. It is just like if you placed a metal object within the two polarities of a magnetic field, the metal object itself will have two polarities. Therefore, if there is any life form formalized in the influence of two polarities, it will have two polarities. For example, you may see the shape of an egg as an ellipse that has two polarities. Actually, scientists have also confirmed that even a tiny cell has two polarities," Master Dong explained.

"Can we then assume that the universe we are living within has the shape of an ellipse just like an egg has two polarities?" Dr. Owen asked.

"Logically, we can assume so. However, we still don't know the truth of it since science is not able to prove it yet," Master Dong said.

The rest of the lecture focused on the introduction and the practice of Normal Abdominal and Reverse Abdominal Breathing commonly practiced by Chinese Buddhist and Daoist Qigong practitioners. After that, different groups of three to four people were arranged for discussion groups. The morning session was over. The afternoon was open for students to practice the different breathing techniques.

The first lecture and discussion had already deeply stimulated and inspired Dr. Owen's thinking. When the day's session was over, since Brian had a four-wheel drive car, he and Xiaoling brought Dr. Owen down to the base of the mountain.

"Here is my car, thank you. It is still early. Would you like to come to my home and sit for a while? It's been a long time. My place is not too far from here," Dr. Owen asked.

Since Brian and Xiaoling had nothing important to do at the retreat center that evening, they decided to follow Dr. Owen's car and go to his home.

As they walked in his front door, Dr. Owen asked, "Brian, I never dreamt that we would meet again, especially in such a place. Where do you live now?"

"We are living together now in the San Francisco area. Actually, it took us only four hours to get here," Brian replied.

"Can you give me your address, e-mail, and telephone number? Just in case I decide to come visit you in San Francisco. You know, my younger son, Robert, is still living there," Dr. Owen said.

"Of course, Dr. Owen. You are welcome to visit us anytime." Brian took his pen from his pocket, found a piece of paper on the table and wrote down the information for Dr. Owen.

"Are you still watching those crystal recordings, Professor?" Xiaoling asked.

"Yes. It is amazing that even though I have been watching them for so many years, often I see something new. However, I began to see some repetition. I am guessing that I may have watched about two-thirds of the entire recording," Dr. Owen replied.

"Do you still record the recordings onto DVDs?"

Brian asked.

"Yes, I do. That way it's easier for me to find the section I want. You know, the crystal recording itself jumps from place to place," Dr. Owen replied. Then, "Come, let me take you to my viewing room." He led Brian and Xiaoling to a corner room where all of the windows were covered by thick black cloths. It was exactly like a dark room. Dr. Owen turned the light on.

"As you see, I have modified the reading system. Now, the disturbances from surrounding vibrations are not as serious as before, however, it is still not as good as what we saw in the underground office," Dr. Owen said.

Since it was impossible to watch all of the crystal recordings, Dr. Owen only demonstrated 20 minutes or so to Xiaoling since this was the first time she actually saw it, even though she had heard about it from Brian many times. She was so amazed to see how the three-dimensional images could be extended to be as large as the entire room or shrunk to as small as a basketball. She was shocked to see the advanced technologies that had been developed in the past world.

They returned to the living room and drank Chinese Wulong tea, Dr. Owen's favorite. Brian and Dr. Owen talked about the past, especially the exploration of the oil mine. Xiaoling just sat there and listened with curiosity. Time passed quickly. Xiaoling helped Dr. Owen prepare a simple dinner while Brian kept himself in the dark room and watched the memory crystal.

"Professor Owen, I can come to pick you up tomorrow morning," Brian offered after dinner.

"That's OK, Brian. I prefer walking up to the mountain. I am getting old quickly. I need exercise," Dr. Owen replied.

"Well, how about I bring you down the mountain again like today," Brian again offered.

"OK. It will be nice to get together as much as we can while you are here. Come tomorrow night again," Dr. Owen invited.

"OK. It's a deal," Brian said. Then he and Xiaoling said good night and left.

After they had gone, Dr. Owen kept thinking about the day's lecture. He searched for similar theories in the DVD recordings of the past world. He could see from the recording that meditation was commonly practiced in daily life at that time. He was wondering if, since the development of science at the time had already advanced about 500 years more than today, he might find some clue about the two polarities of the universe or about anti-matter. From what he knew, the past world had already untied the mystery of anti-gravity and applied it to daily activities. In addition, he also kept thinking about the recording theory of crystal memory through the theory of the two polarities. To him, this new project of understanding two polarities and applying it to a crystal recording was another challenge and excitement in his life. All he wanted was to learn the truth – he wanted nothing for glory, power, or wealth. Since he was nearly 70 years old, all of these had no meaning or temptation for him anymore. He could not wait for the next lecture and discussion session. He wished that Dr. Torr was there with him. He knew that Dr. Torr would be a good partner for discussing all of this. However, he was afraid to contact him and mention anything about the two polarities. He began to read Master Dong's books again. It seemed that he could read his books repeatedly and learn or comprehend new things each time.

Second Lecture

The next morning, Dr. Owen again drove his car and parked it at the base of the mountain. However, he came much earlier this time. He remembered that he had arrived at the meditation hall near the end of the session, at 7:00 yesterday morning. He knew now that the morning meditation began at 6:00. Dawn was the best time for meditation when the surrounding natural energy was changing from Yin to Yang. Therefore, he took off at 4:30 in the morning from his house. When he arrived at the base of the mountain, it was 4:52. Then he walked up step by step with a flashlight he had brought. He didn't have a hard time finding the way since he had been there yesterday, and the road was pretty straight. When he arrived, it was only 5:50, ten minutes early. However, he could already see a few people there, sitting down with their eyes closed. Brian and Xiaoling were among them, sitting near the corner of the room. He picked up a meditation cushion and sat down. Within the next ten minutes, all of the participants were there. At 6:00, Master Dong came down from upstairs and sat down.

"Good morning, everyone!" Master Dong looked at everyone. "Are there any questions from yesterday's meditation?" he asked.

"I found out that it is very difficult to calm down my mind. It was always drifting off with some thought. It's not easy to reach the state of 'the thinking of no thinking' and 'the thought of no thought,'" one of the female participants said.

"Naturally. As I mentioned in the last couple of days, the mind is always the biggest obstacle in meditation. Regulating the mind has always been the most important issue in Qigong practice," Master Dong said. "There are two crucial keys to bringing the mind to the neutral state, that means the state of 'the regulating of no regulating.'"

Master Dong took a look at the group and said, "The first key in reaching this goal is to get rid of the thoughts hanging in your mind."

"I tried and it didn't work. The more I wanted to get rid of it, the more my mind was stuck deeper," a participant said.

"Naturally. The way of handling it is to find the root of thinking. That means to recognize the origin of the thought and then pull the root out. Remember, we have two minds, an emotional mind and wisdom mind. The emotional mind can be disturbed and make you upset while your wisdom mind is rational and helps you calm down. For example, when you encounter a traffic jam, after a long time without moving, you will become impatient and lead yourself to be emotionally upset. However, if you use your wisdom to analyze it and ask yourself, 'Will the traffic improve if I am upset?' Naturally, the answer is no. Once you have recognized this fact, then your wisdom mind will take over. The wisdom mind then says, 'Why don't you listen to the music and relax? You may also use this time to practice Qigong while waiting.' In no time, the traffic moves again. This is the way of pulling out the root of emotional thinking," Master Dong explained.

"Let us ponder a story from Japanese Zen society, about a bold and handsome young Samurai warrior standing before an aged Zen master, asking, 'Master, I have reached a high level of Zen theory and practice, but would like to ask a serious question.'

The master humbly replied, 'May I ask what question you would like to ask?'

'Please teach me about heaven and hell?' the Samurai replied.

The master froze motionless for just a moment and then suddenly snapped his head in disgust and seethed, 'Teach you about heaven and hell? I doubt you could even keep your own sword from rusting, you ignorant fool. How dare you suppose you could understand anything I might have to say?'

The old man went on, becoming more insulting, while the young swordsman's surprise turned first to confusion, then to dismay and hot anger. Master or no master, who insults a Samurai and lives? At last, teeth clenched and blood boiling in blind fury, the warrior drew his sword and wanted to end the old man's tirade and life.

The master looked straight into his eyes and said gently, 'That is hell.'

At the peak of his rage, the Samurai realized this was indeed his teaching, that the master had driven him into a living hell of uncontrollable anger and ego. The young man, profoundly humbled, sheathed his sword and bowed to this great spiritual teacher. Looking into the wise man's aged, beaming face, he felt more love and compassion than he had ever felt in his life. The master, sensing the changed demeanor, raised his index finger and said, 'And that is heaven.'

"Emotional disturbances are created from false illusions in the mind. Do we create heaven and hell in our minds, and keep ourselves trapped in this matrix, or do heaven and hell really exist?" Master Dong asked.

"Once you have recognized this fact, then most emotional disturbances can be stopped," Master Dong said again.

"Then what is the second crucial key to calm down the mind?" a participant asked.

"The second key of calming down the mind is to stop

new thinking from initiating. The key of this is paying attention to your abdominal breathing. When your mind stays at the abdominal area, the Qi will be led downward from the upper body. In this case, it will cool down the brain's function. In addition, when you pay attention to breathing, you will move your mind away from initiating another thought. The emotional mind is considered a monkey mind that is small but unsteady. However, the wisdom mind can be compared to a horse which is big and powerful yet can be calm and controlled," Master Dong explained. "Actually, in order to calm down the monkey mind, you will need a banana. Breathing is a banana. By using this banana, you will be able to lead the monkey into a cage and lock it there. That's why breathing is considered a strategy in Qigong practice."

He continued, "It's been 20 minutes already. I hope everyone focuses on regulating the mind this morning through deep abdominal breathing. When you have reached a semi-sleeping state, you have probably reached the state of 'regulating of no regulating.' When this state has been reached, the truthful subconscious mind will wake up. This subconscious mind is the key of connecting with nature. Now, let us meditate for 40 minutes."

During the meditation, Dr. Owen kept thinking about what Master Dong said. He tried to calm down his mind, but it was not easy at all. He also tried to concentrate his mind on his breathing. However, somehow it would last only a few minutes before his thoughts interfered again. He began to analyze the mind: "What is the mind?" "Is it energy or matter?" "It is neither. However, when it is manifested, it can be very powerful. The mind can create and also destroy. The mind is the key to deciding each individual's life." "How much does today's science understand the mind?" "Not at all." "We still cannot even understand more than 12% of the brain's function." "How can we use this limited understanding to interpret nature? How ridiculous we are!" Dr. Owen's mind kept asking these questions and could not stop. Before he knew it, the early meditation session was almost over and he was hearing Master Dong's voice.

"Now, gradually bring your mind back here. First, interlock your hands and stretch your torso upward a few times. Then, turn your body from side to side while stretching." Master Dong raised his arms and led the class doing the same stretching exercise.

"Next, place both hands on your knees and use them as leverage to move your spine section by section." Again, he led the class through it.

"Now, use the tips of your fingers to tap your head from the center to the sides and from the front to the back. After a few times, use both palms to brush the head from the forehead backward to the rear neck." While he was explaining it, he did the same.

"Finally, close your eyes and make a humming sound of 'Mmm' loudly. This will generate a vibration for your brain cells." He did it while everyone followed. Actually, everyone but Dr. Owen already knew this recovery process since it had been done each of the last three mornings.

After meditation, Dr. Owen went over to greet Brian and Xiaoling. Together, they went to the dining room for breakfast and sat down.

"What could be the possible difference between the minds of today's people and the minds of past or future people? From what I understand about the people in the past world, they could live for around 700 years. What would the mind be like at that time? What was the meaning of life?" Dr. Owen asked.

"I think we won't find out until we are in that situation. I don't know if they had the same emotional bondage as we have today. I also wonder if they had the same structure of a human matrix dominated by emotions that hold back the entire spiritual evolution of man. You know, we have created power, wealth, glory, dignity, honor, pride, happiness, sadness, and so on. After we created them, we have been brainwashed by society and then we kill each other for these false feelings. I just wonder, if we had evolved for another 500 years, would we be still in this emotional bondage?" Brian asked. "Have you discovered any of this from what you have seen of the past world, Professor Owen?"

"Actually, from what I have seen so far, due to a different social structure and mentality at that time, they also had different kinds of emotional conflicts. However, I still need to ponder a lot of the details. I believe I will come to a conclusion soon," Dr. Owen replied.

* * *

"Since there were so many questions about the mind in this morning's meditation session, I think it would be a good idea to discuss it further," Master Dong said at the beginning of the 9 a.m. morning lecture.

"Remember what I said yesterday, Taiji is the natural power which is able to create everything from nothingness. From this Taiji, the Yin and Yang can be initiated or discriminated. In Chinese society, it is said that nature is the Grand Heaven and Earth, which means Grand Universe, while a human is a Small Heaven and Earth, which means Small Universe. The reason for this is because any life form formalized in the Grand Universe will also copy the structure of the Grand Universe. For example, all living forms in the Grand Universe are just like cells of this universe and all of these forms are re-cycled. Naturally, comparing with the life of a universe, all of the lifetimes of these life forms are very short. It is the same in a human body, the Small Universe, which is constructed by countless different cells. Again, comparing with a human life, the lifetime of these cells is short and also re-cycled. Today, scientists have verified that each cell has two polarities and has its own memory. In addition, each cell contains all of the DNA information in the entire body. Therefore, we are able to clone a human simply from a tiny cell," Master Dong said.

"If there is a Taiji in the Grand Universe, then is there a Taiji in the Small Universe? If there is, then what is it?" a participant asked.

"It's a good question. In nature, there is a Taiji or Dao, also called 'God' in the Grand Universe. There is also a Taiji or Dao or 'God' in a human body. If I use the concept of Taijiquan to explain, it may be clearer for you. At the beginning of the Taijiquan movements, you stand there motionless with a calm mind. This state is commonly called the 'Wuji' state since there is no clear discrimination of Yin and Yang yet. Then, once you begin the movements, Yin and Yang are immediately discriminated. For example, forward is considered Yang and backward is considered Yin, right is Yang and left is Yin, upward is Yang and downward is Yin, external physical movement is Yang while internal Qi circulation is Yin. You can see, from stationary to the first move, Yin and Yang have already been discriminated. What makes this discrimination happen is the Taiji. In this case, what do you think this Taiji is in the human body, Brian?" Master Dong asked.

"The mind, sir. It is the mind that initiates the action. Therefore, the mind is Taiji in a human body," Brian answered.

"You are correct. A human mind is able to travel from one galaxy to another instantly without any restriction. Not only that, this mind can be in the past or in the future without bondage. This mind is the mighty God of the Human Small Universe. This mind leads or governs the Qi or energy and manifests it into physical action. Remember scientists have already confirmed that through thinking alone, you can get sick, and through thinking alone, you can heal yourself. In nature, this

Taiji is the natural spirit or 'God' and in human this Taiji is the mind," Master Dong said.

"Then, what are the differences between the natural spirit and the human mind? Does nature have a mind? Why do we differentiate between the spirit and the mind?" a participant asked.

"Well, spirit is truthful without a matrix, while often the mind is not truthful and in the matrix. As you know, our mind has been brainwashed or educated so as to fit in this society since we are born. Since then, we have been trapped in this human emotional matrix. The first chapter of *Dao De Jing* said, 'Dao, if it can be spoken (with words), (then) it is not the true regular forever lasting Dao. Name, if it can be named (with words), (then) it is not the true regular forever lasting name.' Remember, we created everything from our mind, glory, dignity, power, greediness, happiness, sadness, etc. and then trapped ourselves inside. Actually, nature doesn't have emotion. It shows neither mercy nor compassion. Not only that, we also give a name for everything. We define what is black and what is white. We define what is right and what is wrong, and all the others. Once we have created this matrix, then we lie to each other. Actually, honestly speaking, all of us have a mask on our face. That means we are not truthful. The mind is the control of all of this. Spirit is not the mind. All humans in all different societies in the past have experienced it but yet cannot explain what it is. All I know is the natural spirit is truthful and without a mask."

"Then why do we put the mask on?" a participant

asked.

"Well, since this human matrix was created from the beginning of human culture, the entire human society has a mask. If you don't have a mask, then you will be abused in this masked society," Master Dong replied. "The question is, if we continue to put the mask on and dare not to face the truth of nature, then we will be in the emotional matrix forever and human mutual conflict will never stop."

"Then how can we recognize this human matrix? And how can we be truthful?" another participant asked.

"Meditation is the key entrance of this recognition. From meditation, you gradually regulate your mind until all of the emotional bondage can be set free. When this happens, your conscious mind will be suppressed, and your subconscious mind will begin to wake up. Usually, this happens in deep meditation semi-sleeping states. It is the same often when you are in a semi-sleeping state, the truth comes out and this subconscious mind will lead you to the right path of spiritual cultivation."

"Are you implying that the subconscious mind is the key to the entrance of spiritual understanding?" Brian asked.

"Yes, to many scientists, it is believed that gravity is the boundary line of this dimension and the other dimension, and to Chinese Buddhist and Daoist meditators, the subconscious mind is the boundary line of the Yang material world and Yin spiritual world."

"Would you explain it more clearly, please?" Dr. Owen asked suddenly.

"Well, as you know, science today has understood many types energy, however, it still cannot untie the mystery of gravity. If we really understood what gravity is, then we would be able to manipulate it and apply it in daily life. I mean we should able to create anti-gravity. When this happens, then we will not need much energy at all. Simply, through manipulation of gravitational and the anti-gravitational forces, we would have unlimited energy. For example, we could have flying cars without fuel. Many scientists believe that gravity is the borderline of this dimension and another coexisting dimension. If we are able to untie this mystery, we can then travel to another dimension. Similarly, from *The Book of Change (Yi Jing)*, it is believed that there are two dimensions coexisting. One is the material world that has some energy forms, and there is another dimension, the spiritual dimension, which is not yet understood. I explained this a couple of days ago. The spiritual dimension and the material dimension are coexisting and mutually influence each other. It is from this spiritual energy that matter and anti-matter are materialized in this universe. When a living being such as a human dies and enters the recycling process, the spirit will re-enter the spiritual dimension," Master Dong said.

"If we knew how to enter into the other dimension from the dimension we are in, can we travel in the other dimension and then again materialize into matter and re-enter the material dimension?" Dr. Owen again asked. To many participants, his questions were very profound and mysterious. However, to Dr. Owen, these questions might help him untie the mystery of how those people in the past world traveled in the ways that he saw in the crystal recordings. He thought, "It seemed they were able to travel in the other dimension since they had untied the mystery of gravity."

"How could we reach the other dimension, if possible?" Dr. Owen asked again.

"As I know, you must first neutralize the thoughts you have generated in this dimension and allow the subconscious mind to wake up. When you have reached a profound meditative state, your spirit and the natural spirit will unite. This is called 'unification of human and heaven' in Chinese meditation," Master Dong said. "The way of reaching this stage, as I know, is through Embryonic Breathing."

"How about the heaven eye or third eye? Do you have to open it for this unification?" Dr. Owen asked anxiously. He had read Master Dong's book and knew that the third eye's opening was the crucial key to this unification.

"As I know, often when you have reached a deeply profound state, your subconscious mind will wake up. This will provide you a higher level of spiritual sensitivity in communicating with nature. However, this is not a unification of the human and natural spirit. In order to have unification, you must first re-open the 'heaven eye' or the 'third eye.' Once you are able to, then there is no obstacle between your spirit and the natural spirit. When this happens, you will be able to feel or sense a lot of natural phenomenon which other people cannot. That means you will have become a prophet and are able to foresee natural disasters such as earthquakes, tornados, hurricanes, and tsunamis, all of these natural energy changes or disasters. Not only that, you will have the capability of telepathy. That means to communicate with other life forms without speaking," Master Dong explained.

"When you have reached this stage, can you use your concentrated mind to make matter move?" Dr. Owen asked.

"I believe so, if you have reached a profound level. Scientists have conducted some experiments in the past. For example, when sand is dropping from a hole above, if your mind does not interfere, the center of the pile will be right under the hole. However, if you concentrate and keep thinking about moving to the left while watching, it is verified that the center of the pile will be shifted to the left. From Chinese *Yi Jing*, it is believed that the forces of two dimensions are able to influence each other. When there is a change in one dimension, there is also a change in the other dimension. For example, many fortunetellers in the past would be able to tell your fortune from three or four sticks dropped from above. Different arrangements meant a different energy force was developing in the other dimension. Eventually, this force would cause some consequence in this dimension."

"All of these explanations seemed impossible. But what do we really know about nature? Actually, we know nothing compared with all of the remaining mysteries existing in nature. All of these had been experienced both in the West and the East in the past. The question is, how can we do it?" Dr. Owen thought.

* * *

The lecture was over. The morning's discussion had many people wondering and confused. They were doing a lot of thinking indeed. However, to Dr. Owen, since he had watched the recordings of the past world, he knew all of these things were possible.

After the lecture, Dr. Owen, Brian, and Xiaoling went together into the dining room for lunch. In the entire group, probably only Brian could understand why Dr. Owen asked all of those questions. He knew if Professor Owen could obtain the answers from Master Dong, it might lead him to a deeper understanding of the past world.

In Dr. Owen's mind, he remembered what Dr. Torr had told him. The memory in the crystals was stored by synchronized vibrations between two polarities. When this vibration was influenced by the surrounding energy, the information could be recorded in the crystal molecules. If this were the case, then every energy disturbance in this universe would also have been recorded. He kept thinking about all of this and looked at Brian.

"If this universe is constructed by two polarities as Master Dong believes, then any event that happened in this universe in the past will also be recorded. That means if we were able to access the recorded spiritual memory of nature, we would be able to acquire unlimited knowledge from all of the past civilizations in this universe. That also means we would be able to trace back history accurately through this spiritual memory," Dr. Owen said.

"From what I understand, if we could access this spiritual memory through the re-unification of humans and nature, then it would be possible that an individual could receive all mighty knowledge and power beyond anyone's belief," Brian said.

"Yes. That means this individual would be able to use the force or the power of other dimensions to influence the structures of or changes to this dimension. These influences could make an object move or even change one's destiny," Dr. Owen said.

"Would the spiritual energy transform into a life form, or some lower level of energy existing in the material dimension?" Xiaoling asked.

"Theoretically, the material world is a manifestation of the Yin force, that is 'spiritual energy.' That means that if we are able to access the Yin spiritual dimension, we will be able to change anything in the material dimension," Dr. Owen replied.

The discussion was getting more and more weird. It seemed that all of this talk was ridiculous. However, how do we know it was not possible? After all, we still don't know nature. Today's science is only in its beginning stage of development. If we used the technology developed 500 years later to judge today's science, then today's technology would seem like nothing at all.

* * *

Again, the afternoon session was a group discussion. Everyone offered his opinion about the morning's discussion; however, all of the discussions were shallow and did not interest Dr. Owen very much. He kept thinking about the morning's discussion. He could not wait to go home and watch the recording of the past world and hopefully figure out some answers from it.

It was around 6:00 p.m. by the time all the activities were over. Brian told Dr. Owen that he and Xiaoling would like to stay to join the evening's meditation session, even though he had promised that they would visit him again that night. Dr. Owen understood. Actually, he was very anxious to go home and watch the history of the past world. He remembered seeing a section where the Utana had already emigrated to Mars and also had begun to develop the moons Piya (Europa) and Tina (Callisto) of Jupiter. From what he saw, it seemed they were able to travel through another dimension. Stana dimension, the Utana called it. Wasn't this what Master Dong talked about when he spoke of the spiritual dimension? From the technological development at the time, since they had already had anti-gravity technology, it was reasonable to believe that Utana had already had the capability of crossing the boundary line and entering the spiritual dimension.

Dr. Owen took his time walking down the mountain. Brian offered him a ride, but Dr. Owen said he preferred walking today since it was the second-best time of the day - the sun was going down and all of the energy in the area began to cool down. He believed the best time was still the early morning at dawn when clouds covered the tops of the mountains and the woods were filled with mist. As he walked down, a lot of thoughts came to him. He was very excited and anxious to know more about ancient meditation. After watching those recordings for such a long time, he knew all of the crystals belonged to a young Utana named Aidan Stou Buta, who was 285 years old at the time. As he understood, the average age of the time was 700-800 years old. He remembered that Aidan was learning meditation from an old master. Dr. Owen was hoping that he would be able to learn some meditation theory and methods from the past world. Actually, after so many years, he had reorganized all of the information recorded on DVD. Whenever he found a new recording in the crystal, he would place it chronologically into the place he thought it should be. As a result, the information on this new DVD compilation had become more continuous and complete. He had begun to make sense of the entire recording. Now, he was working on a book or report about this past world through the personal history of Aidan Stou Buta.

While he was thinking about this, Dr. Owen came to his parking place. It was much easier to come down than go up. It had taken him only 35 minutes. When he got home, he warmed up some leftovers from last night's dinner with Brian and Xiaoling. Then, after finishing his dinner, he fixed a pot of nice Wulong tea and went to the corner room. He began to search for his DVD recording of the meditation session. When he compared the teaching in the past world with Master Dong's, he was amazed that they were so similar and consistent, especially the concept of the two polarities. Since he was able to learn from two sources at the same time, his understanding improved rapidly. "Alas, I really wish that Dr. Torr could be here with me. He would be a good meditation partner, especially on the theory side," he thought. He could not wait until the next morning's lecture. It seemed that he had learned so much in just two days.

Third Lecture

As he had yesterday morning, Dr. Owen arrived at the meditation hall around 5:50 a.m. Again, he saw Brian and Xiaoling sitting in the same place as yesterday. There were only about ten people there now. They all had closed their eyes, trying to relax their bodies and calm down their minds.

Dr. Owen found the same place he sat in yesterday. Even in just two days, he had become acquainted with almost all 20 participants. To his surprise, the group included a few Western physicians, a couple of retired professors, some engineers, and a few young participants. It was a mixed group and covered all kinds of people. He believed that each one of them had his or her own reason for coming here to learn this meditation. However, almost all of them were interested in searching for the truth of nature, especially the spiritual side. After all, we understand so little about this side. We are still in the spiritual bondage of all kinds of sects. Dr. Owen believed the way of setting yourself free from this spiritual bondage was through meditation and self-awakening.

The first step was daring to open the mind and accept other meditation cultures which had been developed and practiced for thousands of years. He knew that since the industrial revolution, material science had advanced so rapidly that spiritual science had lagged far behind. Traditionally, throughout human history, spiritual and material development were always advancing together at the same pace until modern material science had suddenly bloomed in such a short couple of hundred years. For this reason, now we were enjoying material luxury but felt empty inside. The meaning of life had become shallower in today's world. However, the worst part of it was that due to the fast development of the material sciences, now we had the capability to destroy the entire human race.

Again, Dr. Owen remembered that only a few years ago, both the American and Russian presidents signed an agreement that each country was allowed to have 3,000 nuclear bombs. "How many bombs are needed to destroy the entire human race? Actually, just 100 would do it," he thought. "Are we crazy? Why are we trapped in such a crisis? Can catastrophe be avoided in the near future? How did all of this happen? Isn't this caused because of the human emotional matrix we have created?"

And then, "What happened to the past world? Are we on the same path to self-destruction?" The more he thought of it, the more he needed to find the truth about the past world. Not only that, he deeply believed that what he did to hide the secret of the crystals from the government was rational. He knew that all governments wanted to find new technologies for their weapons development. He also deeply realized that the way of preventing future catastrophe was through spiritual development.

"I wish the government would spend tax money on spiritual science development instead of on weapons," he could not stop his thinking.

* * *

As usual, at 6:00 a.m. Master Dong came down to the meditation hall from upstairs. By now, all the participants were there. He took a look at every one and asked, "How many of you believe what I said yesterday?"

More than half of the participants raised their hands. Master Dong smiled and said, "If you do, then you have been brain-washed."

Master Dong went on, "You should understand that it does not matter what you have heard or read. It is only a personal opinion. Naturally, this includes my books and lecture. They are only my personal belief or understanding. You should always add a question mark to everything you hear and read. If you don't have this attitude, then you can be brainwashed easily. This was how a sect begins, blind belief. You must always keep this in your mind.

"Everything is relative instead of absolute. Often, there is a right thing from one point of view, and it can be wrong from the other angle. Therefore, before you believe something, you must first ponder and try to see it from different angles. After pondering, you will see the logical sense of it. If it does not make sense, then keep searching for the answer and verification. Remember, the reason for your coming here is to find some inspiration and stimulation of your thinking instead of blindly believing," he continued.

"In that case, what you said about gravity and the subconscious mind being the border lines of this dimension and the other, that was only a guess or your imagination?" one participant asked.

"Yes, it is true. We still don't know how true it is until we are able to cross the line. That is the reason that I am so serious in studying ancient documents. These documents were the recordings of all ancient, talented Qigong meditators' lifetime experiences in spiritual development. I hope through studying these documents, I am able to find the correct path for my own study. Actually, all that we have discussed were the conclusions of these documents. I believe that each document is a road sign to lead us to the right path," Master Dong said. "That means this seminar only offers you a possible direction to pursue your goal. After this seminar, it will take you a lifetime to experience it and come out with a new conclusion."

"Isn't this the correct attitude to learning in science? If we are able to keep this open-minded attitude, we should be able to find the correct path for any area of research or study," Dr. Owen thought.

"This morning, I need you to continue yesterday morning's practice. That means learning to get rid of the old thoughts and stop the initiation of new thoughts. Remember, if you can see that all emotional bondage, at the end, is all emptiness, then it is not worth hanging your mind there. You must recognize this fact so that the old thoughts can be dissolved into emptiness. Not only that, you must pay attention to your deep abdominal breathing so the new thoughts will not be initiated. This is not an easy task and impossible for anyone to reach this stage in a short time. However, I need you to practice this morning again and see if you have any questions. Only then, can you be on the correct path when you practice at home after the seminar," Master Dong said.

Everyone closed their eyes and began to meditate. Dr. Owen, though, could not calm down. He had learned so much information in just a few days. He had to ponder and analyze all of the discussions. He had to understand. Without this understanding, he could not calm down his mind and rest. This had been his attitude towards his studies and research ever since he was in college. However, from the last two mornings' meditation practice, he had realized a fact. That was, once he was able to keep his body relaxed and mind calm, he could think more clearly, accurately, and logically. Therefore, first, he followed the deep breathing method to bring his body and mind to a relaxed and calm state.

* * *

After breakfast the morning lecture began.

"Let us continue the subject of the two polarities. If a human is formalized in the field of the two polarities, then a human should also have two polarities. As I mentioned before, scientists today have confirmed that each cell has two polarities. Due to the existence of these two polarities, a cell has the capability of storing a charge and releasing a charge. Not only that, a cell can also have the potential of memories. As you know, each cell includes all of the DNA information or blueprint of the entire body. That is why we are able to clone another entire human from a single cell," Master Dong said.

"How big of a cell? I am just curious," one participant asked.

"Well, it is very small, indeed. Just think about it. It is estimated that on average one trillion cells die each day. From this number, you can imagine how big a cell is. When this cell is used to clone a human, will this human have two polarities?" Master Dong asked.

"I think so. From a theoretical point of view, it should," Xiaoling replied.

"Yes, this has been confirmed by scientists in 1996. On January 23 of 1996, scientists announced that a human has two brains. One is on the top inside the head and the other is the guts in the stomach and abdominal area. The top brain is able to think and record memory, however, the lower brain only has memory. These two brains are connected by a highly electric conductive spinal cord. That means physically, there are two brains, in function, actually, there is one. The reason for this is because the spinal cord is constructed with a highly electric conductive tissue and thus, there is nearly no resistance in it. That means in function, these two brains synchronize with each other simultaneously. Therefore, there are two brains physically, but there is only one in function. There is one, but there are two. The top brain governs the usage of the electricity while the lower brain stores and supplies the charges. For example, when you lift up a marker, your top brain thinks first. From this thinking, an EMF or electromotive force is generated. When this happens, the charges stored at the lower brain will be led upward through the spinal cord and the nervous system. When the electricity reaches the arm, it activates the muscle cells and the action is initiated," Master Dong said as he lifted up a marker in his hand from the waist area to his shoulder.

"Do you mean these two brains are the two polarities of a human body?" Brian asked.

"Yes. Due to these two polarities, all of the cells developed in this field also have two polarities. Since these two polarities have the capability of memorization, all of the cells developed in this field also have memory," Master Dong said.

"How do these two brains relate to meditation, may I ask?" one female participant asked.

"Let us compare this new scientific discovery with traditional Chinese Qigong understanding. The earliest record was in Chapter 16 of the *Dao De Jing* written about 2,400 years ago. Through thousands of years of study and experience, the Chinese began to know these two polarities. The top brain in Chinese Qigong is called 'Upper Dan Tian' while the lower brain is called 'Real Lower Dan Tian.' Dan Tian means 'Elixir Field' which implies the capability of storing Qi or elixir. These two Dan Tians are connected by the 'Thrusting Vessel' (Chong Mai, 衝脈). Remember the word 'thrusting' means 'thrust through very quickly.' Therefore, physically, we have two Dan Tians, in function, we have only one since they cannot be separated," Master Dong said. He picked up the cup of tea in front of him and sipped a little bit. "Remember, this understanding of two polarities has already been existing for more than 2,000 years in China. It was not discovered until recently by Western scientists. As a matter of fact, I believe the Chinese have understood the function of these two polarities for even longer."

This caught everyone's attention. Everyone was quiet and listened carefully.

"The Chinese believe that a human life is constructed by two parts, a physical body and a spiritual body. The lower Dan Tian is able to store the Qi to an abundant level and also release it. It is just like the function of a battery. In fact, this battery deals with the quantity of the Qi. When the Qi is abundant in this Lower Dan Tian, the immune system is healthy and strong. However, when the Qi is weak, then physical life can be sickened or even die. That means this center provides the energy for physical life. However, the Upper Dan Tian, which is located at the center of head, the limbic system, is the residence of the Shen or spirit. When a person is able to keep his Shen in this center, his spirit will be high, and his mental body will be strong. However, if this spirit has been distracted by a disturbed emotional mind, then the spirit will become chaotic and be weakened. Normally, this Shen will depart from the physical body only when a person dies. However, through past experience, when a person is very sick, or in a deeply profound semi-sleeping state, this spirit can also separate from the physical body temporally. Naturally, through deep meditation, often a meditator is able to experience this as well," Master Dong explained.

"You mean the spiritual and physical body could be separated through meditation?" Xiaoling asked.

"Yes, from past experience, many meditators were able to do so. As a matter of fact, as I know, this kind of spirit and physical body's separation has been commonly practiced in Tibetan Qigong."

"Does this mean when we die, actually, only the physical body dies, and the spiritual body continues to live?" one participant asked.

"This is the theory of reincarnation. Actually, when the physical body dies, the spiritual body must find a new residence and be re-born. If this spirit cannot find a new residence, this spirit will be blended into nature and vanish forever," Master Dong said. "Daoists and Buddhists believed that by opening the third eye and through correct practice, the spirit could become independent and survive without re-entering reincarnation. When this happens, this spirit is called 'Buddha' and is able to live forever. That is the meaning of eternal life."

"In that case, how can we cultivate our spirit and achieve this goal?" Dr. Owen asked.

"According to *Bodhidharma's* theory, to reach this goal, you must first build up an abundant level of Qi at the Lower Dan Tian. This Qi can then be led upward to the brain or Upper Dan Tian to nourish the upper brain or activate more brain cells' function. When more brain cells have been activated, more abundant levels of Qi can be stored there. If you know how to focus this Qi and aim it into the third eye area, the third eye can be re-opened. I have translated all of this theory into English from Chinese ancient documents in one of my books, *Qigong - The Secret of Youth*," Master Dong said. "In order to re-open the third eye, you will need not only the quantity of Qi, you must also know how to focus the Qi to a tiny point. It is just like focusing a sunbeam through a lens. The first crucial key of this focus is Embryonic Breathing. Remember, the Lower Dan Tian supplies you the quantity of Qi while the Upper Dan Tian handles the quality of the Qi's manifestation. When you have these two, you can be healthy and live long. Remember, these two polarities and the spinal cord establish a central Qi system. If you are able to manage this system properly, you will be able to conserve your Qi and also manifest it efficiently and effectively. This is the key of health and longevity."

296

"Isn't this system the same as the central nervous system in Western medical science?" Dr. Owen asked again.

"Yes, it is. By now, you should understand that almost all Western science was established by a rule, that is 'seeing is believing.' However, Chinese or many Eastern sciences focus on the feeling or Qi of the body. One approaches from the material side and the other approaches from the energy and spiritual side. The results from both sides should be consistent. If it is not, then one of them is wrong and needs to be redefined," Master Dong replied.

"Then how do we increase the amount of Qi and how do we train our focus so the quality of the Qi's manifestation can be improved?" Brian asked again.

"Well, once you have recognized the two polarities and central Qi system, then you must learn how to keep this energy in this system. In this case, as I said earlier, you will be able to manipulate your energy more efficiently and effectively. The first key of governing the Qi's manifestation is controlling your mind. Remember, whenever you think, the Qi will be led away from its battery, the Lower Dan Tian or lower brain, and will be consumed. If your mind stays at these central Qi systems or two polarities, the Qi will be preserved. This is the first key training of Embryonic Breathing."

"Does this mean you must first learn how to control your mind in order to conserve your Qi?" Brian asked again.

"Yes. When the mind or spirit stays in its residence,

the Qi will stay at this storage place, the Lower Dan Tian. Whenever the mind or spirit becomes chaotic, the Qi's circulation will also become weird and wasted. Therefore, the first step of Embryonic Breathing is regulating your mind to a stage of 'mind of no mind,'" Master Dong said.

"How do you do this?" one of participants asked.

"As I mentioned in the last few days, you must get rid of the thoughts already existing in your mind and second you must prevent the new thoughts from being initiated," Master Dong replied.

"What is the state we are searching for?" Brian asked again.

"Actually, we are searching for a semi-sleeping state as I mentioned the other day. The state of θ wave in EEG (electroencephalogram). Remember, scientists in the 1960s discovered that two brains from two different people are capable of communicating with each other. This was proved from many twins. When one is hurt, the other one, even a distance away, can experience the pain as well. Therefore, scientists created a machine, called 'electroencephalogram' (EEG), to test the brain's function. You know, a brain is constructed by two lobes or two hemispheres. Scientists began to understand that the space between them creates a vibration resonant chamber. When the energy is trapped within, it vibrates. This vibration will cause other brains to resonate if they have the same vibration frequency. Twins can sense each other much easier since they originated from the same genes. Similarly, this kind of telepathic connection can be happening between mother and her children. However, according to ancient Chinese Qigong practice, through meditation, one can make this energy vibration so strong that other brains, even though the vibration frequency is slightly off, can synchronize their vibration. This is called 'forced vibration' in physics. This was also how a dictator in the past who had a high level of spirit was able to influence the surrounding people's thinking and make them follow his wishes willingly. Naturally, this kind of usage belongs to the dark side of the force. Anyway, as known from the past, through meditation training, a person will be able to control another person's thinking."

"Then, how can we train this?" Dr. Owen asked. He was very curious about this because he had seen this kind of practice in ancient times from the past world crystal recording.

"As I explained earlier, first, you must have an abundant level of Qi to activate more brain cells. When this energy is focused at the center of the two lobes, the vibration can be very strong. From past experience, some Qigong masters would be able to widen the band of vibration frequencies and cause a wide scale of resonant vibration. Again, the way of learning this focus is through Embryonic Breathing." Master Dong paused a while and watched the expressions on the students' faces. He continued,

"From the EEG machine, we can classify four groups of brainwaves generated, one is called β wave which records the vibration when a person is very awake. In this wave, normally, there are about 18 thoughts passing through your brain. Then, α wave shows when you are relaxing and there are only about 12 thoughts passing your brain. That means you are more focused and less distorted. This also implies that when you are more relaxed, you are more concentrated. The most amazing part of this is the amplitude of vibration also increased when you are relaxed. You know, from science, the intensity of vibration is proportional to the square of the amplitude. That means the more you are relaxed, the vibration intensity is stronger, that means your thinking is more powerful. Then, when you reach a semi-sleeping state, it is the θ wave. In this wave range, there are only four to six of thoughts passing through your brain. Naturally, again this implies that you are more focused, and the intensity of vibration is also stronger since the amplitude is again increased. However, once you have fallen asleep, you have reached the δ wave. In this range, there is only one or two thoughts passing through your brain and the amplitude is the largest, this implies the intensity of vibration is the strongest. Now, is there anyone of you who would like to tell me that when you are in the thought of no thought, which of these four states are you in?" Master Dong asked.

"The δ wave," one of the participants replied.

"Well, then you would be in the sleeping state in δ wave. That means you don't have thought at all. No, this is not the state you want since you cannot control it," Master Dong said.

"Then, it must be the θ wave," Brian said.

"Yes, the θ wave is the one desired. This is the semi-sleeping state. Your mind is there but also not there. When you are in this state, your conscious mind begins to cease activity and the subconscious mind begins to function. This is 'Wuji' state. This is the profound meditation state described in Chapter 14 of *Dao De Jing*," Master Dong said. "Actually, in the *Dao De Jing*, this resonant chamber between the two lobes of the brain is called the 'spiritual valley' (Shen Gu, 神谷) and the spirit residing in this valley is called the 'valley spirit' (Gu Shen, 谷神). Since we are near the end of this morning's session, I would like to urge you to think about what we have covered this morning and open a discussion this afternoon. I will be here with you this afternoon to share with my experience in regulating the mind. Tomorrow will be the last seminar session; we will conclude with the training of Embryonic Breathing."

* * *

After lunch, Dr. Owen found a quiet place under a very old madrone tree in front of the house and tried to rest a little bit. However, he could not sleep. All of his thoughts were on the morning's lecture. He tried breathing deeply. "Calm down and breathe deeply. Inhale deeply and exhale to lead your body to a higher level of relaxation," he kept reminding himself. In about 20 minutes, he entered a semi-sleeping state while his mind was still connecting with the morning's lecture. It was a strange feeling, even though he had had this kind of experience whenever he was falling asleep or had just woken up from sleep. In truth, he had never paid attention to the feeling. It seemed his mind was there but also not there. At this moment, it seemed all of the usual emotional disturbances were no longer important and they gradually disappeared. His mind was clear but without intentional thought. Unfortunately, when he began to pay more attention to it, he woke up, the semi-sleeping feeling was gone, and the conscious mind had returned.

* * *

Master Dong came down from upstairs at 3:00 in the afternoon.

"As you already know, regulating the mind is not an easy thing. It is even harder to explain how you can actually do it. This is simply because each individual has his own background and emotional bondage. It is not easy to generate a standard rule or guideline to lead you to this path. This regulating process must be done by yourself. Through your pondering and continuous experience, you will gradually regulate your mind to the desired state. In Chinese Qigong society, when you have deeply comprehended and understood the problem and are able to jump out of it, it is called 'Wu' (悟). To Western society, it may be called 'awakening.' Once you have this awakening, you will be able to set your spirit free," Master Dong said. Master Dong took a look at all of the participants and saw that the spirit of learning for most participants was low. It was the afternoon and most people didn't want to put more effort into thinking, especially after the morning session. Therefore, he said, "To help you understand how to regulate the mind, I would like to tell you some stories. From these stories, I hope you are able to grasp the key of regulating your own mind."

This caused a lot of excitement in the group. Understanding the mind through stories would be fun, so everyone paid more attention to Master Dong.

"Often, our mind cannot be calm because of our desires and greediness. There are two stories which I would like to tell you and then we should discuss them," Master Dong said.

A wealthy businessman from the north spotted a fisherman relaxing against his canoe and smoking a pipe. The businessman was dismayed, 'Why aren't you out sailing to catch fish?'

'I caught enough today already.'

'The sun is still high in the sky, you could catch plenty more, couldn't you?' insisted the businessman.

'Why should I?' retorted the fisherman.

'Money! You would have more money!' the businessman exclaimed. 'With a better engine on your boat, you could go to deeper water and catch more fish. Soon you could buy a better net and catch even more fish and make even more money. Finally, you may become rich enough to buy a fleet of new boats, even becoming as rich as me.'

'And then what would I do?'

'Sit and enjoy your life.'

'That is what I am doing now,' said the fisherman.

Master Dong looked at everyone and said, "What do you think about this story? Often due to our ceaseless demands, we are not happy. Greediness has always been one of the origins of unhappiness. If we appreciated everything we have, we would be happy. However, if we always demand or complain about life, then we will be always unsatisfied.

"Here is another story."

In a small village in southern China lived the hardest worker in his community. Day and night he toiled, and year by year his riches grew. As time passed, his hoard of money increased, as did his concern for failure or loss. He worried about how to make more money and how to keep both friends and enemies away from the massive wealth he had accumulated.

He raised the fence around his house and strengthened the walls. He kept putting strong locks on the doors and bars on the windows, until the house resembled a jail. He felt safe and believed himself the happiest man alive as he counted his money all day.

A curious passerby peered in and saw him

sitting there smiling as he counted. He called out, 'Why are you so happy? It seems you're in jail!'

The man answered, 'No! It's not that I'm in jail, it's that you are outside of it.'

"What do you think, friends? Are you happy and appreciate whatever you have obtained or are you always demanding more?" Master Dong asked.

"But if you don't have an aggressive mind in demanding more, then there is no progress, right, Master Dong?" one participant said.

"Yes, it is true. You should have an aggressive mind in cultivating your temperament instead of material things. If you continue in demanding material things aggressively, you will soon be enslaved by material things and forget your original being. I understand that we need material things to survive, however, we should not have a greedy mind. I mean, when you have enough to live comfortably, then it should be enough. Let me tell you another story about the Sixth Chan (禪) (Ren, 忍) ancestor."

When the fifth successor of Chan, Hong Ren (弘忍), had to make his decision to pass the leadership to one of his two most qualified disciples, Shen Xiu (神秀) and Hui Neng (慧能), who were standing right in front of him, he said,

'Please tell me what life is,' he asked.

'Life is just like a piece of a mirror. You must wipe it all the time and keep it clean until there is not even a piece of dust on it,' Shen Xiu said.

Then, when Hong Ren asked Hui Neng about this, he said,

'Bodhi does not have a tree originally, nor is there a shining mirror in front. There are no objects there originally, so how can they be contaminated by dust or mud (objects or emotions)?'

"Bodhi means an enlightened mind. Buddha was enlightened under the Bodhi tree. Shining mirror means a pure and clean Shen (spirit). When you cultivate Shen, the material world disappears, so there is no tree or mirror. With no material concept in your mind, how can it be cleaned of secular emotions and desires?

"That means if you don't take material satisfaction too seriously, you will not be enslaved by material things. Only if your mind is not enslaved by material things, then your spirit can be set free. To Buddhists, the material world does not exist, so there is nothing to be cultivated or considered," Master Dong said.

"Master Dong, actually, the hardest part of regulating the mind for me is getting rid of the thoughts hanging there. How can I handle that?" a participant asked since he had experienced that getting rid of old thoughts was the most difficult task in the last two days.

"Let me tell you another story and see if you are able to comprehend it and apply it into your practice. I hope this story will inspire all of your thinking."

In ancient China, two monks walked down a

muddy road when they came upon a large puddle completely blocking the road. A very beautiful lady in a lovely gown stood at the edge of the
puddle crying, unable to go farther without
spoiling her clothes.

Without hesitation, one of the monks picked
her up and carried her across the puddle, set her
down on the other side, and continued on his
way. Hours later, when the two monks were
preparing to camp for the night, the second
monk turned to the first and said: 'I can no
longer hold this back. I'm quite angry with you!
We are not supposed to look at women, particu-
larly pretty ones; never mind touching them.
Why did you do that?'

The first monk replied, 'I left her at the mud
puddle a long time ago, why are you still carrying her?'

"From this short story, can you see that the root of
thought is in your mind? If you are able to empty this
mind, you have pulled the root out of it. Therefore, you
must find the root of a disturbing thought, ponder it,
and then find the way to get rid of it. Here, I would like
to tell you another Samurai story from Japan."

A boy of ten was playing in his house when a
Samurai swordsman entered and started killing
people. He hid behind a large clothes cabinet.
Through a gap he saw clearly what was happening. The swordsman was his father's enemy, and

the boy was the family's only survivor. The swordsman finished his killing, then left without searching the cabinet.

The boy traveled the country searching for the best Zen (Chan) master. He swore he would become the most famous and skillful Samurai swordsman so he could avenge the murder of his family. He found a master and practiced day and night with vengeance in his heart.

By his early 20s, he became one of the best-known Samurai swordsmen in Japan. He traveled to every corner of Japan, searching for his enemy. But after 25 years of searching, all efforts were in vain, and his enemy seemed to have disappeared from society.

With great disappointment, he entered a deep valley one day where only a few tribesmen lived. He came to a small river, where an old man was rebuilding a bridge, slowly and strenuously moving wood piece by piece. The original bridge had been swept away by a torrent, and the villagers had to travel far downstream to cross the river.

Talking to the old man, he could not believe his eyes. The old man was the one who had killed his family more than 35 years before. Without hesitation, he drew his sword ready to cut off his head. Before doing so, he explained why. The old man freely admitted to killing his family but had one final request.

'This bridge is the only hope for the village.

Allow me to finish building it before killing me,'
the old man asked.

Since the old man's request was good, he
agreed to permit him to finish the bridge, but he
would watch him day and night so that he could
not run away. The avenger built a tent next to the
old man and watched him build the bridge. Progress was slow and time-consuming, and after
six months, he joined in to help the old man finish the bridge to hasten the day of his revenge.

Eating together, talking, and helping each
other, in time they became good friends. The
bridge was completed in the third year. After
completing the job, the old man came to the
Samurai's tent. He had washed his body clean. He
knelt before the avenger, and said, 'It is time for
you to take my life to avenge your family.'

The Samurai found he could not draw his
sword for revenge. He knelt in front of the old
man and said: 'My first life was hatefulness like
hell. My second life is kindness and peace like
heaven. I cannot kill you, otherwise I would also
kill my second life.' So, they traveled together
and treated each other like father and son.

"Do you have a heart for forgiveness? Often, we are
trapped into emotional bondage due to the hate or anger.
If you can see through this and have a forgiving heart,
you will soon see you are in the territory of peace and
calmness," Master Dong explained, watching all the

participants' facial expressions. He could see some agreed and were touched, and others disagreed and felt that the avenger should have carried out his revenge. Then, he asked, "What do you think? Should this Samurai swordsman take his revenge, or should he have the heart of forgiveness?"

"Even though he did not want to kill him, at least, he should not travel with him and treat him like father and son," one participant said.

"Well, that depends on how deep your forgiveness is and how profound your understanding in life is. If you are able to forgive and are able to travel together like father and son, you have pulled the root of hate out completely. However, if the thought of hate is still in your deep heart, then you will not be able to do it. You know, everyone makes mistakes. However, making mistakes does not mean you are absolutely a bad person. Don't you think?" Master Dong said.

Some of participants agreed but still others disagreed. However, this story had already stimulated many people's thinking.

"Another thing which can make a person disappointed and emotionally upset is the mind of expectation. Often, we expect things to be happening as you hope for, however, they came about a different way. When this happens, many people will get upset and become disturbed. As you have probably already experienced many times in the past, the higher your expectation is, the more you are disappointed. Let me tell you a story,

There was a priest preaching in the church to many followers. Suddenly, a person ran in the church and shouted, 'Run! Everyone, run quickly! The big water dam has broken. This town will be flooded in an hour or so.'

Everyone ran for his life. One follower saw the priest was not in a hurry, he yelled, 'Father, run! Quickly run! The water is coming.'

'I'm not worried about it. God will save me. I am not in danger,' Father replied.

After not too long, everyone was gone, and the water entered the town. It got higher and higher so that the priest could not run away anymore. Pretty soon, the water reached his waist and he quickly went up to the roof. He kept praying to God to show him a miracle to save him. In another 30 minutes, the water had reached the roof. He kept praying to God. In a few minutes, a boat came by. 'Father! Father! Let us take you to a safe place,' the person asked.

'Go away! I am asking God to save me,' the priest replied. The boat went away. The priest continued his praying and the water got higher and higher. Another boat approached,

'Father! Father! Let us take you to a safe place,' the person asked.

'Go away! I am waiting for God to save me.' he replied. Again, the boat went away. He continued his praying and the water got higher and higher. Another boat approached,

'Father! Father! Let us take you to a safe place,' the person asked.

'Go away! I am asking God to save me,' Father replied. Again, the boat went away. The water got higher and higher. Finally, the priest died and went to heaven. When he saw God, he said,

'Oh, God! I have been so loyal to you in my life. I have served you for my whole life, why didn't you help me when I prayed for your help?' Father asked.

'Who said I didn't help you. I sent three boats to you, but you refused them,' God replied.

"Don't you think, we make the same mistakes sometimes? Often, we don't appreciate what we have already gotten and expect more or better. When the time comes, eventually, we lose everything," Master Dong said.

"If material things are not important, then what is important, spirit? What are we looking for?" a female participant asked.

"Well, this topic is very profound and big. I remember a story told to me by my master about a very famous archer, Yang, You-Ji (養由基), who lived during the Chinese Spring and Autumn period (722-481 B.C.) (春秋)."

When Yang, You-Ji was a teenager, he was already well known for his superior skill in archery. Because of this, he was very proud of himself. One day, he was in his study when he heard the call of an oil seller just outside his house. Curious, he went out of his house and saw an old man selling cooking oil on the street. He saw the old man place the oil jar, which had a tiny hole the size of a coin, on the ground and then use the ladle to scoop a full measure of oil and pour it from chest height into the jar without losing a single drop, or even touching the sides of the hole. Yang, You-Ji was amazed at this old man's steady hand and the accuracy with which he was able to pour the oil into the jar. He asked the old man: 'Old man, how did you do that?'

The old man looked at him, the well-known teenage archer of the village, and said: 'Young man, would you like to see more?' The young man nodded his head.

The old man then asked him to go into the house and bring out a bench. The old man placed a Chinese coin, which had a very tiny hole in the center, on the hole in the jar. Then, the old man ladled a full scoop of oil and climbed onto the bench. Standing on the bench, he poured the oil all the way down from a high place, through the hole in the coin and into the jar.

This time, Yang, You-Ji kept his eyes wide open and was shocked at the old man's amazing skill. He asked the old man: 'How did you do that? I have never seen such an amazing thing before.'

The old man looked at him and smiled. He said: 'There is nothing but practicing.'

Suddenly, Yang, You-Ji understood that his archery was good because he practiced harder than others. There was nothing of which to be proud. Thereafter, he became very humble and practiced even harder. When he reached his 30s, he was considered the best archer in the entire country and was honored to serve the emperor as a bodyguard. But in his late 40s, he disappeared from the palace, and nobody ever knew where he went.

Thirty years later, one of his friends heard that Yang, You-Ji was on Tian Mountain of Xinjiang Province (新疆、天山), and decided to find him. After months of traveling, he finally arrived at the mountain and located his friend. He stepped in Yang's house and they recognized each other. However, when Yang saw his friend's bow and arrow on his shoulder, he opened his eyes and said: 'What are those funny things you are carrying on your back?'

His friend looked at him with mouth agape and said: 'Wow! You must be the best archer existing today. You have already gone through the entire experience of archery.'

"What do you think about this story? If you think

carefully, all we are experiencing about our life is actually the process of understanding our life," Master Dong
said.

"Often, we find out we don't have time to do what we
want to do. Time is always limited. This has been one of
the reasons that people's minds cannot calm down easily, since there are so many things they have to think
about," a participant said.

"It is true. Our time is limited and there are always
many things that you want to do. The question is; how
do you set your priorities. There is a story about Buddha.

One day, when Buddha came to a river, he
met a 60-year old man there. After the old man
saw the Buddha, he said, 'You are the Buddha,
right? Are you as good as people say? Look at me,
I can wade and cross the river without using a
boat. See if you can do it.' Then, he was so proud
of himself he stepped in the water and crossed
the river and returned.

He looked at Buddha with his pride and expected Buddha was able to do the same, but
Buddha said, 'May I ask how long it took you to
learn how to do this?' Buddha asked.

'Forty years. It took me 40 years,' he replied.

'Wow! It took you 40 years of your lifetime to
accomplish this. Actually, it costs me only 50
pennies to cross the river by boat,' Buddha said.

"I remember, I saw a story in the newspaper once,

and I was very touched by this story. Let me tell you and see what you think," Master Dong said.

A teacher came to the classroom with a jar and many rocks. All of the rocks were just the right size to fit in the hole of the jar. He looked at the students and said, 'I have a demonstration to show you. After you have seen the demonstration, I want you to tell me how this demonstration is related to your life.'

Then, he placed the rocks one by one into the jar until he reached the top and there was no more space for the rocks. Then, he asked, 'Is this jar full?'

'It's full,' the students replied.

'No, it's not,' the teacher said and opened the drawer and brought some pebbles out. He carefully placed pebbles into the gap of the jar and then asked, 'Is this jar full?'

'No, it's not.' The students had learned to be smarter this time.

'That's right,' the teacher said and then brought some sand out of the drawer and placed it into the jar until it had reached to the top. Then, again, he asked, 'Is this jar full?'

'It's not,' the students replied.

'That's right.' Then the teacher poured some water into the jar until it reached the top.

'Is this jar full?' he asked.

'It's full, teacher,' the students replied.

'OK, now, is there anyone that can tell me how this demonstration is related to your life?' the teacher asked.

'It means we can always find extra time to accomplish something in our life,' one student said.

'It's true. However, the most important thing of this demonstration is that if you don't place the big rocks in first, you will not have any chance to place them in since the jar will be filled with pebbles, sand, and water. Therefore, you must first define what are the big rocks in your life and pursue them. I have seen many people who know what the big rocks in their life are, however, they are afraid to face these big challenges. They just kept themselves busy in something not important and found the excuses that they were busy. Once time passes, when they are old, they regret that they have wasted time on small, unimportant things.'

"Finally, I would like to conclude this afternoon's discussion with some wisdom I learned from my White Crane master. He said, in order to fit into this society, you must be round outside and square inside. If you are round outside, you will be able to get along with people around you. But, if you are square outside, you will soon be pushed out from this big, round society. However, you must be square inside so you will aim for a higher level of spiritual cultivation. If you allow your inside to also be round, then your emotional mind will take over and dominate your life. That means you will lose the principles of your life," Master Dong said.

"In order to be round, the first step is learning how to be humble. When you are humble, you can be accepted easily by society. However, if you are always too proud of yourself, you will soon lose friends. I remember that when I was 17 years old, I went to a mountain to see my master. Though I had learned only 18 months of White Crane, I believed that I had reached a higher level than another classmate of mine who had been there for about five years. So, I mentioned this to my master and expected his praise. However, he looked at me and used his fingers to point out bamboo growing around his house and said, 'Little Dong. Look at those bamboo. The taller they grow, the lower they bow!' This sentence had hit me so hard that even today, it still is one of the important reminders of my life. Please think about it and hopefully, you have learned from all of the stories I told you," Master Dong said.

It was 6:00 p.m. already. It was the time for rest and then dinner. Indeed, there were lots of thoughts and inspirations from this afternoon's talk.

* * *

Since tomorrow would be the last day of the meditation seminar, Brian and Xiaoling decided to go to Dr. Owen's home again. They believed when the seminar was over, Dr. Owen would probably not come to the center again. When the afternoon discussion session was over, Brian and Xiaoling brought Dr. Owen down to the base of mountain. Dr. Owen then drove his car and Brian followed him to his home. Along the way, they ordered some Chinese food in Garberville. Once at the house, Dr. Owen opened a bottle of California red wine to celebrate their reunion.

"Professor, I am very curious about the meditation method that was used by those ancient people in the past world. Do you have any ideas at all from what you have seen so far?" Brian asked.

"Actually, I began to recompile the entire recording about eight months ago. There are at least 100 DVDs already recorded. It is not easy to compile such a huge amount of information. I have gone through only one-third of it. However, from this compilation I have obtained a much better idea about this young guy's life. This has helped me to write my report or book about the past world. I had never paid special attention to their meditation methods until a few days ago. I intend to generate a special DVD only for meditation in the next few months," Dr. Owen said.

"It would be so great if we were able to learn some of the methods and knowledge developed by those past meditators who had had 500 years' more experience than us. It would offer us a more accurate direction for spiritual cultivation, don't you think, Professor?" Xiaoling said.

"Will you make a copy for us once you have completed the compilation of the meditation part? We would appreciate it very much," Brian asked.

"That won't be a problem. But you must understand that you must keep these secrets to yourself. The secret of the crystals must be kept continuously. Also, I don't know when I will be able to finish the compilation. You know I am still picking up new things from the crystals. It seems it never has an end," Dr. Owen said.

"That's OK. Xiaoling and I will be staying at the center for Chinese martial arts training for the next three weeks. We have been learning White Crane, Chin Na, and Taijiquan from Master Dong for more than three years. It does not matter how much you have compiled in the next three weeks; would it be possible to give us an updated copy?" Brian asked again.

"Naturally. Will the morning's meditation session continue to go on with the group or will Master Dong meditate by himself after this week?" Dr. Owen asked.

"Based on our past experience, Master Dong will meditate with the group - of course with different groups - for the next five weeks of summer retreats. Unfortunately, Xiaoling and I can only take three weeks more and then we must return to San Francisco for work. You know, meditation has always been an important part of training in all Chinese martial arts. Do you want to join us?" Brian said.

"I will think about it. I like the morning meditation session. After my last few days' experience, I feel that my mind is clearer, and I am able to concentrate better. Do you think Master Dong will mind if I join only the morning session?" Dr. Owen asked.

"Not at all! I am pretty sure that you will be welcome.

But you should know that there will be no more morning Qigong lecture except about 20 minutes of discussion before meditation," Brian replied.

"I understand. I just like to be around that environment when I meditate. Somehow, I had more inspiration and felt my Qi was stronger in that valley," Dr. Owen said.

"Yes, it is true. The Qi is strong there. Many of us have also experienced the same thing," Xiaoling said.

After they had dinner, they sat down and had some good Wulong tea that Dr. Owen purchased off the Internet. Usually, the Wulong tea purchased in any grocery store was a lower class of Wulong tea. Though it is cheaper, it does not taste as good as high quality Wulong tea.

"Since you will still be here for training for the next three weeks, whenever you like, you are always welcome to come here. I need some companionship anyway. As a matter of fact, I have two extra bedrooms. If you like you may sleep over," Dr. Owen said.

"That will be great. I would like to watch more of those crystal recordings. When we have time in the evening, we may drop by and stay over," Brian said.

They talked about the past world, the clothes those people wore, the vehicles they drove and flew, the social structure, and many unusual customs at that time. However, they mostly remained curious about the meditation practices and why the catastrophe of the past world had happened. Even though Dr. Owen had already had some idea from watching the crystals, he still needed more time to conclude his theory.

"I will send you a copy of the report when I finish it. It may take me a couple of years," Dr. Owen said.

At about 10 p.m., Brian and Xiaoling left. Since they all had to get up early again, they all needed their sleep. This was especially true for Dr. Owen since he had to get up even earlier. It would take him about 30 minutes to get to the base of the mountain and another hour to climb up there.

Last Lecture

As usual, at 6:00 a.m., Master Dong came down to the meditation hall from upstairs. After he sat down, he said, "It will be the last morning's meditation for most of you who just take the Qigong Meditation seminar. If you have any questions from the last few mornings' practice, this will be the last chance for you. All I hope is that after what you have learned this week, you can carry this meditation habit home and practice by yourself. If you go back to the same old lifestyle, you will have wasted your time here," Master Dong said.

"Master Dong. When I took a rest yesterday afternoon, through deep breathing, I was able to bring my body and mind to a higher level of relaxation and calmness. When I entered the semi-sleeping state, my mind became clear and began to think about the subjects we discussed yesterday morning. When I began to think about it, I could comprehend the deep feeling of it. However, when I paid attention to the subjects, I began to wake up and everything was gone," Dr. Owen said. "The

322

question I have is, how can I keep myself in the semi-sleeping state and at the same time still have the conscious mind direct my thinking. It seems the subconscious mind and conscious mind cannot be existing at the same time."

"Well, this is the most difficult part of Embryonic Breathing. You want your thoughts to be there but also not there. I mean 'the thinking of no thinking.' It is not easy for me to explain this to you. You must feel it and practice by yourself. I can offer you two examples of this state. It is said, 'Like a stone chime suspended from West Mountain.' A Chinese stone chime is shaped like a heart and there is a thread tied up at the center on the top of this heart. When it is hanging, the chime moves freely following the winds. The West Mountain is a high mountain that can see everything underneath. When a stone chime is hanging down from a cliff of the West Mountain, one way the chime is able to see or feel everything underneath it and also moves freely following the surrounding energy, the other way, it is connected to the top of the cliff with a thread.

"The spirit, or subconscious mind, is just like the chime and the thread is the conscious mind. One way, you must allow the chime to move freely, so the thread cannot be thick, and the other way, your thread must be strong enough to keep the chime hanging there. When the thread is thick, your conscious mind is too strong and when the thread is too thin or broken, you will have fallen asleep. I wonder if you are able to comprehend this meditative state from this example. If you are able to reach this state of meditation, you will feel your physical body disappear and become transparent. That means all you feel is the energy instead of the physical body. This is a very high level of calmness and relaxation," Master Dong explained.

"It seems it is not easy to figure out the real feeling of this state unless you are able to reach it. Isn't that right?" Brian said.

"Yes. If I use another example to explain to you, you may get a better idea. For example, you are flying a kite. The kite is flying high and can see everything underneath. This implies your mind is clear and neutral. However, the kite must be able to fly freely following the current of the wind. This implies your subconscious mind must be free without any bondage. However, if the thread connecting the kite and your hand is too thick, the kite will be restricted and fall. Therefore, you must have a strong but thin thread for this connection. This connection is the conscious mind that is still governing the situation. If this connection is broken, the kite will go out of control and disappear," Master Dong said again. "Remember, the mind is the border line of the conscious mind and the subconscious mind connecting to the spirit. When the subconscious mind is awakened and the conscious mind ceases activity, the spirit can be set free and raised up. When this happens, you have connected your spirit with the natural spirit."

"Why did we create this human matrix? Is it supposed to be this way?" one participant asked.

"Yes. This is the path of spiritual evolution. When we

make mistakes, we learn. Every time we learn, the spirit will be moved to the next level. We were born with five sensing organs: the eyes, the nose, the mouth, the ears, and the feeling heart. These organs are designed to help us collect information around us so our spirit is able to learn and grow. However, when humans abuse these five organs and become emotionally trapped, then the emotional matrix is generated. Again, this is also a path of our destiny. We must be trapped in this emotional bondage so mistakes can be made and experienced. The more we suffer, the more we learn, and the more our spirit grows. The question is, how much do you want to stay in this matrix. Remember, this matrix is there to help you comprehend the meaning of life," Master Dong said.

"In Buddhist society, there is a saying, 'As long as you have a subconscious mind, you will have a lotus seed. Through meditation, this seed will bud and grow. It will continue to grow until one day it emerges out of the mud and above the mud. When it blooms, it is pure and clean.' In Chinese Buddhist society, it compares the emotional matrix as emotional mud. When you are in the mud, you cannot see clearly, you cannot hear clearly since all of your feelings are covered by the mud. You are in pain and blind. However, most people will continue to stay in the mud for their whole lifetime. However, someone, someday, will wake up and realize that he does not want to stay in the mud anymore. Then he must search for his subconscious mind and begin to wake up. The way of making the subconscious mind grow out of the mud, or emotional matrix, is through meditation and self-awakening."

The entire group kept quiet and listened. Many of them wondered about what Master Dong said and were confused. However, Dr. Owen, after nearly 70 years of life, and also from watching the recordings of the past world, could comprehend this meaning deeply. "What is the meaning of our lives? What will the destiny of the entire human race be if we are continuously trapped in emotional bondage and conflict?" Dr. Owen thought. "Isn't the meaning of life to experience life so the spirit can grow?"

"Now, let's meditate," Master Dong instructed. "I want you first to calm down and relax your body through deep breathing. Once you have entered the semi-sleeping state, I want you to ponder the meaning of what we have discussed. Remember, if you handle it correctly, your conscious mind and subconscious mind can coexist. We have only 30 minutes this morning."

Everyone closed their eyes and began to meditate. It is not easy at all to reach a semi-sleeping state. Dr. Owen, however, had by now grasped the crucial key of reaching this stage. "Breathing is the crucial key. Just regulate your breathing and make it deep, slender, and soft," he kept reminding himself. In just ten minutes or so, he had already entered the stage of calmness and steadiness. His subconscious mind had gradually been set free. Today, he learned an important trick to keep himself in a semi-sleeping state. This trick was to continue with his deep breathing and try to make it softer and deeper. He was very successful. Time passed so fast.

To others, it might be 30 minutes but to Dr. Owen, it seemed like only ten.

* * *

This morning's lecture would be the last one. Tomorrow, almost all of the participants would go home except for a few who would continue to take seminars in the following weeks. Master Dong came down from upstairs.

"This morning," Master Dong began, "we should focus on practicing the method of Embryonic Breathing. As I mentioned during the last few day's sessions, we talked about the quantity of the Qi and also the quality of the Qi's manifestation. You already know the quantity of Qi came from abdominal breathing and the Qi can be stored in the Lower Real Dan Tian or Second Brain. You have also learned that the quality of the Qi's manifestation depends on how much you are able to focus by neutralizing your emotional disturbances. You must have also experienced the difficulty of regulating the mind.

"Now, let us reveal some of the secrets about regulating the mind which have been passed to us. First, you must recognize the structure of the brain. The brain is constructed by the Cerebrum, Cerebellum, and also Limbic system. As scientists know today, the Limbic system, situated at the center of the head, is responsible for primitive emotional responses. That means the Limbic system responds to an emotional touch without thinking, just like the behavior of a baby. However, from Chinese ancient understanding, this area is called the 'Mud

Pill Palace' (Ni Wan Gong, 泥丸宮) which is related to our subconscious mind. It is truthful and pure and reacts without a mask. That also means that our spirit resides in this area. That is why this area is called 'spirit residence' (Shen Shi, 神室). This place is called 'Mud Pill Palace' because, first of all, the Chinese believe that we came from Mud and will return to Mud eventually. Actually, you Westerners have the same saying that we came from the dust and go back to dust. Pill implies the two, small, pill-like glands, the pineal gland, and the pituitary gland. Palace means a big hall which will echo sounds, and this implies the spiritual valley or energy resonant chamber formalized by the two lobes of the brain." Master Dong watched for the students' expressions while he talked. Then he picked up a marker and drew a rough sketch.

"If you are able to locate this center through feeling, you will be able to lead the Qi there and at the same time cease the activity of thinking. That means the mask on your face will drop and the subconscious mind will wake up. This process is just like when you are falling asleep. Remember, when your exhalation is longer than your inhalation, you are leading the Qi outward for manifestation. When your inhalation is longer than exhalation, you are leading the Qi inward for storage. For example, when you are happy and make a sound of 'Ha' your exhalation is longer than your inhalation and you feel warm. However, if you are sad and cry, or are scared, your inhalation is longer than your exhalation while making the sound of 'Mmm'; you are leading the Qi inward. In this case, you will feel a chill. For the same reason, when you are awake and your mind is outside of the body, your exhalation is longer than inhalation and the Qi is led outward and consumed. However, when you sleep, your inhalation is longer than your exhalation and the Qi is led inward. Therefore, normally, when you sleep, it will take about three hours for you to lead the Qi inward to the Limbic system. When this happens, the pineal gland and pituitary gland will be functioning, and hormones will be produced. At this falling asleep stage, your conscious mind ceases activity; however, the subconscious mind will be stimulated and respond to your 'primitive emotions' and dreams will be initiated," Master Dong said.

"Does that mean if we are able to lead the Qi to this Mud Pill Palace, then we will be able to cease the conscious mind's activities and calm down our thinking?" Brian asked.

"Yes. The difficult part is feeling this center that is situated right in the center of the head, between your two ears. If you cannot feel it, how can you lead your Qi there? For example, if you wish to move your body from here to the door, you must know where the door is. If you don't, you won't be able to lead yourself there. Now, I would like all of you to close your eyes and try to locate this center and see if you are able to find it. You will have three minutes to search for it," Master Dong said.

Everyone closed his or her eyes and tried to find this center through feeling. Three minutes passed very quickly.

"How many of you were able to find it?" Master Dong asked. A few participants raised their hands.

"Are you sure or was it only your visualization? You know you must be able to feel it or sense it. If you have visualization, you have placed your mind somewhere else and do not really feel it," Master Dong said.

"It is true. The feeling is not clear at all especially since it is very difficult to keep your mind from searching. Your mind just jumps from one idea to another," Xiaoling said.

"It will take time. However, there is a trick that allows you to feel this center. Remember the sound of 'Mmm' that we have been practicing at the end of meditation in the morning? This sound is generated from the bottom center of the spiritual valley, the Limbic system. Now, everyone, try again. Close your eyes and make a loud sound of 'Mmm' and see if you are able to feel the origin of this sound which makes the entire valley vibrate," Master Dong said. Everyone tried a couple of times.

"It's amazing. Now that you mentioned it, I can really feel this center," Brian said.

"Actually, this sound is commonly used by humans, for example: crying, sighing, chanting, or humming. This sound has been known to be able to stimulate vibration of the brain cells. This sound is called the 'awakening sound' in Buddhist society.

"The way of leading the Qi inward to this center is to inhale longer than you exhale. Not only that, you must have a 'Mmm' sound in your mind. You should not actually make the sound since this will lead the Qi outward. This will direct you to the feeling of this center. Now, I need every one of you to try again with this trick and see if you can find it." All of the participants tried again.

After three minutes, "Tell me now, how many of you are able to feel this center?" Master Dong asked. More than half of the people raised their hands.

"When you return to your home, I want you to continue your practice and search for this spiritual center. Once you have found it, you must also find the center of gravity, I mean your physical center. This place is where the Real Lower Dan Tian, or the center of the Second Brain, is. In other words, your battery."

"How do you know this is the real battery or energy storage place of the human body?" one participant asked.

"Well, think! A human began from a single cell and then multiplied until the entire body was completed. Tell me, if this cell is still alive, where will this cell be?" Master Dong asked.

"Theoretically, it will be situated at the center of gravity," Brian said.

"That's correct. This place is the center of the physical body and energy at the beginning. This place remains the center of the physical body and energy when a human is completed. Remember this center is where a woman carries the baby. Actually, the baby is growing in the mother's Qi center," Master Dong explained.

"How do we find this center then?" one participant

asked.

"Actually, it is easier to find this center than the upper center. If you move the front and rear side of your abdominal area at the same time, you can locate this center very easily. Naturally, your mind will be in the front and the back at the beginning. However, after you have practiced for a while and reached the stage of 'regulating of no regulating,' you will find the center easily," Master Dong said. "Now, everyone, try it and see if you can find it."

The group closed their eyes and searched for this center. After three minutes Master Dong asked, "How many of you are able to find it?" At least half of the participants raised their hands.

"Once you have found the upper polarity, the Mud Pill Palace, or Limbic system and the lower polarity, the Real Lower Dan Tian, or Second Brain, then you synchronize these two polarities at the same time. I mean, when you inhale, you lead the Qi to these two centers at the same time and when you exhale, you simply relax and allow air out by itself. If you do so, you will lead the Qi inward to this central energy line and conserve it. Once you are able to do so, the final stage of Embryonic Breathing is to lead the Qi down from the upper polarity to the lower polarity, or Real Lower Dan Tian to store it there. When you inhale, you lead the Qi down to the Real Lower Dan Tian and when you exhale, simply relax and allow the Qi to dissipate to the intestines and stored. Remember, through this practice, the Qi will return to its residence. You will be in the Wuji state, calm and peaceful. That also means you are returning to the beginning first cell of a human. This is the beginning of life, or Embryonic Breathing. Once you are able to practice Embryonic Breathing smoothly, you will then be able to manipulate the Qi efficiently in order to preserve it or to manifest it as you wish," Master Dong concluded.

"What do you mean to preserve it or to manifest it, Master Dong? Can you explain that more specifically?" Dr. Owen asked.

"Well, once you are able to manipulate your Qi's action, then you can either store it to preserve it, or to lead it out with your mind for manifestation efficiently. For example, in summertime, when the energy in the surrounding environment is plentiful, it will be the time to lead the Qi inward to store it and also to use it to wash the bone marrow. You know, when the Qi in the bone marrow is healthy and abundant, blood cells can be produced properly. This is the secret of youth. However, when wintertime comes, you will need to lead more Qi outward to strengthen your Guardian Qi (Wei Qi, 衛氣) or aura, as you say, to defend against the cold environment. In this case, your immune system will function healthily," Master Dong said.

"How do you do this, Master Dong?" one participant asked.

"Remember, whenever your inhalation is longer than exhalation, you are leading Qi inward. When your exhalation is longer than inhalation, you are leading Qi outward. All of this is controlled through your mind and breathing," Master Dong said. "Theoretically, if you have built an abundant level of Qi and stored it at the Real Lower Dan Tian, or the lower polarity, your physical body will be strong. This is the root of Muscle/Tendon Changing Qigong. However, if you lead the abundant Qi upward to nourish your brain and activate more brain cells for function, then it is the Brain-Washing Qigong. The first one is for physical life while the second one is for spiritual life. That means for enlightenment." Master Dong pointed out the two different polarities on the sketch behind him as he talked.

"Does that mean that if we wish to re-open the third eye, we must lead the Qi upward to nourish the brain cells?" Dr. Owen asked again with great curiosity. He needed to confirm this practice since he knew this was the major practice in the past world.

"Yes. However, the most important, crucial key of re-opening the third eye is not just technique. It is your mind. You must be truthful to yourself and other people. Remember, why is our third eye shut now? According to Chinese Daoist society, it was because once we knew how to use our brain to play tricks and lie to each other, we intentionally closed it so other people could not read our mind. The reason for this is that when you have opened your third eye you will have the capability of telepathy. That means you can read people's mind and also people can sense your thinking as well. Remember, different brains are able to communicate with each other. Therefore, if you are not truthful, you will continue to shut down the third eye. That is why Chinese

Daoist called themselves 'Zhen Ren' (真人) which means 'truthful person' since they must be truthful so they can open the third eye. This was also the reason that when a person had opened his third eye, he retired in the deep mountain. You know, since he was able to read peoples' minds, it would make masked people feel uncomfortable," Master Dong said and took a look at the clock hanging on the wall.

"It is almost noon now. We will finish this morning's section. Since today is the last day of the seminar, we will continue to discuss the subject of Embryonic Breathing this afternoon then finish after," Master Dong said.

* * *

After lunch, Brian and Xiaoling took a walk and Dr. Owen, again, went to the meadow to sit under the madrone tree. He closed his eyes and again tried to recreate the same semi-sleeping feeling he experienced yesterday. However, his mind told him that he must ponder everything he had learned in the last few days. This was the last day for him to ask questions. He must compile all of the thoughts in his mind. He knew all of the information he had learned could be the crucial key to understanding the spiritual development of the past world. He began to think about the meaning of Taiji, the two polarities theory, the two polarities of the human body, Embryonic Breathing, ... Before he knew it, he fell asleep. He had not had enough sleep in the last few days because of too much thinking and too much excitement.

When Brian and Xiaoling came to wake him up, Dr. Owen realized that it was almost 3:00 p.m., time for the afternoon discussion. They immediately entered the meditation hall and sat down.

Afternoon Discussion

Master Dong came down to the meditation hall from upstairs at 3:00 p.m.

"Well, since this will be the last session for discussion, I believe it is a good idea that we summarize what we have covered in the last few days. This will help you remember once you return to your homes," Master Dong said.

"First, you must understand the meaning of Taiji or Dao. In the universe, Taiji is the natural power that is able to create things. If this Taiji is applied into a human body, this Taiji is the mind - that includes the conscious and subconscious mind. The conscious mind is the matrix that we have created while the subconscious mind is the mind which is still natural and connected with the natural spirit, or the Dao.

"Second, you should understand and continue to ponder the two polarities of the universe. From these two polarities, all things grown in these two polarities will also have two polarities.

"Third, through the concept of the two polarities, there are two worlds coexisting: a material world, and a spiritual world. As you know we have understood the material world to a very high level, however, we still know very little about the spiritual world. It is because of this reason we should not and cannot use today's material science to understand or to analyze the events or phenomenon of the spiritual world.

"Fourth, a human is constructed by two parts: a physical body and a spiritual body. As we know from the past, after the physical body dies, the spiritual body will separate from the physical body and be reincarnated.

"Fifth, there are two polarities in a human body, one is located at the center of the head and the other is situated at the center of gravity, or the center of the physical body. While the lower polarity or the second brain is used to store Qi, or bioelectricity, the upper polarity is the control center of the Qi's manifestation. The lower polarity is the center of physical life while the upper polarity is the center of the spiritual life.

"Sixth, gravity is possibly the boundary line of the material dimension (material world) and the spiritual dimension (spiritual world). The subconscious mind is also the boundary line of the material world and the spiritual world. Therefore, once we are able to untie the mystery of gravity, we can then step into the spiritual dimension. Not only that, if we are able to lead our mind to subconsciousness, we can then also step into the spiritual world.

"Seventh, while scientists today still cannot untie the mystery of gravity, we know, from the experiences of past masters, that through meditation, we will be able to wake up our subconscious mind and reach the spiritual world.

"Eighth, it is possible that when a person is able to reach the spiritual world, he may be able to manipulate this spiritual energy to influence the material world.

"Ninth, when a person has opened his third eye, he will have the capability of telepathy. In addition, he may be able to use his mind to influence other people's subconscious mind and control their thinking.

"Tenth, the key of re-opening the third eye and reaching the spiritual world is through the practice of Embryonic Breathing. Therefore, you must search for your spiritual center and also your energy center or physical center. Then, you must learn how to build up a more abundant level of Qi and store it in your energy center, or second brain. Not only that, you must learn how to neutralize your emotional mind, so you are able to concentrate your mind on your spiritual center. Through these two basic trainings, you can then have the quantity of Qi and quality of Qi's manifestation. This will lead you to health, longevity, and also enlightenment." As Master Dong summarized the ten important points of this seminar, everyone wrote them down.

"Next, please make groups of three to four people. I hope you can discuss the entire seminar and write down all questions or doubts you have. Then, I will need you to ponder these questions when you practice over the next year. If there is any question that you cannot find the answer to, then we will discuss it when we meet again this time next year," Master Dong said.

The entire class had been divided into five different

groups. Each group chose a leader and began the discussion. However, after nearly two hours of discussion, it seemed there were unlimited questions and doubts. When it was the end at 6:00 p.m., everyone began to pack for their travels home. There were two groups of departures, one tonight and the other tomorrow morning.

While people were packing, Dr. Owen went to see Master Dong. "Brian told me that you will continue to have the morning session every morning. I wonder if I can join you since my home is not too far from here," he asked.

"Naturally. You are quite welcome. You always have some profound questions that inspire my thinking. Remember, tomorrow morning, 6:00 a.m.," Master Dong said with smile.

* * *

The next morning, Dr. Owen arrived at the meditation hall at 5:50 a.m. as usual. The group was very small, only about six people. This was because some people had left the previous night and some others were getting ready to leave this morning. The van was going to leave at 8:00 a.m. to go to the Eureka/Arcata airport. Brian and Xiaoling were at the morning meditation since they were staying for a few more weeks. There was not much of a discussion beforehand, and meditation began right at 6:00.

Right after meditation, Dr. Owen went to ask Master

Dong a question. Brian and Xiaoling went along.

"When does the next seminar begin, Master Dong?" Dr. Owen asked.

"Tomorrow. Most people will arrive this afternoon."

"Is it possible to stay and ask you some personal questions this morning after breakfast? I didn't ask before since these questions may sound weird to many people in the class," Dr. Owen asked.

"Well, I have nothing planned this morning. It will be nice if we can sit down and talk. Brian and Xiaoling, will you also like to join us since you have known Dr. Owen for many years?" Master Dong said.

"Actually, I was going to ask your permission for this very same thing. Xiaoling and I also don't have any plans this morning and I know it will be very busy this afternoon when the new group arrives," Brian said.

"In this case, why don't you come upstairs to my study so we can have some good Chinese Wulong tea," Master Dong said.

"That would be great since I love good Chinese Wulong tea," Dr. Owen said.

At 8:00, Master Dong was in the parking lot to say goodbye to those people who were departing. Then he returned to his room upstairs. At about 8:30 a.m., Dr. Owen, Brian, and Xiaoling went to Master Dong's study and knocked on the door. Master Dong opened it and led them into his study. There was a hot pot of water boiling and a traditional set of teapot and cups on the table. This was the first time that Dr. Owen was part of a traditional Chinese tea service. First, Master Dong asked everyone to sit down and relax. He then put a proper amount of Wulong tea into the tiny traditional Chinese purple clay teapot and poured the boiling water onto the tea leaves. He covered the lid of the teapot and gently shook it a couple of times, then poured the tea out to wash the four teacups.

He explained, "This is called washing the tea. There is some tea oil on the tea leaves, and it will make the tea taste bitter. The first step is to wash the leaves to get rid of the tea oil and also use the washing water to warm up the teacups."

Master Dong quickly poured the boiling water into the pot again and let it sit there for about one minute. He immediately poured the tea out into a separate container, and then distributed the tea into four cups.

"Here is your first cup of tea. Though the teacup is small, the tea is strong. Drink it slowly," Master Dong advised.

"Wow! This is very good tea. This is the best tea I have ever had. What kind of Wulong tea do you use?" Dr. Owen asked.

"Dongding Wulong (凍頂烏龍) that means 'frozen top Wulong.' The Wulong tea produced on the top of high mountains," Master Dong said.

"But I have used the same kind of tea, and it did not taste as good," Dr. Owen said.

"Well, then it is the way of preparation. If you don't do it at the right temperature and right time, the tea does not taste as good," Master Dong replied and poured more boiling water into the tea pot. Again, he waited a little more than one minute then poured it into the container quickly. Again, he shared the tea with everyone.

"I have a few questions. Do you believe that there are some extraterrestrial intelligences existing in this universe?" Dr. Owen asked.

"Of course. Since the universe is so big, how can we be the only intelligence in this universe? I believe many of them have already reached a very high level of spiritual development and some others are still under development just like humans on earth."

"If there are and they have reached a very high spiritual level, then shouldn't we be able to communicate with them through spiritual communication?" Dr. Owen asked again.

"I believe so. Once you are able to reach the other dimension, I mean the spiritual dimension, there are no limits to time or space. I believe that spiritual energy is able to travel from one end of the universe to the other end instantaneously. I also deeply believe that if we have reached a profound level of spiritual development, we will be able to acquire our knowledge from other intelligences without even seeing each other. The Chinese always believed that there is a spiritual memory in this universe and this memory is the accumulation of knowledge and history of all different intelligences existing in this universe. Therefore, if you are able to vibrate and synchronize with this spiritual energy, you will acquire all of the information recorded in this universe," Master Dong said.

"This spiritual communication is called 'Shen Jiao' (

神交) and means 'spiritual communication' and the spirit that is able to acquire all knowledge from nature is called 'Shen Tong' (神通) and means 'spiritual comprehension' in Chinese Daoist society," Master Dong explained.

"In that case, is it possible for one highly spiritually developed person to use his spiritual vibration to influence other people's subconscious minds and make them do what he wishes? Is mind control possible?" Dr. Owen asked.

"This had been proved possible in the past both in the Western and Eastern spiritual societies. It is also believed that is why a dictator is able to brain wash people surrounding him to execute his wishes. Think, if a dictator's spirit is low, he will not be able to control the people around him. Usually, a dictator controls people around him by brainwashing and also by fear. However, if any high level of spiritual person uses his spirit to abuse another's life, then he is considered evil or the dark side of the force," Master Dong said.

"Then, how about making an object move without touching it. Can this be done through the spiritual dimension?" Dr. Owen asked curiously.

"From past experiences we know it is possible. As I explained in the seminar about the spiritual dimension and material dimension, though there are two dimensions, actually in function, there is only one. That means there is a spiritual energy connecting these two worlds together. If you are able to reach the spiritual world from the material world, theoretically you should be able to use the spiritual force existing in the spiritual world to influence the material world."

"Doesn't this mean that if someone has reached the spiritual world, they would be able to control the material world? Is it possible that human science has reached a stage that allows them to control spiritual energy in the spiritual dimension with a machine? If this is so, then this will be the most powerful weapon ever to exist in human history," Dr. Owen said.

"Does this also mean that through machines, a human's subconscious mind can be brainwashed?" Brian suddenly spoke his thought.

"Then, it would be a weapon of mind control instead of a material weapon," Xiaoling said.

Everyone was quiet. Now, all of them realized that if any government were able to access the spiritual dimension with a machine, then that government might be able to control the world. The reason that Dr. Owen asked all of these questions was because of what he had seen, from pieces of the past world recordings, that it seemed that the past world had already reached the stage of reaching the spiritual dimension through a machine. If gravity was the boundary line between two dimensions, then there was no doubt that Utana was able to access the spiritual dimension since anti-gravity technology had already been applied in daily life.

"Will humans reach the same level of scientific development in 500 years?" "What happened to the past world? What was the reason for the catastrophe?" "Will humans have the same destiny in the future?" Dr. Owen kept thinking in his mind.

Soon it was lunchtime. They went downstairs to the kitchen and grabbed a simple lunch. After lunch, Dr. Owen said good-bye to everyone.

"See you tomorrow morning," Dr. Owen said.

"I am sorry that I forgot to tell you that there is no group morning meditation tomorrow. This is simply because the new group will have just arrived and needs time to settle down. However, you are welcome to join the morning after tomorrow," Master Dong said.

* * *

It was about 3:35 p.m. when Dr. Owen arrived home. As he was getting ready to take a nap, the telephone rang. He wondered who it could be. There were only a few people who knew his number: his close family and a couple of friends.

"Hello, this is Dr. Owen."

"Hi, James! This is Edward," Dr. Torr's voice came over the phone. What a surprise! Dr. Owen and Dr. Torr had not talked to each other for many months except for exchanging a few letters.

"Wow! This is a very good surprise indeed," Dr. Owen said.

"I made this call from a cafeteria near my home. I still don't trust my home phone. I believe that as long as I am not using my home phone, it should be safe for us to talk. You know, I will be retiring in a few months. It's not worthwhile for them to keep me monitored. How are you doing, my friend?"

"I am fine. Actually, I feel better than ever. I am learning meditation now and learning a lot of things which allow me to interpret the scenes I saw from the past world recordings. I wish you could be here with me," Dr. Owen said.

"Actually, I had a minor heart attack last week. That made me think of you seriously. I wish I could be there with you too, my friend."

"Are you OK now? Why don't you take some time off and come here to relax for a few days? It will be great to see you and talk to you about the past world."

"I had the same thought. I am just wondering if it will be too much trouble for you."

"Don't be ridiculous," Dr. Owen said. "I will be very happy to introduce you to Master Dong and my student Brian, who I've mentioned to you several times. He was one of the four students who got involved in the project, remember? When would you like to come? All you need is to get a ticket to Eureka/Arcata airport, and I will pick you up."

"How about next Friday?" Dr. Torr suggested.

"That will be great! Brian and his girlfriend, Xiaoling, will still be here studying with Master Dong."

* * *

Friday afternoon, at 4:30 p.m., Dr. Owen was at the airport waiting for the plane's arrival. It was five minutes late. This made Dr. Owen more anxious than ever. He kept looking at the sky, trying to see the appearance of the airplane. Finally he saw a small, two-engine propeller plane emerge from the thick clouds. He recalled his first meeting with Dr. Torr in a Japanese restaurant. "It's been eight years. How fast time has passed," he thought. A smile appeared on his face when he thought of Richard saying, 'Dr. Torr is a weird guy and cannot get along with anyone.'

Dr. Owen thought, "I am glad that he has become one of my best friends."

The airplane landed and taxied to the terminal. It had been nearly four years. Their last meeting was on the boat in Virginia Beach when Dr. Torr secretly passed the crystals and the recording device to him. As Dr. Torr came down the steps from the airplane, he saw Dr. Owen standing outside of the waiting area. He waved his hand and Dr. Owen waved back.

"I am so excited to see you again, my friend," Dr. Torr said with red eyes. "If my heart attack had been more serious a couple weeks ago, I may never have seen my friend again," he thought.

"Welcome, Edward!" Dr. Owen stepped forward and hugged him with tears in his eyes. He had not been so emotionally touched since his wife's funeral. He had been feeling so lonely until he joined the meditation seminar with Master Dong. It seemed there was so much to say, but at the same time, he did not know how to get started.

"Have you ever been in a redwood forest? I mean huge redwoods?" Dr. Owen asked.

"No, I think I have wasted too much of my time in study and research. I have heard of the giant redwoods and seen them in photos, but I've never really seen them."

"Well, from Eureka to my home there is an alternate route through 33 miles of The Avenue of the Giants. Let's take that one. You can see the trees. The best part is traffic is not as busy as the freeway so it is more relaxing. What do you think?" Dr. Owen asked.

"It will be great to see those trees. But you know, my main reason for coming here is that I missed you. Plus, I would like to know about your study and research on the crystals."

When they arrived at The Avenue of the Giants, Dr. Torr was very excited to see the giant trees. They drove slowly and stopped whenever there were some attractive sights. However, it did not matter what else they were doing, the conversation always came back to the memory crystals.

By the time they arrived home, it was already 7:30 p.m. Dr. Owen showed Dr. Torr around his house, the rooms, and the surrounding land. It was still light out at this time in June and the sun had just disappeared on the far end of the mountains. Finally, he brought Dr. Torr to the corner room where the crystal reader had been set up.

"I have spent as much time here as possible. I am compiling the entire set of recordings chronologically onto DVD. It is not an easy job. However, gradually, I am able to put them together piece by piece," Dr. Owen said.

"Since it is not possible for me to see all of the recordings, I will be very happy to hear about what you have seen and come to understand about the past world," Dr. Torr said.

"Let's have some dinner first and then some nice Chinese Wulong tea. I have learned the traditional Chinese way of preparing the tea. It tastes much better."

After dinner, Dr. Owen prepared some tea the same way Master Dong had the other day.

"Wow! It really is better. When can I meet Master Dong?" Dr. Torr asked.

"I think Sunday morning will be the best time. That is the day that the old seminar group leaves and the new group comes in. There is a gap between 9 and 12 in the morning for him."

"Well then, let us chat tomorrow and see Master Dong Sunday morning."

Since Dr. Torr was suffering from jet leg, they decided to go to bed early and get some rest.

* * *

"Good morning, James! You got up early. It's only 6:00 a.m." Dr. Torr was on his way to the kitchen to get some water. When he passed the living room, he saw Dr. Owen was getting ready for meditation.

"Well, this is the normal time we did meditation on the mountain. Why did you get up so early?"

"You know, it's 9:00 a.m. in Washington, D.C. Actually, this is late for me already," Dr. Torr replied.

"In that case, why don't you join me for meditation. It takes an hour."

Dr. Owen helped Dr. Torr set up a meditation place and then explained what he should do for the first step.

"Just sit comfortably. Inhale deeply and then gradually allow the air to go out. While you are exhaling, simply relax your body and use your thoughts to lead your feeling downward. This will help you settle down your energy," Dr. Owen said.

After half an hour, Dr. Torr could not sit any longer. He got up and went outside to sit on the porch and watch the sunrise in the morning. The woods were filled with mist and the tops of mountains were covered with clouds. This was a scene that he could never have seen in Washington, D.C. He felt so peaceful, especially after 30 minutes of relaxing meditation. Though he could not calm down his mind easily, he had obtained some benefits simply by calming his physical body and taking deep relaxing breaths. He felt this should be his life after he retired in about ten months.

At about 7:10 a.m. Dr. Owen came to get him for breakfast and then fixed some good tea. Both of them took their tea outside to sit on the porch.

"I think for safety reasons, you should not expose those crystals, reading device, and DVDs in the room. I guess there are no burglars in this mountain area, however, you should still be careful. You know, maybe the FBI will come here to find you," Dr. Torr suggested.

"I thought it should be safe here. But maybe it's better if we can think of some solution for this. You know,

I am still compiling the files and occasionally reading the crystals."

"Maybe I can help you redesign the reading device so it is portable. In that case, whenever you are not reading the crystals, you can simply hide them someplace. Naturally, you cannot hide them in the house. That's the first place they would search," Dr. Torr said.

"If you can help me redesign it, I will find a hiding place outside of the house," Dr. Owen said.

"What have you learned in the last few weeks from Master Dong's seminar?" Dr. Torr asked, changing the topic.

"First, I understand that there are two worlds coexisting, one is the material world and the other is the spiritual world. The spiritual energy can be formalized into matter and the matter can be converted into spiritual energy. When spiritual energy travels in this universe, there is no time limitation. This spiritual energy is able to influence the structure of, or change, the material world. I mean, when there is any change in spiritual energy, the manifestation can be seen in the material world. These two worlds cannot be separated. There are two worlds, however, in function, there is only one," Dr. Owen explained.

"We already know that we understand a great deal about the material world, but we know almost nothing about the spiritual world. Have you seen anything fantastic in the past world?" Dr. Torr asked.

"As you know, they had already unlocked the mystery of gravity. They had also applied anti-gravity technology to daily life. From what Master Dong said, gravity and the subconscious mind are the boundaries of these two worlds. There are two ways to reach the other world. One is through understanding the science of gravity and the other is through meditation. When you are in a deep meditative state, the subconscious mind will awaken, and this will connect you to the spiritual world," Dr. Owen explained, then sipped a mouthful of tea. "There was a recording in the crystals about how the Utana were able to travel from Earth to Mars instantly through the spiritual dimension," he continued.

"You mean the Utana had already been to Mars about 12 million years ago?"

"It seems so. However, the recording about this was very short. All I know from what Master Dong has said is that it is possible to build a mind-control machine through the crystals' vibrations. Through vibrational synchronization, a person's subconscious mind can be controlled. Do you know of any of this kind of development in any government on earth today?" Dr. Owen asked.

"Yes. My information is that Russia, China, and America are all searching for a way to create a mind-control machine. You know, once you can control your enemy's thinking, you have conquered them. Future wars will not be fought in the material world. Instead, there will be a war of minds through brain-washing machines."

"I know that, theoretically, that is possible. Since a

person's brain can be like a radio station and another brain can be just like a radio receiver. When the wave-lengths of the vibrations are the same, the thinking can be synchronized. If we are able to create a machine to influence our opponents' thinking, that will be the greatest weapon ever developed," Dr. Owen said.

"That is the reason why we cannot reveal the secret of the crystals to the public, especially to the govern-ment. If we do, all of the human race will soon lose the ability to think freely and have spiritual freedom."

They could not help but talk about all of the possibil-ities of the near future on Earth.

* * *

The next morning, at 7:30 a.m., they took off and drove the car to the base of the mountain. Then they walked up. It took longer than an hour this time because Dr. Torr was not used to this kind of hiking or mountain climbing. They stopped often to rest. As they were walk-ing up, they saw a van coming down. "It must be the group who is departing this morning," Dr. Owen thought.

"You walked like this every morning the last few weeks?" Dr. Torr said, looking at Dr. Owen.

"Yeah, it was harder at the beginning. However, after a while it gets easier and easier."

Finally, they reached the top. When they entered the meditation hall, Dr. Owen spied Brian and Xiaoling sit-ting and talking. They stopped when they noticed Dr.

Owen's and Dr. Torr's appearance.

"Good morning, Professor. We were just wondering where you've been for the last couple of days. You didn't come for morning meditation," Brian said.

"Yes. Remember I told you a few days ago that I might have a good friend coming to visit me? Here he is. This is Dr. Torr."

"Ah! The Dr. Torr you've mentioned many times in the past! Great to meet you, sir." Brian was very excited and shook Dr. Torr's hand, then introduced his girlfriend, Xiaoling.

"Where is Master Dong? I would like to introduce Dr. Torr to him," Dr. Owen asked.

"He just went upstairs around 8:30. He should still be up there.Let's go up to pay him a visit," Brian said.

They went upstairs and knocked on Master Dong's study. When he opened the door, Dr. Owen apologized for disturbing him.

"Hi, Master Dong, I'm sorry to bother you, but I would like to introduce my best friend, Dr. Torr to you," Dr. Owen said as they entered.

"Welcome! Come in and sit down. Brian, can you help me bring up a couple of more chairs from downstairs?" Master Dong asked.

Brian went out while Master Dong began to prepare tea to serve to his guests.

"James told me that you prepare a very good Chinese Wulong tea. It is very true. This tastes so different," Dr. Torr said when he took a sip.

"Well, I also learned this from my Long Fist master.

Whenever I visited him in Taipei, he always fixed this tea for me. Actually, this tea was given to me when I visited him last year," Master Dong said.

During this first meeting, they just talked about some casual matters and had a very nice chat. After about an hour, they said goodbye and decided to go for a walk around the facilities of the center. Master Dong stayed in his study and prepared for the next seminar.

* * *

In the following three days, Dr. Torr helped Dr. Owen redesign his system for reading the crystals, making it much smaller. Now it could be moved easily. Dr. Owen decided to hide it outside under the electric meter, in a hole, covered with a rock. To look at it, you'd never know. It was just a rock that had been sitting there for many years. The spot was completely sheltered under the roof and fairly waterproof in design, so Dr. Owen didn't worry about rain damaging the device. The space was big enough for him to hide his almost 100 DVDs as well.

The next day, the day of Dr. Torr's departure, Dr. Owen and Dr. Torr felt like brothers. They talked to each other openly, without a mask on their thoughts or emotions, both feeling glad to have a friend of such depth and understanding.

As they drove to the airport, Dr. Owen asked, "Why don't you move in with me after your retirement?"

"That is very tempting James. I like it here very

much. However, I must think about it carefully. I might cause you problems, especially involving the FBI," Dr. Torr said.

"I'll finish my preliminary report about the past world in a few months. I'd like to send you a copy to read. Just treat it as a novel or a fantasy story."

Dr. Torr left California, and Dr. Owen again concentrated his time on his meditation practice, studying the past world, and writing the report.

Chapter 7
Summary

After Dr. Torr went back to Washington DC, he couldn't concentrate on his research. All he thought of was the beautiful mountains and forests of Northern California, and of the things he had seen on the DVD of the past world. He missed Dr. Owen's companionship after only one week of being home alone with his thoughts. One day, after he'd gone home from work at the government's research center, he picked up the phone and dialed Dr. Owen's number.

"Hi James. How are you? I just wanted to call and thank you for the excellent time we had together. I really appreciate our friendship."

"Hi John, I have missed you since the first day you left. It's so great to hear from you. You should come more often," Dr. Owen said.

"While I was flying back from San Francisco, I decided that I think I would like to take you up on your offer. You know, I'll be retired in less than a year."

"That's great news! You know you are welcome. I'd very much like to have you here, since you've been my greatest colleague and friend. Well, when do you think you'll move here then?"

"Probably May of next year."

"That's so great. Well, I'm making great progress with the novel I told you about when you were here," Dr. Owen said.

"Yes, I remember. I'm sure it'll be a good story." Dr. Torr knew he couldn't say a single word regarding 'crystals,' 'lost civilization' or 'history' since he may very likely still be under surveillance before his retirement.

"I believe I will have the first draft completed in five months. I will send you a copy. I hope you can find time to read it and offer me some suggestions."

"Naturally! I am already excited about reading it," Dr. Torr said.

Following this conversation, they called each other often and chatted. They talked about California, and where to buy good tea online, and discussed many aspects of Qigong theory, especially the concept of the two polarities, Yin and Yang.

While Dr. Owen continued his writing over the following months, he also continued to watch and record information from the crystals and gain a deeper understanding of this ancient history. He began to see some of the recordings repeat, more and more often. He began to feel that he may have viewed most of the recorded data, and he felt that he now had a very good idea about the society, politics, and life of the past world, and especially about the 285-year-old engineer, Aidan Stou Buta of Utana. His novel would simply be titled *The Past World*.

Six months later, Dr. Owen completed his 357-page-long story and sent a copy to Dr. Torr. Since this novel

appeared to be a work of fiction describing an unbelievable story of the past, and there was nothing mentioned
of their shocking discovery in the oil reservoir or of the
crystals, Dr. Owen believed that it was safe to send a
copy to Dr. Torr. He also sent copies to Brian and to each
of his sons. Even if the FBI intercepted and saw it, this
story was just a fantasy of something impossible, that
no one could ever believe to be true.

About the Author
Dr. Yang, Jwing-Ming, Ph.D.

楊俊敏博士

Dr. Yang, Jwing-Ming was born on August 11th, 1946, in Xinzhu Xian (新竹縣), Taiwan (台灣), Republic of China (中華民國). He started his Wushu (武術, Gongfu, 功夫) training at fifteen under Shaolin White Crane (Bai He, 少林白鶴) Master Cheng, Gin-Gsao (曾金灶, 1911-1976).

At sixteen he began the study of Yang Style Taijiquan (楊氏太極拳) under Master Gao, Tao (高濤). At the age of eighteen, he entered Tamkang College (淡江學院) in Taipei Xian (台北縣) to study Physics. In college he began studying traditional Shaolin Long Fist (Changquan, 少林長拳) with Master Li, Mao-Ching at the Tamkang College Guoshu Club (淡江國術社, 1964-1968). In 1971 he completed his M.S. degree in Physics at the National Taiwan University (台灣大學). In 1974, he came to the United States to study mechanical engineering at Purdue University. In May 1978, he was awarded a Ph.D. in Mechanical Engineering by Purdue.

In 1984 he gave up his engineering career to devote himself to research, writing and teaching. He has presented seminars around the world to share his knowledge of Chinese martial arts and Qigong. He has visited Argentina, Austria, Barbados, Botswana, Belgium, Bermuda, Canada, China, Chile, England, Egypt, France, Germany, Holland, Hungary, Iran, Ireland, Italy, Latvia, Mexico, Poland, Portugal, Qatar, Saudi Arabia, Spain, South Africa, Switzerland, and Venezuela.

Dr. Yang founded YMAA (Yang's Martial Arts Association) in 1982 (ymaa.com) in Boston, MA. Currently, YMAA is an international organization, including 56 schools in Argentina, Belgium, Canada, Chile, France, Holland, Hungary, Iran, Ireland, Italy, Poland, Portugal, Spain, South Africa, the United Kingdom, and the United States. Dr. Yang has written more than 40 books on martial arts and Qigong. He also published 71 videotapes and more than 20 DVDs. His books and videos have been translated into French, Italian, Spanish, Polish, Czech, Bulgarian, Russian, Hungarian, Portuguese, and Farsi. He was awarded the French Prix Bushido book award for his groundbreaking writing on the subject of Qigong.

He was voted by Black Belt magazine as "Kung Fu Artist of the Year" in 2003 and has been named by Inside Kung Fu magazine as one of the ten people who have "made the greatest impact on martial arts in the past 100 years."

Made in the USA
Lexington, KY
20 November 2019

57387554R00238